Driven

Andrea Badenoch lives in Newcastle. She lectures part-time and co-edits *Writing Women*, an annual anthology of new voices. Her first novel, *Mortal*, was published in 1998 and is also available in Pan Books.

Her new novel, *Blink*, a hauntingly resonant novel set in the early sixties, will be published in Macmillan hardback in March 2001 (priced £10).

Also by Andrea Badenoch in Pan Books

MORTAL

Andrea Badenoch

Driven

PAN BOOKS

First published 1999 by Macmillan

This edition published 2000 by Pan Books
an imprint of Pan Macmillan Ltd
Pan Macmillan, 20 New Wharf Road, London N1 9RR
Basingstoke and Oxford
Associated companies throughout the world
www.panmacmillan.com

ISBN 0 330 36926 1

3 5 7 9 8 6 4

A CIP catalogue record for this book is
available from the British Library.

Phototypeset by Intype London Ltd
Printed and bound in Great Britain by
Mackays of Chatham plc, Chatham, Kent

For Jay, Miriam and Naomi

Acknowledgements

Several friends were generous with their time and expertise and helped me research details for this book. I am very grateful to Barry Stone. Thanks also to Mick Cook, Ian Jordan, Fiona Kearns, Steve Manchee, Paul Miller and Sean O'Brien.

We have done with Hope and Honour, we are lost to
   Love and Truth,
We are dropping down the ladder rung by rung;
And the measure of our torment is the measure of
   our youth.
God help us, for we knew the worst too young!

Rudyard Kipling

Prologue One

Jasmine was chopping up a half-rotten stable door when she saw the car approaching. It was red and determined looking and it bounced along the uneven track to the farm. She called the dogs and shut them inside the house, because they were noisy and aggressive with strangers.

The ground had been frozen solid for more than two weeks and there was no firewood, apart from that salvaged from the decaying buildings. Jasmine intended to use the door and then the roof of the derelict stable in order to light the kitchen stove and heat some water.

She saw two ladies inside the approaching vehicle. It was a Fiat Uno, she decided, not particularly new. They stopped and parked carefully, beyond the deep ruts of hard mud that were the yard. Then they picked their way gingerly in their city shoes towards the house. Jasmine held her axe and regarded their pale legs, their neat suits with coats over the top, their leather shoulder bags. One of them had a clipboard and a biro. The other held a small tape recorder.

Jasmine knew they were social workers. She'd read their letters. When they'd telephoned, she'd insisted her mam was indisposed. Her tone suggested chronic sickness but in fact Lola, her mother, was watching videos and drinking cheap Spanish wine in bed, running an electric fan heater in her room which Jasmine knew they couldn't afford. She wasn't ill, but she'd stayed in bed all winter, her hair matted, her nightdress and woolly jumper malodorous, expecting Jasmine, her eldest daughter, to do all the work.

'Good afternoon, dear,' said one of the ladies loudly. She was the sterner of the two. 'I believe you are all expecting us?' She made her way purposefully towards the front door. She had the air of someone used to getting her own way.

Jasmine jumped sideways into the dilapidated porch, blocking their entrance. She knew she must prevent them going in at all costs. 'You can't go in,' she said, without apology.

'You must be Jasmine,' said the kinder-looking official.

Jasmine frowned. She was very small for her age. Her pale freckled skin was stretched tight over her face, emphasizing her pointed features. Her thin red hair was dragged into a skinny plait. She was thirteen years old but this lady spoke to her as if she was about six.

The tape recorder clicked.

Jasmine had lived on this ruined smallholding for as long as she could remember. They were near Teesside, a few miles from Middlesbrough on a polluted rural-urban fringe known only for its ugliness. Her mother, Lola, was an ageing hippy, tired now of what she called 'the good life' but too lazy to move on. She'd spent the last fifteen years grazing a few sickly animals and raising organic vegetables, downwind of ICI. What hope that had ever been invested in this project had long since disappeared. She couldn't even remember her old optimism or ideals.

Different men, attracted by Lola's voluptuous body, had arrived, tried to help, become discouraged and then moved on. Now, as well as looking after the farm, Jasmine cared for her feckless, drunken mother and the twins, Peony and Mimosa. They were in the grip of a hard winter. All she wanted to do was leave. She resented her mother's idleness, the stale smell of her bed, the growing pile of unwashed crockery and empty bottles littering the floor of her room.

'I can't talk to you now,' she insisted. 'I've got to . . .' She was about to say 'find something for the dinner', but changed it to 'do my homework'.

The ladies each gave her a hard look. 'None of you go to school,' the strict one said.

'Oh, the twins are at school,' Jasmine lied. She took a deep breath. 'A special bus comes and picks them up at the end of the lane.' She prayed that the two girls would not suddenly appear, filthy and giggling. They never went to school. They hadn't been for years. She imagined them running over and grabbing the tape recorder and the clipboard, possibly even the shoulder bags. They were out of control, like wild animals. Their antics made her tired. 'They'll be late tonight,' she added quickly. She didn't want these nosy parker social workers to stay, hanging around, waiting to see her sisters. She had a bizarre thought, which she expressed. 'They're at their violin lesson.'

'Do you go to school?'

Jasmine hadn't been to school for eighteen months. 'Oh yes, but I'm off today. I had a bilious attack.' She knew she was undersized but otherwise a picture of health. She paused. 'Last night. Spewed up everywhere. Dodgy frozen scampi. It's OK though, I'm better now.'

The questions continued. Jasmine fielded them as best as she could. Yes, the twins were healthy. No, her mother was perfectly all right, she was fine. No, no one else lived with them. A man? No, there was no man. Yes, they had welfare benefits and they knew about free school meals. Of course they had a washing machine.

'We would like to see inside.' The strict lady moved towards the door.

Jasmine knew her rights. Holding up her axe, she stood firm. But she also knew that these ladies could take the twins away and put them into care. They could do the same to her. The three of them could end up fostered or, even worse, in a children's home. She pictured the inside of their dwelling; its empty larder, the long-abandoned freezer, the broken lavatory, the dismal, leaky attic room where she slept next door to the twins. She knew her mother was probably drunk and asleep in her stuffy, darkened lair, her electric fire burning away money they didn't have. 'No.' She sounded very definite. 'It's not convenient.'

The tape recorder was switched off. The younger lady filled in a laborious form. She had started to shiver. 'Well then,' she said. She sneezed. 'We'll be going.'

'Is that it?'

'For the moment.'

The strict one sighed. 'We'll be back,' she threatened. They began to walk away.

Jasmine watched them, relieved but her face completely impassive.

They stopped and looked up at the pockmarked roof, the crumbling chimney. One of them pointed at a rusting transit van. As they stood there, a chicken emerged from

4

its window and fluttered to the lifeless ground. They shook their heads and got into their Fiat.

Jasmine noticed that the winter sky was stained both black and orange. A few white flakes appeared from no-where. She scanned the fields, her anxiety moving away from the visitors and focusing on the whereabouts of the sheep. She hoped it wouldn't snow again. She had dug them out of a drift earlier in the week.

The car disappeared slowly along the track, its tail lights blinking as it joined the road. She went back to her chopping block, raising her axe above her head. At that moment a clod of frozen dung hit the side of her neck. She heard girlish laughter and scuffling. Mimosa and Peony appeared, dressed in long velvet skirts and lacy shawls, stolen from their mother's wardrobe.

Jasmine put down her axe. 'Look at you both,' she said, exasperated.

The twins' faces were smeared with jam. They had straw and peacock feathers in their straggly hair. Mimosa offered the same chicken that had recently emerged from the van. Its neck hung lifeless and broken. Peony held out a wizened turnip she'd found in the barn. 'Dinner,' they suggested, in unison.

'Go and light the stove,' ordered Jasmine.

'Light it yourself,' said Mimosa.

'We're going down to Mam's,' insisted Peony, meaning their mother's room. 'We're cold.'

'It's telly time,' insisted her twin. 'It's *Rug Rats*.'

'It's *Blue Peter*, later.' They joined hands, shrieking and jumping for joy, then they went inside.

*

At six o'clock, the stove blazing and the chicken roasting, Jasmine stood at the sink, peeling the turnip. She'd dug some frozen carrots and cut off the black bits. She'd made herself tea but there was no milk.

Suddenly, there was a commotion outside. The dogs were barking frantically, but in a way that indicated pleasure. Jaz went to the door. Another car was coming along the track. Like the dogs, she recognized the sound of the engine. It was a vintage Ford Escort. She felt a rush of pleasure which was immediately replaced by annoyance. She went back to her duties at the sink.

The front door banged and there was a blast of air. A tall, fat man appeared noisily in the kitchen. He was red-faced and jovial. He sniffed the air appreciatively then held up a Tesco's carrier bag. 'I went shopping,' he said cheerfully.

Jasmine smiled but refused to acknowledge him. She kept her back turned.

This was Lola's current boyfriend. His name was Blow and he was a used car dealer from Sunderland. He'd been around for about three years, part-time, and although he was kind and generous he was also unreliable. Jasmine liked him, not least because he was patient with the twins, but she knew he would never ease her burden. He was too weak, too indecisive and too lazy to be of much help.

For reasons Jasmine couldn't understand Blow shared her mother's bed and referred to her as his 'Queen'. He dumped the bag on the table, raising a cloud of chicken feathers. With big gestures he produced frozen pizzas, breakfast cereal, baked beans, three bottles of wine. 'Howzat!' he declared, as proud as a child.

Jasmine opened a can of beans and emptied it into a

pan. Blow uncorked a bottle and poured a glass for her mother. 'You were supposed to get food two days ago,' she said to him. Her voice was sulky, quiet. 'What am I supposed to do? Magic tricks?'

He moved towards the door, still grinning widely. He was wearing a suede car coat and a back to front baseball cap. His round cheeks were shining and his stomach protruded over the top of his trousers. He gave her a friendly wink.

Jasmine was suddenly furious. 'I've told you,' she shouted, 'and I'm not telling you again. I'm sick of this. You promised to get shopping. You're two days late and there's nothing here.' She pointed to the items on the table. 'What've you done with the child benefit? You had a hundred pounds to spend.'

Blow turned around, put the glass of wine on the mantelpiece then came over and tried to stroke Jasmine's cheek. 'What's bugging you, little baby?' he crooned. 'What's bugging little Jazzy Razzy?'

'Don't start that,' she yelled in his face. She backed away, dumping the pan of beans on the stove then opening its door, throwing in more wood. 'I've had enough. Those Authorities have been here. Those nosy parker ladies. What can I tell them? And there's no hay left. There's no chicken meal. The twins are almost starving. I give you all our money and you come back with fucking wine. Fucking pizzas . . .'

Blow opened his hands in a gesture of apology. He shrugged and smiled. 'I've sold that Roadster. The MG you polished up – I told you I would.' He blew her a series of kisses. 'I've got money . . .'

Jasmine picked up the pan of boiling carrots and hurled it at him. He jumped aside and it hit the wall.

There was an upward rush of steam and a clatter. The twins appeared in the doorway, whooping and yodelling.

'I'm out of here!' Jasmine yelled. 'All of you. You bastards. D'you hear me?' She took a deep breath. 'D'you really hear me?'

'Bastards!' repeated Mimosa, rushing in and stamping hard on the scattered, half-cooked carrots. 'Fucking pizzas!'

'Fucking bastard pizzas!' repeated Peony, running and sliding through the squashed vegetables and spilt water.

'I'm going to London. I tell you. I'm going away!'

'London!' screamed Mimosa, careering into the table, raising more feathers and overturning the wine.

'London! Fucking bastard London!' screeched Peony even louder, pushing over her sister, fists flailing. 'LUN DUN! LUN DUN! LUN DUN!'

Blow leaned against the mantelpiece, laughing. He clutched his sides.

Jasmine would not allow herself to cry. She tossed her apron into the sink full of peelings and water. She kicked the stove. She was white and shaking with anger as she slammed out of the room.

Prologue Two

The headlines were everywhere – blazing from news-stands, jumping out from TV screens in shop windows, moving fast, high up on a glass wall, from right to left, right to left, where they were broken only by the time, 18.36, and the temperature, 34. The words kept repeating 'Bonfire Bodies. Bonfire Bodies – More Human Remains.'

Jaz, formerly Jasmine, saw all this but averted her eyes. She heard the same message through her head-phones, crackling on Capital Radio as she jogged down Shaftesbury Avenue. She imagined a burnt, blackened hand and immediately turned off her Walkman. She pictured suburban wasteland, somewhere beyond the city, with a petrol can and someone's charred cotton skirt. She sniffed the London air and could detect only car fumes, doughnuts and drains. She was relieved to be in the centre of things, amongst the crowds. Here, it was safe and anonymous.

Jaz was hot and her sports bag bulky. She stopped and bought a can of Dr Pepper, rubbing its damp coolness across her brow. As usual, the busy street made her feel invisible. She could sense people's eyes focused else-where, not meeting hers. She loved the anonymity when she ran around London, the impersonal bustle. No one was interested in her. After a childhood with only her family for company, miles from anywhere, this new life gave her a sense of freedom.

Later, Jaz sat outside a pub near the Strand, underneath a blue and yellow umbrella which advertised Pernod. The atmosphere wasn't French – there was too much traffic and the pavement was rather narrow. Nevertheless, the weather was warm and the huddles of London office workers, liberated at the end of Friday, were cheerfully making the best of things.

The golden light cast long shadows. Cars and buses moved through a shimmer of exhaust. Overhead, a helicopter beat and hovered like an insect against the deep, clear blue. The evening air was gentle and from a nearby café there wafted a smell of onions.

It's like being on holiday, Jaz thought to herself. She was with her two best friends, Harmony, who was known always as Harm, and Tracy, whose name they usually shortened to Trace.

Harm was brown-skinned with crinkly Afro-Caribbean hair, rolled into dreadlocks. She had an hourglass figure which she emphasized with cheap, fashionable clothes which were both too short and too tight. Trace was tall and lanky with cropped blonde hair. She always wore jeans. She had the sort of face which was both beautiful and ugly at the same time, the kind often seen in the more avant garde style magazines, but if it was ever suggested to her that she might try modelling, she simply snorted with derision.

Jaz was sipping canned orange slowly through a straw whilst her friends drank double Bacardis which were half price because of Happy Hour. 'He's given me a straw,' said Jaz, scowling through the open door at the barman.

'That's because you look about twelve,' answered Harm.

Harm and Trace, like Jaz, were sixteen years old. All three were runaways and had been surviving home-lessness and unemployment in London for some time. At present, they were staying in a hostel in Tower Hill run by the Little Sisters of Hope, which was known by inmates simply as the Little Sisters. They'd been there for six months. Today, their discussion was mainly centred on the relative merits of moving out and moving on. They tried to take decisions together. They believed in standing by each other.

'I hate that young Little Sister,' said Harm. 'You know, the one with the moles.'

'Sister Teresa? She's a stupid cunt,' agreed Trace. This was an expression she'd picked up recently from another girl at the hostel and she'd begun using it indiscrimi-nately, pleased by its power to shock.

'She got big personal problems,' giggled Harm, 'and one of them's her fat arse.'

'Problems?' said Jaz. 'She's giving me problems. No one speaks to me like that.' She sounded defiant. She was still smarting from a barrage of Sister Teresa's self-righteous abuse, delivered only that morning, in the refectory. 'I won't have anyone talking to me like that. Not any more. Who does she think she is? I'm telling you, I'm out of there.' She kicked her sports bag, indicating that she'd already left.

'She thinks we should be grateful,' commented Harm. 'For the charity.' She drained her glass. 'I have to say, I quite like the showers. And the breakfasts. There's a lot to be said for the breakfasts.'

'I'm not going back.' Jaz had made up her mind. 'She can stuff her fucking charity. And her showers. I'd just as soon take my chances on the streets.' Adamant, she gave her leftover vouchers to her two friends. Not for the first time, she thought that within the threesome she was the outsider, the one most likely to break away.

Harm and Trace, as inseparable as ever, decided not to decide. Then they thought they might stay a few more days, perhaps another week. Neither wanted to settle permanently in the Little Sisters' place, they said, becoming long-term charity cases. They dismissed such an existence as sad. They agreed that hostel dwellers were generally losers but saw themselves as free. 'We're just bumming along, using the facilities,' Harm insisted.

'We'll stick around,' said Trace. 'Like, you know. Take advantage. Do our laundry.'

'We'll catch up with you later,' agreed Harm, shrugging. 'Next week.' She sighed. She sounded more worldly, more mature than her sixteen years. 'It's one day at a time in the big bad city.'

A man on the next table held a copy of the *Evening Standard* in front of his face. The familiar headlines glared. 'Bonfire Bodies – New Lead.' After a while he folded the paper and placed it next to his pint. He leaned back and looked at the girls in an interested way. Jaz gave him a hostile glance but Harm smiled. 'Have you got a light, mister?' she asked, even though her own lighter was obvious. The man stretched out his arm, holding a match. He was about thirty-five, with longish dark hair combed behind his ears, an earring, and side-burns. He was slightly overweight and wore jeans and a tight white T-shirt which strained across his belly.

Harm bent forwards and whispered something to him. He smiled and shook his head. Jaz and Trace pretended not to notice. They both knew that Harm went with men, briefly and routinely, for quick money. She never missed a chance. It was something she'd always done and they'd given up trying to stop her.

The man was not embarrassed. 'Would you all like a drink?' he asked confidently. He had a London accent. He stood up, his expression open and friendly. 'Why don't I buy us all a round?'

'Thanks,' said Harm, in no way offended by his refusal. 'Two large rum and blacks and a Fanta.'

Jaz was relieved, both by the man's unwillingness to go with Harm and by his manner, which was reassuring and ordinary. She decided he was OK. She noticed his Millwall FC anorak, slung across the back of his chair. When he returned, she mentioned the team's prospects.

'I'll join you,' he said, pleased, and somehow innocent, moving his chair next to Jaz. 'So where're you from, darling? You new here?'

The daylight ebbed away and the sky turned purple. The office workers left and were replaced by tourists and two rich-looking couples in evening dress. The traffic died. A police car sped past, its siren wailing, and empty buses accelerated and rattled. An old man wearing sandwich boards shouted something about the end of the world.

Jaz chatted to the man. She described her mother's smallholding but didn't say that she'd run away from

Teesside. She told him she'd been staying in a hostel but didn't intend going back. She tried to give the impression that she'd come to London for work. 'Do you work near here?' she asked.

He shook his head. 'On the buildings, but not here. Down the East End.'

She noticed that his teeth were uneven and pointed.

Harm and Trace were drunk. They giggled over the problem page in *Sugar*, leaning together like children. Trace had never learned to read. 'Go on,' she said to Harm, 'go on, read me some more.'

Harm waved her cigarette wildly. She carried on reading from the magazine. Her voice became louder and emphatic. ' "I'm in love with my biology teacher." Christ, listen to this!' She laughed, holding the page away from her face, spilling some of her drink. 'Listen to this, Trace. It genuinely says this, no joke.' Her words were slurred. 'This is the frigging headline, right? "Classroom Love." This is unbelievable.'

Trace spoke to Harm in a loud stage whisper. 'Do you think this girl's like, you know . . .' she giggled, her hand over her mouth, 'a stupid cunt?'

Harm continued, adopting a soppy voice. 'It's the real thing. I love him and he loves me. I know we're made for each other. The problem is I'm only fifteen and I've missed my period.'

Trace laughed. 'I don't get this.' She was always a bit slow on the uptake.

Harm continued reading. ' "We've only done it standing up. We do it in the technology room during the breaks. He says because we're doing it standing up, I can't get pregnant." ' She dropped the magazine on the table. 'Can she be serious? This girl, she signs herself "Boyzone Fan". Is she for real?'

Trace laughed too. 'She's definitely a stupid cunt.'

'Biology!' spluttered Harm. She put her drink down.

Both Harm and Trace's laughter was now out of control. 'The technology room!' squeaked Harm.

'The stupid cunt!' shouted Trace. They held onto each other for a moment, rocking in their seats. The other customers on nearby tables looked over quizzically. Some of them seemed offended. The magazine slid to the ground.

Jaz didn't smile. She examined a beer mat.

'You don't drink?' asked the man, gently.

She shook her head.

'Not at all?' His mouth was near her ear. He was ignoring the others.

She was conscious of his attention. He was now very close, too close. She wondered if he was about to kiss her. She had decided she liked him, not least because she felt she already knew him. It was something to do with his big build that made him familiar. He reminded her of Blow. She could smell his aftershave and the beer on his breath. She shook her head again. She never discussed alcohol.

'I'll get myself another pint.' He stood up.

Harm, still laughing, gestured towards the table top, which was full with glasses. 'Two large thingies and a . . .'

The man smiled. 'Sure,' he agreed, disappearing inside the bar.

Harm took a deep breath and almost recovered her composure. 'He's nice,' she said, gesturing, pretending to admire his backside. 'Fat, but quite good looking.'

'You've scored there, Jaz,' added Trace, still gasping a little for air. 'He's got money.'

'Don't forget to do it standing up,' added Harm loudly.

Trace's laughter pealed out again. 'Find a technology room. You've got to find a technology room.'

The man reappeared and walked towards them. He carried another pint and two more Bacardis.

'Hey you!' Harm waved both her arms again. 'You can only do it to Jaz if you do it in a technology room.' She was swaying in her seat. 'It's the only safe way. Standing up. I read it somewhere!'

'Shut up,' said Jaz quietly. 'Just shut up, you two. If you don't go soon, you'll be locked out by those nuns.'

Harm and Trace stood up, holding onto each other, steadying themselves with the table, making sure they swallowed the drinks which had just arrived. 'She's right. We have to go. We're going to a technology room in Tower Hill. It's got showers. It's got bloody Little Sisters.'

'They're all stupid cunts,' offered Trace.

The man looked at Jaz. 'You going?'

'No.'

'You want to come with me? I've got space.'

'Maybe.'

'I'll finish my pint.'

Fifteen minutes later, after her friends had staggered off, Jaz picked up her sports bag and prepared to leave with the man.

As she stood up, he was clearly surprised by her size. 'You're very small, aren't you?'

'I'm eighteen.'

'I'm Keith.' He winked. His face was kind.

Jaz thought that he was quite attractive, but certainly old. She wasn't sure what to say.

They walked together down a side street. He didn't put his arm around her or stand too near. 'I did a trial for Millwall's youth squad,' he said, clearly pleased that she knew about his team. 'Trouble is, I never had the ankles.'

'The ankles?' repeated Jaz.

'Dodgy Achilles.'

There seemed to be no adequate response to this, so Jaz stayed quiet.

'I've got a car along here.'

'A car?' Jaz was surprised. She didn't know anyone in London who had a car. 'What kind of a car?'

'Mark II Zephyr. Nineteen sixty,' he said proudly. 'Canary yellow and cream.' He gave her a strange, sidelong stare, as if she might have some objection to the idea.

Jaz was pleased. She remembered the succession of old cars she'd watched Blow restore. 'I love old cars,' she said reassuringly. 'I'm a car freak.' With relief, she realized they had something in common.

The hot day had turned into a heavy, oppressive night. Jaz was conscious of dampness under her arms, a weight which seemed to press down from the dark buildings on either side, and the smell of refuse coming from the back of restaurants.

'Here we are,' said Keith, turning into a narrow rear entrance. His car was parked in a tight bay, between buildings. It was covered in a tarpaulin, as if he'd been expecting rain. He dragged this off and the Zephyr was illuminated in the glow from a street lamp.

Jaz let out a low whistle. 'Amazing,' she enthused. She

was genuinely impressed. 'Beautiful.' It was one of the best she'd ever seen.

'Highline,' Keith pointed out.

'I can see that.' Jaz took a few steps backwards.

'I prefer the highlines.'

'You've had the headlamp cowls chromed?'

He nodded, clearly pleased. 'Yeah. And the wheel arches – see them?' He paused. 'Rebuilt.'

Jaz walked around the vehicle, then surveyed it again from the front. The Zephyr had big chrome bumpers and a shiny grille with a period AA badge. She dropped her bag, put her hands on her hips and shook her head slowly. 'It's terrific. It's totally . . . fab.'

He unlocked the passenger door. 'Get in,' he said.

Jaz threw her sports bag in the back and slid over the bench seat. She took a deep, appreciative breath. It was a unique smell of old plastic and leather. Keith climbed in next to her and she realized again why he was so familiar. His height, his bulk, his long wavy hair and now his car – everything about him reminded her of Blow. As he turned the key in the ignition she was suddenly back on the farm, sitting next to Blow, admiring his latest acquisition, talking cars.

'Just listen to that,' he said. The engine gave a low growl.

'Straight six,' she offered.

'Needs a new clutch.' There was a slight judder as they moved off. 'I've got one ordered, though.' He paused. 'It's under control.'

They drove along Fleet Street, the car purring like a cat. Jaz noticed there was a collection of tax discs neatly secured behind the one displayed on the windscreen.

He'd kept them all. Blow had always done this with his best cars. It was a sign of fanaticism.

Soon Jaz caught a glimpse of the river. She realized they were heading east when she saw the dome of St Paul's. 'There's St Paul's,' she said, making conversation. Every time they turned a bend, she slid towards him on the slippery leather seat, so that their arms touched. She let this happen. She took another deep breath, this time for courage. 'Do you mind if I drive?'

Jaz loved driving. She had learned in her mother's tractor on the farm when she was eight. Then when Blow arrived, with his succession of second-hand vehicles, he let her manoeuvre them around the fields, the lanes, then, later, the quiet country roads. She was a good, instinctive driver. Blow said she was a natural. She considered driving to be her best talent, her greatest skill – the one of which she was most proud.

Keith pulled over. 'Why not?' he asked. 'Watch that clutch. It's tricky.'

Jaz got out and went around to the driver's door. Keith slid across onto the passenger side. She felt a flutter of excitement in her chest. She hadn't driven a vehicle since she'd left home, two and a half years before. She turned the key and started cautiously, slowly, waiting for the clutch to rebel. She got the measure of the engine. There was virtually no traffic but she'd never been on a main road in her life. The speedo said twenty. She was nervous. They crawled along. She was wary of the pedals. Gingerly, and in order to avoid a stationary bus, she moved out into the middle lane. After a few more minutes her confidence grew. She realized she'd already passed the hostel run by the Little Sisters of Hope. 'I was living around here,' she said, 'until very recently. Where are we going?' She accelerated to get through an amber light. 'This is great,' she added. 'This is totally brill.'

She saw a taxi rank ahead on her right and then the unmistakable figures of Harm and Trace. They were talking to a trio of drivers. She slowed and waved, proud to be driving.

'What's up?' asked Keith.

Jaz hooted at her friends. They turned and saw her.

'Come on,' said Keith. 'Never mind them.'

Jaz drove past the taxi rank and was aware of Harm and Trace coming out onto the road and then waving and running behind her. 'They're drunk.' She shrugged and accelerated away.

Keith gave her some directions. They were now in the East End. Jaz saw a sign saying East London Tabernacle. After about fifteen minutes, they entered a warren of small streets. 'Slow down,' he instructed. 'See these lock-ups?' They were adjacent to a row of railway arches. 'Stop here.'

Jaz got out of the car.

Keith unlocked a door, then parked the Zephyr out of sight. 'It's not far,' he assured her. 'My gaff's just up the road.' They set off, again walking two feet apart. For the first time, Jaz felt scared. They had come a long way and this was an area unfamiliar to her. Groups of Asian teenagers stood around on street corners outside grocery shops and video rental outlets which were still open. A sign said Wedding Saris. There was a smell of foreign food and occasional noisy bursts of car stereos.

'Let me take that,' said Keith, grabbing and then shouldering Jaz's sports bag. He started singing 'I'm turning Japanese, Oh yes, I'm turning Japanese, I really think so.' He sounded jolly and a little old-fashioned, like someone's dad.

Jaz was silent again. They walked for what seemed like a long time. The streets and alleys became more and more empty. The road had potholes and cracked drain covers. They passed large buildings, like hospitals, which were deserted, with stained bricks and broken windows. The dark purple-orange sky faded to black at the edges. Jaz was aware of pools of urine, gaping pavements, uprooted cobbles. She wished she hadn't come.

'Not far now,' Keith assured her.

Jaz hesitated at a small junction.

He turned around and looked down at her. 'Don't worry,' he said, reading her mind. 'I don't like sex.' He noticed a squashed drinks can in the gutter and flicked it up with his foot, bounced it on his knee then shot it expertly across the road. A dog started barking. Jaz noticed a group of drunks arguing in a pub doorway. As they turned a bend, she could see open space and several bunches of homeless men grouped around bonfires. Keith walked in the direction of the first blaze.

Jaz followed him. She was aware of bottles being shared and the familiar mixture of old and young, destitute and ordinary, alcoholic and sober. There was the usual combination of laughter, argument and weary silence. They regarded Keith and Jaz with interest, but didn't speak. She glanced at their faces, feeling the heat. It wasn't a cold night, it was close and warm, but she knew they lit fires from habit and from the strong need to make a focal point in the urban wilderness. She'd joined such a group herself, in the past, on more than one occasion.

There was no one amongst them that she knew. It

occurred to her again that she was a long way from her own patch. Keith carried on walking. Further on and around another corner Jaz saw more fires and more huddles. One or two makeshift shelters were already housing individuals who'd settled for the night.

Keith continued up the street but suddenly stopped. 'Here,' he said.

Jaz looked about. There were tall tenement blocks on either side, most of which seemed unoccupied. Their doors were boarded up with wood and corrugated iron, as if they were scheduled for demolition. She tried to get her bearings. At the end of the row, about thirty yards away, was the second patch of wasteland they'd crossed, with its glowing fires. She wanted to remember the way they'd come. She didn't like being lost.

Keith turned directly into a narrow slit between the flats. It was pitch black, and Jaz paused. He grabbed her arm. He pulled her roughly and she stumbled against him.

'Easy,' he said harshly. 'Steady on.'

Jaz could see nothing. She was conscious of his tight fingers and his breathing which had become a little heavy. There was rubble under her feet. They stopped. A hinge creaked and her eyes started to adjust. She could see a tiny green metal entrance inserted in a much larger, older wooden door. She was reminded of a tannery which had frightened her in a Middlesbrough back street when she was very small. They stepped inside.

Keith still had hold of her arm. 'Home sweet home,' he said in a gruff voice.

Jaz blinked. 'What is this?' She was afraid. She felt a change in Keith's manner. He had become threatening, even rough.

He dropped Jaz's bag. She picked it up with her free hand. Then, still holding her, he pushed the small door shut, wedging a short plank under it to keep it closed. His hand groped for a light switch. There was a click and a pale glimmer shone from a low watt bulb strung between some rafters. Jaz looked around. The building was old and damp with crumbling walls. There was a strong smell of mice, mould and rotting plaster. In a corner were new bags of cement, sand and a pile of bricks.

Keith propelled her down a corridor. 'Come and have a look at this,' he said. After a moment she was aware of emerging into a big dark space. He pressed another switch, illuminating a decorator's lamp which hung from a pair of step ladders.

Jaz gasped. Before them was the foyer of an old cinema. It was spacious and had once been very grand. There were marble stairs curving away upwards bound by iron balustrades hung in places with dusty cobwebs. There were ornate rococo walls and ceilings, a wooden booth under a sign saying tickets, framed, stained prints of long dead stars. The tiled floor was broken and in places dug up. The air was musty and stale. Again, there were signs of building work – trestles, planks, cement and other evidence of repairs or a conversion which had been abandoned.

'What is this place?' Jaz's voice was small and scared.

'It's empty,' muttered Keith. 'Bricked up. Been empty for years. Supposed to be the Calcutta Road bloody Arts Centre.' He sniffed aggressively. 'The Lottery never coughed. Bastards. Not a good enough cause. Not good enough for those bloody Lottery sods.' He mimicked someone on television. 'Just come on down.' His tone suggested resentment, anger, disappointment.

'You worked here, didn't you?' Jaz stared into his face. He met her eye and she realized his face had become strange, almost distorted. His eyes were staring and his mouth compressed in fury. He looked mad. He lifted a hand, his finger pointing into the air. He raised his voice. 'I still work here. And I'm not leaving.'

Jaz was aware of her heart beating. She'd imagined she'd been heading for a cheap rented room, or a temporary, anonymous bed and breakfast with old furniture, a dirty cooker, a lumpy settee. She'd stayed in many such places in London.

In the pub he'd seemed nice and friendly and quite good looking. She'd wanted him to fondle her, undress her, make a small fuss of her. She'd expected brief love-making, then a hot drink, a blanket and a safe place to sleep. She'd imagined waking up, having breakfast, kissing him lightly, moving on. He would have given her money, maybe arranged to meet her again. It was the usual pattern. It's what had happened every other time.

This place, this derelict old cinema miles from her usual area, and Keith's tight grip, his fanatical expression, were not at all what she'd expected. The situation was weird. This meant it was unpredictable and therefore dangerous. She knew she was in trouble. She looked around. There was a thick, looped chain and a padlock across what must have been the main entrance to the building.

'Come on,' he said.

Don't panic, she told herself. He pushed her through a new fire door into a room which had been recently constructed at the side of the ticket booth. It had ceiling spotlights, rows of new blue chairs which had become white in places with mildew, a rolled carpet, still in polythene, and a life-size cardboard cut-out of the men from *Reservoir Dogs*. At the front there was a small screen. A tiny cinema had been created within the vast body of the original, decaying building, and then left to deteriorate.

'You said an Arts Centre . . .' Jaz turned round in time to see Keith disappearing. In a couple of seconds he'd closed the door, locked it and extinguished the lights. She was alone and in the dark.

'You're shut in,' Keith confirmed. His voice was very muffled, from behind the soundproof barrier. 'What a shame.'

Jaz experienced a rush of fear. Her head swam and her knees went weak. She had a sensation as if her heart was leaping in her chest. She bit her lip, willing herself not to faint. He's a weirdo, she thought frantically. I'm a goner. She tried hard to see in the blackness and reached out, taking two nervous steps forward in order to hold onto the back of a chair.

After a while, there was a whirring noise and something appeared in front of her. She blinked, realizing it was a beam of projected light, shining on the small screen. A bright rectangle about four feet by six took shape and then diminishing numbers flashed up inside. She realized she was looking at the start of a film. She glanced behind her. Above her head, a projector shone the white triangle down into the room, and Keith stood behind it. He spoke again. 'I'm going to kill you, little girl.' His voice was quiet. He was no longer behind the soundproofing. He was very close. He spoke softly and menacingly. 'Yes, I am.'

Jaz felt sweat break out all over her body. First it was

hot, but it immediately became cold. She shivered, and looked at the screen.

A young Princess Margaret appeared, pale and grainy, wearing a pink suit and matching shoes. She shook hands elegantly, smiled and waved, received flowers, walked alongside a crowded pavement.

Jaz realized, with a shock, that the amateur film had almost certainly been shot in the street outside the building which now held her prisoner. She could see the flats, the old cinema façade, with the name Essoldo, and at the end of the road, the open stretch of wasteland where tonight there burned bonfires.

'I'm going to kill you,' Keith repeated. 'I'm going to do you like I did all the others. Then I'll put you on a fire.'

Bonfire Bodies, thought Jaz. She remembered the news headlines which had tried to intrude into her consciousness all day. She'd ignored them but had been unable to shut them out completely. Bonfire Bodies. They're here, she thought, those murders. They're not miles away. They're here, in London. Keith's doing it. He's using those bonfires. They're lit by the neighbourhood homeless, and then he uses them to get rid of the girls he's murdered.

'No one knows you're here,' said Keith. He sounded almost reasonable. 'No one knows I'm here. They won't look for anyone in this old place. No one comes here now. You won't be found.' He paused, then chuckled. 'Until you're roasted meat.'

Jaz took several deep breaths. She understood from the tone of his voice that he was enjoying this. He was excited by her fear. He doesn't like sex, she remembered. This is what turns him on. He gets off on this. This is his thing – the terror, the panic, the desperation of young girls.

A sensation rose up in her chest which was stronger than any of those feelings. She was aware of it growing and feeding greedily on the adrenalin which pulsed through her body. This new emotion took the place of her fear. It was anger. Keith's sadism was making her angry. 'Fucking bastard,' she said.

'What's that, girlie-wirlie?' he replied. 'What's that?'

Jaz was furious. Her fury took over, took control. She felt it welling up and spilling out, just as it always did. 'I hate you, you fucking bastard.' She shouted at him in a way that suggested she'd never known fear. Then she swallowed and lowered her voice. 'What's the matter with you anyway?' There was a silence, broken only by the fan spinning quietly on the projector.

Jaz then forced a laugh – deliberate, disparaging. Her anger made her hate him. She wanted to mock him. 'I think I know. I know exactly what your problem is, fat boy.' There was a pause. 'We just . . . freak you out, don't we? Us girlie-wirlies. You can't cope. Can't manage it, can you? Ugly old wanker. That's what's wrong with you. Your dick doesn't work.'

He didn't answer.

'You hear me? Wanker?'

The film in front of her flickered, then went off. The room was in total darkness again. Jaz imagined Keith coming back downstairs, maybe with a weapon. She was too angry to be afraid. Her anger was her defence, her courage. She was ready for him. She shouldered her bag and clenched her fists.

The screen became illuminated for a second time. She glanced up and behind. His outline was still visible.

'What've you got up there, arsehole? Porno films?'

A still image in black and white appeared. It was an old photograph of the cinema, looking huge and impressive. Painted on the side wall of the building was the word 'talkies'. Passers-by were dressed in old-fashioned clothes. Several other slides clicked into view. They were all of the cinema, taken at different times in its history. There were street vendors, crowds, trams, horses and carts. It was clear that in the past the area had been a lot more prosperous and populated than it was today. One or two photographs showed the interior of the building. It had contained mirrors and painted murals.

Jaz heard a noise. It was the key in the lock. The slide carousel continued to rotate upstairs, but Keith had returned. He opened the door and a chink of light shone through. He stepped inside, leaving the door ajar. Jaz prepared herself for a struggle, but he didn't come towards her. Instead he moved into the centre aisle and gestured at the screen. 'It could have been like this again,' he said, almost conversationally, 'if only they'd had the vision.'

At that moment there was a clatter and the babble of raised voices. Keith jumped, visibly surprised. Jaz instinctively took a few quick steps towards the door and flung it open. Keith lunged, then stopped in his tracks.

The dimly lit foyer was filling with people. There were shouts and jostling. Jaz blinked and emerged amongst them, her eyes smarting. Two women grabbed her. She realized, in a dazed instant, that they were Harm and Trace. They started dragging her towards the corridor which she knew led to the unlocked side door. She looked back at the surprising crowd. It milled and pushed its way into the new, small cinema, where briefly Jaz had been held prisoner. There were thirty or forty men and they seemed united, determined. Some of them were unkempt and dirty. Others were wearing blankets. Jaz couldn't take it in. The scene was surreal. Who are these people? she thought. Some of them waved sticks, others broken bottles. They surged, in a mob, towards the room where Keith was trapped. I know them, she suddenly decided. They're the men from the bonfires, the same people I passed on the way here. She tried to stop, to wait, wondering what would happen, but her friends continued to pull her towards the exit.

In a few seconds the girls were outside. 'Come on,' Harm insisted. 'Don't worry, they know. They know everything. He's been using their fires. Me and Trace, we know two of them. They used to doss in Stamford Street, last winter. We told them he'd brought you here.' She took Jaz's bag. 'Don't you see? All his victims were homeless. Runaways. There's a lot of angry stuff going down around these parts. We asked them for help. The posse was ready – they just needed info.'

'Yes,' Trace agreed. 'They thought this place was empty.'

'That creep's had it,' Harm continued. 'We have to get away.'

Jaz, led by her friends, one holding each hand, retraced her earlier footsteps back to the spot where Keith had hidden his car. Surprisingly, it seemed to take no time at all.

The streets were deserted. A single police car cruised past, unaware and nonchalant, then disappeared. As they approached the lock-up, Jaz saw that a black cab was idling. The driver grinned and looked at his watch. Jaz recognized him. He was one of Harm's regulars – someone from the taxi rank, the one she'd passed earlier, near the Little Sisters of Hope on Tower Hill. Jaz knew he routinely traded rides with Harm, in return for blow jobs. She turned to her friends. 'You're amazing,' she said.

They jumped inside. The cab moved off. Jaz lay back and closed her eyes. She heard the engine climb through its gears and felt the vehicle gain speed. She let out a huge sigh. 'Oh God,' she whispered. 'Thank Christ you got here.'

'Of course we got here,' said Harm gently. 'We've got to stick together. We shouldn't have separated.'

'How did you . . .'

'Don't ask.'

'I'm asking.'

'We saw you waving . . .' began Harm.

'We were worried . . .' Trace stroked Jaz's sleeve. 'Poor Jaz.'

'Saw you going past us, near the Little Sisters. At that taxi rank. Really slow. Like a snail. Then you speeded up. We jumped in the taxi and followed you here. Then we tailed you on foot.'

'We saw you,' interjected Trace. 'Waving. You were in a fancy car, with that bloke.'

'So?' Jaz was bewildered.

'You don't know?' Harm turned to Trace. 'I told you she didn't know.'

'Know what?' whispered Jaz.

'It's been all over the news, all day.' Harm was insistent. 'The man they want to question about those fires. The bodies in the East End. He drives a shiny yellow old car, a Ford Zephyr. It was on the news. In the papers. I can't believe you went and climbed into it, with that pig. Willingly.' She whistled. 'You got in it with him and went for a drive.' She turned to Trace. Her voice was a mixture of exasperation and relief. 'What's it with this girl? What exactly does she think she's doing? Is Jaz dumb, or what?'

Trace pursed her lips and looked out of the window. There was a bright star visible in the dead-night city sky, between the buildings. 'It's obvious what she is. She's a stupid cunt.'

Chapter One

Much later, when it was all over, after she'd been away on holiday and come back again, Jaz told everyone that she'd celebrated her twenty-first birthday at the best hotel in London. She said it with a smile and a shrug, but it was true. Her party was held in a luxury hotel, but not in the glowing dining room or the sumptuous lounge. It took place in a tiny scullery off the side of the kitchen. She crouched on the floor there, almost hidden by an industrial dishwasher and a trolley of stacked plates. Trace and Harm were the guests and they sat alongside and toasted her birthday with champagne, sipped from antique crystal glasses. Jaz joined in with chilled tomato juice, the colour of blood. She never drank alcohol. This was still one of the many rules which she used to run her life.

'These little gobfuls are nice,' said Harm, scooping up exquisite hors d'oeuvres from a polished platter and stuffing them into her mouth.

'I'll find some more,' offered Trace vaguely. 'There's loads of them, somewhere.' Trace was helping out at the hotel, off the record, no questions asked, cash in hand. What this meant was that every weekend and sometimes during the week, she took charge of the dishwasher, the crockery trolleys and sink-loads of precious metal and glassware that required 'hand rinsing'.

She stood up, wearing her regulation overall and hairnet. She went into the kitchen with confidence, smiling, mingling with foreign chefs, their stressed sous-chefs and calm, overtrained waiters in red cummerbunds. They all ignored her. She pushed another trolley of dirty dishes towards the scullery, this time bringing a half empty bowl of salmon mousse, more hors d'oeuvres and a paper carton, containing olives. Jaz and Harm dug into the glass bowl with silver spoons. 'These black things are weird,' said Trace, handing around the olives, 'but you get used to them. Better than the snails.'

Jaz was happy. This, she decided, was one of the best birthday celebrations she'd ever had. She was glad Trace had organized this, pleased she had such good, reliable friends. She pursed her lips thoughtfully, sipped her drink, remembered another good party when she was eleven. Blow had come back to the farm that morning in an open-topped Armstrong Siddeley. The chrome was crazed and pitted and the hide seats were mildewed but he pulled up outside the door hooting the horn and giving a mock gentleman's wave. Jasmine and her sisters were excited. They climbed all over the bonnet. 'I've just bought this from a duchess.' He grinned. 'Go and borrow your ma's finery. We're all going for a drive.'

Jasmine, her mother and her two little sisters searched through the big old bedroom wardrobe for hippy Indian cotton, lace, feathers, velvet and fur. They found leather boots and costume jewellery. They tried on hats. Blow squeezed into an old dinner suit. The family drove to Middlesbrough in his new old car where they turned heads and stopped traffic. They had tea in Burger King and Blow said they should eat as much as they liked, because it wasn't every day that someone special was eleven.

Jaz chewed on an olive and refilled her friends' glasses with champagne. Around the corner from their scullery, the kitchen was now busy. Even the waiters were running and raising their voices, but in their own special, private party corner, it seemed peaceful, wrapped in its cloudy, damp, dishwasher air. Harm burped quietly and announced that she'd had enough to eat. She eased her back away from a hot water pipe, sighed and stood up. 'S'pose I better go outside,' she suggested, 'for a ciggie?'

'Yes,' agreed Trace. 'This is a smoke-free zone.' She laughed. 'You could go and sit in the lounge.' She cleared their dishes from the floor, stacked some expertly in her sink, packed the rest in her dishwasher, closed it and switched it on. The jets roared.

'It's been nice,' said Jaz. 'Thanks.' She stood a little stiffly as Trace bent down and kissed her cheek.

'It's OK,' said Trace, stepping back and wiping her damp brow with the back of her hand. 'It's not every day your mate turns twenty-one.'

'What about that champagne?' asked Jaz.

Trace smiled. 'Come with me.' The three friends walked through the jostling kitchen. Harm ducked the flailing meat cleaver in the raised hand of an assistant's assistant. Instructions were shouted in French. There was sizzling and a flash of flame and Jaz closed her eyes for a second as two live lobsters were dropped into a steaming cauldron. 'Come on,' insisted Trace, catching both her friends by the arm, but not one of the kitchen staff bothered them.

They went down a corridor which led to the back of

the reception desk. Computer monitors winked, white on green. Above, on the marble counter, enormous vases of lilies were mixed with white roses. Only one uniformed receptionist was on duty and she was talking on the telephone. She giggled and swivelled from side to side on her high stool. Beyond her stretched the wide, glittering lobby lit by a dazzle of chandeliers. A group of guests in dinner suits talked and smoked. Two small children ran from the staircase towards the open door of a lift. Outside, a row of taxis idled. 'Wait here,' Trace said.

Harm and Jaz stood in the shadows. Trace slipped unnoticed in front of a computer and tapped for a moment on its keyboard. The receptionist didn't turn round but laughed again down the phone. 'You dirty beast!' she exclaimed.

Jaz turned to Harm. 'I didn't know Trace understood computers,' she murmured. 'She can't even read.'

Harm smiled. 'She understands what she needs to understand,' she replied. 'Never underestimate Trace.'

Their friend returned. 'You better go now,' she said.

'What've you done there?' asked Harm, pointing to the monitor.

'Taken care of the champagne,' Trace whispered. She smoothed her overall over her thin hips. 'I've just put it on Dustin Hoffman's room service account.'

Jaz and Harm stepped out, laughing, into the warm night. Harm lit a cigarette. Her mobile phone rang and she took it out of her bag. She exchanged a few words. Jaz knew it was Wesley, her current pimp. He had a client waiting for her in Belgravia.

Harm sighed. 'Time to earn a crust. I'll be going.' Her

words were slurred and soft. 'See you later, alligator.' She grinned. 'Happy Birthday.' She blew out a stream of smoke. Steadying herself against a lamp-post, she bent down and kissed the top of Jaz's head, then wandered away into the darkness. Jaz listened to her stilettos clicking for a moment above the hum of distant traffic.

She looked up at the BT tower and noticed that behind it, the moon was as full as an eye. The streets were empty, comfortable and strange. She passed several door-ways where street people had bedded down under cardboard for the night. A ragged man came into view, then lurched past, pulling a tiny handcart. She switched on her Walkman, adjusted her headphones then set off at a steady jog in the direction of Tottenham Court Road. She imagined that she was one of the few people left on earth. The city is mine, she thought. She was happy.

Jaz lived in south London. For the last six months she'd been staying with Fat Andy, a friendly car thief, sharing his council flat in the badlands near Peckham Rye. She'd reminded him about her birthday, two nights before. They were in bed and she'd caressed his big stomach in a way she knew he liked. He was drinking Tia Maria from a plastic tumbler and reading *What Car?* magazine.

'You thought about my present?' she'd asked.

'What d'you want?'

'You know,' she murmured. She moved her hand downwards, gently. 'You know what I want.' She licked around his mouth, delicately, then her tongue probed inside his lips.

He tossed aside his magazine, put his drink down and

rolled heavily onto his back. 'Don't tell me.' He sighed. 'I know.'

'I know you know.' She climbed on top of his bulk and pulled on the child's nightdress, which was covered in pictures of Minnie Mouse. He'd bought it for her and it was the one he most liked her to wear.

Her body was small and thin, like a young girl's. 'I want to drive your car. You know I do. All around London. I want to drive it like I'm going to drive you.'

Andy rolled her pink nipples in his fingers, groaning slightly. Jaz was almost as flat-chested as a ten-year-old. 'Like what?' he asked, 'you sexy little baby.'

'Like crazy,' she laughed.

He kneaded her bony hips for a moment then raised his head. She knew the routine. She turned, leaned forwards and slipped a nipple between his lips. He sucked it greedily then fell back on the pillow. He always said the same things. 'Little baby, do it to me. Do it nice.'

'OK?' she said, as she guided him between her legs.

He shuddered and sighed. 'Nice. That's nice.'

Her hands pressing on his shoulders, she moved her hips quickly up and down. 'On my birthday?' she insisted. 'The Lotus Cortina? Is that a deal?'

Jaz jumped off a bus and ran lightly towards the estate. Her good mood was evaporating. Fat Andy hadn't come home last night and she'd waited on her own most of the day. She knew he might not keep his promise, but the thought of driving his car for the first time had kept her in a state of excitement for hours. Eventually, she'd admitted to herself that he wasn't coming. Her anticipation turned to anger. She'd tried his mobile for the tenth time but it was still switched off.

When Jaz had left the flat to meet Trace and Harm at the Savoy, she'd been furious with Andy. Now she was no longer emotional, just resigned. It's time to move on, she thought, running across the concrete courtyard. This wasn't the first time she'd decided to leave him, but she felt a stronger resolve than usual. She'd had enough.

I'm sick of living with a man I hardly know, she told herself. I'm sick of this feeling that I don't really understand him. Jaz felt close to only part of him. He wanted her to pretend to be much younger than she really was, and this had become a tiring game. He was secretive and evasive about many things. He'd forgotten her birthday.

Jaz felt a sense of relief at the prospect of change. Maybe he's back, she thought. If he's back, I'll drive the Lotus Cortina, but afterwards, I'll leave him anyway.

She pictured the shiny car, ermine white with its green flash and polished chrome, and the image led her to thoughts about Blow. He too had been big and fat with great old cars, and he too was unreliable. For some reason, she suddenly felt a pang of regret about leaving home and Blow and her sisters. This was followed by another feeling she couldn't name. What do I want? she thought. She decided at that moment to quit London and return to Teesside. Having a plan made it easier to dispel unwanted emotions and regrets. It gave her a sense of purpose. Only for a visit, she thought. I'll just stay for a while. See how they're getting on. Blow would let her drive his car, she was sure. He'd let her do anything she liked. He'd let her drive all his cars.

She remembered how in the months before she'd left,

he'd come into her bed a few times, late at night after her mother was asleep. He made the springs creak. He'd liked exactly the same things that Fat Andy liked. She'd been thirteen years old. She'd sat on top of him in the moonlight and she had worn a little girl's nightdress. He said he loved her. She never told tales. She never told anyone. Because of this, she knew he'd never deny her anything.

Slightly breathless from running, but not tired, Jaz entered the flats through the underground car park. It was twelve thirty. The Lotus Cortina was parked, gleaming and sleek on its low suspension, in Fat Andy's bay. He was back. A few teenagers stood around, sharing a joint, but Jaz knew they wouldn't touch the car. Fat Andy was known and respected on the estate.

Inside the building there was a sour odour and the strip lights were harshly bright. Jaz waited for the lift then decided it wasn't working. She started on the stairs, two at a time. From the doors she could hear televisions and arguments and a baby crying. The sourness was replaced by the smell of frying onions. Her trainers tapped quickly and evenly as she maintained a rhythm. She glanced at her watch. She was three seconds within her normal time. On the twelfth floor she stopped to catch her breath. A Vietnamese man passed her on his way down. He smelled of garlic and carried an extra large bottle of gin. He did not meet her eye. Jaz continued her rapid ascent. On the sixteenth floor, breathless, she began to unlock Fat Andy's door, but it swung open against the pressure of her hand.

It was oddly quiet in the flat. She'd been expecting

television or loud music or the jangle of Fat Andy's banjo. There were no lights on. 'Andy?' she called, pressing the switch in the hall. The small table by the door was overturned and the telephone was on the floor. Jaz picked them up and restacked the directories. 'Andy?'

She turned on the kitchen light and glanced inside. Her heavy breathing steadied but she was tense and wary. She went into the living room. The computer monitor was on and it cast an eerie glow. She walked over, pressed a key and examined the words that came up on the screen. It was an e-mail. 'Vinnys NOT a happy man', she read. 'Vinny says he wants his proparty back STRATE away. He wants his disk. Allrite? Allrite you Peckham git?'

Something bad had happened here. Jaz felt her pulse quicken again, but with the ugly, irregular flutter of uncertainty and fear. She looked around. The room was a mess. The sofa was on its side and a chair was broken in pieces. CDs and computer disks were scattered. Cups, plates and playing cards were strewn across the floor. Glasses were broken. A framed photo of Andy and his previous girlfriend, Princess, was smashed on the hearth. There was a smell of whisky and Jaz saw a bottle had been flung against a wall, streaking it brown. Andy's banjo was lying face down in the debris. She swallowed hard. This wasn't a burglary. Nothing was missing and no one on the estate would ever bother Fat Andy.

She went into the bedroom. It was in complete darkness. Jaz paused, aware that her brow was sweaty but not because she'd been running. Her whole body was suddenly clammy with a sense of dread. Something very bad had happened. This is scary, she thought to herself. This is very scary. Her fingers felt for the string that turned on the light. She couldn't find it. There was a strange smell and a chilly, nameless kind of quiet that was unnatural and new to the room. At last her groping fingers located the cord and the bed was suddenly illuminated. 'Andy?' she whispered.

He lay on his back, his boots dangling, toes pointing inwards. One hand was above his head, the other below his throat. Blood had oozed through his fingers and coagulated. It covered, thickly and glutinously, his neck, chest, waist, arm and half the bed. It had run down and made a large, sticky-looking pool which hadn't entirely sunk into the carpet. Jaz stared. She had seen blood before but never so much. It smelled strongly, salty, like fresh meat. She felt the urge to scream and cry out but held a hand over the bottom half of her face. The cold stillness of the room and the blood that had stopped flowing meant one real, definite thing. Fat Andy was dead. She went over and touched his raised hand. It was ice cold. It didn't feel like human flesh. His face was ghastly white, his eyes half closed, his mouth slightly open as if in surprise. His cheeks were like sunken, grey dough. Jaz couldn't move. She examined with her eyes the gash in his neck which reminded her, at that moment, of a woman's sexual parts. 'Andy?' she said.

Later, thinking about this night, Jaz would find it strange, remembering how quick and decisive she'd suddenly become. She turned and left Andy, left him lying there, left the bedroom, turning off the light. She was able, temporarily, to dismiss both shock and outrage. For the next fifteen minutes, her only thoughts were that she'd made a big mistake by being here and that it was necessary, imperative to get away. Far away. She shouldn't have come back tonight. She should never have stayed in this flat, lived here. She'd been trapped. She'd abandoned her freedom. For six months she'd been a fool. I'm a mug, was all she could think. What have I got myself into? Jaz, you're a mug. You're a stupid idiot.

She searched the rooms for her few possessions and packed them in her sports bag. From the mantelpiece, she took an old photograph of her twin sisters, Peony and Mimosa, which was undamaged. She picked up the smashed frame from the hearth and extracted the picture of Fat Andy and Princess. She decided to keep it as she had no other to remind herself of him. She found his jacket in the living room and took a fold of money and small change. She pocketed his leather driving gloves and his Filofax. For ten seconds she held the keys to the Lotus Cortina, staring at them, tempted, before tossing them aside.

She knew that her departure needed to be speedy, silent and unremarkable. She wasn't going to take the car. Not now. Not yet. She had to become the same homeless, unacknowledged shadow she'd previously been. She didn't want trouble. She didn't want the attention that would come from driving Andy's car. For a few mad months she'd broken her code. Living in a proper flat, with the same man, day in day out, had been an error of judgement. It wasn't her style. Now she would resume her former life where invisibility and safety were the same thing. She didn't want to be noticed. She certainly didn't want to be caught up in the glare that follows the discovery of a murder.

She locked the outside door. She ran down the stairs and across the deserted courtyard. She sprinted towards

Camberwell New Road. She ran and ran, heading instinctively towards the river. At Blackfriars she stopped and leaned against a wall. She was at last exhausted. She knew of a wide doorway nearby which was draught-free. She was relieved to find it unoccupied. Before settling down she found a phone box. She dialled 999 but hung up when asked for her name. Instead, she phoned the police station on Peckham High Street. 'Don't ask me anything,' she insisted. She gave the address of the flat and checked it was recorded correctly. 'Fat Andy's dead,' she then added. 'Get round there now.'

'What was that, Madam?'

'Fat Andy's dead.' As she said these words again the tears started flowing. She realized she was in shock. There was a pain in her chest which was nothing to do with running such a long way. She was on the verge of losing control. 'Andy,' she sobbed. 'My Andy. Someone's done him in.'

Chapter Two

The early morning traffic woke Jaz at four thirty. She'd
become unaccustomed to sleeping outside, so despite
feeling very free, she was also stiff and cold. A thin sun
glimmered from below the skyline. She stood up,
stretched and then remembered. Her life in Peckham had
come to an abrupt close. She had been ready to end
it herself, but she'd wanted merely to disappear. Such
violence, such a brutal snuffing out of Fat Andy's life was
unbelievable. She was appalled.

Jaz had lived on the streets for a long time and wit-
nessed lots of unpleasant scenes, but seeing Andy like
that, a person who was normally warm and cuddly and
alive – seeing him like a butchered animal spread over
their bed – this was the worst thing she'd ever had to deal
with. An unfamiliar emotion spread from a pain at the
centre of her chest and through her undersized frame,
before lodging in her mind. She considered this sensation,
deciding the only word to describe it was grief. Grief
mixed with yesterday's shock. Her mind was racing and
her body was trembling.

She picked up her sports bag, put on Andy's gloves
and her Walkman and set off, across the river. The
Thames was liquid silver streaked with grey. The sky
was changing from orange-mauve to blue and overhead

a helicopter hammered and swooped, frightening a flock of gulls. Jaz was the only person on the bridge and she walked quickly, then even quicker, before breaking into a gentle jog. The morning air was at its freshest, before the cars poisoned the day. She breathed evenly, concentrating on maintaining a rhythm. She increased her pace. As she sped up Farringdon Road, the exertion of running had its usual effect. All thoughts of Fat Andy and the carnage at his flat disappeared temporarily from her mind. She remembered instead that only yesterday, on the night of her birthday, she'd decided to return to Teesside. Now, this idea was compelling. She wanted to get as far away as possible from the flat, from Peckham, from London.

Ahead, on a bend, a vast hoarding advertised a building society. A delicate child was shown, ten times life-size, surrounded by apple blossom and cradling a dove. Suddenly, sentimentally, Jaz felt a desire to see the twins. Her sisters would make her feel better, she was sure. She remembered their small bodies, their silky cheeks and long eyelashes. It didn't occur to her that they must be seventeen years old. She still thought of them as young children. For the first time in years, she missed them. She thought of the way their golden hair lay across their brows, ragged and uncombed, hanging down in strands, hiding the innocent smoothness of their little-girl necks, their bony shoulders. She could imagine them only as they had once been. Peony and Mimosa existed forever in her mind as nine-year-olds, together and inseparable, playing carelessly amongst the mud and debris of their mother's ruined farmyard.

Jaz approached the Angel and slowed to walking pace. A group of women wearing overalls emerged from the

Tube station. They were cheerful and smiling, extending to her the complicity of early morning workers. London is a secret at five a.m., Jaz thought to herself – a precious secret known only to a handful of its inhabitants. She avoided their gaze. There was no way she wanted to belong to London now; be a Londoner. Instead, she needed to escape.

Jaz spent the day walking and running, covering several miles. She tried to contact Trace at the hotel, to tell her what had happened, but the receptionist said she knew no one of that name. Then she rang Harm's mobile and left a message, merely saying she was going away for a while, and not to worry. She was concerned that they would hear of Fat Andy's death and start panicking. She resolved to keep trying them until she could explain what had happened at the flat.

She sat in a park, ate a sandwich, then slept for a while on a bench. She hitched a couple of rides. Later, at a service station somewhere on the M11, acting out of habit she decided to ask someone for money. It was eleven p.m. She glanced around the lobby but couldn't see a woman. She went over to the café, but the diners were all men, lorry drivers and travelling salesmen. Even the staff, serving behind the hot counters in red waist-coats and bow ties, were male. She noticed two young men in overalls who were about to leave. They walked towards her at the entrance, each sipping a can of Pepsi.

'Hello, boys,' Jaz said too loudly and with confidence, 'I've got no money. Going to give me some?' She looked them in the eyes, in turn, and stood too close, using her sports bag to block their path. They stopped, surprised.

Automatically, politely, one searched in his pockets for change. He became flustered and embarrassed. Without examining it, he handed her a crumpled note. He didn't meet her gaze.

Jaz stepped into the restaurant and grinned. She smoothed out the cash. It was ten pounds. At least I can still hustle for money, she thought. I haven't lost my touch. She hadn't done this for a long time, but she knew that in the near future she might have no choice. Everything was uncertain. She was homeless again. The days and weeks ahead had an unknown quality that might demand anything – not least the use of her old street skills.

The café was called the Planet Suite and it was air conditioned. The low light fittings were ringed orbs. The ordinary food was imaginatively named. Using the ten pounds Jaz bought a large coffee, a Saturn Burger and a Milky Way ice cream. As she sat down she noticed that her plastic table top was a map of Mars. Outside was the straight corridor of the motorway, the thrum-thrum of lighted cars, empty fields and the real moon, hanging in the distance like a dirty plate. Jaz stirred her cup and glanced around. She thought to herself, this place is just a universe of lonely souls.

A few men studied tabloids, drank tea, slapped the bottoms of sauce bottles. For an instant each one was known to her – there was a neighbour from Peckham, a teacher from her school, a social worker she'd had sex with at the hostel in Hammersmith – but then, at each moment of recognition, their unfamiliar features focused and she knew she was amongst strangers. I'm tired, she thought a little bleakly. It's night-time. And there's miles and miles still to go.

After finishing her food, Jaz bought a second cup of coffee. The men around her arrived, left and arrived. They glanced at her without curiosity. She took the blotting paper doilies from between her cups and saucers and tore them into thin shreds. Sitting quietly, but restless, it was impossible not to think about Andy, lying with his throat cut on the bed where she'd slept with him for the last six months. She remembered a long smear of blood, brown and thick, across the blue pillowcase. The image of him dead kept cutting across thoughts of him alive. She tried to think of him settled in his armchair, drinking Scotch, big and jolly, always pleased to see her, but the grisly corpse in the bedroom kept returning to her mind.

She remembered the e-mail message on the computer screen. 'Vinnys NOT a happy man.' Reluctantly, Jaz thought about what this could mean. It was a threatening statement. Vinny from the Island was dangerous if he was unhappy. People tried to keep him happy at all costs.

Vinny dealt in cars. His legitimate business was run from a wide-fronted, brash showroom and its adjoining forecourt, both filled with new and second-hand Mazdas, all acquired legally. However, his legendary wealth was the result of another enterprise. Vinny employed a team of thieves who operated throughout east London and the City. His expertise lay in changing the identity of stolen cars and then selling them abroad. He specialized in Jaguars and BMWs, stolen to order, but he was prepared to handle any car that was new, gleaming and expensive. He paid well but demanded total loyalty. Fat Andy had worked for him for several years, supervising all the work on the streets. This meant he recruited and fired the thieves, specified which cars they were to steal, and handed out their wages.

Jaz drained her cup. She had worked for Vinny too, but not recently. She'd met Andy in a queue outside a Chinese takeaway and admired his Lotus Cortina. They started chatting about classic cars. That night, they arranged to meet again and once she had discovered his line of work, Jaz persuaded him to take her on. For a while she was his star thief, earning special commendations and a bonus. When she decided to quit an unsatisfactory squat in Kensington, Andy suggested she stay at his flat. After they started sleeping together, he'd asked her to stop stealing cars and reluctantly, she agreed. He said it was unsuitable work for a woman. What he meant was, he didn't like his girlfriend doing it. Vinny understood. He knew he had to let Jaz go. Vinny was familiar with the nuances and etiquette of male pride, and Fat Andy was not only proud but indispensable. Or at least he had been.

Jaz thought about the tiny office at the back of Vinny's showroom with its girlie calendars and battered desk. Vinny, she knew, sat there for hours, wiry and energetic in his dark suits, talking rapidly down the phone in his Greek accent, fixing deal after lucrative deal. He had contacts all over Europe. He had gold rings on his small, hairy hands, a compact, muscular body and dark eyes, one of which had a habit of wandering sideways, out of control, giving him a stupid look. But Jaz knew that Vinny from the Island was no fool. He was ruthless and clever and not a person to offend. She wondered what Andy had done. He'd said Vinny was ungrateful. He'd said he wanted a better deal, more money and responsibility. He wanted to be cut into the operation as a partner rather than a lackey. Whatever had happened between them, Andy had ended up dead.

Vinny was not a happy man. He wanted his property back. Andy had a disk belonging to him and because of this and probably other reasons, he had killed Andy or ordered him killed. Jaz was in no doubt: Vinny had done it. Of this, she was absolutely certain.

After another half hour, Jaz walked over to a games machine and fed the slot with her few remaining coins. Trying to be animated, she pressed several buttons and a stream of lucky silver cascaded to her feet. She was aware that all the men in the café were staring. She collected the coins together and went into a phone booth.

She checked in Andy's Filofax, then pressed the numbers of Vinny's mobile. It was twelve forty-five but she knew he suffered from insomnia. He was hyperactive and a gambler. Fat Andy had told her of his habits. He would be sucking Rennies for his heartburn. He was probably playing roulette at a down-market Chinese casino off the East India Dock Road.

The phone was answered immediately.

'Vinny! Companero!' She always called him this. 'You fucking Greek bastard, it's Jaz.' She pressed her hand against the pain in her chest.

There was a pause. 'Hello darlink,' he replied. His voice was always unnaturally high, making him sound effeminate. 'How yous keeping?'

Her voice became very cold. 'Why did you do it? You're a complete shit, you know that?'

'What you mean, darlink? What you want?'

'Vinny, don't piss about. I've left London. You can't find me. D'you think I won't shop you? Turn you in? You evil fucker. I know what's gone down in Peckham. D'you think I won't contact the Old Bill?' Jaz hung up. She wanted to make Vinny's sleep patterns even more troubled. She felt a rush of pleasure. She'd never liked him. Now there was nothing to stop her from harassing Vinny on his mobile, any time she felt like it. She decided to ring him again the next day.

Outside, the exit road curved away like a dark snake. Jaz needed to hitch a lift but felt reluctant to face the night. She picked up her bag and stepped out into the warm wind, then jogged across the car park. A mother and father unloaded two sleeping toddlers from the back of a Ford Escort. Jaz noted their roof-rack loaded with luggage and their window stickers showing previous holiday destinations. She thought of her own family and of Peony and Mimosa and how they'd never been anywhere on holiday apart from a day trip to Redcar sands. I'm going home, she thought to herself.

She ran past the petrol station and down the slip road towards the motorway's convoy of lorries, its buzz of anxious cars. I'm going home, she thought again. She stopped and turned around. The family with the sleeping children entered the service station. It shone like a friendly island in the sea of night. Jaz stood on the grass verge, hesitated, then loosened her hair, letting the wind stir it around her face. She felt smaller than ever in the darkness. She stood casually for a moment, her thin hip jutting, then she stretched out her arm.

A car stopped immediately. It was a new Mondeo, red and throaty. It throbbed lustily at her side. The driver leaned over and opened both the passenger and the rear door. There was a blare of music. She threw her bag on the back seat then climbed in next to him. As she clipped together her seat belt he turned down the volume of the

CD. Jaz noted that he was about twenty-seven, smart and smelled of scent. He smiled, accelerated and cruised over into the sparse but fast moving outside lane. Jaz inspected his suit, his gleaming collar, a faint shadow on his jaw, a nervous pulse in his temple.

'Michael,' he said. 'I'm only going as far as Cambridge.'

Jaz smiled and took off Fat Andy's driving gloves, turned round and tucked them into her sports bag. She recognized his flat friendly accent. She'd heard it in hostels all over London.

'Call me Mike,' he added self-consciously. 'I'm from Leeds.'

Jaz decided at that moment she could do with a bit of short-term help from Mike. She was in no hurry and she was tired. In an instant she had assessed both Mike's affluence and his susceptibility. He's not a weirdo, she thought to herself. He's ordinary and safe. He won't give me any trouble.

'Hi Mike,' she replied, moving closer and placing her right arm behind his head rest in a gesture that was both innocent and seductive.

With a strained roar from the engine he overtook a BMW. He was trying to impress her. Jaz decided he was a good driver but not as good as Fat Andy and definitely not as good as herself. One thing she'd learned from Blow was not to overwork a car.

Mike took a cigarette out of a packet on his lap and pressed the dashboard lighter. 'It's a dangerous game,' he said, 'thumbing lifts.' He inhaled. There was a silence. 'D'you always travel this way then?'

Jaz adopted a slightly breathless, babyish tone. It was one she'd sometimes used with Andy when she wanted her own way. She exaggerated her northern accent. 'Only with nice lads. Nice lads with decent cars.' She sounded at least six years younger than she actually was. She sounded under-age.

'Your mam and dad. They know where you are, luv?' He changed gear and his hand brushed her knee. He pretended it was an accident.

'That's all right,' Jaz murmured softly.

The Mondeo ate up the miles. A cool breeze blew on Jaz through the vent at her side and Mike played a Levellers album. Soft guitar music filled the small space. She was suddenly sleepy and for a moment wished more than anything that they were the only two people in the universe. Travelling at high speed in a fast car, late at night on the motorway was one of her favourite things in the world. She closed her eyes, pretending she was in a space rocket, circling the earth. It was so peaceful, she wanted it to go on for ever.

After a while, Jaz told Mike that she loved animals and that when she left school she wanted to study veterinary science. She invented an elderly godmother in Leeds. She could read Mike. He was excited by her presence in his car and pleased and flattered. He thought she was a wayward child. She built up the fiction. 'My older sister's a lesbian. She's sixteen. She's got fat legs.'

'You got a boyfriend, then?'

'No. 'Fraid not.'

'Good.'

'Is it?'

'Yeah.'

Jaz dozed again, almost happy. She woke up as the car curved, slowing, leaving the steady rhythm of the motorway. Instantly alert, she took in road signs, an all-night pizzeria, a double-decker bus. 'Where are we?' she mumbled, pretending to be confused.

They paused at a roundabout. 'I'm not going much further,' Mike said.

Jaz straightened, yawned, reached for her bag. 'Best drop me here then,' she said in a neutral voice, 'so's I can get another lift.'

'I can always take you to my place,' Mike offered, very hesitant. He pulled into a lay-by and turned towards her, his empty palms upward in a gesture of honesty and helplessness. 'It's no trouble.'

Jaz pretended to be shy. Her hair fell forward hiding her face. 'OK,' she agreed, sounding like a little girl.

'You sure?'

'I'm sure.'

Later, in Mike's bed, Jaz stared at the brown walls, the chrome alarm clock, the single plain white bathrobe hanging on the back of the door. This wasn't a woman's room. She held her hands over her nipples. Mike was next to her, propped on pillows, talking to Japan on the phone. The bed was soft and clean. Jaz wished that he was speaking to a wife or even a girlfriend. She felt almost sorry for him. She leaned over and stroked his thighs.

Mike put the phone down, switched off the light and turned towards her. Jaz's mind immediately moved to that distant place which makes feigned sexual interest possible. Out of habit, her expert hands travelled over his body. She held him and kissed his neck. She rubbed her chest against his and wrapped her legs around him. He was fleshier than she expected and at first his gentle passivity encouraged her. She kissed his lips fiercely, her hand travelling down his back, finding the crack in his buttocks. After a few more moments she realized he was not responding. 'What's the matter?' she whispered.

He rolled over onto his back. 'I'm sorry,' he said finally.

'It's OK.'

'No it's not. It's never OK.' He sounded desperate. 'I thought you'd be . . .' He paused.

'What?'

There was another awkward silence. Outside a siren announced an ambulance.

Jaz suddenly realized the nature of the problem. 'You thought I'd be a virgin,' she supplied. She'd been acting a part, but she'd not acted the right one for Mike. He'd wanted a naive and innocent female, not one who was experienced and knowing.

She stared at the space around the window blind where the orange light from a street lamp gleamed dully. When she heard him crying, she pretended to be asleep.

The alarm clock said seven a.m. Jaz touched Mike's cheek, checking he was still unconscious.

He breathed deeply and regularly. She slipped out of bed and with practised stealth, dressed in silence. She combed her hair with his comb and removed forty pounds from his jacket. She took the loose change from his trouser pocket. A box on the mantelpiece contained some gold cufflinks which she removed. Finally, without disturbing him, she slid his watch off the bedside table.

In the hall she was relieved to see that the burglar

alarm was not switched on. There was no complicated locking mechanism on the front door. In an instant, she was outside in the street where the morning rush hour was starting to build.

Chapter Three

Jaz had never been to Cambridge before. She wandered around, mingling with the crowds. A lot of people carried cameras and guidebooks. She wondered what it must be like to be a tourist and go somewhere on holiday. She thought again how she'd never been on holiday in her life.

After leaving another message for Harm, she bought a postcard showing two students in a punt and scribbled on the back 'Going up north for a visit, don't worry,' and sent it to Trace, care of the kitchen at the hotel. Jaz wasn't confident she'd receive it. It was likely that she had moved on to other casual employment by now.

It was hot in the bright sunshine and she bought an ice lolly. At one point, near some traffic lights, she thought she saw Mike in his red Mondeo but realized immediately that the registration number was different. Thinking of him with a mixture of pity and distaste, she found a shop with a sign in the window saying 'We Buy gold' and sold his watch and cufflinks for two hundred and fifty pounds.

Jaz had lunch in McDonald's, ordering a McChicken Sandwich and a strawberry milk shake. As she sat munching, she watched diners come and go and thought about how people from all walks of life ate at McDonald's, even men who were almost certainly university dons. She tried to keep her mind occupied but, inevitably, thoughts of Fat Andy came crowding in. The now familiar pain spread across her chest and she placed a hand on the centre. She could feel a rhythmic pulse. My heart is breaking, she thought. I was going to leave him, but now he's dead. I'm suffering. If only I'd stayed in and waited for him. If only I hadn't insisted that he come back for my birthday. If only I'd never met him. She repeated this new phrase in her mind. My heart is breaking.

She remembered Andy using the same words. They'd just had a row. She leaned her head in her hand, sipping her milk shake, picturing the scene in the flat. Andy didn't like Harm and Trace. He didn't like Jaz going out in the evening without him.

'They're my best mates,' she'd argued.

'They're slappers.'

'They saved my life!' Jaz was very angry. Not for the first time with Andy she felt trapped. 'We've been through all sorts together, us three. We're the nearest any of us has to family. They're more like my sisters than my real sisters. Who the hell do you think you are? I've only known you a few weeks.'

The quarrel ebbed back and forth.

'First you make me give up my job . . .'

'Nicking cars isn't a job . . .'

'Then you start telling me who I can and can't see . . .'

'I'm only saying . . .'

Jaz picked up her sports bag and went into the bedroom and stuffed it with clothes. She returned. 'I'm out of here,' she said. 'I'm not listening to any more of this fucking shit, you telling me what to do.' She took one of the photos off the mantelpiece. It was the picture of

Peony and Mimosa, dressed as angels. She packed it away. 'I'm going.' She pulled the zip and shouldered the bag. 'Pissing right off out of here.' She walked towards the door. 'Goodbye.'

Fat Andy was sitting in the armchair, his head in his hands, leaning forwards. He peeped at her between his fingers. As she opened the door he raised his head. Jaz turned and saw that his face was wet. He looked very sad. 'My heart's breaking,' he said.

Jaz was amazed. She stopped in her tracks. 'What?'

'My heart. You're breaking my heart.'

She put down her bag. She was pleased. He'd told her he loved her, but only in bed, when he wanted certain things. She hadn't believed him. She went over and wrapped her arms around his head, pressing his face to her chest. 'It's fine,' she said repeatedly, 'I'm sorry, everything's fine.' Her anger had vanished. His heart was breaking. She was at a loss for words. 'It's fine. Really. It's fine.'

Jaz stirred her milk shake with her straw and pressed her hand even harder against her chest. It occurred to her that she had never felt grief like this before and that the pain was physically sharp. Tears pricked her eyes but refused to fall. She wondered what had happened between Andy and Vinny and how things could have got so very bad between them. Andy must have pushed Vinny too far. He was never any kind of match for Vinny – he wasn't devious or clever enough and he wasn't cruel. In any case, Vinny never let anyone push him. Never. He demanded total loyalty. He demanded respect.

She finished her meal and went outside, into a phone

box. She dialled the number of Vinny's line in his garage but he didn't answer and she was asked to leave a message. She spoke angrily but quietly. 'Companero? You greasy pile of shite? Guess who? You'll not get away with this. You'll not, I repeat, not get away with this. I'll do you. I'm going to do you. You evil fuck. You Greek bastard.' Until yesterday, she'd never dared speak to Vinny like this. She realized she'd always wanted to. She wondered what the point of it was, but she hung up the phone feeling a tiny bit better.

Later, Jaz boarded a tourist bus and sat on the open-air top deck. She stayed there for an hour and a half, going round and round the town, listening to the same recorded commentary. It was reassuring to do such a predictable, innocent thing. It made her feel more like other people.

She remembered the first time she'd sat on such a bus. It was a cold, dark night in Sunderland and they'd driven there in one of Blow's old cars. It was late, a time she'd normally be in bed. She was with the twins. They parked, got on the bus and climbed the stairs. It was breezy and Blow wrapped the three of them together in an old blanket from the stable. The memory of the rough wool and the rank horse-smell was still with her. The bus drove in the darkness to the promenade but there was no moon and the sea was as black as the sky. Jaz remembered the sharp jabs of the twins' elbows and the way Blow had leaned towards them, his arm along the back of their bench, his breath sour with beer. The invisible sea rolled to and fro and they waited, unsure what was happening. Suddenly the air around them burst into a blinding dazzle of light. Peony screamed, and Jasmine's heart lurched in her chest. There was an explosion of colour. A brass band, somewhere below them, blew out the national anthem in a deafening, resounding blast. The bus started to move, driving slowly along, and above them were flashing Santas and snowflakes and the glare of a million light bulbs. 'It's the Illuminations,' exclaimed Blow, excited. 'Aren't they something, girls? You've just seen 'em switched on.'

Jaz sat on the bus, her mind wandering. She tried to imagine olden times, when the students wore gowns and worked within these ancient colleges with dusty books and quill pens, but thoughts of Fat Andy kept returning. She remembered the horrible quiet in the bedroom where the body had lain, the dreadful stillness of the corpse. She recalled the scent, the chill of death, the blood on the carpet.

I am a free person now, she reminded herself. I can do exactly as I please, just like in the old days. I was going to leave him anyway. I know what I'm doing. I know what I want. I'm going home. She was surprised that these realizations did not make her feel better. She got off the bus and jogged in the direction of a big modern hotel which she'd noticed earlier in the day.

She checked in and hung a 'Do Not Disturb' sign on the outside of her door before closing it firmly. Jaz loved hotels and even feeling as bad as she did, she went through her routine of lying down on the first bed, then bouncing on the other, like a child. She pressed a button which raised and lowered an external shutter and then she tinkered with the controls of the air conditioning. She made herself a cup of coffee, drank it then took a shower using the complimentary gel and shampoo. She wrapped herself in thick white towels and switched on the TV. She drank several non-alcoholic beverages from the mini-bar. There was nothing about the murder in the news. She rang Harm's mobile again. This time she answered.

'Look Harm, no questions, but I'm in Cambridge. Andy's been killed . . !'

'Jesus Christ, Jaz! What's happened?'

'Fat Andy's been killed. Murdered. I don't want to talk about it. I'm going home to Teesside, just for a bit. Tell Trace. Don't worry. I'm OK.'

She hung up, then picked up the phone again and rang room service to request three newspapers and a bacon sandwich. She combed through the papers but there was nothing about Fat Andy. Evidently a murder on a south London council estate was not remarkable enough to interest the national dailies. Jaz drew her curtains and climbed into bed. She knew she had enough cash to stay in the hotel for a while but was conscious of wasting resources. She decided to continue on her journey home the following day.

She picked up the phone again. Slowly and remembering the number whole, like a familiar place name, she pressed each separate digit carefully, her anticipation and fear growing with each electronic beep. She hadn't phoned home in years. When the ringing tone began, she almost hung up. Her heart was hammering and her mouth was dry. She pictured the empty hallway with its bare and rotting boards, the crazy lean of the dilapidated porch, the old-fashioned bakelite phone, dusty on the windowsill. She imagined the bell, echoing up the dead, damp space of the stairwell and the clatter of the twins' boots.

'Yes,' answered her mother. 'Who is it?'

Jaz's stomach lurched. Her mother never answered the phone. She'd expected Blow, or one of the girls. 'Lola?' she said. 'It's Jasmine.'

There was the briefest of pauses. The line hummed with a thousand ghostly conversations linking south and north. 'Well then,' her mother said. She sounded discouraged, just like she'd always done, but surprisingly sober. 'Well then.'

Jaz explained that she was on her way home.

'You've just caught me,' her mother said, as if she was at the start of an errand.

'I'll be a day or two yet,' Jaz explained, almost apologetic.

'That's not what I mean.' Her mother went on to say that she was leaving the farm, going the next day. Everything was sold. The fields were to be built over with starter homes.

Jaz listened to this, barely able to comprehend. Her mother's words buzzed in her head like a fly.

'And not a minute too soon,' said her mother. She sounded weary but at the same time more decisive than she'd ever been before.

'What about,' Jaz whispered, then paused. 'What about the others?'

Her mother's tone didn't change. 'What others?'

'The twins . . . Are they . . .'

'Peony's in town with a good-for-nothing labourer and twin baby boys. Mimosa's at Newcastle College making sculptures out of papier mâché.'

'And Blow . . .?'

There was a silence. Her mother sighed. 'Well of course. You wouldn't know.'

'Know what?'

'Blow's no longer with us.'

'You mean he's left?'

She sniffed, then coughed. 'Dead.' She paused. 'Crashed his car the same night as Princess Diana.'

Jaz gasped. There was another stab of pain in her chest, the same as before. She pressed her hand to the spot once again. 'What . . . what on earth was he doing in . . . Paris?'

'Don't be bloody stupid. He crashed on the A1, just north of Leeming Bar. He lost control, caused a pile-up, and everything caught fire. They had to use dental records to identify him.' She coughed again, then sighed.

Chapter Four

·

Jaz held the phone away from her face and stared at it in disbelief.

'Hello?' she heard her mother say. 'Hello?'

Purposefully, slowly, she replaced the receiver.

A few minutes passed. She watched the numbers on the clock radio change: 20.45, 20.46, 20.47, 20.48.

Blow is dead, she thought. Fat Andy is dead. She fiddled with the TV remote, turning the set off, then on again, without the sound. She got up and filled the kettle and switched it on, then forgot about it. After a while, she lay flat on the bed, clutching the pillows to her stomach. 'Oh, no,' she said aloud. It came out as a groan. 'Shit, shit, shit.'

A few tears ran down the sides of her face and into her ears. She sat up and wiped her nose. Outside, below in the street, a succession of emergency vehicles raced by, their sirens sounding.

Both of them, she thought. Both Blow and Fat Andy. Both dead. It seemed beyond all reason. She picked up the phone, intending to call Harm, but replaced it without dialling.

She realized, not for the first time, that the two of them – Fat Andy and Blow – were, in a curious way, the same person. They were very alike and she'd loved them.

She ran this word through her mind a few times. Love. She'd loved them. Yes, she loved them but never desired them. She'd loved them even though they'd let her down. The pattern had repeated itself.

I thought the world of them, she said to herself, realizing that this quaint expression was one she'd learned long before, but never in connection with her own feelings. She said it aloud, 'I thought the world of them.' She'd never admitted this, or even considered it, when they were alive. Love was a subject she never acknowledged, an emotion she always suppressed – but she felt it now. They were loved. Both Fat Andy and Blow, as if they were one. She pressed her hand again onto the place in her chest where she felt the wound. It was the pain of an empty space. It was an acute sense of loss.

She climbed back into bed but couldn't sleep. Instead, she kept imagining a scene where either Blow, or Fat Andy, or sometimes both of them curiously merged, were repairing the sills on a white, ex-police Ford Capri. Lying on their backs, heads partially hidden, they were drilling holes, then filling them with Waxoyl to keep the metal rust-free. 'How's it going?' she pictured herself asking, several times, always placing a steaming cup of tea on the ground.

'It's a right bastard,' they each said resignedly. 'This gunge. It's terrible when it drops in your hair.'

At two a.m. she sat up and tried to watch a Sky movie but couldn't understand the storyline. It was very complicated. The gangster in the sharp suit who was killing everyone reminded her of Vinny. He was bigger and better looking, and had an American accent, but he had the same mean, squinty stare. Suddenly she pictured Vinny, dressed in the gangster's clothes with the same machine gun, mowing down Blow and Fat Andy, as if they were nothing. Then, in her mind, she saw him with a knife at Andy's throat. She blinked. She saw a quick, nasty image of the neck wound, but the next moment she imagined him speeding up the A1 in his new Mazda 626 and, in a fit of road rage, deliberately running Blow off the carriageway.

Vinny's to blame, she thought. It's all Vinny's fault. She dozed off then, leaving the lights and the TV switched on.

She woke at five with a stiff neck and an angry sensation growing in her stomach. Anger was taking the place of grief. In an instant she remembered. Blow and Fat Andy were both dead. That fucking Vinny, she thought. She stood up and looked at herself, naked in the mirror. She clenched her fists. That evil spivvy bastard. I'm going to get him for this. He's not getting away with it. She picked up a damp towel from the floor and hurled it towards the bathroom. 'Vinny,' she said aloud. 'You shit. I'm going to get even with you, if it's the only worthwhile thing I ever do.'

She went back to bed and turned things over in her mind. Her anger made her feel strong. She wasn't afraid of Vinny. She had been once, but not any more. She knew he was clever, but then so was she. His viciousness and power could be matched by her determination. She was in a better place to take him on than Andy had been, not least because he wouldn't take her seriously. She wasn't sure how she was going to damage him, but she was determined to make him suffer.

A few certainties began to take shape in her mind.

Number one, Fat Andy and Blow were dead. Number two, Vinny was going to face the consequences. Number three, Harm and Trace were her very good friends and could be called on for help if necessary. This is what I'm going to do, she thought. I'm going to sort out the Greek bastard. She felt a little better. Things suddenly seemed very clear.

She was reminded of a phrase of Fat Andy's. It was one he'd used a lot and he'd repeated it to her endlessly when he was training her to steal cars. 'Stay calm,' he used to say. 'Stay focused. Stay cool.' She said this aloud several times. 'Stay calm, stay focused, stay cool.' She knew that she had to return to London. She wanted revenge. She would go in the morning, quickly, without wasting any time.

Chapter Five

At seven o'clock, Jaz ate a light breakfast, sitting alongside a few silent businessmen. They eyed her curiously over their newspapers whilst ordering extra coffee. Later, in the hotel lobby, she peeled off a few bank notes – part of the proceeds from the sale of Mike's jewellery – and paid her bill.

In the car park, she was pleased to discover there were no surveillance cameras. She walked around, weighing things up. Finally, she selected a 1994 VW Golf with a sticker in the back window which said 'Country-side Campaign'. Jaz was unsympathetic to this pressure group, despite her semi-rural childhood. She believed in the Right to Roam and thought fox-hunting was a sick joke.

She picked up a loose half brick from the edge of the paving. Leaning against the vehicle, her body shielding her action, she broke a quarter light and lifted up the button on the driver's door. She slid inside the car, rummaged in her bag for a pair of screwdrivers, then tossed her belongings onto the back seat.

She waited for a moment as two Japanese men with briefcases walked through the car park and disappeared. She looked at her watch before hitting the steering cowl hard, cracking it open. She threw the brick out of the window, levered the cowl with the large screwdriver, broke it cleanly then discarded the plastic pieces. Using both hands she stabbed the implement into the ignition, leaning against it, ramming it with the weight of her chest until she felt the soft metal around the keyhole open like a wound. Quickly, using the smaller screwdriver, she inserted its blade into the damaged inner barrel and moved it gently up and down. The soft alloy disintegrated, some of it falling to the floor at her feet. She leaned to the side and squinted into the hole she'd created. Satisfied, she repositioned the small screwdriver inside the mechanism and turned it carefully. The engine coughed and awoke with a guilty sigh. Jaz glanced at her watch again. Two minutes. Not bad, she thought.

At that instant, a hotel receptionist arrived and braked her Fiesta at the entrance to the car park. She was yawning, stretching, about to start her shift. She pressed her remote and raised the security barrier.

Jaz drove forward, towards the exit, as if she was in a hurry.

Politely, the young uniformed woman beckoned to the Golf, indicating that it should have priority.

Jaz gave her a thumbs-up as she turned out into the traffic.

The journey south was uneventful, if slow. The motorway was busy. Jaz opened the glove compartment and listened to a few CDs. She found a pair of Versace sunglasses which she put on and decided to keep.

In London, she took the advice of a radio presenter and turned off the main road early, only to get held up near Wood Green for half an hour because of a burst water main. Frustrated, she abandoned the Golf near Archway, took a Tube to London Bridge and changed to a train for Queen's Road. She put on her headphones and jogged steadily in the direction of the estate where she'd lived with Fat Andy. It was only very recently, she thought. It was not that long ago.

She'd decided to take Andy's Lotus Cortina. She couldn't manage without wheels if she was going to get even with Vinny. Her plans were still a bit vague, but she was certain that she'd need a car. Andy's Lotus Cortina was the only one she really wanted and he couldn't stop her driving it now. He's dead, she kept thinking as she ran towards the estate. Fat Andy's dead.

She paused for breath at a bus stop on the main road. It was another hot sunny day. She wiped her sunglasses then replaced them and rubbed her brow with the back of her sleeve. A homeless mother, whose headscarf and sallow skin suggested eastern Europe, begged for coins outside a launderette. Two women with deep, fake tans walked past with pushchairs, ignoring her. Jaz noticed for the first time that the seats at the bus stop were broken and the perspex of the shelter was scored with a thousand cigarette burns. Old newspaper stirred along the pavement, listless in the heat, a lazy dog scratched itself and a group of children, skiving off school, giggled in the doorway of an abandoned hairdresser's, passing around a magazine.

A middle-aged man lurched across the road, muttering. One of his arms was inside a metal hospital crutch and his other hand held a carrier bag full of empty bottles. Jaz recognized him as a former neighbour but avoided his eye. The homeless woman called out to him but he seemed not to hear.

Jaz hesitated, wondering if her reasons for coming here were more complicated than just taking the car. Maybe it was something to do with the place being home. She felt confused. It was, after all, the only proper home she'd had since leaving Teesside more than seven years before. I was living here, she reflected again with sadness. Only recently. Not that long ago. She blinked her eyes rapidly to avoid tears. Last week, she thought, everything was normal. She pressed against the pain in her chest with the palm of her hand.

She was unwilling to make her way towards the estate. Without wanting to, she imagined the final scene in the flat. She remembered the way Fat Andy's dead feet had pointed inwards, toes together, helpless and sad. She couldn't go there and there was no one she wanted to see. She examined her watch. The sun was bright and high and her pale face smarted in its strong urban rays. There was a smell of soft tarmac, drains and a whiff of an Indian takeaway.

A silver Mercedes drove past slowly. Three men lounged inside, behind the darkened windows – two of them black, the other white. There was the flash of gold jewellery, the impression of expensive sports clothes. Jaz watched as it circled the block, disappearing, then reappearing from behind the flats. It made another leisurely circuit then paused twenty yards from the bus stop. She knew these men were drug dealers and that they were involved in estate-based crime. She also knew their car – Fat Andy had supplied it, via Vinny, in return for cash, and she herself had stolen it to order the previous year.

A window of the Mercedes glided down and there was a sudden blast of rap. One of the black men looked at Jaz but her eyes were hidden by her sunglasses and she pretended not to notice. He was holding a phone. He pursed his lips in a kiss then spat confidently. She still didn't respond. He grinned then shrugged. The window was raised, extinguishing the music. With indifference, Jaz lifted, then quickly plaited her thin sandy hair in a tight braid, knotting it at the ends. The car cruised away.

She took another long hard look at the flats. This estate, she knew, was different from the real world. It was more extreme, more bizarre. It was a place where a young mother, crazy on drink and drugs, had thrown her three-year-old daughter out of a sixth-floor window. It was a place where an old man had lain dead and unde-tected in his bedroom for two years. It was a place where a teenage boy had been set alight and left to burn in a stairwell.

Jaz moved her sports bag from one shoulder to another. The rows of windows glittered symmetrically. The concrete oblongs were grouped together like strangers around their tract of empty wasteland. The fore-court and walkways seemed deserted. Jaz took a deep breath and purposefully walked over. 'Stay calm,' she said aloud. 'Stay focused.' She entered the dark and mal-odorous space beneath the flats that led to the under-ground car park.

Fat Andy's car was still there. She saw it immediately, gleaming in the half light. One of its back tyres was a little flat, but otherwise it was perfect. She wanted it and was determined to take it. It had been Fat Andy's and he never let her drive it, but it was no use to him any more. She walked towards it. Hello, you shining beauty, she thought. I want you. You're rare and gorgeous. You're mine.

She didn't have the right key but she knew that this wasn't a problem. Despite its superb styling, its spunky Lotus twin cam engine, its mint condition, it had useless sixties Ford locks which could be picked with a hairpin. Jaz pulled a large keyring out of her sports bag and selected an old double-sided chrome key which she wiggled in the lock of the driver's door. At first it wouldn't work. She turned to a pillar behind her and rubbed both sides on the concrete, filing it down. She tried again and this time she was successful. She unlocked the door, inserted the key in the ignition and turned it. The engine rattled then died. The battery was flat.

At that moment the Mercedes reappeared. It stopped about twenty yards away and reversed into a parking space. Jaz knew she had to ask for help. She went over to the car and smiled shyly at the white man, who was now sitting alone in the front. He opened the door.

Jaz sniffed. There was a smell of marijuana.

'Hi, doll. How you? You OK?' He was thin and young with a shaved head and a weasel-like expression. He had a conversational style which avoided the use of verbs.

'Elvis.' This was his real name. 'I need a jump start. Can you give me a hand?'

'No worries, doll.'

He drove over, got out and handed her the leads. Between them they had the Lotus Cortina firing in a minute.

'Sorry about Andy,' he said.

'Yeah, well. He fell out with that fucking bastard, Vinny.'

'His boss?'

'Yeah. Vinny from the Island. That Greek bastard.'

Elvis gave her a quizzical look.

74

'The police must think it was you lot. I bet they do. They blame you for everything. You and Peppy and Big Boy.'

He spat on the ground. 'Those coppers on the High Street? Pure harassment, doll. Intimidation.' He slapped the roof of the Mercedes. 'The Old Bill? Me in there twice, overnight, in a cell.' His mouth became a thin line. 'A victim, me. Police brutality. My brief? Complaint to the whatsisname. The Ombudsman. Ongoing, doll. Ongoing. What else? Big Boy's brief? Racism.'

Jaz closed the bonnet of the Lotus Cortina, slid inside and revved the engine a little. She checked the oil pressure. She raised her voice. 'I'm going to tell them it was Vinny. I think they'll pull Vinny. It won't stick but it might give you a break.'

Elvis took his jump leads and got back into the Mercedes. 'All right, him, that Andy,' he mused. 'An OK bloke. Never, you know, not Andy . . . Us? Knife in the neck? Not us.' He raised both hands in a gesture of innocence. 'You know? Straight up, doll.'

Jaz took her foot off the accelerator and let the engine idle. She looked into his hard south London face. It revealed generations of criminality. His eyes were like black pebbles. His mind was full of deals, coercion, cash, violence. He had no hobbies apart from drugs, no friends outside the gang and no family that he bothered with. She knew he'd kill anyone as soon as look at them, if there was a reason. But Fat Andy had never given him a reason.

'I know it wasn't you,' she said. She didn't like him. She wanted him to go away.

He gestured towards Fat Andy's car. 'His motor? You?'

'Yep. I need wheels. Been thinking about going on

holiday. Soon.' She shrugged, dismissing him. 'Cheers, mate.'

Elvis set the Mercedes in motion. 'Help with that flat tyre? Yes or no?'

She shook her head.

'Well, you around, I expect. Yeah?' He reparked, locked the Mercedes and slouched away, his hand raised in farewell.

Jaz changed to the spare, turned the Lotus Cortina then drove out, emerging into the late morning sun. For a few minutes, driving again, getting the feel of the car, she was elated. She put on her shades and headed towards the police station on Peckham High Street. It was twelve a.m.

Inside, within the stuffy anonymity of the waiting room, she gave a false name and an address which was a few doors away from where she'd been living with Fat Andy. When she was asked for a date of birth, she invented one which indicated she was only fifteen years old. 'It's about that killing,' she said, adopting a London accent. 'That fat geezer with his throat cut.'

After a short wait she was taken to an interview room by a plain-clothes officer who was working on the case. He was surly and wordless, as if he expected her to waste his time. He gestured to a chair, then seated himself behind a desk.

Jaz stared at him as he slowly copied her details onto another form. He was very clean, with a pale blue shirt and patterned tie. He was young, too young. His nails were manicured. His hair was shiny and shaped in a way that suggested he'd just been to the hairdresser. She pictured him in a department store, selecting expensive cologne. She wondered if he sat behind a desk, writing, all of the time. Maybe writing was his job. He didn't look like he fought any kind of war on the streets. 'Well?' he said.

She felt irritated by his unfriendly manner, his clerk's hands. She could feel her anger growing. She took off her sunglasses and put them in the top pocket of her denim jacket. 'I don't have to hang around here,' she told him.

'I'm sorry?' He pretended to look puzzled. He thought she was a child.

She stood up. 'This is frigging public spirit, mate, wasting time, coming here. This is my citizen's duty. I've got better things to do, me. This is neighbourhood bleeding watch.'

He frowned. His eyes were the same colour as his shirt. 'Why aren't you at school?'

Jaz returned his gaze, then shrugged. She glanced at the door, as if she was thinking of leaving.

He suddenly smiled, nervous, as if remembering some training he'd sat through once, ages ago, on inter-personal skills. 'How can I help?' he said, his tone more polite. He fiddled with his pen.

'That fat bloke. He was my neighbour. You came and spoke to my mum. She didn't know nothing, but I knew him.'

The policeman raised his eyebrows. 'Drugs?' he suggested casually.

'Nah, nothing like that. It was cars. He used to nick cars for a living. It was Vinny what did him. He's the one. He had a grudge, like. They'd argued.' She was insistent. 'Vinny from the Island.' She gave the address of Vinny's garage on the Isle of Dogs.

He looked unimpressed.

'Well write it down, then.'

He began writing. He said lazily, 'Just bring me up to speed. Run that past me again.'

Jaz repeated the address. She spoke quickly. 'It wasn't a drug thing. It wasn't, see? I know there's been a lot of all that going down on the estate, but this was different. The fat bloke, he wasn't into drugs. Not dealing. Nothing big time. Sure he smoked a bit of grass, but he mostly stayed away from the bad guys.' She had a sudden vision of Andy, big in his armchair, rolling a joint on the back of an old Jimmy Hendrix album cover. Fat Andy was an old hippy. He was a pacifist. He supported CND. 'He hated guns, knives, all that shit. He didn't like violence. It wasn't his scene.'

'That's not what we've heard.'

There had been two other murders and one stabbing on the estate in the last few months. They were all drug-related crimes. Elvis had been 'harassed' about these matters too. The police clearly thought, with Fat Andy's death, that they were tramping over familiar ground. Jaz knew they saw the flats as a no-go area, where everyone who was killed or injured probably had it coming.

'Listen to me, will you?'

He pursed his lips.

'You must have fingerprints, forensic stuff.'

'Yeah,' he agreed, 'like telly.' He smirked. '*Prime Suspect. Crimewatch UK*. Nick Ross, Jill Dando.'

Jaz wanted to hit him. She pressed on. 'Vinny's got a record. You'll have his dabs here somewhere, on your computer. I'm telling you, he was in that flat, that night. He killed the fat guy.'

'You saw him?'

She took a deep breath. 'Sure I saw him,' she lied. 'I saw him on the stairs.'

He wrote hurriedly for a few moments.

'Covered in blood,' she added for good measure. She knew she had his attention at last.

'Why haven't you come forward before?'

'I'm here now, aren't I, smart arse?'

'We'll need to take a statement.' He picked up the phone. He sounded excited. 'I've got something here,' he said. 'A witness.' He replaced the receiver and stood up. 'Wait here please,' he glanced at his notes. 'Miss Smith.' He walked to the door. 'I'll be back in a minute.'

Jaz counted to ten, then left the room, retracing her steps to reception. The duty sergeant was arguing with an old black woman who was surrounded by plastic carrier bags, apparently full of rubbish.

Jaz's heart was beating fast. She left the police station and ran off lightly in the direction of the supermarket car park, where she'd immobilized the Lotus Cortina. She stopped at a phone box and dialled Vinny's number at the garage. She heard him pick up the receiver. She imagined his small, monkey-like hands. 'I've shopped you, Companero. I've told the police. This is Jaz and I've only just fucking started. But don't worry, I'll keep in touch.'

Chapter Six

Jaz didn't believe that Vinny would actually be arrested for Fat Andy's murder. He might be picked up and questioned; he might even be held. This was as much as she could hope for. Vinny's tracks were always well covered and in any case he might not have done the deed himself. He sat at the centre of a complicated web of crime, giving lots of orders. He employed two minders, a pair of brothers, known behind their backs, jokingly, as Reggie and Ronnie.

She had a sudden, unwanted vision of the pool of blood at the side of Fat Andy's body, the way it had thickened, like packet soup. Is it possible that the brothers did it? she wondered. Jaz knew these brothers slightly. She'd met them a few times when she'd worked in Vinny's racket. She remembered introducing them to Harm, who'd become a favourite of theirs for a while. They were both big and bald and wore gold bracelets and expensive tracksuits. They had exceptionally good manners and were always quiet and polite. When they weren't working for Vinny they managed a gym on the Mile End Road.

Fat Andy liked Ronnie and Reggie. He referred to them as his mates. He drank with them regularly in a pub in Limehouse. He said they tried to persuade him to join the gym and work out on the machines but he'd always laughed at this idea. He was too lazy to exercise, too fat to make the effort. He told her he always changed the subject. Jaz had wondered, but never asked, what the three of them talked about. Andy said they were hard, but fair. He insisted that they were very sound and had their own moral code. Jaz wasn't sure what this meant, but it didn't seem likely that it covered slashing the throat of an old friend. It was more likely to be Vinny himself, she reasoned. Everyone knew he was vicious. It was rumoured he'd stabbed his two cousins in order to get control of the business. This may or may not have been true.

Jaz knew that the police would follow up her information. It had been too blunt and unambiguous for them to ignore. Officers would appear, with clear directives, asking questions at Vinny's garage.

She pondered the likely scenarios. Perhaps he would buy them off. He'd been doing this for years, in connection with his car exporting racket. Alternatively, he'd throw up some kind of effective smoke screen and they'd quickly resume their enquiries in Peckham, trying to nail Elvis and his gang. Jaz knew she mustn't underestimate Vinny. He'd been operating an illegal business for many years and no one had stopped him. All she could hope for was that things might become unpleasantly hot for him, for a while. It would serve him right, but it wasn't enough. It wasn't the answer. The bastard had to be properly punished. She needed a better plan.

Jaz got back into the Lotus Cortina. She drove slowly up the Old Kent Road, acclimatizing herself to the car's needs and possibilities. It seemed old-fashioned at first, a little stiff but, within its limits, responsive. It took her a while to get used to the clutch. Initially the pedals seemed soft, but after a couple of miles they were OK. This was a car without any modern refinements. Jaz realized that it didn't allow for excuses or half measures. She was in complete contact with the road and with the engine. There was no padding, no nannying, no leeway. The gear box had strong opinions. Any sloppiness on her part was immediately noticeable. She was aware of sharpening up her technique, of doing things properly. It didn't tolerate anything less than superb driving. After a while she realized that, well handled, the car drove like a dream. The engine purred like a cat or roared like a tiger at exactly the right moments. This was real driving. On a clear stretch of road, approaching the river, she let out an excited cry. She was exhilarated. She understood all at once why Fat Andy, who could have possessed and driven any car in Britain, had chosen this model. He'd loved it for more than its beauty. It was a car-lover's car. It was the real thing. It was perfect.

Jaz crossed the Thames at Blackfriars and went up into Clerkenwell. She stopped outside a newly improved, luxury development, where under the internal courtyard, there was a private car park. She opened Fat Andy's Filofax, then turned the car down the slope and tapped the resident's code into a key pad on the security barrier. Inside were alarms and surveillance cameras. Here, the car would be safe. Jaz didn't know how Andy had come by this number but it was always a useful place to leave the Lotus Cortina. He had made a list of such havens. She left her sports bag and jacket, taking only Andy's

Filofax and the wad of banknotes she'd acquired in Cambridge.

She went into a café and took off her sunglasses. It was quiet but the waiters were tense and speedy as if limbering up for a sudden rush. The food looked complicated, so she ordered a risotto from the blackboard. She turned down a free glass of house wine. The Spanish posters on the walls and the background music made her think again about holidays. Spain, she thought. The rain in Spain falls mainly on the plain. She pictured a dusty, rainless plain with cacti, cattle and a pair of flamenco dancers holding castanets. In the distance were mountains.

After she'd finished eating, Jaz called Harm's mobile from a payphone on the wall. Wesley answered. He sounded pleased to hear from her. Jaz remembered how good-natured and warm he was and not for the first time wondered about his career choice. She pictured his round, shiny black cheeks, his toothy grin. He seemed too kind and too gentle to be a pimp. He was into personal development and vegetarianism. Perhaps Harm's clients behaved well because he always set a good example. Jaz asked him if he knew about Andy.

'I'm sorry, honey. I didn't know the guy but I'm truly sorry. This is one mean, sad old town.' He sighed. 'One real messed up universe.'

'Can I speak to Harm?'

'She's working. She's in a hotel on Kingsway, then next stop, Portland Place.'

It occurred to Jaz that Harm had come a long way since turning tricks in back alleys and taxis when she was sixteen. 'Wesley, listen. Tell her to meet me at five in that pub in Covent Garden. You know, the one where the old guy in the bowler hat plays the piano? It's important.'

'Sure now. And you take care of yourself, honey. Shed some tears, of course, but stay, you know, centred. Staying centred, that's the karmic thing.'

'Bye then, Wesley.'

'Remember I love you, honey.'

Jaz sat outside in Covent Garden, at a pub table in the shade, watching jugglers and a fire eater entertain the tourists. One hand was pressed against her chest. Blow is dead, she thought. Andy is dead. They are both dead. She imagined their flesh disintegrating and falling off the skeletons underneath. She thought of worms, maggots. She closed her eyes.

Next to her, half hidden in a doorway, a group of ragged, dirty men passed a bottle to and fro, ignoring the jollity. They were arguing drunkenly amongst themselves, locked into their own world. Inside the pub, the pianist played Beatles' tunes.

At exactly five o'clock, Harm emerged from a black cab and clip-clopped towards the pub across the cobbles. It was still sunny and she cast a long shadow. She was wearing a leopard skin print lycra dress, very short, which hugged her generous curves. She was just, but only just, voluptuous, rather than too fat. Her heels were very high, at least six inches, and as she walked, her breasts bounced. Her Afro hair, newly plaited and oiled, was caught on top of her head in a big gold clip. She waved at Jaz and smiled, showing the gap between her front teeth.

Jaz saw people looking at Harm. The homeless men

ignored her, too lost in their own concerns, but other male eyes travelled up and down her body. Their womenfolk glanced with hostility before turning away. Jaz stood up and waved back.

Harm called out loudly, 'You still having trouble getting served, little one? I'll go in myself.' She emerged with an elaborate, decorated cocktail and a bottle of Perrier for Jaz. 'Got you a whole bottle. Those glassfuls are just a rip-off.'

'How's business?'

Harm shrugged. 'I got your messages. Sorry to hear about your bloke.' She examined Jaz's face for a moment. 'You upset or what?'

'Vinny did it.'

'Vinny from the Island?'

Jaz nodded. She was suddenly angry again. She put on her sunglasses, then took them off. Her voice was tense. 'There was some problem between them. Andy felt he wasn't getting a big enough piece. Wanted to be cut in properly, something like that. Aggro was building up.' She stopped and thought. 'I know they argued a few times. Andy wasn't happy. He talked about setting up on his own.' She hesitated. 'Although I doubt if he ever would. He wasn't . . . energetic. He wasn't driven.'

She had a vision of Fat Andy in bed in the mornings, half awake, his big hand silencing the alarm. He hated getting up. He always groaned and dozed, demanding a cup of tea. It took him an hour to pull himself together. She helped him on with his socks. Made his breakfast. He moved slowly around the flat, like a lumbering bear.

'Anyway, when I got back that night, there was this e-mail. The night he was killed. Andy must have taken something of Vinny's because it said something about

Vinny wanting his property back. Whatever it was, he ended up dead.'

Harm reached over and placed her dark, round hand, covered in rings, on top of Jaz's sleeve. 'I'm sorry.'

Jaz leaned back, disengaging herself. She had problems receiving sympathy. 'So am I. Life's a shit. You told Trace?'

'Of course. We've been worried. Not knowing where you were.' She paused. 'How're you feeling?'

'OK.'

'You don't seem OK.'

'I'm fucking angry.'

'You're always angry. You let anger hide your real feelings.' She reached out and briefly touched Jaz's arm again. 'Right?'

Jaz sighed. 'You're starting to sound like Wesley.' She changed the subject. 'You know those brothers that work for Vinny? . . . You know, Vinny's boys, Ronnie and Reggie?'

Harm stifled a laugh. 'Christ, don't let them hear you calling them that.'

'You remember them?'

'How could I forget? Those were the bad old days. I'm doing better than them now.'

'D'you think they kill people? Could it have been them?'

'What d'you mean?'

'Vinny. D'you think he ever gets them to kill people? Could they be the ones?'

Harm paused, sipping her cocktail then opening and closing its little paper umbrella. She lit a cigarette. 'Doubt it. Mind you, they never talked to me about their work. But they were quiet. Polite. Mostly it seemed, if they wanted something, they just turned up together, stood around looking threatening and that was enough. They didn't seem violent. They were more like window dressing. Vinny's reputation always went before him. No one crossed Vinny. Ever. As far as they were concerned, they did their job, quietly. Ran their gym. They seemed to care for nobody, except each other.'

'I thought they quite liked you.'

Harm raised her eyebrows, giving Jaz a pitying stare. 'What?'

'Well, you were round there often enough.'

Harm pursed her lips. 'Business is business.' She sounded annoyed.

'Look, Harm,' Jaz said hurriedly. 'I'm sorry, but I want a favour. I want you to talk to them.'

Harm exhaled heavily. 'Oh God, please . . . give me a break.'

'Yes, Harm. Do it for me. Go on. Find out what you can. Please.'

'What for?'

Jaz hesitated. 'Vinny killed Andy. I know he did. I've told the police, but they'll just go through the motions. I want to pay him back.'

'Keep out of it, Jaz.' Harm frowned. 'Just keep out of it.'

'No. I'm not going to keep out of it. I owe it to both of them. To Andy and to . . .'

'What the hell do you think you can do?' Harm was exasperated. 'So Vinny killed Andy. OK, I buy that. It's possible. He's a bastard. He'll stop at nothing, everyone knows that. He's unforgiving. That's what I've always heard. But what are you going to do about it? You'll end up in big trouble, Jaz. I mean it. Stay out of it. Vinny's bad news. He's one mean, nasty guy.' She stubbed out her half-smoked cigarette.

There was a silence. Harm finished her drink and went inside to get another. She sat down again without speaking. She looked serious and disapproving.

'If you don't go and talk to them, I'll go myself.' Jaz swigged some Perrier from the bottle.

Harm sighed and rested her head in one of her hands. She thought for a moment. 'I guess you will. And there's nothing I can say to stop you.'

They sat together for a moment in mutual recognition of this fact.

Harm stared at her colourful drink. Then she looked at Jaz. 'Remember that time you got kidnapped by that nutter and locked up in an old cinema? He was one mean motha.'

Jaz stared at the table.

Harm waited a moment. She sighed. 'What do you want me to ask them?'

Jaz relaxed a little and smiled at her friend. 'Facts. Ask about Fat Andy. What happened with Vinny. What went wrong and why. Maybe even . . . why Vinny killed him.'

Harm flashed her lighter at another cigarette. She was irritated again. 'For heaven's sake. Can you remember who we're dealing with here? They're not going to tell me anything, are they?'

'Just find out anything you can. Use, you know . . .' She gestured at Harm's large breasts. 'Your feminine charm.'

Harm picked a slice of orange from the rim of her glass and sucked it. 'I hoped I'd never see them again.

They were downmarket. East End trash. I was well out of there.'

'Just this once.'

Harm sighed heavily. 'Two conditions.'

'Being?'

'Number one, you stay away from them. You stay away from Vinny.'

'For the moment. I'll promise that. Just for the moment.'

Harm nearly protested, then stopped herself. 'Number two.'

'Yeah?'

'You don't tell Wesley.'

'Wesley won't go with you?'

Harm smiled fondly. 'Wesley couldn't handle it. Wesley handles . . .' she paused, 'a different kind of client.'

'OK.'

Harm fished in her bag and produced a couple of mobile phones. She handed one to Jaz. 'Here. Keep this. You've got my number. Use it. Stay in touch. I'll ring you if I find out anything.'

'Where's Trace?'

'She's chamber-maiding for a few weeks. A place on Bayswater Road.' She rummaged for a pen and wrote down a number. 'The Grand Bahama.' She smiled for the first time. Jaz was relieved. Harm had a beautiful smile. 'The Grand Banana. She's living in. You can ring her there.'

'Thanks, Harm.'

'Stay centred.'

Jaz laughed. 'Stay centred yourself.' She took another swig of Perrier and got up to leave.

Chapter Seven

Jaz slept in the car, parked up in another safe haven near Parliament Square. The next morning she bought a bacon sandwich from a street vendor and ate it hungrily, studying Fat Andy's road atlas. She wanted to go to a place called Hartley Wintney. It turned out to be much farther from London than she'd imagined. She discovered it was necessary to go west past Richmond and then get on the M3, which would take her down through Surrey. It'll be like going on holiday, she thought.

She found a garage and filled the tank. The Lotus Cortina was thirsty. With a sense of setting out on a journey into uncharted lands, she bought more sandwiches, chocolate, a packet of Eccles cakes and two bottles of Evian. She also bought an inflatable cushion and blew it up, because the driver's seat was very low. She took out the photograph of Andy and Princess and the one of Peony and Mimosa dressed as angels, examined them and put them on the passenger seat. Then she put on Andy's driving gloves but after a couple of miles took them off again, as they were much too big for gear changing.

The trip across London was slow. It was a very hot day. She needed the noisy fan to cool the car's interior, and drowned it out by listening to the Lightening Seeds on her Walkman.

As she expected, the car attracted attention. Because it was so immaculate, so old and so classic, it turned heads. Highly polished, the bodywork and chrome were dazzling. Dawdling along, hemmed inside the dull, sleek caravan of contemporary European motor-style, snaking its way through Chiswick, Twickenham, then Richmond, Andy's Lotus Cortina purred like a sex symbol and shone like a star.

Some drivers, awe-struck, hooted in appreciation. At other times, stationary for a moment at traffic lights and junctions, Jaz was aware of closer scrutiny, a kind of voyeurism. Usually, this came from middle-aged men. Jaz knew these were the true aficionados. Cortina-crazy in their youth, they suddenly recognized the model they'd always wanted, but never managed to possess. This car, this fabulous construct of metal and glass, had once been their dream. Their mouths gaped. They wound down their windows. Some tried to speak. Jaz didn't look at them. She tapped on the wooden rim of the steering wheel and sang a tune to herself. She hid behind her sunglasses. She knew their eyes would be grazing the car's lines, its perfectly preserved curves. Some might be reaching through their windows, their hands empty and gesturing, unable to touch what had never been attainable. Deliberately, she stepped on the accelerator as soon as she was clear. She knew she was leaving them disorientated, shocked, almost weeping. For the whole of the rest of their day, they would be alone with her after-image, wracked by nostalgia, regret, lust.

*

Once she'd reached the motorway, Jaz thought about her reasons for making this trip. She was on her way to see Princess, who up until a year, maybe eighteen months ago had been Andy's steady girlfriend. She picked up the photograph again, studied it, then threw it back on the seat. She'd decided during the night that it was necessary to break the news of Andy's death. People should be told. His passing had been too insignificant, she thought. He needs more than one mourner. She pressed her hand to her chest. I'm not enough, on my own. I didn't even know him well or for long. Jaz cruised down the outside lane, trees, fields and pylons flashing by. She knew that she wanted Fat Andy to be mourned in an appropriate way. He might have been a petty criminal but he'd mattered to her. He'd mattered . . . She thought of nights she'd lain by his side with the wind roaring round the high rise and police sirens blaring and the sound of screaming somewhere down the stairwell. He'd slept like a giant baby and the mound of him next to her, peaceful and oblivious – this had made her feel safer. Not safe, but safer. It had been the same with Blow. He'd offered a kind of security. 'Andy.' She said his name aloud. 'Andy.' She wanted his life to have meant something. This was another thing she had to do. It was another purpose, another reason for sticking around.

Jaz had never met Princess but she'd seen old videos, and the photo that was now beside her had sat until that final night on Andy's mantelpiece, alongside her own of Peony and Mimosa. Princess had smiled warmly at her in Andy's flat every day for six months.

Princess was a large blonde woman with a pretty face and small gold spectacles. In some ways she reminded Jaz of her mother. She had the same tawdry rock-chick glamour. Developed by Lola and her contemporaries in the early seventies, it was a combination of femininity, loucheness and rebellion. Princess was simply a more up-to-date version. Jaz had spoken to her on the phone. She had a braying voice which Andy referred to as her posh school gush. He mentioned her often, without rancour but with a kind of resigned sadness.

Jaz had never felt jealous. She considered this now. She decided she'd not minded the ever-present ghost of Princess in the flat. She hadn't been threatened or made insecure by another woman's taste, her property, or by her smiling mouth on the mantelpiece. Andy had been Princess's lover. He hadn't been hers. For Jaz, Andy had been a protector and a friend rather than a lover.

This was an interesting moment of self-analysis. She understood it had been the same with Blow. Blow had been her mother's lover, not hers. As far as Jaz was concerned he'd been protector and friend.

She let her mind wander over this realization as she drove south. She'd relished the security these men had offered her, but finally found it wanting. In both cases, she'd felt close to them for a while, but ended up being let down.

She hadn't cared for the sex. They'd liked it because of the games she'd played – not only looking like a child, but behaving like a child. They'd been turned on by those fantasies, all that role-play. They'd liked dominating her, pretending she was very young. They'd liked her wearing childish clothes, her hair in bunches, talking in a baby voice. She'd done this to please them, when they wanted sex. It hadn't seemed like much, she hadn't really minded. But she hadn't enjoyed it. Not when she was thirteen and not when she was twenty.

Her relationships with both had foundered whenever she asserted herself, tried to get her own way. She wondered how these men related to their real partners. Her mother and Princess were fully grown, buxom, loud-mouthed women – the exact opposite of the part she'd played.

She stayed in the outside lane and maintained a steady seventy. The Lotus Cortina drove like a dream. The inside and middle channels were full of heavy lorries and coaches of tourists. The road had become straight and boring and now the suburbs on either side were dull.

Jaz considered the fact that everyone who had been important to her was part of a twosome. Andy had never really got over Princess. Blow loved her mother. Peony and Mimosa were like one person, as were Harm and Trace. She seemed to exist as a hanger-on, a spare part, a surplus number three.

She asked herself if she would ever fall in love, like people did on television, and have a proper relationship. This would presumably involve equality, desire, quarrels, holidays, trips to the supermarket. Maybe she'd have children of her own and a solid pine kitchen in a proper house, with a tumble drier. The idea was ridiculous.

She wondered if she'd ever meet a man who wanted her because she was a real woman, rather than a little girl. Will I ever have a normal life, like other people? she thought. Is this what I really want? She expertly manoeuvred the car through the middle lane and off onto the slip road near a place called Bagshot. Will I ever be happy?

*

Princess had lived with Fat Andy for a long time. She was a few years older than him, maybe almost forty. When she met him, she was unemployed and staying temporarily with her father. Andy had gone to their house in Weybridge to pick up a BMW which Vinny was acquiring legally. Her father was away on business at the time. Andy often told the story of his first meeting with Princess – it was his favourite anecdote.

When he arrived there was a collection of cars outside in the street and on the drive. He wondered how he was going to get the BMW out, as it was probably blocked in the garage. He noticed a straggly, slightly embarrassed-looking group of men outside the front door. They were weighed down by camera equipment. He walked past them and rang the bell. After a delay, Princess opened it. She was completely naked. She told him to come in, and he followed her into the kitchen where she gave him a Heineken. He said afterwards that he'd tried to act cool, as if everything was totally normal, but he was, for once, at a loss for words. He watched her apply mascara and hairspray. After a while she disappeared out the front door. He next saw her in the back garden leaning against a tree. Her long blonde hair partially hid her large breasts and stomach. The photography club surrounded her in a semicircle, clicking and fiddling with lenses. Andy joked that they never had film in their cameras, although he said that Princess always hotly denied this, insisting they were serious artists.

Fat Andy ended the story by saying that he waited until the men had left in order to drive away the BMW. Princess eventually reappeared, wearing a caftan, and Andy gave her Vinny's cheque. She said she was bored and after a brief flirtation on her father's driveway, agreed to accompany him back to London. She arrived at the flat with no luggage, but stayed for six years.

He'd told Jaz that there'd been a lot of arguments, mainly about money. Like him, Princess was extravagant, but she was less lucky when it came to acquiring cash. She worked as a travel agent, a bank clerk, a doctor's receptionist. Andy said she got the sack more times than all the people he'd ever known in his life, all counted together. She was discontented. She didn't enjoy working, but she didn't like being at home. Eventually, whilst employed by an upmarket osteopath in Highgate, she met a wealthy client – a South African diamond importer, called Pillay, who had a bad back. In what Fat Andy described as 'no time', she'd married him and settled in Hartley Wintney.

In the village, Jaz stopped at a corner grocery where an Asian woman in a sari was adding water to a bucket full of cut flowers in the doorway. 'Hi there,' said Jaz in her friendliest tone, 'how much are these?' She picked up a colourful bouquet.

As she was paying, she asked innocently, 'Do you know Princess Pillay?' The name conjured up an image of a bejewelled Eastern temptress.

The woman handed over her change and deftly wrapped the blooms. Her eyes met Jaz's for the first time.

Jaz showed her the photo.

The shopkeeper glanced at Princess's toothy English smile.

'I've been employed to find her.'

The woman was wary, a little frightened. She glanced again at the picture. 'Find her?' she repeated. 'Is she in some trouble?'

'Oh, no,' replied Jaz, breezily. 'She's inherited money.

A long-lost aunt. The probate's being held up, and until the solicitor finds her, the estate can't be divided.' Jaz had heard these comments once on a TV film and memorized them, knowing they would come in useful. 'She's a beneficiary. She's married to a South African, that's all I know.'

The woman smiled nervously. She looked Jaz up and down and decided because she was so small, she wasn't threatening. 'At the end of this road, turn left. You'll see high rails with gold tops. Big house. Nice one.'

'Cheers,' said Jaz. She turned to leave.

'Excuse me, miss.' The woman was holding out a newspaper. 'Can you please take this? My delivery girl never turned up this morning.'

The house was single storey, mock-Georgian with a triple garage. It was expensive looking, with dead windows. It stood back from the road, surrounded by gilded railings and a collection of low, gloomy trees.

Jaz sat in the car, eating her lunch, wondering what she was going to say. She saw the curtains twitch a few times. After a while, the front door opened and a woman appeared. At first Jaz assumed she must be at the wrong house. If this was Princess, she certainly looked a lot different from the old days. She walked down the drive towards the car. Her face was hidden by a wide-brimmed straw hat and she wore a silk floral dress with a matching fitted jacket – the kind of outfit Jaz associated with weddings. She carried a bulky clutch bag.

Jaz rolled down the window.

The woman had stopped in her tracks. 'Oh, I thought . . .'

'You thought I was Fat Andy.' Jaz examined the face under the hat.

The woman was middle-aged. Her face was dull and plump, covered in thick foundation.

'Are you Princess?'

'Who's asking?'

Jaz recognized her voice. She was totally different from her photo. She'd not put on weight, but the formality of her clothes, the expensive tailoring, the matching shoes and bag, made her matronly and staid. She wasn't wearing her little hippy glasses and this revealed the lines around her eyes. Her lips were painted suburban pink.

Jaz opened the car door. She tapped the side of the Lotus Cortina. 'This is Andy's car.'

'I know it is. Who the hell are you?'

'Jaz. We've talked. On the phone. I've brought you these.' She picked up and handed her the newspaper and the bouquet. 'Can I come in?'

Princess seemed completely nonplussed. She held the flowers and paper to her breast. Her mouth had a slack look.

Jaz wondered if she was just surprised, or maybe drunk, or even tranquillized. 'Look,' she said more insistently, 'we need to talk. Were you going out somewhere? Can I give you a lift?'

Princess glanced over her shoulder at the house. She seemed afraid. 'You can't go in there. It's not possible. My husband, he isn't . . !' She paused. 'He isn't . . .good with visitors.' She hesitated. 'Just a minute.' She walked back to the house and disappeared briefly. Then she came out again, closed the front door and walked towards the road. She'd left the newspaper but still carried the flowers. 'You can take me if you like. I'm going to Basingstoke, to a Conservative ladies' luncheon. William Hague is speaking.' She tittered. 'I do what I'm told these days.'

Jaz opened the passenger door. Princess put the flowers and her hat on the back seat, climbed into the front and sighed. 'I haven't been in this car for . . .' She eased the seat belt across her substantial bosom and clicked it together like an expert. She stroked the dashboard approvingly. 'Where is he?' She glanced back at the house. A shadow crossed the window. Her voice changed. She was suddenly urgent. 'Quick. Let's get out of here.'

Jaz drove down the road then followed a sign indicating the M3. She eyed Princess curiously. Not that long ago she'd had a pert face and her body had been soft and inviting. Now things were reversed. She seemed corseted and restricted and her face had completely lost its tone. It was doughy, with soft jowls. Her hair was still long but it was rolled into a bun. There were streaks of grey at her temples. She wasn't attractive any more and her new style didn't suit her. She'd lost her freshness, her excited vitality that Jaz had noticed on Andy's home movies. She'd become bourgeois and defeated. Princess sighed, and Jaz thought she sounded depressed. Her breath smelled of gin.

'I'm afraid I've got some bad news,' Jaz said.

'Don't tell me. He's left you.'

'No, it's not that. He's . . .'

'You've left him and pinched the car.' Suddenly she laughed, a little wildly. They joined the motorway. 'Yippee!' Princess called out. 'Let's go!'

Her words sounded forced, even false, as if she was trying to recapture some long-lost pleasure. There was definitely something wrong with her, Jaz decided. She was drunk and miserable. She was possibly mad.

'You've taken his car! The fat bastard probably had it coming. I want to go faster!'

Jaz took a deep breath and stepped hard on the accelerator. The road was very quiet. 'He's dead.'

Princess looked straight ahead. 'Let's go faster! Faster!'

'Fat Andy's dead.' Jaz paused for effect. 'Vinny cut his fucking throat.' Jaz had not intended to be brutal, but Princess was so strange and distant she didn't know how to communicate with her. She had a sudden vision of the blood on Andy's shirt, a clot of it in his chest hair. She remembered the smell in the bedroom. Stay calm, she reminded herself. Stay focused.

She looked at the speedo. They were doing eighty and the engine was humming. She took it even higher. 'I'm sorry. It's a shock. I'm sorry to tell you like this. Maybe I should've phoned.'

'Faster,' Princess said. 'I want to go faster!' Jaz accelerated again. She overtook a lorry. On either side of the motorway, trees flashed past and there was a slight smell of burning coming from the hot road. 'Oh God,' Princess shrieked, 'it's just like the old days.' Jaz noticed she was crying. Her make-up was streaked by two black lines coursing through heavily powdered beige. They were going at a hundred miles an hour. It was too fast. Jaz saw a sign advertising a Little Chef and pressed on the brake. They slowed rapidly. Princess sighed again, either in relief or disappointment. Her emotions were all exaggerated. They turned up a slip road and into the car park.

Princess sniffed and took a handkerchief and powder compact out of her bag. Her excitement waned as quickly as it had arisen. 'That was great,' she said flatly, as if she'd been bored.

'Are you hearing me?' Jaz asked, pulling into a bay.

'Andy's dead. That's what I've come to tell you.' She could feel herself getting angry. The woman wasn't listening.

Princess patted her cheeks with a powder puff, mopping up the tears but making her face look even more caked. 'No he's not.'

Jaz sat back and stared at the horizon. There was a grim suggestion of distant factories and office blocks. Flags flapped listlessly outside the café, advertising kiddie meals.

Princess put away her powder and took a small bottle from her bag. It was a quarter of gin. She took a substantial swig then put it away.

Jaz felt at a loss. 'What can I say to you?' she asked.

'That fat bastard's not dead because he's on the telly every night. He's doing really well for himself. Typical, isn't it? I stuck with him for the best years of my life and what was he? He was a small-time car thief with no real money, dodgy friends, a grotty flat. He was nowhere.' She paused for emphasis. 'I had to work myself, you know, to pay the bills.' She sniffed again, self-pityingly, got the bottle out and drained it. She swayed slightly towards Jaz. 'I left him and now what's happened? He's suddenly on the telly. It's the nine o'clock news and big black cars and Downing Street. He's in the papers. What is he now?' She turned to Jaz enquiringly. 'Is he some sort of bodyguard?'

Jaz knew, from her experiences with Lola, that Princess was now very drunk. She might stay quiet and incoherent, or she might not. She might shout or get violent. She might be sick. She wanted to get her out of the Lotus Cortina. Fat Andy's old girlfriend might not dress like Lola any longer, but she was behaving like her. Jaz remembered the misery of her childhood. Her mother had been like this – unpredictable, out of control. Jaz didn't like it. Princess was making her nervous. She wanted rid of her. 'Why don't I call you a taxi?' she asked gently.

'A taxi?' Princess was suddenly angry. 'Why would I want a taxi? You're taking me to Basingstoke!'

Jaz didn't want a scene. Princess was big, but unsteady. It might be possible to bundle her out of the car and dump her here, but this would leave Jaz feeling guilty. She still wanted to do right by Andy. 'OK,' she whispered. She drove back out onto the M3. A sign said 'Basingstoke 5 miles'.

They continued in silence. When they got to the town Princess gave monosyllabic directions. They slowed outside a featureless building near an ugly shopping centre. 'Take me to an off-licence,' Princess demanded. 'I can't face this lot without a drink.'

They found a small shop which sold wine and spirits. Jaz waited while Princess bought more gin. When she got back in the car, her mood had swung again. She was cheerful. 'Take a look at these, if you don't believe me.' Opening her bag she produced a bundle of newspaper cuttings and tossed them onto Jaz's lap.

Jaz removed an elastic band and spread them out. They were a collection of photos, torn from the *Telegraph* and *The Times*. At first they seemed to be straightforward press shots of the Home Secretary. Some were very recent and had been taken at the party conference. One was at Heathrow. Another was at a press briefing, about the problem of homelessness in the capital.

Princess leaned over. Her finger jabbed into Jaz's knee. 'There he is,' she said.

Jaz held the picture and turned it towards the light.

She realized what Princess meant. Standing behind the man who was the focus of the photograph, half out of frame, was a large male chest in a double-breasted suit.

'That's him,' said Princess, pointing again.

Jaz examined a second picture. Again, in the background was a bulky figure. This time she could make out his double chin, the outline of a ponytail. This shadowy figure was very similar to Fat Andy. She picked up a third cutting. Here, the man in question was at the front of the picture, as if hurrying to get out of shot. He was immaculately dressed, his long hair was carefully groomed and secured, he looked confident, even complacent, rubbing shoulders with the country's leaders – but he definitely resembled Fat Andy. It was clear that Princess had been deluding herself with this fantasy for a long time. Jaz leafed through the pictures. She'd collected them for more than six months.

'Well,' Jaz said. 'It looks like him, but . . .'

Princess picked up the pile, rolled it tightly, then stuffed it back into her clutch bag. 'So, he's too good for both of us now,' she said, almost conspiratorially. 'He's cruising around in limousines, not even doing his own driving. What's he up to? What's he doing? D'you think he's shacked up with some lady MP?'

Jaz felt the pointlessness of trying to argue. She started the car and drove her passenger to her destination.

Princess seemed to be aware, even through the haze of too much gin, that Jaz was unconvinced by her collection of pictures. 'You get yourself in front of a telly,' she insisted. 'Just watch the news. He'll be on for the next few nights, with this new vagrancy White Paper everyone's talking about. There'll be press conferences and meetings. Watch him get in and out of those cars. He's usually got a label hanging on a chain around his neck.' She opened her new half litre of Gordon's, took another long swig, then squeezed the bottle into her handbag.

Jaz felt suddenly irritated – overwhelmed with a sense of having wasted her time and energy. She had been unsuccessful in her mission. Fat Andy still had no mourners apart from herself. She put her hand on Princess's arm, detaining her, then let go, slightly repelled. 'He never mentioned family,' she said. 'Did he, I mean does he have family?'

Princess reached into the back for her hat. She jammed it on her head, pushing loose strands of hair inside. 'You mean you've never met his mother? That hideous old bat in Pimlico?'

Jaz picked up a pen from the parcel shelf beneath the dashboard, then pulled out Andy's Filofax from under the driver's seat. 'Is her address in here?'

Princess looked puzzled.

'Just write down the address, will you?'

Princess scribbled across two pages. She burped quietly. 'I think this is right. It's something like this.'

Jaz watched as she walked towards the Conservative club offices, tottering slightly, her bulging bag under her arm, her other hand holding her hat which was caught in a spiteful breeze.

Chapter Eight

Jaz spent the night in a lay-by on the A30. She didn't care for parking on the road – the Lotus Cortina was an ostentatious vehicle to sleep in and its locks weren't safe. She feared being surprised by a passing weirdo. However it was the best possible option, other than a hotel, and she didn't want to waste more money. She had a meal in the Little Chef then found a suitably quiet spot, parked and slept in the back, with her head on the inflatable cushion. She was unconscious for six hours. When she awoke, stiff but refreshed, she drove back to London, thinking about Hartley Wintney and her unsuccessful attempt to find a mourner for Fat Andy. At least I've got his mother's address, she thought. Princess was a disaster, but tomorrow, I'll go and see the mother.

At nine o'clock she hid the car in a side street on the Isle of Dogs, overlooking the Thames. It was a bright morning and the sun, still low on the skyline, cast long, cool shadows. She stared at the glittering water and the Millennium Dome which crouched on the opposite bank like a pale, sleepy beetle.

Stay calm, she reminded herself. Stay cool. There was a lot to be done. Her life had suddenly become full of purpose. She pressed the pain in her chest. It burned, this morning; it was worse. Vinny will be punished, she assured herself, and Fat Andy will be mourned.

She polished the dashboard and the steering wheel of the Lotus Cortina with her sleeve. The interior was immaculate. A small air freshener in the shape of a pine tree swung from the fan switch. Andy had forbidden smoking and eating in the car. Guiltily, she picked up some crumbs and dropped them out of the window. I'm living here, she reasoned. Andy never actually lived in the Lotus Cortina, so it was easier for him. However, I must look after it as best I can.

She remembered several Cortinas from her childhood. Back in the eighties, Blow was nostalgic for them and bought and restored three or four. 'The car of my youth,' he used to declare, whenever he appeared with another one. 'We loved these. Had them in all colours. Knew them inside out, back to front. I spent more time with Cortinas than with my girlfriend. Or family. We were all the same. All the lads. Cortina crazy.'

Jaz remembered a cold autumn day, not long before she ran away from home. She'd just finished seeing to the hens and she was leaning against Blow's latest Cortina in the yard outside the farmhouse, worried about her sisters. She shivered and pulled Lola's old fur jacket around her thin frame. Just then, she heard a shriek and turned and saw the twins. She was relieved. They were fine. Peony and Mimosa had tied their ankles together and grasping each other's wrists, had formed their bodies into a giant loop. They steadied themselves like gymnasts, and as Jasmine watched they began rolling in a slow circle down the grassy slope, away from the house. Steadily and without losing their balance, they turned as one, gathering momentum. All at once, Jasmine felt lonely. They never include me, she thought. They're one person. They're one girl in two bodies.

Blow appeared, grinning. He opened the bonnet of the car, excited about his latest acquisition. 'Sixty-nine Mark II 1600 GT,' he informed her. 'It's the two-door. Rare as hen's teeth. See the colours?'

Jasmine stepped back and examined the white bodywork with the green stripe. She could hear the twins' laughter, but didn't look round at them again.

'Not a real Lotus Cortina,' he continued regretfully, half disappearing into the engine, 'but it's the nearest I could find. Lotus colours.' He tinkered with a spanner. 'I never had a Lotus Cortina. Never. None of us did. We all wanted one. Like a dream.'

After a moment, as she expected, he started singing. Do wah diddy diddy, dum diddy do. He always sang this when he talked about Cortinas and his friends in younger days. There she goes, justa walking down the street. He turned a spanner. Singing Do wah diddy diddy, dum diddy do.

Jasmine joined in, hoping the twins would hear. She looks good, she looks fine, canna really make her mine? She always imagined this song was about a Cortina. The song and the car were linked in Blow's mind. Do wah diddy diddy, dum diddy do. She believed this to be the kind of song they always sang in the sixties. It sounded innocent, friendly and full of hidden meaning.

Blow stopped singing suddenly. 'Damn!' he said.

Jasmine looked.

He pointed to the near-side inner wing.

'What's wrong with it?'

'See that rubber? That's the top bush. Suspension's bulging like a hernia.'

'What does that mean?'

'It means I'll have to remove the strut and replace the effing bush. That, or wobble like jelly on the bends.' He sighed. 'These struts are rock solid.' He leaned on the car and bounced the wing. He shook his head. 'Road holding, I won't get. Not unless I do it.'

Jaz sat for a while, thinking. Cortina crazy. She pictured Blow and Fat Andy as teenagers. Blow was young in the sixties. Andy was young in the seventies. She imagined a happy, simple time with open roads, jolly policemen on bicycles, steam trains, women with chiffon head-scarves tied over candyfloss hair. A gentle, predictable world, she thought, compared with today. A world where everyone knew who they were and where they were going. Not like now. I'll take the car on holiday, she decided, when all of this is over. I'll go somewhere nice, with Harm and Trace. Somewhere old-fashioned, a long way from London. We'll be Cortina crazy too.

She crossed her arms over the steering wheel and leaned forwards, trying to direct her thoughts towards the moment. Pull yourself together, she told herself. Stay focused. She tried to recall times recently when Fat Andy had appeared troubled. After he'd insisted she leave the gang, she'd become largely out of touch with what went on at the garage. Fat Andy had never been one to share his problems. However, he'd complained about Vinny. Jaz imagined him pacing across the living room at the flat, a glass of Scotch in his hand. It was rare to see him in a bad humour, but this had happened several times.

He'd said that Vinny didn't realize his true worth. He'd said that without himself there'd be no gang and without the gang there'd be no stolen cars. 'He pays me well,' Andy had said to her. 'It's not the money. It's just that he doesn't listen to me. He keeps me right out on a limb.'

Another time he'd come home late at night, pale-faced and angry. Jaz sat up in bed, alarmed. She'd opened her arms to him and he'd lain down next to her, upset, still in his clothes. 'That Vinny,' he whispered. 'He's too much. Sometimes he really is too much . . .'

'What's happened?'

'You know Davey, in the gang? PhD drop-out? Gob full of long words? He got nicked this morning. Lifting a Megane Scenic. God knows what he was up to. You know his head's always in the clouds. Anyway, he's banged up now in Brixton. Vinny sent the boys over to his gaff, told them to break in, look for anything incriminating, anything that might link him to the garage. They came back with his dog.'

'You mean Blackie?'

'Yeah. That's the one. Well, the boys brought it back with them. For why? Because there was no one to feed it or look after it, that's why. An act of kindness. Well, what does Vinny do? Vinny took one look at it . . .' He paused, horrified. 'You know what he did? Guess what Vinny went and did?'

'What?'

'Snapped its little neck, that's what. In one move. Killed it. Like he'd done it lots of times before. Took him three seconds.' Andy was disgusted. 'The Greek bastard.'

'You're kidding!'

'I wish I was. I've got to go and tell Davey tomorrow. Vinny said it would teach him a lesson. Teach him not to be so careless.' He was silent for a minute. 'Snapped its poor little neck . . . little Blackie. Then he got in his car and drove away.' He brushed away a tear. 'Davey's finished, of course. Sacked. And now he's got no dog either. Have you ever known such a sadistic bastard as that Vinny?'

Jaz got out of the car. Vinny's legitimate workforce had been busy for at least an hour. She crossed the road. Behind the showroom, separated by a back alley, were the workshops. Sweet fumes emerged from the paint shop where cars, both legal and otherwise, were given new clothes.

Jaz didn't want to meet Vinny accidentally. Her plans weren't entirely clear yet, but she couldn't see any value in a confrontation. She walked past a hooded, spraying figure, lost behind a mist of blue. Further along was the repair shop. She peeped inside. Nearest the door, a few yards away, a mechanic lay underneath a VW Passat. She knew by his long legs and big boots that this was Pete. The place was too noisy to attract his attention so she picked up a small stone from the street and aimed it at his crotch. She didn't hear him curse but he emerged in an instant.

Jaz beckoned to him urgently. 'Sorry,' she mouthed.

Pete grinned, stood up and joined her outside. 'Make it quick, Jaz, I'm on time and a half. Another customer in a hurry.'

Jaz looked up at him. He was very tall. 'Vinny there?'

'I don't think so. Why?'

'Go and have a look, will you?'

Pete loped off in the direction of the shabby cubby-

hole which was Vinny's office. He reappeared, shaking
his head. Jaz regarded him appreciatively. He was lanky
with long ginger hair, like her own, only his was thicker,
a richer colour and more shiny. He wore stained blue
overalls unbuttoned on his chest. Both his ears were
pierced. He had a self-conscious, modern walk, which
suggested he knew his sexual value. His young face was
chiselled and bony. His complexion was like porcelain.
Jaz had always thought his features belonged to a concert
pianist or a poet rather than a mechanic. Similarly, his
hands, although always dirty, were elegant and beauti-
fully moulded.

Jaz whistled as he approached. 'You just get more and
more tasty, Pete.'

He blushed, taken by surprise.

'Licking you all over wouldn't be hard.'

He looked at the ground and muttered, 'What for . . .
I mean why d'you want Vinny?'

'I don't. You heard about Fat Andy?'

He nodded, raising his eyes to meet hers. 'Yeah. I
heard he got done in, like.' He paused. 'Sorry. No one
here knows nothing. No details.' He leaned in the
doorway, trying to regain his composure, struggling to
look casual. He scratched his balls and pretended to
yawn.

Jaz knew he was nervous, but he wanted to appear
cool. He was only eighteen. She was just about to tell
him that Vinny had killed Fat Andy, then changed her
mind. If he didn't believe her, then she'd lose him as a
contact.

'How about a drink tomorrow night?' he said hesi-
tantly and blushed again. He was doing his best.

'Well, you're not wasting any time.' She smiled at him.

She'd always fancied Pete. He had a nice body, his face was as pretty as a girl's and more importantly, now, he might prove useful. Whatever revenge she planned for Vinny, she'd need an insider. She took a step towards him, reached up and placed her index finger on his chest, in the gap of his overalls. 'Where?' His skin was hairless. She ran her finger lightly up and down.

His face was now bright red, but he was pleased. He suggested a time and a pub on Poplar High Street. 'It's karaoke night,' he said. 'Good laugh.'

He moved backwards, away from her, grinning shyly, then turned and lowered himself onto his trolley. Jaz noticed that his flush had extended from his face over his neck and onto his pale chest. She waited for him to disappear under the VW Passat.

She looked about. The coast was clear. She dodged behind a Skoda then ran across the floor of the workshop to the corner where Vinny had his office. The door was open and she went inside. A poster of Pamela Anderson wearing ragged bikini and handcuffs was blue-tacked to the back of the glass. A calendar, showing a woman wearing nothing, hung on the wall. Jaz wondered about this choice of decoration. Everyone knew Vinny was gay.

There was a lingering smell of aftershave, mixed with kebabs. The light on the answerphone was flashing and there was a pile of new faxes. Jaz looked at Vinny's computer. It was old. There was no modem. She slid the floppy out of the disk drive. She opened a drawer of the desk and found a plastic rack holding a dozen more disks: customer orders and repairs. She removed these, then took a small screwdriver from her sports bag and used it to unscrew the cover from the chassis of the computer. She glanced round the door. There was no one nearby. Working quickly, she located, then unfastened the hard disk. She took it out and examined it. Then she put everything in her sports bag including the faxes. She wiped the messages off the answerphone, then pressed record. 'Hi there, slimeball,' she hissed. 'Companero? It's me again. I've fucked up your computer here. I've got your files.' Unobserved, she left the building.

Later, at West India dock, she parked the Lotus Cortina, put on her Versace sunglasses and walked over to the side of the wharf. It had become a hot, breezy day and tourist boats ploughed back and forth. A group of children waved at her and some of them raised cameras. She could hear the recorded commentary, pointing out the sights of the capital. I'm going on holiday, she reminded herself, when this is all over.

The Thames was high, lapping against the sides, the water blue-grey and oily. Jaz dropped the faxes into the current and watched them swirl away. She tossed the floppy disks as far as she could and they scattered then sank. She threw the hard disk way out into the river. You've seen nothing yet, she thought to herself. She pressed her chest. The pain had eased slightly. You've messed with me, you fucking bastard, Vinny. And this is just the beginning.

Later, Jaz drove over to Peckham. Vinny's disks had reminded her of the e-mail she'd discovered on Fat Andy's computer just before finding his body. It hadn't been sent from the garage. Vinny must have a computer at home, she thought. She could remember the message almost word for word. 'Vinnys not a happy man. Vinny wants his proparty back strate away.'

She pictured the disks disappearing in the Thames. She was reminded of Fat Andy talking about a computer disk which contained the details of Vinny's illegal car exporting racket – his contacts in Europe, their specific orders, details of the ringed cars with both their old and new identities. I wonder if I threw it in the river? she thought. It seemed unlikely that it would be unprotected, in a desk drawer.

Andy had always joked that with this disk he could set up on his own, making a clean line between the thefts and the export, cutting Vinny out of the middle. Jaz had never taken him seriously, but now it suddenly seemed more than likely that Andy had stolen the disk. This must be the 'proparty' which Vinny wanted back so badly. He needed to protect his contacts and he wouldn't want this evidence of his covert business dealings to fall into the wrong hands. Jaz tried to remember the scene at the flat. There had been signs of a struggle but the place wasn't ransacked. She remembered that Andy's computer disks and CD roms had been strewn across the floor. She knew that if Andy had stolen Vinny's valuable disk, he wouldn't have left it lying around. She had a good idea where he might have hidden it.

Jaz stopped the Lotus Cortina near the estate where Fat Andy had died. She sat and considered. She still didn't want to go back to the flat. She had a key, but she knew it would be boarded up. It was, after all, the place where an unresolved murder had been committed, very recently. She brought to mind police programmes from the TV. She pictured yellow scene-of-crime tape, sealing off the area, possibly even a police guard. She imagined a body bag on a stretcher and forensic experts with tweezers and plastic bags, picking over the dirty carpet. In any case, she thought, I couldn't go back in there. I couldn't face it. It was too horrible. A vision of Fat Andy's dead, staring eyes flashed before her. His eyes had been the worst thing. They were unlike real eyes. In death, Fat Andy's eyes were more ghastly than anything she'd ever dreamed of.

She waited. She ate a bar of chocolate and drank a can of Dr Pepper. I could do with a shower, she thought. She watched two teenage boys drag a sobbing toddler up the street. A third followed behind with his pushchair. The wind had dropped and it was too hot. A dog tore open a bin liner and started rummaging. A woman, over-dressed in a raincoat, pulled a shopping trolley towards the launderette. The homeless mother in the headscarf was still in position with her baby, her supplicating hand outstretched. She made low, inarticulate sounds. Next to her was a young boy who held a piece of cardboard. 'Work-less and hungry', he'd written in red felt tip pen.

Jaz plaited her hair tightly and pinned it in a small clump on the back of her head. She looked in the mirror. Her fringe was too long. It hung in dry stands. The sun had caught her face, creating a rash of freckles. Her eyelids were pink.

Eventually the silver Mercedes came into view. As usual, it was moving at twenty miles an hour. Elvis always drove slowly around the estate and its neighbouring streets. It was a statement of ownership. One day, Jaz thought, he'll start giving a regal wave, like a member of the royal family.

She followed the Mercedes into the underground car park and drew up alongside it. Big Boy and Peppy got out immediately. Peppy staggered. He seemed disorientated and weaved towards the lift. Big Boy noticed Jaz and raised a hand in greeting. Jaz nodded. He followed behind Peppy, his large backside wobbling inside silky jogging bottoms. He disappeared.

Jaz stepped out of the Lotus Cortina and slid into the back seat of the Mercedes. Elvis was in the driving seat, wearing a set of headphones. The tinny sound suggested something heavy and rhythmic. Elvis moved his skinny body up and down in time to the beat. Jaz looked at the spots on the back of his neck, his shaved head. He was wearing a white shirt. She tapped him on the shoulder. He turned round defensively, pulling off his headphones. When he saw Jaz he smiled. He switched off the engine. 'Doll. How do!'

'Elvis, listen. Will you do me a favour?'

'Maybe.' Despite his clean, pressed shirt, he looked as if he hadn't slept for days. His skin was shiny and grey and his breath smelled of chemicals.

'Can you get into Andy's flat?'

He laughed. 'Your make-up, yeah? Doll? That it? Or your birth control pills?'

'Are the police still there?'

'They's not here now. 'Cept for harassment of course. 'Cept for Peppy's intimidation and false arrest. 'Cept for . . .'

'Can you get in?'

Elvis pursed his lips. 'Board on door. New. Padlocks.'

'What about the window?'

'Sixteenth floor. Yes or no?'

'Can you get in, Elvis? I'm serious.' She explained what she wanted and where to look. She told him about the loose polystyrene tile on the bathroom ceiling.

Elvis reached over and lifted her T-shirt. His mean little eyes met hers. 'Is it worth a shag? One now and one later?'

Jaz nodded. Stay calm, she thought. Stay cool. She slipped out of her jacket, pulled her T-shirt off and undid the button of her jeans.

Chapter Nine

The next day, on Oxford Street, Jaz approached a man selling the *Big Issue*. 'Hi, Davey.'

Davey was the ex-student, turned car thief, who was sacked by Vinny after getting caught by the police. Fat Andy had paid him off, cleared his fines and treated him generously. Davey had remained grateful. Jaz knew he was still in touch with the other members of the gang who worked the streets. She bent down and stroked his new dog. It was another collie, similar to Blackie.

'How's tricks?' Davey enquired. He grinned down at her, showing toothless gums.

Jaz was half expecting this friendly unconcern. Some news travelled on the grapevine, other news didn't. For some reason, no one seemed to know about Fat Andy's murder. She couldn't explain why. 'Fat Andy's dead.'

Davey took a shocked step backwards, jerking his dog's lead. The magazines slid from his grasp but he caught them before they dropped.

'I knew you didn't know. No one knows. I don't get it.'

Under the street grime, Davey's face had lost its colour. 'Hey man, it's nothing I've heard about. How the hell . . .?'

'I knew you'd be surprised.'

He took a tissue out of his trouser pocket and blew

his nose. 'Surprised? I'm gutted.' He sat down on his haunches, placing his magazines on the pavement.

Jaz bent towards him. 'Murdered.'

Davey was astonished. 'Murdered? Bloody hellfire!'

Jaz didn't hesitate. 'Vinny did it. Vinny killed him.'

'Never?'

'Yep.'

'You sure?'

Jaz was ready for this. 'I was there,' she lied. 'I saw everything.'

Davey paused, then said angrily, 'Why?'

'Dunno. Prestige? Power? Andy wanted more. Thought he deserved more.'

Davey was silent. Then he whispered, 'That Vinny was always a complete bastard.' He looked as if he might faint. He paused. 'Mephistopheles,' he muttered. 'A man without morals.'

'Yep.'

'I can't believe it.'

Jaz straightened up. 'Well, believe it. Put the word out. I don't know who's paying the boys now, doing Andy's job. But you make sure you tell them. Andy always did right by them. You tell all the boys.' She turned and walked away.

'They won't work for Vinny,' Davey called out, 'once they know about this.'

Jaz smiled to herself grimly. I know that, she thought. The gang's finished.

Later, sitting in the Lotus Cortina and using the mobile phone, Jaz rang the number she'd been given for Trace. She'd already been to Pimlico and discovered that the address of Fat Andy's mother supplied by Princess was that of a block of mansion flats, respectable and staid, which appeared to be occupied by well-to-do elderly people who had cleaners and chauffeurs and help with their shopping. Andy had never mentioned his mother. He'd never talked about his family.

The phone rang for a long time. Eventually it was answered by a foreign-sounding woman. 'Yes, please?'

'I would like if possible,' Jaz spoke very slowly, 'to speak to Trace.'

'Who?'

'Trace. One of your chambermaids.'

There was a silence. 'Who is this, please?'

'I'm Jaz. I'm a friend of hers.'

'Ah, OK, OK. Tracy. Yes, one moment please.'

Jaz waited for several minutes. Eventually Trace picked up the phone. 'Hello, Tracy speaking.'

'Hi, Trace, it's Jaz.'

Trace gasped. 'Jaz! We've been so worried! Where are you? Where've you been?'

'I'm OK. Listen. When are you free?'

'I'm sort of free now.'

'Will you do me a favour? Meet me in Churchill Gardens, off Grosvenor Road?'

'Why?'

'I'll tell you when you get here.'

'OK. I'll be . . . three quarters of an hour.'

Sitting in the car, perspiring gently in the heat, Trace listened in silence to Jaz's account of the events on the night of her birthday. She'd already heard a version from Harm, but she wanted to hear it from Jaz herself. When

Jaz had finished, Trace sat for a moment with her head in her hands. 'That's so terrible,' she whispered.

Jaz knew she would cry. Trace hadn't really known Fat Andy, but she was empathic and very sensitive. Jaz waited until she composed herself. 'I have to tell his mother. This is really important to me, Trace.'

''Course it is.'

'Andy's been done in and no one seems to know. No one seems to care.'

'We care, Jaz. We both care.'

'I'm not even sure if there's going to be a funeral or whatever. The murder wasn't in the papers. It's as if it doesn't matter. Just another killing on the estate. As if it was . . . ordinary. I've got to tell people. Andy would want everyone to know. He'd want a big production number. He'd want his people there for him.'

'Where, Jaz? At the funeral?' Trace glanced over at Jaz. She looked confused.

'No, not a funeral. That would be meaningless. I mean, he'd want people to be hurt for him. He'd expect concern, discussion. He'd want people to be angry and upset and bothered. And no one is. It's really getting to me. I mean . . . he had a life. He was a person with a life . . .'

'Of course he had a life, Jaz. He had . . . a beautiful life.' Trace wiped her eyes.

'That's right. And I want to tell his mother that it's ended. She may not know. It's right and proper that she should know. I want you to come with me.'

Trace was sympathetic but bewildered. Jaz waited patiently for a while, then explained again. It was always necessary to run things past Trace more than once. She was slow on the uptake, but once she'd absorbed something, she never forgot it.

'Why do you want me to come, Jaz? I mean, I'll come, but wouldn't it be better for you to see her, you know . . . one to one?'

After the episode with Princess, Jaz knew that she didn't want to go alone. 'I just do, OK? I want you to come.'

'OK.'

'And there's another thing.'

'What?'

'I need a shower. Can I come back with you to that hotel afterwards, and use a bathroom?'

'No problem.'

Jaz parked near the mansion block and took off her sunglasses. She fed the meter. She was just about to ring the bell when the main door opened and a maid emerged with a shopping trolley. She nodded and let the two of them through without question. The hall inside was dark, with wood panelling and a coloured, tiled floor. A grandfather clock ticked patiently. A vase of sweet, droopy roses scented the air. It was the kind of place where old people waited to die.

Jaz took the marble stairs two at a time with Trace at her heels. They went up to the third floor. The lobby was thickly carpeted and a large, elegant window gave a view of neighbouring rooftops.

Jaz rang the bell.

'What are we going to say?' Trace whispered.

'I don't know. We'll play it by ear.'

There was no reply. Jaz rang again. 'Shit, I hope she's in.'

After a while, there was a rattling and the door opened a fraction on a security chain.

'Hello,' Jaz said loudly. 'Hello. This is Jaz. I'm Andy's girlfriend. Your son, Andy. I'm with a friend. We want to speak to you.'

'Go away,' said a voice from inside. It was a woman speaking. She sounded very discouraging.

'No, we're not going away. Let us in. It's important. About your son.'

'No one comes in here.'

'We won't be long.' Jaz felt desperate. 'How about if we just talk to you in the hall?'

There was a long silence. Then to Jaz's relief, the chain was dropped and the door opened.

Jaz was expecting an old lady. The woman in the hallway was very tall and slim. Her pale hair was elaborately dressed in a sixties style, rolled in a bun on top with a deep pleat at the front, like a nurse's cap. She wore silk trousers with a matching tabard and a long string of beads. The first impression was one of glamour. 'Come in,' she said. She now sounded resigned. Jaz and Trace followed her down the hallway. Jaz realized she was, in fact, old. She walked stiffly, her back was bent and she had an old woman's elbows.

They entered a dark room which smelled of urine, overlaid with sandalwood. One table lamp was illuminated but it was draped in a coloured scarf. There were several low sofas and tables and wall hangings which seemed to depict scenes from the Kamasutra.

'Sit.'

Jaz and Trace sat down together.

The woman was indistinguishable in the shadows. She switched on another dim lamp, her back turned, then lit a stick of incense.

Jaz took in an oriental rug and cushions, an elephant carved in ivory, a hookah. The impression was one of an eastern bazaar.

Andy's mother faced them, then crouched awkwardly on a small leather pouffe. It was a young movement, but executed with difficulty. Her face, too, was disturbing. She had once been beautiful but her cheeks had fallen into low, baggy folds and her neck was a concertina of creases. Her mouth and eyes were surrounded by deep lines. Onto this ruined canvas, she had applied a great deal of make-up. Her lips were pearly pink, her eyes decorated with false lashes so long and black they looked like insects. She smiled. Her teeth were false and badly fitting. Jaz was reminded of a ghoul in a horror film.

'We're sorry to bother you,' said Jaz. She was non-plussed. She felt Trace grope for her hand and squeeze it.

The woman grasped her knees, tilted her head to one side and smiled. She appeared to be posing. After a few moments she said, 'I don't have visitors. Not these days.' She sighed theatrically. She had a posh, actressy voice.

There was a silence. 'It's, er, a nice day,' said Trace shyly. 'Like,, you know . . . sunny.'

'Oh, I never go out.' The woman gestured at the heavy brocade curtains which blocked all natural light. 'I haven't been out since 1987.'

There seemed to be no reply to this. Jaz decided to dispense with small talk. 'I was Andy's girlfriend,' she began.

The woman's pencilled brows lifted in surprise. The furrows in her forehead were like a ploughed field. 'I

don't know you,' she said. 'I only know that plump girl
with the little round glasses. Princess. The one who won't
work.'

Jaz was relieved. At least this was the right flat. At
least this crazy-looking woman was talking sense.

'No, she went away. I was with Andy for the last six
months,' she paused, 'of his life.'

Her response was immediate. She was sharp, Jaz
realized. 'What do you mean "of his life"?'

'Andy's dead.'

Her mouth fell open and she raised a hand to cover
it. 'He can't be. I saw him on the television.'

Jaz realized that she'd seen the same lookalike that
had confused Princess. 'No, that wasn't him. I don't know
who that is. Forget him. Andy was killed at the flat in
Peckham. He was murdered. I'm sorry to have to tell you
like this. Why weren't you informed? Through . . . you
know . . . the usual channels?'

The woman stared, her hand at her mouth, her
painted eyes wide with shock.

'Can I get you anything?' asked Trace timidly. 'Cup
of tea?'

The woman nodded. She gestured and Trace disappeared in the direction of the kitchen.

'The usual channels don't apply,' she said. 'Not with
me.'

'I'm sorry,' said Jaz. This was very difficult. She half
wished she hadn't come.

'Are you quite sure?' Her voice had become a croak.

Jaz nodded.

'I told him he was mad, living down there amongst
all those gangsters. Drug addicts. I told him he should
move out of London. It would have been possible, in his

line of work. I mean, computer programming . . . You can do that anywhere, can't you?'

Jaz decided not to contradict her. There was no point in telling her about Vinny. It wouldn't help.

'He was a good boy.'

'When did you last see him?'

'Oh, I don't know. I lose track of time. It was before Christmas.'

Jaz wasn't sure how to keep the conversation going, but she knew she couldn't just leave. 'The police haven't been to see you? What about a funeral?'

'No, no one's been here. Only my charlady.' She stood up shakily, then lowered herself onto a sofa nearer Jaz. She sank into the cushions and leaned back. 'I can't go to a funeral,' she whispered. 'I never go out.'

'It's OK.' Jaz wanted to reassure her. 'I just wanted to tell you, that's all. Andy would have wanted you to know.' She saw two tears trickle down the woman's cheeks making streaks in her foundation.

There was a silence between them. A whistling kettle sounded, then stopped. Jaz could hear a neighbour's radio and the faint hum outside that was the noise of London. She stared at the floor. The carpet, once beautiful, was old and stained.

Trace came back in holding a tray. She plonked it heavily on a table, rattling the cups. 'This is beautiful china,' she said. 'Spode. They've got some at the Dorchester, but it's not as nice as this.' She poured the tea.

The woman sniffed and blotted her face with the back of her hand. 'He was adopted,' she said suddenly, bending forward to pick up her cup. 'Taken away.' Her hand shook a little. 'I had them both adopted privately. Both boys. Jason and Justin. That's what I called them.' She smiled at the memory. She gazed away into nothing. 'They were darlings.'

'Both of them?' asked Jaz. 'What do you mean, both of them?'

Trace blew on her tea noisily.

'They were twins.' The woman's voice had become dreamy, almost sentimental.

'Andy had a twin?'

She sighed again. 'They were separated. Adopted separately. Cruel, but that's how it was. I was desperate.'

'What happened?'

She settled back on her sofa, composed now, as if she had told the story many times. She continued to stare into space, nursing her cup and saucer. 'I was with Mickey first,' she said, 'before he met Marianne.' She smiled to herself. The memory appeared to have replaced all emotion about Fat Andy. 'They were wild times. Paparazzi. Night clubs. Parties.'

Jaz watched as Trace spooned sugar into her cup.

'I'd been modelling,' the woman continued, 'a few commercials, a few walk-on parts at the Old Vic. I was the Revlon Girl back in 'sixty-two. Mickey was very sweet. Not at all like they tried to make out in the papers. I was a lot older than him, of course.'

'What's she on about?' asked Trace in a loud whisper.

'Shh!' said Jaz.

'I'd been engaged twice. Once to Neddy, he was the son of a Duke. Then to Mario. He was a top hairdresser. Mickey swept me off my feet. He was so . . . real.' She turned her head and stared at a framed photograph on a side table. It was a signed print of the Rolling Stones.

Jaz followed her gaze and the penny dropped. 'She means Mick Jagger,' she whispered. She stared at the woman. Her voice, she decided, had a brittle, false note. She didn't believe her.

'It was a while before I met Brian. When I did, it was love at first sight.'

'Brian?' queried Jaz, humouring her.

'Brian Jones. You must remember him. He was the original rhythm guitarist. Before Ronnie Wood.'

Jaz shook her head. It seemed rude to say she wasn't even born then, that her own mother was still a child. She glanced at Trace. She knew she'd probably never heard of the Rolling Stones. She had no sense of history.

The woman continued. 'He was the one who drowned. In his swimming pool.'

Jaz saw Trace's expression change. She was so empathic about calamity. She stared, horrified. 'His swimming pool! Really? What happened?'

The woman clearly wanted to tell her story in her own way. 'Brian and I were together for a few months. Let me tell you, dears, they were the happiest months of my life.' She paused. 'I was a mother to him, in a way. But he treated me so well.' She held out a hand. It was long and bony, like a claw, and on it sat a huge diamond. 'He bought me this.' She turned her hand towards herself and admired it. 'He bought me a lovely car. An E-Type Jaguar.'

'Roadster or hard-top?' asked Jaz automatically.

'Oh, yes.'

'All-synchromesh gearbox?'

The woman looked offended.

'What year was it? Have you still got it?'

'No, of course I haven't. Anyway. As I was saying.' She drank some of her tea, then returned the cup and saucer to the tray. 'We were in love. He went away on a tour and I did a very silly thing.'

'Crashed the E-Type?'

Trace elbowed Jaz in the ribs.

'I started seeing this boxer. He was a black fellow from the United States. Very handsome. He was as gentle as a lamb, but his people. Oh, my dears!'

'Oh, no, poor Brian,' sympathized Trace, as if she knew what was coming.

The woman smiled. She began directing her words towards Trace. 'Yes. You're right, dear. It was a mess. I was a fool.' She sighed. 'A silly young fool.'

'He drowned.' Trace said this in a way that made her sound familiar with the whole story, but Jaz knew she wasn't. She was just sad about the tragedy.

'There were horrid scenes when I went back to Brian. I just wanted the boxer to get on with his prize fight or whatever it was and go back home.' She sighed. 'But he was in love with me.'

'Oh, no!' exclaimed Trace. Her sympathies were now being pulled the other way.

'It was a love tangle.' The woman stopped talking and picked up a magazine.

Jaz realized she was at the end of her narrative. 'Brian Jones drowned.' She wanted to get back to the subject of Fat Andy.

The woman nodded.

'It wasn't an accident?'

She shook her head.

'That's awful,' said Trace.

'And you were pregnant,' added Jaz.

The woman's head sank onto her chest. She looked defeated, vulnerable. 'I was told they were twins. I didn't know what colour they would be. The boxer disappeared after the swimming pool incident. There was a big fuss. The official version was an accident, but everyone on the inside blamed me. No one would speak to me. I got no invitations any more. The phone never rang. I was persona non grata. I moved in here and became a ghost, dears. When the boys were born I couldn't cope. I got depressed. I mean, how was I supposed to know what to do with two babies? I just wasn't equipped. I was a celebrity, not a mother.'

'You said adopted?' Jaz prompted.

'Two private adoptions. An old school friend arranged it. I rang her up, absolutely desperate. She provided the childless couples. They paid well.' She thought for a moment. 'The right sort of people, of course.'

'The twins were separated?'

'Yes, I told you. Justin went to Bournemouth. Jason went to Highgate. I thought I'd never see them again. I never did see Jason again, but Justin turned up about four years ago. He'd traced me somehow and said his name was Andy. He had all sorts of papers and documents. I thought he wanted something, but he didn't. He was a good boy, a good-natured boy, a computer programmer. He was a surprise. He was rather ordinary, but I thought that was probably a good thing. He came to see me from time to time.'

'Andy's dead,' reminded Jaz. She didn't want to be brutal, but she thought the woman's grasp on reality was a little thin. She didn't want their visit to be a waste of time.

'Dead,' repeated the woman sadly. 'First lost. Now dead.'

Trace slid from her seat, kneeled in front of the

woman and stroked her hand. 'We're very sorry,' she murmured.

Jaz stood up abruptly and pulled Trace to her feet. 'We've got to go,' she said. 'We'll see ourselves out.' She made for the door, pulling Trace's arm. In moments they were outside in the street.

'She was sad,' said Trace. 'We shouldn't have just left her there like that.'

Jaz walked quickly towards the car, with Trace following. She unlocked the Cortina, got inside and slammed the door. As Trace climbed into the passenger seat, Jaz put on her sunglasses then started the ignition with a furious gesture. 'I didn't like her,' she said. 'Talking all that shit about the Rolling Stones. And she sold those babies, probably to the highest fucking bidder.' She paused. 'And she was very ugly. She had false teeth. She gave me the creeps.'

'You know something?' said Trace. 'You swear too much.'

Jaz fired the engine.

Trace was silent. Then she said, 'You know that woman on *Absolutely Fabulous*? The blonde one?'

Jaz turned out into the traffic and, still angry, quickly wound down her window.

Trace considered again for a moment. 'She'll look like Andy's mum one day. The way she carries on, that's where she's heading.'

'Trace,' said Jaz. 'Shut up. Start giving me directions, like now. I've got to have a shower.'

Chapter Ten

The hotel in which Trace worked illegally was more like a private health club. It was called Hotel Grand Bahama. Behind its regency exterior there was a fitness suite, chiropody and massage rooms, a beauty salon and a warm turquoise pool surrounded by palm trees. Middle-aged women wandered around in white towelling robes and mud packs.

Jaz had been expecting a quick, lukewarm shower in a maid's attic. Instead, in the luxurious staff quarters, Trace handed her a yellow overall with a tiny palm tree embroidered on the chest, white tights and a pair of white lace-up shoes. 'Put these on,' she said. 'We all wear these.' Jaz examined the unfamiliar garment as Trace pulled off her clothes and wriggled into her own overall. Then Jaz transferred her attention to Trace. Her hemline was very short because her legs were so long. Jaz undressed and donned hers. She hadn't worn a skirt for years. It was much too big and came halfway down her calves. 'I've got a date tonight,' she confided.

Trace giggled. 'Who with? Anyone I know?'

'Yes. He's called Pete. Do you remember him? You met him once or twice. He's a mechanic at the garage where Andy worked. Where I used to work.' It occurred to Jaz again that Pete might be a very useful ally. 'He lives near there. On the Isle of Dogs.'

Trace considered. 'Yeah ... He's that tall, pretty boy ... Nice.' She glanced at Jaz. 'You ought to get your hair done while you're here. I'll take you to the salon.'

'What exactly do you do here?' Jaz enquired.

'Clean the rooms, of course. But we wear the same uniform as the nurses and hairdressers and everyone.' She grinned. 'The manageress reckons we're just one big, happy family.'

'Until they don't need you any more,' exclaimed Jaz impatiently, 'until the job centre coughs up, or someone answers their advert in the *Evening Standard* and they have to start paying National Insurance.'

Trace frowned. 'Don't be like that,' she said, 'it's nice here. I like it. Except for the food. The guests pay hundreds of pounds and all they get to eat is leaves.'

Jaz wandered around. In her uniform, she immediately blended in. She went back to the staff quarters and had a shower. In the laundry room, she ran her own clothes through the washer-dryer. She ate a salad in the dining room next to a table full of large ladies discussing carbohydrate. Then she went down to the pool and sat naked in the jacuzzi.

Jaz found the onslaught of probing bubbles a strange sensation. She lay back and opened her limbs like a starfish. It was pleasant, she decided, sensual. She thought about sex and closed her eyes, imagining Pete stroking her thighs, his gestures both caressing and firm. She touched herself between her legs, excited, as a jet of warm water played against her body then inside it. She sighed with pleasure, but at that instant, unable to help herself, her fantasy switched to Fat Andy and to Blow.

Their faces and their insistent fingers, merged as one single, needy person, filled her thoughts. 'Little baby,' they whispered, handling her. With a splash she stood up, cupping water into her face, trying to free her mind of the image. She stepped out of the pool. I don't like this, she thought.

Later, egged on by Trace, she went into the hair and beauty parlour. The decor here, unlike the pastel reassurance of the rest of the premises, was modern and stark. Even the floor was made of chrome. Because it was a slack period, the therapist, Kayleigh, wearing the same uniform as her own, trimmed and styled Jaz's hair. She was very talkative. She urged Jaz to use conditioner. She said she was from the Isle of Wight.

Kayleigh was the mistress of a thousand potions. They were kept in a glass cabinet, locked with a key. She suggested a facial and then an eyebrow wax. Jaz drew the line at a top-to-toe fake bronzing, but her new friend persuaded her to have her contours defined with blusher, her cheekbones highlighted and her eyelids outlined with pencil. She coated her lips in orange gloss, then gave her the small tube. 'Keep this and use it,' she said.

As they were finishing, Trace appeared. She was holding Jaz's sports bag. 'Jaz. Your phone was ringing.'

The two of them went back to the staff quarters. Jaz put on her own clothes and phoned Harm. Wesley answered. He sounded upset. 'You better get over, Jaz,' he said. 'We're in a very, very negative energy field here.'

'Where's Harm? What's happened?'

'Harm's been harmed,' he said. He wasn't joking. He sounded as if he'd been crying. He sniffed a couple of times and hung up.

'What's up?' asked Trace anxiously.

'Come on,' said Jaz. 'Something bad's happened to Harm.'

Trace gave a little cry. In an instant she dragged off her overall, tights and shoes. She wasn't wearing a bra or knickers. Not for the first time, Jaz admired her gawky beauty. She wriggled into her jeans, a clean belly top and her flip flops. She yanked her fingers through her short, thick hair. In under a minute they were away, running towards the Lotus Cortina. In three minutes they were on the road, heading for Wesley's place in Shepherd's Bush.

Wesley had a spacious studio flat above a pork butcher. A homeless man was crouching in the doorway, holding out his hat, but in their hurry Jaz and Trace merely stepped over him. Wesley opened the door wordlessly and gave them a bleak stare. They followed him in. There was a strong smell of cooking meat coming from below. Trace grimaced. Like Wesley, she was a vegetarian.

Harm lay on the settee wearing a pink cellular blanket. Her face was bruised and swollen. Her bottom lip was split and blood, now dry, had collected in the corner of her mouth. One of her eyes was blackened and half closed. When she saw her two friends, she attempted to smile. Trace leaped towards her and then knelt at her side, burying her face in the blanket. Jaz sat at Harm's feet. Wesley disappeared to make coffee.

'My, my, Jaz, you look like Miss World,' joked Harm. Her voice sounded muffled. She could hardly open her mouth. 'You're wearing make-up!'

'I've a date,' Jaz muttered. 'You remember Pete from the garage? Lives in Poplar?' She paused. 'Shit,' she said, staring at Harm's injuries. 'Look at you. Who did this?' There was a lead weight in her stomach. She knew the answer.

Trace, her face still hidden, started to sob.

'Wesley?' Harm called out. 'Wesley? Can you come here?'

Wesley reappeared. He seemed desolate. He was carrying a tray with four mugs of instant coffee.

'Be a good Wesley,' said Harm. 'Go and get me a milk shake from McDonald's. Banana flavour. With a straw. I can't drink coffee. It just makes my bladder ache.'

Wesley looked miserable. He said nothing.

'Take Trace with you.'

He pulled on a bomber jacket.

Trace was still crying. 'Shut up, Trace,' said Jaz aggressively.

'Come on, Trace,' said Wesley. They both went out.

'This was my fault, wasn't it?' Jaz inserted one of Harm's cigarettes between her damaged lips and lit it.

Harm inhaled gratefully. 'Forget blame,' she said. 'We made a mistake, that's all.' She raised her hand with difficulty and flicked her cigarette ash onto the floor.

Jaz picked up an ashtray from the table and put it into her other hand. 'Ronnie and Reggie.' It was a statement rather than a question. 'Mile End Road.' Jaz stood up, paced across the room, then back again. She clenched and unclenched her fists. I'll fucking kill them, she thought. I'll kill Vinny. Her mouth felt very dry. She bent down and picked up her mug. She watched Harm smoke, noticing that her knuckles were grazed.

'They took me to an Indian restaurant,' said Harm. 'They were all right at first. We chatted and had a curry and a couple of beers. Then they took me back to the gym, paid me and we did the business. It was just like the old days. One watching the other, straight fucking, no extras. Then swapping around. It was afterwards, when I mentioned your bloke, that things turned heavy.'

'What did you say?' asked Jaz.

'I said he'd been murdered. I told them I hardly knew the guy, but that you were upset. I asked them if Vinny was behind it. I didn't cut corners, I just came out with it.'

Jaz stamped across the room and back, twice.

'They wanted to know where you're living,' Harm continued. 'Said they were looking for you. Wouldn't believe me when I said I didn't know. Jaz is a homeless person, she just stays anywhere, I said. You know that, boys. You know Jaz – what she's like. She's gone back to her old ways.' Harm sucked on her cigarette again, then extinguished it. 'They weren't having any of it. They tried to beat it out of me.'

'A mistake,' said Jaz. 'Going there was my mistake.'

'It was all a mistake. I shouldn't have gone. They're cheap. Always were cheap. They're not nice people.' She thought for a moment. 'And I know them. Another mistake. These days I only do business with men I don't know. Avoiding repeats. I don't want to get to know them. I don't want to talk to them. I shouldn't have gone back to the Mile End Road. Too much history there, too much baggage. It was another life.'

'I'm sorry, Harm.' Jaz drained her coffee and dumped the mug on a table. She was too angry to feel guilty. Guilt would come later.

'I'll recover. Worse things have happened. But you need to watch out, Jaz. They're after you.'

Jaz thought for a moment. 'They think that Andy took something belonging to Vinny.'

'Maybe they think you have it.'

'Did they say so?'

'Not exactly . . .'

'Do you think they killed Fat Andy?'

'They didn't answer questions, they asked them.' She grinned ruefully.

Jaz felt frustrated by the lack of information. She was not only angry, she was impatient. 'Yes, but what do you think?'

'I think they might have done, if Vinny told them to. They're Vinny's heavies, after all. If Vinny wanted Andy dead, then . . .' she paused, pursing her lips. 'They were the ones. Stay away from them, that's what I'm telling you.'

The front door slammed.

Harm spoke hurriedly. 'Remember that cinema weirdo who was going to kill you when you were sixteen. Remember the mess you were in that time. Don't do anything stupid.'

Wesley and Trace came in. He handed Harm her milk shake then left the room. The atmosphere was charged.

Trace resumed her place at Harm's side, her cheek on the blanket. 'A bad man,' she muttered. 'They're all of them bad men.'

Jaz paced back and forward again. She punched the air. 'The bastard,' she muttered. 'That fucking bastard Vinny.'

'A bad bastard,' Trace repeated vaguely. She sat up on her haunches and reached for a mug of coffee. 'You'll get killed one day, doing this awful job.'

Harm sipped through the straw. 'Where are you staying, Jaz, anyway? Just out of interest.'

Jaz shrugged. 'Fat Andy's car.'

'Don't take that batmobile anywhere near Stepney, that's all I can say. You'll stick out like the Boy Wonder.' She drank the milk shake steadily. 'You know what was funny? Typical of them? They beat me up, then called me a taxi. They even helped me on with my coat. They're vicious thugs, but they've got like . . . you know . . . perfect manners.'

Jaz moved towards the door. She needed to get outside. 'Come on, Trace.'

'Be careful, Jaz,' said Harm. 'Forget that Pete. Stand him up. Just stay away from the East End.'

Jaz dropped Trace back at her hotel then, disregarding Harm's advice, set off for Poplar High Street. She was supposed to be meeting Pete and she was late.

It was a beautiful evening. The light was soft and mellow and it was warm. The sky was high and blue. London seemed unlike itself, bathed in gentle, almost southern sunshine, its colours continental, its pedestrians wearing shirtsleeves and skimpy dresses, cheerful and relaxed.

Jaz thought of Italy, Portugal and Greece. She remembered everything she'd ever absorbed about such places on TV holiday programmes. Fat Andy laughed at her for watching them. 'I'll take you there,' he'd said once. 'I did all that stuff in the seventies. On the Magic Bus. But I'll take you, if you want.' Jaz suddenly remembered the way his hair, on that last evening, was matted and dead, like an animal run over on the road – thick and full of blood.

About half a mile from her destination, Jaz parked the car at the side of a police station. Fat Andy had always said that if there was nowhere else, it was a reasonably safe place. Jaz wasn't confident but then she remembered that she herself had never stolen a car from outside a police station. Not once.

She checked herself in the mirror. She wasn't sure about the make-up but decided to leave it on. She applied a little more lipstick from the free sample she'd been given. She sniffed her hair. It smelled of coconuts. It was straightened and with the extra benefit of Kayleigh's protein treatment, it hung in deep, smooth curves to her shoulders. It looked thicker and more glossy. The kinks and dry wisps had been eased away. Her fringe was even and manicured. Jaz decided at that moment to put her anger and frustration and revenge plans temporarily to one side. She was out on a proper date and she was almost pretty. She looked like a woman rather than a child.

As an extra precaution, she immobilized the car. She jogged the half mile to the pub, not too fast, to avoid getting sweaty. The place was large, on a corner. It had an excess of overflowing window boxes which cascaded garish flowers down its walls. A few tables were occupied outside and the sound of karaoke came from within. Someone was attempting an old Kate Bush hit, but they couldn't reach the high notes.

Jaz paused and smoothed her T-shirt. She had brought her sports bag but had left her jacket in the boot of the car. She checked her jeans pocket. The photo of her twin sisters was folded inside. She still had a roll of money, left over from her trip to Cambridge.

Pete was sitting alone. Jaz paused at the bar and looked at him. She ordered a lemonade. He was wearing a baggy black shirt and a green silk waistcoat. His hair was held in a ponytail. He looked more New Age than she was expecting. As she walked towards him she noticed that his white jeans were clean but deliberately ripped and frayed at the knees. His ankles were white and bony above black plimsolls. He saw her but didn't smile. She was ninety minutes late.

'Sorry,' said Jaz lightly. 'My friend Harm's been beaten up. I was at her bedside. You know, helping.'

Pete frowned. 'Harm?'

'I think you've met her. She used to hang out with those brothers on the Mile End Road. The big ones who work for Vinny.' Jaz was thirsty. She drained her glass.

Pete thought for a minute. 'Black girl? On the game?'

'Yep.'

'Occupational hazard, I should think.' Pete turned the long words slowly over his tongue.

There was a sudden blast of music. Jaz turned to the stage. An elderly Chinese man picked up the microphone and started dancing stiffly, like a puppet. He sang the opening to the Spice Girls' 'Wannabe'.

Pete finished his pint. He stood up to go to the bar. 'Want anything?'

Jaz shook her head.

He smiled. She knew she was forgiven. 'Never drink, do you?'

'No. My mother's a drunk.' She paused. 'An alcoholic.'

Pete nodded sympathetically.

When he returned, Jaz moved next to him on the bench seat. He rested his arm along the back, behind her, in a gesture that was both casual and enclosing. 'You don't mind me drinking?'

'Oh, I don't care what other people do.' She laughed. 'I need a few friends, you know.'

'Your hair looks nice,' he said.

'I had it done in a really posh place. My friend Trace works in this hotel. Called the Grand Bahama.'

'The Grand Banana?'

'Bahama,' Jaz laughed. 'People go there to lose weight.'

They chatted about various things. Jaz was surprised to discover he didn't share her enthusiasm for cars. He said when you fix other people's cars all day you don't want to think about them in your spare time. Jaz could see his point. Both Blow and Fat Andy had spent a lot of time fixing cars, without their passion becoming dimmed, but then they weren't doing it day in day out, non-stop, for other people, for a wage.

She changed the subject. They discovered they both liked football. Jaz expected him to be a Millwall fan but he supported Palace. They discussed Sunderland's new Stadium of Light. 'I never go back up there,' said Jaz. 'I was going to but . . .'

'But what?'

'My sisters have moved on. Grown up.' She took out the photo of Peony and Mimosa, dressed as angels, and showed it to him.

He smiled.

She folded it and put it away. 'My mother had a farm, but it's been sold . . .' She was going to mention Blow, but stopped herself.

'I'm sorry about Andy,' Pete said, as if reading her mind.

'So am I.'

'I hope you don't think . . .' He stopped, then tried again. 'I hope you don't think . . .'

'That you're taking advantage of the situation? No I don't. I don't. OK?'

'It's just that . . .'

142

'It's OK, Pete, honest.' She paused. 'Being on my own all the time doesn't help.'

He picked up her hand and kissed it, looking into her eyes. His touch was like an electric shock. Jaz hoped he hadn't felt her jump. She realized that his confidence had grown. He was no longer shy. She smiled and withdrew her hand. She was beginning to feel a little out of control.

'Where're you staying?' he asked.

Jaz didn't want to tell him she was homeless. She had a feeling that he wouldn't approve. 'With friends,' she lied.

He got up to go to the bar. Jaz watched his small rear and noticed that his lovely hair was tied back with coloured braid. He had young arms. She felt a surge of desire. What am I doing, she thought, with Blow dead, and Fat Andy dead? Why am I with someone else? She turned the question over in her mind. She placed her hand on the centre of her chest. The pain was still there. She was still grieving, but the situation with Pete was quite different and separate from anything that had happened with Andy or Blow. This had nothing to do with them. Then she remembered Fat Andy telling her to loosen up. He was a hedonist and he'd found her tightly strung and unadventurous. Enjoy yourself, girl, he'd kept saying. Find some pleasure in life! She looked at Pete, buying the drinks. He had bony, boyish shoulders. He was young and because of this he made her feel mature. She wanted him.

Andy would have approved, she thought. He would have found this need more normal and acceptable than my usual cold style. She smiled to herself. Maybe I just needed to find the right person.

Pete came back with half a pint for himself and a lemonade. Then he walked over to the stage. He was joining in the karaoke. He selected a song. He climbed up as the opening bars of Simply Red's 'Stars' started playing. Jaz was worried, and grasped a beer mat. She started shredding it, but immediately he began singing she realized everything was fine. He had a great voice. He sounded just like Mick Hucknall. He was a gentle New Age man. He turned to face her, singing something about falling from the stars and landing in her arms. People turned to stare at Jaz. She was embarrassed but very pleased.

It was dark outside. The window boxes gave off a faint, summery perfume. They walked away from the pub, down the warm, deserted street, holding hands. Pete carried her bag. The sky had turned purple. His flat was a short distance away. It was medium rise with balconies covered in plants. He tapped a keypad outside the entrance and the big glass door swung open. The lobby was brightly lit and a uniformed man sat behind a screen like a bank clerk. He saluted as they passed by, on their way to the lift.

'What is this place?' asked Jaz.

'It was a council gaff,' he replied, 'but it was bought out by a private company. They put the rents up, did a bit of decorating. They made the entrance more secure and hired that con-serge.'

'Who?'

'That con-serge. That bloke. He stops the trouble-makers from coming in. It used to be hell before. Kids, winos, homeless dossers, beggars. Now it's sort of OK.'

Jaz coughed.

They got into the lift. 'Have you been here long?'

'All my life. My mum died and I stayed on.' A bell rang and the door opened. Jaz noticed that they were on the third floor.

Pete's living room was spartan but clean. Jaz was surprised. She'd expected his mother's old furniture, floral wallpaper and carpet. Instead, the walls were white, the floor sanded and the sofa and chair were black cotton. A small lamp was already burning by the window. He turned on the CD player and went into the kitchen to make tea. Jaz looked around. There was a framed print of the Zodiac on the wall and a poster with paintings of various weeds. On closer inspection, these turned out to be herbal remedies. She examined a row of books. There were a few crime novels but they were mostly concerned with astrology, herbalism and homoeopathy. There was a music magazine with a cover picture of the Verve. She looked out of the window. This was the back of the building but she couldn't quite see the river. They were surrounded by blocks of flats of varying heights. There was a deserted market place below, the stalls empty of their goods and awnings. Dominating the skyline, symmetrical and proud, glowed Canary Wharf, as elegant as a space rocket, as huge as a mountain. A plume of white vapour drifted from its tip, revealing then obscuring its upper outline, before being blown into the night air.

Pete returned, holding two mugs. They sat down and chatted about astrology. Jaz privately thought it was nonsense but she played along with it. She told him she was a Gemini and he looked up her date and time of birth in one of his books. He told her that her ascendant was Leo, which was the same as his.

'Does that mean we get along?' she asked, 'or the opposite?'

He replied by stroking her hair. 'You look different,' he said. 'You look kind of . . . softer.'

'I'm wearing make-up,' she replied. 'Do you like it?'

'I don't usually dig it, but it looks nice on you.' He laughed. 'I was worried about tonight.' He paused, searching for words. 'Because you're older than me and everything. But when I saw that you'd put make-up on and had your hair done, just for me, just for my benefit, I felt . . .' He laughed again. 'Flattered.' He leaned towards her and kissed her cheek. His hand fingered the waist-band of her jeans. His other arm encircled her and drew her close. He kissed her tenderly, on the lips, on her neck, on her forehead. 'Your hair smells wonderful,' he whispered. 'What is it?'

'Coconut oil.'

His lips returned to hers and he slipped his tongue inside her mouth, probing gently. He undid the button of her jeans and slid down the zip.

Jaz felt very relaxed. She was enjoying his attention. She was passive, lying back in his arms, responding, but in a minimal way. As he kissed her she realized what was different. He wasn't expecting her to actively please him. In fact, the reverse was true.

Jaz had been with lots of men but usually in return for something – money, accommodation, a favour, a meal. This meant that she had to do what they wanted, maybe even going as far as pretending to be someone she wasn't. In bed with Fat Andy she'd been required to be a little girl. In any event, she'd always concentrated on the needs of these men rather than her own. Now, with Pete, he seemed to want nothing except to be with her. He was only interested in pleasing her.

Gently, he removed her jacket, then her T-shirt. His

hands brushed over her nipples and he kissed the hollow above her collarbone. Jaz realized that she was excited. She felt desirable. She was being properly appreciated, for herself. She concentrated on the sensations of being fondled. I like this, she thought. The relief of not having to focus on his needs, or on her own hard-won techniques, gave way to a languid sense of relaxation. Her mind drifted to a distant place which allowed her body to enjoy and respond to physical sensation. His lips grazed her neck. Gently he sucked her ear lobe. His hands stroked her back. 'Is that nice?' he whispered. 'Do you like that?'

She sighed and opened her eyes. He was smiling at her. 'Do you want to go to bed?' he murmured. He pulled her hand and she stood up and followed him into the next room. She helped him slide off her jeans and pants. Kneeling on the floor in front of her, he buried his face in the hair between her legs. The room was dark but the bed cover gleamed. Jaz held his head against her body then carefully stepped backwards, sitting then lying on the bed. He continued to kiss her – his mouth exploring her stomach and inner thighs then returning to the delicate folds between her legs. Jaz spread both her arms and her legs wide in this act of surrender that she had never dared allow herself before. She held her breath as an acute sensation built up, swept through her body and was then discharged. She made a small, involuntary cry.

There was a brief pause as he drew back but she held up her arms and gathered him towards her in a gesture that signified both gratitude and relief. 'You're beautiful,' she heard him whisper. 'I've always thought so.'

Pete had a single bed. They lay on their sides facing

each other, talking and giggling. His youth was refreshing. Jaz found herself being genuinely childish, rather than pretending. She told some silly jokes. She made rude noises with her hands and armpits. He laughed immoderately and talked about school.

She explored his body and discovered it was hard and thin with clearly defined muscles and bones. After a while, she climbed on top of him, gently coaxing him with her hands towards orgasm. Then, turning over, she let him enter her for his release. They made love again, dozed a little then continued. He was so young he had lots of energy and wasn't at all worried about having to get up early the next day. After several hours she snuggled backwards into the concave line of his body and slept. When she awoke, light shone through the thin curtains and she discovered he had gone.

Jaz stretched across the narrow bed and sighed. She felt wetness ooze from her vagina. She held up the covers and sniffed the scent of sex. They hadn't used condoms. She did a rapid calculation and decided that this was OK. She looked around the room. The painted floorboards were covered in a thin, colourful Indian rug. In a corner, there was a rowing machine and a pile of weights. There was a print of a famous painting of water lilies, which she couldn't name. The room was clean and bare, but pleasing. She sighed contentedly.

After a while her thoughts inevitably returned to Fat Andy and Blow. Despite her night with Pete, the pain of their loss was still there, physically manifested in her chest. She pressed it with her hand. She thought again how both the dead men would approve of her new relationship. This was comforting.

Her mind moved on to the question of Vinny. This

forced her out of bed. She washed, retrieved her scattered clothes and dressed. Her hair had returned to its normal thin-looking, flyaway state, so she plaited it tightly. She turned on the television in the living room. The Home Secretary was making a speech about the government's plans to deal with homelessness and begging. He called it the new deal on Clean Cities. Jaz half listened, cynically, dismissing his concerns as platitudes. She'd heard this kind of talk before. Not only his solutions, but even his definitions of the problem had nothing to do with the reality of life on the streets. She'd been there and knew it well. What do you know about hardship, she thought, you fat cat, you tosser? You designer dressed, feather-bedded wanker. As she was about to switch off the TV the camera panned and she froze in surprise. 'Andy!' she said aloud.

A man stood near the Home Secretary. As the politician moved off the platform, he followed him down some steps. In two seconds they were both gone. The bland face of the morning newsreader appeared. Fucking hell, she thought, it couldn't be . . . She remembered the comments of both Princess and Fat Andy's mother. Was it possible? It had to be. The likeness was uncanny. There was only one explanation. This had to be Fat Andy's twin! She switched off the television and closed her eyes, trying to bring an after image of the man to mind. He had Andy's exact profile, with its triple chin, soft cheeks and slightly hooked nose. His hair was long like Andy's, and the same colour, but straighter and smooth, drawn back tightly into a ponytail. He had the same bulk, the same enormous stomach but he was very smartly dressed in a suit with a white shirt and patterned tie. As Princess had suggested, he wore an identity badge on a long chain around his neck. She took a deep breath. Why had Andy never mentioned him? But then she remembered she knew nothing about Fat Andy's life. She hadn't known about his mother, about his glamorous if curious origins. That information had been shared with Princess, but not with her.

She realized that she had to speak to this man. He would be a proper mourner. He would be the chief mourner. He would understand. She paced back and forth across the room. Both Princess and Andy's mother had responded to the news of his death in a less than satisfactory way. A twin brother would be different. Jaz knew about twins. Twins were one person in two bodies. She would find him and tell him his twin was dead. She owed it to Fat Andy. This was absolutely clear.

She made the bed and opened the bedroom curtains, letting the bright sunshine flood in. There was a leafy balcony, covered in pot plants. This room overlooked the street. She glanced down. Her heart lurched. Two men were standing on the opposite pavement. One was leaning against a lamp-post, the other paced slowly to and fro. Their bald heads gleamed. It was Ronnie and Reggie.

Jaz bunched the edge of the curtain in her fist. Her mind was racing. A surge of adrenalin expelled the last of the calm, contented feeling that had been with her upon waking. She felt her muscles adopt their customary tense, ready state. Her mouth became a thin line, her eyes narrowed. A series of options flashed across her mind. She had to get out without being seen. She had to retrieve the car. She had to disappear. Another thought crowded in. That bastard Pete had betrayed her. He'd set her up.

Vinny and his gang were onto her, and they'd used Pete as a trap.

She strode around, angry, looking for something to steal. There was nothing that was both valuable and portable. She made a note of the phone number and then walked out of the flat, leaving the door wide open. The hi-fi and television were clearly visible from the landing. The room, with its modern decor, venetian blind and rubber plant, looked inviting, even prosperous. 'You shit,' she muttered. 'I hope this place is fucking stripped when you get home.'

She ran along the corridor. The only way out seemed to be down. The back of the building was inaccessible from the public areas. It was a line of closed doors.

She went up the stairs two at a time. On the next floor, halfway along the corridor next to the rubbish chute, there was a narrow metal staircase leading up to a hatch. This was secured with a small padlock. Breathing heavily, Jaz climbed the steps and rummaged in her bag for her smallest screwdriver. She swore to herself. An old woman emerged from a flat opposite and looked up, hands on hips. She examined Jaz quizzically as if expecting to see a naughty child. Holding onto the handrail, Jaz leaned out and towards her. She flicked open her small wallet, pretending to show ID. 'Satellite TV,' she said huskily. 'Service agreement.'

The woman frowned and disappeared without a word.

Jaz prised away the screws holding the catch on the exit. In seconds she was on the roof.

There was a stiff breeze and the sun was already hot on the back of her neck. The street was quiet. She walked over to the low parapet and looked down. The flats were not very high, but without protection the drop seemed dizzying. She could just make out the bald head of either Ronnie or Reggie, still at his post. His shoulders had the resigned droop of someone who was prepared to wait all day.

A helicopter swooped overhead and she felt the disturbance in the air. Combined with the wind, this gave her the feeling of being blown too hard towards the edge. She stepped backwards. The next-door building was two storeys down. Jaz considered staying on the roof until Vinny's men had given up and gone home. She looked around. There were a few satellite dishes, cables, pipes and a large, rusty water tank. It would be possible to sit it out. Just then she heard a shout. Turning, she saw a man emerging from the hatch. His bulky shoulders were through, and then, awkwardly, his stocky legs. He was wearing a purple silk tracksuit and new trainers. He spoke into a walkie-talkie and gestured to her to come towards him. He shouted again, but his words were indistinct, carried away by the wind. It was Ronnie or Reggie. He'd made his way up from the street.

Jaz looked down again. The building next door had a fire escape on the back. She swallowed hard. Maybe. I could jump it. Just. She didn't allow herself time for reflection. Hugging her bag she ran towards the man as if answering his call. He was a purple blur. When he was only yards away and without missing a beat she swung round on one heel and accelerated back towards the edge. She heard him shout again. The wind whistled in her ears and her heart pounded. She looked up at the clear blue sky and then across the rooftops. Without losing speed and without looking down, she felt one foot touch the parapet as she flung herself into space. The free fall was terrifying.

She landed on her feet. A sickening jolt surged from her ankles up through her thighs. She toppled forward onto her knees, winded. Her stomach felt like water. She breathed heavily for a few seconds, her eyes tight shut. She'd made it. She was on the roof of the building next door and she'd put a huge gap between herself and her pursuer. Drawing in a few more sharp breaths she stood up, testing her ankles. Stay calm, she told herself. Stay cool. She was shaking but she was OK.

Turning she saw Ronnie or Reggie waving from above, his walkie-talkie clasped to his ear. He looked small and helpless now, gesturing wildly. She ran over to the fire escape. It was old and rusty but as she gingerly stepped on it, she sensed it was secure. In a couple of minutes she was down and in the back street. She crossed the market place where traders were setting up for the day and entered a maze of narrow passageways between flats, then ran in what she hoped was the direction of the car. Emerging she saw a sign for the Blackwall tunnel and heard the roar of the main road. She felt hot, sticky and red-faced. A group of young Asian children, on their way to school, eyed her curiously and smiled. 'Good morning,' said one of them politely.

She bought a can of Coke from a corner shop, set off at a brisk walking pace, then a steady jog, hoping she was approaching the police station where she'd left the car. She found it without too much difficulty. There were two leaflets under the windscreen and a dollop of bird mess down the passenger door. Otherwise it was as she'd left it. She got in, recovered her breath and massaged her ankles. I must wash this car, she thought. She put on her sunglasses. Within a few seconds she was away. I need a plan, she decided. She wasn't going to let them beat her. She wanted revenge.

Chapter Eleven

Jaz spent another night in the car, parked in a secure covered area reserved for barristers in Lincoln's Inn Fields. This was another one of Fat Andy's safe havens for the Lotus Cortina, where he'd somehow managed to familiarize himself with the security measures. He'd recorded the information in his Filofax.

She lay on the back seat, her head on the inflatable pillow. She found it hard to sleep, not just because of the discomfort but because her mind was full of her night with Pete. She kept remembering things they'd done and what she'd said to him – revealing things, silly things – and now she felt humiliated. She loathed herself for confiding in him. She'd been a fool. She'd been off her guard and now she felt ridiculous. She vowed to herself that such a thing must never, ever be allowed to happen again. Sex was a means to an end, that was all. She didn't need it and she didn't want it, for any reason other than convenience. Pete would suffer for tricking her. She would have to think of a way of paying him back – the only thing was, her list of enemies was growing. He'd have to take his place in the queue.

She deliberately changed her memories to ones of Fat Andy. She pressed her hand on her chest and felt the pain. She recalled a night out in a pub in New Cross with all the members of the gang. They'd just completed an order from Denmark and stolen and delivered twelve BMW 750s. However, this wasn't the reason for the celebration. Andy had suggested a drink because one of the boys, Lem, had exchanged contracts on a house in Blackheath.

'It's something and a half,' Lem told everyone. 'Original features. Fireplaces and that. Plus it's got a bidet and a power shower.' Lem was a short, weasly thirty-year-old who at one time had been a professional boxer. 'It's a step up,' he told everyone, 'from a council house off Southwark Park Road.'

'We'll all come round,' suggested Fat Andy, 'when you've had a chance to settle in.'

Lem took Andy's hand and shook it formally. 'I owe it all to you,' he said.

Andy chuckled and called for another round of drinks. He was always very generous in pubs.

'I mean it,' insisted Lem. 'Now I can move me old mum and me sister and kiddies. Down there, it's like paradise. There's the park and there's no beggars or riff-raff. The air's clean.' He looked close to tears. 'It's heaven.'

Andy took him in his arms and hugged him. Lem seemed like a little boy, squashed against that massive chest.

'I mean it,' he repeated, as he was released. 'You've set me up, Andy mate, in this job. This is the best job I ever had. I'm flying high.' He paused. 'You're the guv'nor, you are, Andy.'

There was a murmur of approval. They all raised their glasses. 'To Andy!' they called in unison. Jaz was pleased and proud.

Fat Andy was flushed. He slapped a few backs. 'Let's

go through,' he announced, pointing to the back room. 'I've got the landlady to put on a spread.'

At nine a.m. the next day, Jaz called on Trace at the Hotel Grand Bahama and borrowed a leotard and trainers from the staff room.

'I wish I knew what you were up to,' said Trace, holding the lycra garment against Jaz's back, to check the size.

'Fat Andy's dead,' replied Jaz. 'I've a few things to sort, that's all.'

'Since that fat man was killed,' Trace offered reflectively, 'you've been running around like a . . . pea in a pod.' She sighed. 'No . . . I mean a bug in a rug. What do I mean?'

'What do you mean, Trace? That's a very tricky question.' Jaz sounded impatient.

Trace continued, her good temper intact. 'What happened to that other one, that Pete? At least he's nice looking. Gorgeous. And he's been asking about you.'

Jaz was just about to leave, but stopped in her tracks. 'Pete? How do you know about Pete?'

'You told me about him. He's the reason you had your hair done.' She paused for a moment. 'You know something? His hair's the same as yours.'

'He's been here?'

Trace nodded.

'What?' Jaz was aghast.

'Early today. About eight o'clock. He was looking for you. He thinks you're staying with friends. I told him you're sleeping in the car.'

Jaz clenched her fists. Her voice was angry. 'He had

no right . . . Coming here . . . the bastard.' She turned on Trace, her voice raised. 'Tell him nothing, right? Don't tell him a thing. I don't want him to know anything about me. I don't want to see him.' She felt close to tears and struggled to control herself. 'Trace, are you listening to me? What did he want? He has no right to hassle my friends.'

Trace was puzzled. 'He was really nice. He said you two were, you know, going out. I knew he meant shagging, but he was being polite and he was really concerned. He said he wanted to get hold of you, reckoned you'd left his door open and all his stuff was nicked . . . But he wasn't angry. More worried.'

'Tell him nothing!' Jaz was shouting. 'Nothing! He's a wanker and a liar!'

Trace put a finger to her lips. 'Shh!' she said urgently. She looked towards the door. 'Do you want to get me the sack?' she whispered.

Jaz hesitated. She swallowed hard. She looked at Trace's kind, mystified face and felt guilty. 'Why don't we meet up later?' she asked, struggling to get her voice back to normal. 'I'm sorry. I didn't mean to shout. I'm a bit strung out. I'll ring you. We could catch up on . . . news.'

Jaz knew that she'd not only been neglecting both Trace and Harm, she'd also been putting them in danger. Harm had been beaten up. Pete was now bothering Trace. It was a mess. The whole thing was a mess and it was her fault. The three friends didn't usually have secrets from one another. But she'd told them only a tiny bit of the truth. 'How's the invalid?' she asked.

Trace sighed. 'Pretty good, considering. Up and about. I just wish she'd stop . . . you know . . . what she does.'

'She's not going to, is she? Not now she's making real money.'

'You're right. She's not. But she takes such chances.' Trace paused. 'And she thinks cleaning hotels is a mug's game.'

Jaz squeezed her arm briefly, then left.

She set off immediately for Ronnie and Reggie's gym on the Mile End Road. She parked at the rear then crossed the road, watching the front of the building. People were waiting impatiently. At ten fifteen a woman in sports clothes appeared and opened up. She was followed inside by three beefy-looking men, two small teenagers who looked like jockeys and a gaggle of women wearing shorts and sweat bands. Cautiously, Jaz joined them as they climbed the stairs. At the top, the woman with the keys stood behind a desk. She smiled apologetically at the customers. Jaz approached her, forcing a grin. 'I'm new here,' she said. 'Can you explain things?'

The woman yawned, then smiled. She was young and pretty with long magenta hair loosely tied up on the top of her head. She was either tanned or dark-skinned, although her black eyes suggested origins which were not British. 'Sorry,' she said. 'I've been run ragged this morning. I'm behind. What can I tell you? You can sign up for a year's membership, pay by instalments and use all the facilities. I can show you around later. Or you can pay three quid and join in the aerobics class. It's just about to start. It should have started at ten.'

'I'll join the class. See if I like it.' Jaz paid the money and followed the woman in the direction of the changing rooms.

'Any health problems? Heart? That kind of thing?'

'No.'

'Done this before?'

'No, but I'm very fit. I run a lot.'

'If you have any problems, just stop and rest. It's not a test. Work at your own pace.'

'Don't worry. I'll be fine. Are you leading the class?'

'Yes.' She pushed open a door. Women were wriggling into leotards or skin-tight leggings with brief midriff-revealing tops. Some were applying make-up. They were mostly tanned and toned, although two outsiders, each standing in a corner, were overweight. They pulled on baggy T-shirts, to conceal their flab.

The instructor peeled off her tracksuit, revealing pert muscles and perfect curves.

'How well do you know the owners?' Jaz asked.

There was a rueful grin. 'Fairly. Why?'

Jaz stepped out of her jeans. 'Are they likely to be around this morning?'

The instructor moved towards the door, followed by her eager protégées. 'No. They're never in before three. They mostly cover evenings because that's when we get the boxers in – and the footballers.' She grinned. 'I'm Kormal, by the way.'

Jaz felt self-conscious in her yellow leotard with its embroidered palm tree. It was big and wrinkly. She thought it looked stolen. In the exercise studio she faced a floor-to-ceiling mirror where everyone stood, unsmiling, critically regarding themselves and each other. Several of the women were old. They had crêpey necks and thin, backcombed hair, but their figures were perfect. Jaz looked at her own thin legs, her flat chest. Why had she been so stupid as to imagine that Pete desired her? She didn't look like a woman. She looked undersized and pre-pubertal. She hated herself for being small. She hated herself for being duped. Even more, she hated him. You bastard, she thought. Just stay away from me. Stay away from my friends. She tried to push these angry thoughts aside as the music started.

The first movements were gentle and repetitive. Jaz stepped to the left, then backwards and forwards making small arm movements. This is for pensioners, she thought.

The instructor had her back to the group and everyone copied her. She moved gracefully like a dancer. Jaz noticed that her breasts and bottom were quite big but they were very firm. I'd give anything to look like that, she thought. Maybe I'll get into body-building. Maybe I need a high protein diet. Maybe I'll take steroids.

The music was very loud and it gathered pace. Jaz felt her heart beating and her breathing quickened. She struggled to follow the steps which were becoming slick and complicated. Sweat ran from her brow into her eyes. Her leotard was sticking to her chest and back and her shoes felt moist. She was required to kick her legs high and spin round. Her arms dipped and flailed like wind-mills. She glanced at the older women. They were bouncing at high speed from one end of the room to the other, following the impossible movements like robots. They were perfectly composed. Jaz started to gasp and her head felt light. She drove herself on. Her muscles were protesting with fatigue. Her chest was bursting. At the very point where she felt it was impossible to con-tinue, the tempo eased slightly. They were cooling down. She felt shaky. She was relieved. She struggled to breathe normally, mopping her face with her hands. She looked in the mirror. Her skin was red and blotchy. My God, she thought, these women go through this torture maybe two or three times a week. They're amazing.

Back in the changing rooms most of them stripped off and disappeared into the showers. Jaz sat on a bench, recovering. 'I thought I was fit,' she said.

Kormal rubbed herself briskly with a towel then got back into her tracksuit. She wasn't even tired. There was a faint sheen on her brow, but otherwise she looked normal. 'You are. That was high impact. An advanced class. Most newcomers wouldn't attempt it, or they'd stop halfway through. You did very well.' She disappeared to answer the phone.

Jaz rested for a while as the other women prepared themselves for the outside world. One by one and in groups, they gradually disappeared. Jaz had a shower and dried herself with one of the towels provided. As she was leaving the cubicles, she saw a handwritten notice, sellotaped to the wall. 'Please look after your Proparty. Management not Responsable.' She recognized the spelling. Ronnie or Reggie had written it. They'd also sent Fat Andy the e-mail on the night of his death. The style was unmistakable. She paused, staring at the sign. She remembered in an instant why she'd come.

Back in reception, clutching the phone to her bosom, Kormal was pacing backwards and forwards alongside the desk. 'I just can't,' she said into the receiver, exasperated. 'What can I do? Damn! Why does it have to be like this?' She put the phone down. She looked close to tears.

'Problems?' asked Jaz.

'I've got to go. That was the blasted receptionist, phoning in sick. Again. But I can't stay. I've got to pick my little girl up from playgroup in a few minutes. I'm already late so I'll have to close the gym.' She seemed scared. 'I'll have to tell those men in the weights room to go home. The bosses will go off it . . .'

'Why don't you get the little one, then come back? How long will you be? I don't mind sitting here for a while.'

Kormal looked very doubtful.

'Don't worry. I know Ronnie and . . .' She swallowed hard. She adopted a cockney accent. 'I mean the owners. Your bosses. They're my cousins. Their old Mum, well, she's my Great Auntie May. I was only saying to her the other day . . .'

Kormal glanced at her watch. She seemed very harassed. She looked at the desk drawer.

Jaz had seen the cash box when she arrived. 'Go on. I won't touch anything. You can trust me.' She pointed to the opening times and the schedule of fitness classes displayed on the wall. 'I can answer the phone. If anything comes up that I can't handle, I'll ask them to ring back.'

Kormal was both desperate and convinced. She ran off down the stairs. 'Forty minutes,' she called out.

Jaz answered two phone enquiries then peeped into the weights room. The beefy men were pumping iron. Next door, one thin teenager was pedalling and the other was running on a treadmill. There was a smell of sweat and talcum powder.

Various acts of sabotage ran through Jaz's mind. She knew she could cut off the electricity supply in such a way that it would take a trained electrician a whole day to repair. She was also capable of damaging the plumbing. The phone system could be ruined, the security alarms confused. It was all possible. The thing was, she didn't want to get Kormal into trouble. If anything went wrong, she'd probably be held responsible. She was nice and a bit desperate and she probably needed the work.

Instead, Jaz spent the time examining the premises thoroughly and making a detailed mental sketch plan. She discovered that a back entrance led onto a fire escape and the door was wedged open with a chair, to create a through-draught. Below, there was a car park where she could see the Lotus Cortina. Two of the women who had been in the class appeared with some shopping, got into a red Polo and drove off. She went back into reception and made a note of the gym's phone number. Switching on the computer, she printed out a list of the members' names and addresses, folded it and put it in her pocket, then stole a couple of sheets of headed notepaper. She rummaged through the drawer of the desk and found a set of Mazda keys and a remote on a chrome ring. A paper label was tied to this, on which was written the words 'spairs'. She left these, but opened the computer's e-mail box and typed in a few lines. Remembering the details of the message to Fat Andy, which they'd sent before he was murdered, she decided to emulate the style. 'Jaz is not a happy girl. Jaz has got Vinny's property and she's going to give it to the police. You Stepney gits.'

Chapter Twelve

Jaz waited in a sandwich bar near Victoria coach station. She'd phoned the Hotel Grand Bahama on the mobile.

It was a very hot day and Trace arrived wearing denim cut-offs and a skimpy white top which revealed her flat stomach. Sensitized by her experience at the gym, Jaz admired her long, lean figure, her strong jaw, her wide mouth. 'I know I've said this before, Trace, but you could be a model.'

Trace slid behind the table and grabbed a gulp of Jaz's milk shake through the straw. She raised her eyes to the ceiling in an expression which said 'I've heard it all before!'

Jaz studied her perfect skin, her thick, badly cut blonde hair, the slant of her oval eyes and the jut of her cheekbones which were almost oriental. She knew, of course, that Trace couldn't handle modelling on her own. Her IQ was too low. 'I'll tell you what, I'll be your manager.' She was more than half serious. It suddenly seemed like a good idea. 'You just stand around in purple lippie and posh frocks and I'll look after the business side.'

'Shut up, Jaz.'

'You've got a foreign-looking face. You know that?' She was aware that Trace had been brought up by a series of foster parents. 'Do you think your real mum could have been Chinese?'

Trace didn't smile. 'My mother was from Leytonstone. She left me in a dustbin at the back of a betting shop.'

'That doesn't mean she wasn't Chinese.'

Trace picked up the pepper pot then slammed it down hard. 'She wasn't Chinese. Right?'

'OK, OK.'

'She wasn't Chinese. Have you got that?'

Jaz thought for a moment. 'There's nothing wrong with being Chinese.'

'Just shut up, won't you?'

Jaz drained her glass. The straw made funny, gurgling noises which she deliberately prolonged.

Trace laughed. She was always entertained by childish things. Her good humour was restored. 'I suppose my dad might've been a chinky,' she offered, chuckling to herself. 'But no one ever said.'

Trace ordered an all day vegetarian breakfast with double soy sausages and extra fried bread. She always ate as if she hadn't seen food for days. 'That bloke came back,' she said, sucking up a forkful of baked beans. 'Again. You know you said to tell you if he did? What's wrong with him, exactly? The girls at the hotel think he's after me. They got all giggly.'

Jaz frowned. She'd thought about telling Trace about Ronnie and Reggie and her need to avenge Fat Andy's death, but she'd dismissed the idea whilst waiting for Trace to arrive. She didn't like lying to her and keeping her in the dark but she knew she wouldn't be able to handle it. Trace hated violence. Also, she had a tendency to get muddled. Unless things were spelled out to her in great detail, several times, she made mistakes. Jaz decided that the less Trace knew about her current problems, the better.

'He's not nice,' she stressed. 'He let me down. He's only pretending to be interested in me.'

Trace cut up a sausage and chewed for a moment. 'You sure? He seemed pretty keen to me. He was carrying a new telly in a box and said it was your fault it got pinched . . .'

'What did you tell him?' She remembered she'd told Trace to tell Pete nothing.

Trace thought for a moment. 'That you'd said to tell him nothing, absolutely nothing at all, that you don't want to see him, that he has no right to bother your friends and that he's a wanker and a liar. That's what you said, isn't it?'

Jaz squeezed Trace's hand. 'Word for word.'

'He's really upset.'

'I don't care.'

'He said again that you left his door open and all his stuff was nicked.'

Jaz smiled. 'That why he's upset?'

'No. I think it was the "wanker and liar" bit. I thought he was going to cry.'

'Good.'

Trace shrugged. 'We all thought he was looking sexy in those overalls.'

Later, they strolled along the Embankment. Jaz put on her Versace sunglasses. 'How's it going at the hotel?' She asked. 'Any chance of a permanent job?'

Trace shook her head. She was eating a KitKat. 'Don't want one.'

The river glittered and a tourist boat ploughed past, its loudspeakers announcing the Oxo Tower and the South Bank. The air shimmered in the heat and two tiny aeroplanes, high above, trailed white spume.

'I like moving around because I've always moved around. My foster parents were all short term, till I ran away, then there were the children's homes. You know I don't like being tied down – it's what I'm used to.'

'You know what I was thinking the other day? I was driving along in the car and I wondered if I'd ever get married. Have a life, like normal people in adverts. You know, a fitted kitchen, cook-in sauces, stuff like that.'

Trace snorted.

'I'm serious. I'm twenty-one. You're twenty. What have we got to show for anything? I've got a car and a change of clothes and no boyfriend. What've you got? I mean, what exactly is the point of it all?'

'It's not even your car,' Trace agreed. She stopped and leaned on the railing looking out at the water. A flock of gulls circled and landed, bobbing on the current like ducks. She thought for a moment. 'I've got Harm and you,' she murmured gently.

Jaz said nothing. Sometimes, Trace made her feel humble.

'I'm OK, you know? I don't have any plans. That suits me.'

Jaz picked up a flat pebble and skimmed it across the water. It skittered near a gull. Disturbed, the bird flapped its wings, rose, then settled again.

'Be careful of that poor seagull, Jaz.'

'Why haven't you got a boyfriend?' Jaz had always wanted to ask Trace this, but had always felt too inhibited.

Trace gripped the railing and squinted her eyes

against the sun. She sighed. 'I don't want one. I had a lot of . . .' She paused. 'I had a lot of trouble . . . with a man in a children's home. It went on for three years. One of the senior staff. I was only little. It sort of put me off.'

'You mean you were abused?'

Trace said nothing but her silence was affirmative.

'My mother's boyfriend used to mess around with me,' Jaz confided. 'Have I ever told you that?'

'Yes,' said Trace. 'You mentioned it once.'

'The thing was, I didn't mind. I liked it. I hated my mother and I felt I was getting my own back. Also, he was nice. He was kind to us. He taught me to drive.'

'That's OK then. If you didn't mind. Not minding makes it sort of all right, I guess.'

'Actually, looking back, I think he was the reason I shacked up with Fat Andy. I didn't know it at the time, but Blow and Fat Andy were really very alike.'

Trace linked Jaz's arm. 'You see, the thing was with me, I like . . . minded a lot. I really minded, I hated it. He always hurt me but then he told me it was my own fault. He said I made him do it and I believed that for a long time. I blamed myself for feeling bad. It made me feel like . . .' She stopped.

'What?'

There was a long silence.

'Nothing.'

'Nothing?'

'Worth nothing.'

They continued walking. The trees drooped in the heat. A woman led a small girl by the hand who was licking a melting ice cream. She was dressed in a broderie anglaise pinafore and her little socks were trimmed with white frills.

'I can't think of myself as, you know . . .'

'Attractive?'

'Right.'

There was a silence as they continued their stroll. There was a frown on Trace's brow, as she remembered.

A man on a unicycle approached them on the pavement. Jaz saw him first. 'Look!' she called out. He came closer. He had a bald head and a very serious expression. His hands were clasped behind his back. He nodded without smiling as he sped by.

Trace laughed delightedly.

Jaz was relieved. 'You know the other day? We went to see Andy's mother?'

'Yep,' answered Trace. 'She was mega-sad.'

'You know she talked about twin sons?'

'Yep. Do you think it was all, like, made up? Just lies?'

Jaz considered. 'No. I mean I reckon the bit about Brian Jones and the Rolling Stones was fantasy. But I do think she had twin sons. And I want to try and find him. Fat Andy's twin.'

'You want to tell him about Andy being murdered and everything?'

'Like I told his mother. It's important to me. I feel . . .'

'It's your duty?'

'Something like that. It's something to do with what I was saying earlier. Like . . . what's the point of everything? What am I doing with my life? Since Fat Andy died, I've had a kind of . . . purpose.'

'Probably best if the brother didn't know. You thought of that? Maybe he doesn't even know he had a twin.'

'No. He should be told. I know about twins. I bet he sort of realizes already that something's wrong and it'll be driving him crazy. Like he's lost his shadow or something.

Whatever he knows, he'll feel bad. He'll feel . . . loss. He just needs to have it confirmed.'

'Is that so?'

'Yeah. Twins are like that. Sort of psychic. They know about each other. Once my sister Mimosa fell down an old well on the farm and her twin Peony was half a mile away and she still came running to raise the alarm. Another time, Mimosa was at a swimming gala and Peony was at school. They hardly ever went to school so this must've been when they were very young. Anyway, Peony was given the belt by this mean old cow who taught religious studies. It was probably illegal, you know? At the exact moment it happened, Mimosa swam to the side, got out of the water, went and got changed and walked back to school. The teacher tried to stop her, but she wouldn't be stopped. "My sister needs me," is all she would say. You see, that's the thing about twins. They're sort of linked. It's really very, very weird.'

Trace thought for a moment. 'How're you going to find him?'

'I've seen him on the television.' Jaz carefully explained to Trace about the Fat Andy lookalike who seemed to accompany a famous politician every time he appeared. 'It's him,' she insisted. 'No doubt.'

Trace was bewildered. Patiently, Jaz ran through it all again.

'I don't see how you're going to meet him,' argued Trace. 'You can't just go up to him outside ten Downing Street or somewhere and talk to him. You'll get arrested.'

'That's where you come in.'

Trace raised her eyebrows. 'Me? What can I do?' She thought for a minute. 'I know. Why don't you send him an e-mail? At the Houses of Parliament or something? Or you could ring them up at *News At Ten* and ask Trevor McDonald to pass on a message.'

Jaz smiled. Her own suggestion sounded just as unlikely, but she thought it would work. 'Trace, I want you to get a job in the Home Office. Like that one you had last year in Kensington Palace. Cleaning windows. Remember?'

'Of course I do.'

'Suss out who he is. Check out if he's got an office somewhere.'

Trace was silent.

'Please. It means a lot to me.' She handed Trace the photo of Fat Andy and Princess. 'He's a dead ringer for Andy.' She paused. 'Bad pun.'

Trace took the picture wordlessly.

Jaz knew that Trace's history in the black economy, with all her hundreds of contacts, made her employable almost anywhere. She'd worked in Harrods, Lambeth Palace, the Harbour Club, London Central Mosque. She worked for cash in hand, filling in, and no kind of security screening ever seemed to apply. She'd done Bill Clinton's laundry. She'd replenished the toilet rolls in the hotel bathroom of Michael Jackson. She once sat at the feet of Tony Blair, looking for his contact lens in the carpet.

'What about the Grand Bahama?' Trace was sulky.

'Fuck the Grand Banana,' replied Jaz. 'If they didn't need you they'd dump you tomorrow without batting an eye.'

Later Jaz drove over to Peckham. She sat around for a while in the car, feeling very hot. There was no sign of the silver Mercedes. She immobilized the Lotus Cortina and went up to the flat she'd shared with Fat Andy for six months. She stood outside for a while holding her chest where the pain was located. The entrance was boarded over and on it some joker had spray-painted the words 'Dead Cunt'.

Downstairs, she knocked at the armoured door of the flat which Elvis shared with Big Boy and Peppy. There was no reply. An old woman shuffled by carrying four bags of shopping. Jaz offered to help but she was too suspicious to agree. She held the bags closer defensively.

'D'you know where the boys might be? The ones who live here?'

The woman was clearly relieved that Jaz wasn't a mugger. 'Try the Duke of Salisbury,' she suggested. 'If not, then Jiggers or Riggers or whatever they call it now. The one that used to be the Old King's Head.'

Jaz crossed the estate. A group of homeless people stood around a scorched patch of earth where the remains of a settee smouldered, giving off black fumes. The sun was hot and their grouping at the fire seemed more from habit than necessity. Jaz recognized one of the women. She was holding a bottle of Lilt and talking dully to herself. Jaz remembered she was Joan. She was from Scotland and she was nice. They'd once doubled in a hostel room and Joan generously shared her food, her blankets, her money, without being asked. Jaz went over and tapped her on the arm. 'Hello,' she said, gently. It would be nice to pay Joan back, she thought.

The woman was startled and took two steps sideways, cradling her bottle. She glared at Jaz without recognition. She looked older and tired. She carried on muttering. Jaz glanced around the group. It was impossible to break in. Everyone seemed too dispirited to talk or make eye contact. It was like a scene from a war, she decided, where people had lost so much, there was nothing left to do or say.

Jaz continued on her way and went into the first pub. There was a thin haze of smoke and the rattle of a pinball machine. The place seemed almost deserted but she saw Big Boy's gigantic back partially concealed in an alcove. The three friends were hunched over soft drinks looking tired and ill. Elvis leaned back when he saw Jaz and blew a desultory smoke ring. 'Hi, doll,' he said, indicating a chair. 'A pew.'

Jaz bought them each a Coke and a Kaliber for herself. She sat down. 'Have you managed to get that . . . property?'

Elvis forced a grin. 'Maybe,' he said.

Big Boy nudged Peppy, they picked up their drinks and cigarettes and with a nod to Jaz they retreated to the pool table in a far corner.

'What's the matter with you three? You look like party time at the morgue. You're not telling me the drugs are finally catching up with you?'

Elvis sighed. 'A bit of bother,' he offered.

'Police harassment?' enquired Jaz.

'No. Trouble at Felixstowe. Consignment impounded. Those thieving customs bastards. Then the Merc. Torched down New Cross. Serious combat, doll. The art of war. Yes or no?'

Jaz thought about their beautiful car. 'Oh, no! What a waste!'

There was a silence. They swallowed their drinks. Elvis sighed again. He felt in the pocket of his jacket and produced a box of matches. Then he pulled out an envelope. 'Yours?' he asked.

Jaz glanced inside. It was a computer disk. 'Where d'you get it? Hidden where I said?'

Elvis nodded.

'How did you manage to get in there? That flat's so tight it looks like Rampton Special hospital.' She paused. 'Like your place.'

He shrugged.

'Thanks, Elvis.' There was an awkward pause. Jaz knew she'd promised him more sex, in payment. 'Do you want to do it?'

He leaned back, swinging his chair, and looked at her with narrowed eyes. Then he grinned. His teeth were bad and his gums were blackish and unhealthy. 'Fact. In total confidence, doll, I's shattered,' he whispered. 'I's depressed. Get it up? Not today.' He paused. 'Another time, definitely.'

Jaz carefully froze her face into a neutral expression in order not to display relief. She took the disk out of the envelope and examined it, then finished her drink. 'Thanks,' she said.

Elvis regarded her for a moment. 'Peppy hallucinate Fat Andy the other night. Down the basement, at the flats. A friggin' ghost. After his old car.'

'Too many drugs,' replied Jaz.

'Peppy's brain full of holes.' He sighed. 'A ghost, doll. A spectre.' He paused. 'Something for us?' he said thoughtfully.

'Yeah?'

'Wheels. We nothing in this fight without wheels.'

Jaz considered this. She was pleased. She was running low on funds. 'What had you in mind?'

'A Jag? An Audi? Big enough. Fast. Reasonably flash.'
He paused. 'Not white, though. Bad luck. Bad *feng shui*.'

'You'll leave it up to me, then?'

'Yeah, doll. You's more the motor girl than us.' He
reached into his pocket again, pulled out a roll of notes
and handed it to her. 'Five hundred,' he said. 'Another
five delivery.'

'When?'

'Yesterday.'

Jaz parked in the safe place in Lincoln's Inn Fields, put
on her headphones and jogged down Holborn towards
the City. Traditionally, this had been her most well
trodden beat when she'd worked for Vinny as a car thief.
She slowed to a dawdle. She felt a little nervous and
realized that to some extent she'd lost her nerve. Like
anything, car crime is perfect only with practice, she
thought to herself. Apart from the ride back from Cambridge and the liberation of the Lotus Cortina she'd been
out of action for a long time. She wasn't entirely sure
what the manufacturers were doing now to stop thieves.
They were constantly improving their systems. She
wasn't on top of it. This was worrying.

She walked around the City, feeling out of place
amongst the male suits, the briefcases, the expensive
sandwich outlets, the bijou boutiques selling shoes and
contact lenses. She saw a few appropriate vehicles – new,
fast, expensive – but they were very exposed. After an
hour she wandered in the direction of the river and
crossed it at London Bridge. She felt hot. She pulled her
T-shirt out from her jeans and wafted it up and down.
Stay cool, she told herself. She was carrying her denim

jacket and sports bag which contained her tools. Elvis's roll of money was making her hip pocket bulge. Stay calm, stay focused. She knew that if she lost her self-assurance, then she would fail. She bought a can of Dr Pepper and sat on a bench to drink it. She thought about holiday destinations. Malaga. She rolled the name around her mouth. Morecambe Bay. Montreal.

She glanced across the road. At that moment, her heart lurched and her limbs changed from hot to icy cold. A brand new Mazda sports car had pulled up opposite. Two men emerged simultaneously, struggling from the small interior cabin. Both had shiny bald heads and pastel coloured linen suits. They each smoothed the creases in their jackets and shook their baggy trouser legs. They were Ronnie and Reggie. A third, smaller man eased himself out, very slowly, from the tiny space which was normally a parcel shelf in the back. He was wearing a conventional dark suit and tie and carrying a briefcase. He placed this on the pavement, stretched like a monkey, grimaced in mock discomfort, then laughed. Jaz noticed his wandering, squinty eye. It was Vinny.

He picked up his case and spoke into an entryphone on the nearest doorway. In a moment, the brothers followed him into the narrow, dilapidated building. Immediately they climbed some stairs. She drained her can and tossed it into the shrubbery, then crossed the road. There was a row of brass and chrome plates outside the decaying offices advertising the names of insurance agents and mortgage brokers. On the ground floor there was a cranial osteopath.

She examined the car. It was a demonstration Mazda MX5, racing bronze, low and sporty. It was gleaming and desirable. 'You lovely little thing, you,' she said under her breath. She walked around it. Alloy wheels, she thought, front air dam skirt, contoured headlights. She whistled aloud, 'Just let me have you, you sexy little baby.'

She looked at her watch then opened the buttoned top pocket of her jacket and carefully removed a spent match and a used piece of gum. She chewed on the gum briefly, then checking that the coast was clear of pedestrians, she placed a tiny piece on the end of the matchstick and inserted it into the lock of the driver's door. She bent down, pretending to adjust a shoelace. She manoeuvred the chewing gum until it held open the little metal flap inside, then, carefully, she removed the matchstick. She stood up and waited as three Indian women in saris passed by. The traffic on the road was busy but drivers were looking ahead to a series of lights and she was confident they wouldn't notice her. She felt in another pocket and produced a yellow tennis ball, cut in half. She placed this over the lock and keeping her body very still, she whacked it silently with the bottom of her right hand, forcing the air from the half ball into the lock. Nothing happened. She tried again. On the third attempt, the central locking of the car disengaged with a quiet clunk. She glanced up the stairs of the office building. There was no sign of anyone.

She waited a few seconds, watching the traffic. Then she heard it. 'Yes!' she said aloud. She was in luck. A fire engine was approaching, its lights flashing and sirens blaring. She opened the driver's door, setting off the alarm. She tossed her jacket and half ball onto the passenger seat and in a quick gesture reached inside, pulling the lever to open the bonnet. The fire engine was passing, its noise drowning out the Mazda's frantic wail. Alongside the engine, tucked away but still visible she located the shiny case of the alarm and using all the strength she possessed, ripped it out. It was silenced as the fire engine turned left at the lights. She closed the bonnet and glanced again up the stairs. A couple of teenagers walked past looking at her quizzically. She got into the car. She was breathing rhythmically and sweat had broken out on her brow. Mazda, she thought to herself. Mazda, Mazda. Stay cool. Stay focused. I know. I know it's the same system as BMW. She put her hand into the well in front of the passenger seat, prodded up behind the fascia and dragged down a spaghetti of wires. She examined them briefly, pulled four apart with her pliers, then connected them in a different sequence. It was tricky. She disconnected a fuse. Let that be right, she thought. Stay focused. Stay cool.

She opened her bag and took out the larger screwdriver. Then she broke off the steering cowl and penetrated the ignition. 'Come on, baby,' she murmured, 'come on.' She felt it give, like soft putty. Once inside and with the smaller implement she turned the exposed, inner mechanism. This is the moment, she thought. Stay calm. The car started gently. She sighed and moved the seat forward, then checked the time: two hundred and thirty seconds. Not bad, she thought. Not my best, but then the stresses were huge.

She drove east, through Southwark. She felt enclosed, like being in the cockpit of a plane. The gearstick had a slick, short throw action which she liked. The suspension was taut, the acceleration positive. She listened with pleasure to the throaty rasp of the exhaust. She played with the electric windows and listened to Capital Radio.

A while later, Jaz checked into a guest house on Lambeth Palace Road and parked in the enclosed yard at the rear. The owner was a large Jamaican woman who Jaz had found, on several other occasions, to be kind but not inquisitive. She was happy for her to have a long, deep bath and to lend her a dressing gown while she laundered her clothes. She cooked up a skillet of spicy food and the two of them sat quietly in the back yard, alongside the Mazda and the dustbins and the washing line, eating chicken and yams and drinking homemade lemonade. 'That's a darling little car,' she said to Jaz.

'Isn't it?' she agreed. 'Isn't it just fab? Not for long though. I'm getting rid of it tomorrow.'

Later, upstairs in her room, Jaz used the mobile to phone Vinny's garage. She was connected to the showroom. 'Tell that fucking Vinny I've got the demonstration MX5,' she told the bewildered salesman. 'The bronze one. Tell the companero that Jaz has got it and she might sell it tomorrow. Sell it or torch it, or drive it into the river. Tell him Jaz hasn't fucking decided what to do with it yet. But she will.' She hung up.

She rang Trace. 'What's happening about the Home Office? Any luck?'

'I can do the House of Lords. Floor buffing and brasswork.'

'No good.'

'Thought not.'

'Get onto it, Trace, will you?'

'I am onto it. I'm definitely onto it.'

'You know you can do it.'

'I'll do it. Right?'

'Thanks, Trace. I appreciate it.'

Trace sniffed. 'Where're you staying?'

'Lambeth. Trevor McDonald's place.'

Trace laughed. She knew the place. 'Mrs McDonald's?'

'Yeah.'

'In the attic?'

'Tell Harm, will you? You know she worries.' She hesitated. 'Not that Pete! Is that clear? Tell that bastard nothing.'

'I know, I know.' Trace spoke as if she was rehearsing. 'Whenever he shows up, tell the pretty ginger boy nothing. Nothing at all.'

Chapter Thirteen

Jaz was aware that she couldn't deliver the Mazda to Elvis unless it was repaired. For this, she needed spares. She lay on her bed in the narrow attic room in Lambeth, waiting for dark and studying Fat Andy's Filofax. One of the codes he'd listed would disarm the security at Vinny's garage. She thought she knew which was the right one. She wished she could ring Pete to check. She felt fresh outrage about his double-crossing hypocrisy. He could have been really useful to her, if he hadn't turned out to be such a rat. As it was, she was determined to get even with him, as soon as she had the time.

It was risky, but she felt more confident about stealing spares from Vinny than she did about trying to negotiate unfamiliar premises. She knew where to go inside Vinny's storeroom and she knew where everything was kept. When she was working for him, Andy had always insisted that she help make good the damage which the team inflicted on stolen cars. He said he trusted her to do it well and that it was a question of having pride in the job.

Because of this, she knew what to expect – there were cameras at Vinny's, and sirens, but no razor wire, nor Alsatian dogs nor helmeted men with truncheons waiting around in vans.

At midnight, she borrowed a door key from her obliging landlady, jogged to the safe haven, collected the Lotus Cortina and set off for the Isle of Dogs. It was a warm, cloudless night with a sliver of white moon. She listened to an All Saints CD on her Walkman and drove with the windows open. The city was quiet, even subdued. She had a sense of London's massive energy, calmed and somnolent, enjoying the balmy stillness of the air, preparing itself for tomorrow and another hectic day.

At Vinny's place, the forecourt was closed for the night, but the showroom, with its rows of gleaming Mazdas, was brightly lit. Jaz drove into the narrow cobbled road behind. She got out and glanced around. The alley was dark and deserted. There was a smell of engine oil and paint. She took the number plates of the stolen sports car from the boot of the Lotus Cortina and looked around again. She could hear a train in the distance, river sounds and the raucous shouts of nearby drunks, but she was unobserved.

Vinny's paint shop, his body shop and parts storeroom were linked single-storey buildings, across the lane from the back of the main garage. The doors were covered by metal security shutters and the windows had grilles – except, she hoped, for a single one. She walked to the corner. As expected, a tiny window was accessible. It was on the end of the body shop, and she knew it led into the overused lavatory. Quickly and stealthily, using the handle of her large screwdriver, she broke its glass. Immediately, there was a pungent smell of urine. With her jacket wrapped around her arm, she cleared the frame of shards. The access was very limited but she hoped she could struggle through. She went in feet first, holding aloft the Mazda's plates. Her shoulders got stuck, but with a few wriggles she was inside. As she opened the door there was a whirr and the bright pop-pop of photographic flashes. Then the alarm went off. She ran across the line of the camera and then beyond it, blinking, struggling to see. The noise was deafening. She said a quick, heartfelt prayer, hoping the security system hadn't changed. She located it inside a cupboard in a corner of the room. Holding the plates under one arm, she tapped in the code, memorized from Andy's Filofax, straining to see the worn numbers printed on the illuminated plastic pad. Suddenly the noise and flashing camera were extinguished. The blackness and the silence were like a fog. Jaz's heart was beating hard and her stomach felt knotted and tight. 'Stay calm. Stay focused,' she whispered, 'stay cool.' Her ears were ringing, as if they'd been punched. You've done it, she thought, groping for a light switch. Jaz, you're a lucky bastard. You've done it and you're in.

In the storeroom Jaz paused at the small vinyl-topped counter, at the side of which was a computer. She remembered that during the day a thin, bored man with greasy hair usually stood here, resting on his elbows, chewing gum and reading the *Sun*. He wore a baggy grey overall coat which was never washed. When necessary he tapped listlessly on the keyboard and sold Mazda spares to the public. As well as this, unhelpful and slow, he secured necessary parts for both Fat Andy and the legitimate mechanics in the garage. He was called Mr Slipper. No one called him by his first name because no one liked him. Once Pete had said he had a personality disorder. She recalled complaining to Andy when, without speaking, he'd repeatedly rubbed his crotch against her body in the confined space between the racks. Andy must have had a word with him because he never did this again. However, he'd continued to be patronizing, as if she understood nothing about cars.

She noticed that the place had been tidied and the racks redesigned. In fact the place looked cleaner and more sterile than a dentist's surgery. Mr Slipper must have quit, she decided. Someone else was in charge, with a passion for order. There was nothing littering the floor. Two body shells in grey primer were hung from the ceiling like modern works of art.

On the computer, Jaz brought up the parts she wanted, one by one, noting down the reference numbers. It took a moment to locate the new ignition, immobilizer, door locks, keys and steering cowl within the new system. The whole place had been streamlined. Then, using the familiar numbers of the combination lock, she opened the old-fashioned safe under the counter. On the top shelf she found a box of unallocated registration documents for new cars. She took one which referred to a Mazda MX5. Underneath were sets of plates. She found the ones which matched the documentation and swapped them for the plates taken from the stolen car. She took a deep breath. She was a little calmer now. She decided, on impulse, to take two extra documents and sets of plates, for good measure. Both referred to the Mazda 626 which she knew was an upmarket saloon. They might come in useful, she reasoned. They would be missed, eventually, but with some luck no one would notice for a while.

Having obtained everything she needed, she wrapped it all in her jacket and dropped it outside in the lane, then went back and reset the alarm. It made a long low drone until she closed the lavatory door. Standing on the edge of the stinking bowl, she forced her shoulders through the window. As she climbed out, a needle of glass pierced her knee. She picked up her booty and got back into Fat Andy's car, then rested for a moment, breathing steadily, rubbing her face with her hands. She thought about fixing the damage to the stolen Mazda. She would do it in Lambeth tomorrow, in daylight. Then she would drive over to Peckham and collect another five hundred from Elvis. The car had only one hundred and seventy-five miles on the clock. It was worth over sixteen thousand pounds. He better be grateful, she thought. He owes me. I'll never need to have sex with him again after this. Thank God.

She wound up the windows of the Lotus Cortina. She was just about to drive off when she realized this was an opportunity missed. She remembered the three thugs in their designer suits, struggling from the Mazda MX5 earlier in the day. They'd killed Fat Andy. They'd slit his throat like a helpless animal. She pictured the brothers pinning him down while Vinny wielded the blade. They'd left him bleeding to death on his bed. On her bed. The bed she'd shared with him for six months.

His lifeless face came into her mind. His mouth had been open in surprise or because of a partially spoken protest. It was like the mouth of a dead fish, formless but rigid. Not me, he seemed to say. Not me. Not now. I'm not ready. Tears came to her eyes. He wasn't ready, she thought. He definitely wasn't ready. Not many people enjoyed life as much as Fat Andy.

And all for a computer disk, which they'd then failed to find. They'd taken his life for a few contacts, names of a bunch of dodgy characters over in Holland or Germany. For the lousy details of a string of hot vehicles.

Nicking cars is one thing, Jaz reasoned. But killing people is in a different league. It was not on. It was unacceptable. It demanded punishment. She crossed her hands on the steering wheel and leaned her head in her arms. This was very clear.

The pain in her chest was suddenly worse. It was like a knife. A hot, burning knife. 'Andy should be properly avenged,' she said aloud. 'I owe it to him.' She had never been so sure of something, so directed, so purposeful. It was almost enjoyable, this conviction, this belief.

Another thing was obvious. Stealing a car, even a neat sports car like the MX5, from a crooked motor dealer was hardly an adequate response. He'd been mildly inconvenienced, that was all. Everything she'd done to Vinny, so far, was pathetic. She had to do more. Andy would expect more. Anything else was weak and cowardly. She took a deep breath and, repeating the whole process, went back inside.

She turned on one light in the body shop but still managed to crunch her shin on an engine which had been removed from a front-ended saloon. She swore and glanced inside. Out of habit, she was looking for bloodstains on the upholstery.

At the far end of the building was the paint shop. She made her way there, having decided on a plan. She turned on the lights. There were no vehicles, just a wide open space with three pairs of ghostly overalls hanging on hooks along one wall. She went over to the oxyacetylene gear and, awkwardly at first, attempted to open the twin bottles. The valves were stiff and the key hurt her fingers. She licked her hand and rubbed it on her jeans. With a second attempt she was successful. She glanced around the room again and went over to the large drum of cellulose thinners in a corner. She began overturning it. It was one third full. As she lowered it onto its side, the contents slopped out, clear, like water. She felt the coldness of the liquid as it splashed her legs and a sting as it touched her cut knee. She dropped the drum and jumped back as it spread across the floor. The sharp, addictive smell was both choking and heavenly.

Quickly, she dragged the oxyacetylene bottles in their metal frame away from the spilt thinners, into the doorway. She turned the circular valves to open the gun and flicked the flint lighter. Adjusting the oxygen level, she made the flame small, blue and pointed. Holding the torch aloft, she felt a rush of adrenalin. Her jeans and boots were wet. One false move and she could burst into flames. She turned, looking behind her. She knew she had a straight run out, through the body shop to the lavatory window. She would have a minute, maybe two. Without pausing to consider, she tossed the torch, flinging it the entire length of its tubing onto the edge of the puddle. As she turned to run, there was a bright flash behind her and a roar.

In seconds, with the level of human energy which is only ever produced by fear, she was out of the window, into the Lotus Cortina and accelerating away. In her rearview mirror she could see a glow. As she raced down the deserted Manchester Road there was a huge bang. She smiled. The acetylene bottle had exploded. The fire must have really taken hold.

Jaz parked the car by the river at Blackwall. She felt elated. She grasped the steering wheel and laughed out loud. The smell of the thinners from her jeans and her feet was heady and overpowering. She wondered if it was making her high. She opened the driver's door to get some fresh air.

She was reminded of a night at home, on the farm in Teesside, a few weeks before she decided to leave. Her mother was shouting and she'd gone to listen outside her bedroom door. Lola was drunk and in bed. She was yelling at Blow. 'You're a lousy provider,' she'd accused him, 'a lousy, rotten provider.' She kept repeating the phrase, as if she was proud of it. 'That's the long and the short of it. A lousy, rotten provider.'

Blow murmured softly, trying to calm her down. It wasn't working.

'You should get rid of those cars. Never mind polishing the buggers, just sell them. Sell them and bring some money in. Why should I keep you? You lousy, rotten provider.'

Jasmine heard Blow continue to speak in a placatory way. He was trying to be patient. He pointed out that the farm was losing money. He said his car dealing was subsidizing the farm and they still needed hay. They needed chicken meal.

'Don't you blame me! Sell that Austin Healy!' Lola had screamed. 'Why d'you want it? Who d'you think you are? James bloody Bond?' She was far gone on cheap Chianti and couldn't listen to reason.

Later, Jasmine heard Blow calling her name. She was skinning and gutting a rabbit on the kitchen table. His head appeared around the door. 'Give me a hand out here,' he said, 'soon as you've got that critter on the stove.'

After a while, she lit the gas under the saucepan and went out to the porch. The dull light of the miserable

November afternoon was slowly fading. The sky was purple and grey. It was very cold. A few starving chickens huddled together out of the wind which blew mournfully across the fields. The farm looked sad and hopeless. Blow was dragging an old gate into the barn. Jasmine pulled on her wellingtons and a disintegrating fur jacket which had belonged to Lola. He pointed towards a disused pig sty. 'Bring the wood from that into the barn,' he called to her.

The two of them laboured together for an hour. They built a bonfire out of rotten buildings and gates, fence posts, a roll of old lino and an abandoned armchair. When it was twelve feet high, Blow told her to get a can of petrol.

'It won't work,' said Jasmine knowingly, 'if you use petrol. Insurance men aren't daft.'

Blow scratched his head and considered. 'OK. We'll do it the Boy Scout way, then. Get some dry leaves, some twigs, a box of matches.'

As the fire caught hold, the twins appeared from nowhere. They shoved chicken feathers in their hair and ran around whooping, pretending to be Red Indians. Blow pulled straw bales and disintegrating trestles from the sides of the building. 'Keep away!' he shouted at them desperately.

They went suddenly quiet and stood together, holding hands. 'What's he doing?' asked Peony.

'What's he doing?' repeated Mimosa.

The fire licked along planks and bales towards a wooden wall.

They were subdued. 'He's burning down the barn,' whispered Peony, in an awestruck voice. She looked worried.

'Does Mam know?' asked Mimosa. 'Does Mam know he's burning down her barn?'

Jasmine took them each by an arm and led them outside. The three of them stood silently on an incline above the structure and watched as it caught alight. After a while Blow appeared, his face blackened by smoke and sweat. Breathing heavily, he joined the girls who were huddled together in the cold wind. Then, as the flames flickered towards the roof and the first crossbeam fell inwards, the heat began to warm them and the twins' excitement returned. Clinging together they started jumping up and down. 'One man went to mow,' they sang, irrelevantly. 'Went to mow his meadow. One man and his dog, went to mow his meadow!'

The fire soared and roared, turning the dark sky orange. In the distance, the penned animals cried out in fear. The smoke billowed like fast time-lapse clouds and the twins' song became a rhythmic chant. 'One man went to MOW! One man went to MOW!'

Jasmine felt a lump in her throat. She was angry, tense but also pleased. The way the barn was collapsing into this inferno of her own making was both strangely beautiful and satisfying. Blow stood slightly apart, his hands in his pockets. 'That's one hell of a blaze, Jasmine,' he said.

As Jaz sat in the Lotus Cortina, gazing at the river and the lights and the dark brown of the London night, a bright shower like a giant red firework suddenly burst upwards then cascaded down on the limits of the roofline. After a few moments, flames reached up above the buildings and the stark outlines of the cranes, illuminating the sky. Sparks flew like fireflies. It took her a moment to realize that this was her own handiwork. Vinny's repair shop was burning.

She licked her lips but her mouth was very dry. Sirens announced a convoy of engines speeding towards the blaze. Soon, a helicopter swooped above her, then inwards, over the Island.

Jaz thought about the heat that had come from the burning barn, up on the farm on Teesside, eight years before. She stared at the distant glow, pretending that she could feel its warmth, smell its acrid smoke, see the roof beams and walls implode. Just then she thought she heard the twins' raised voices, united in song. They sang one brief verse. Then, 'That's one hell of a blaze, Jaz,' someone seemed to say, close to her ear. She was startled. The imaginary, approving voice was not that of Blow. It was Fat Andy. He was grateful.

Chapter Fourteen

At some point during the night Jaz fell asleep in the car. When she awoke the sky was a blend of grey and orange, but in the spot above Vinny's garage, a black smudge proved that her fire was still burning. She got out and stretched and realized that her cut knee was stiff and painful.

Jaz drove back to Lambeth. She was no longer elated, but she was satisfied. It was a Saturday and still early, so everywhere was quiet. She parked the Lotus Cortina in the lane behind Mrs McDonald's yard. As she got out of the car, she knew something was wrong. The gates were open. When she looked inside, the Mazda MX5 was gone. Her heart jolted. She glanced around and cursed. She hadn't disabled it in the way she would have done her own car. In fact, she hadn't taken any precautions at all. She herself had dismembered the manufacturer's anti-theft devices. She'd left it completely vulnerable. Any halfwit with a screwdriver could have driven it away. One of the local lads had stolen it, she decided. You stupid cow, she said to herself. You cretin. You look after the Cortina like a precious baby but then go and neglect a real flash and dazzle car that would tempt any teenage joyrider.

She walked through the yard to the back door. She

could see her landlady through the kitchen window. She was holding a scrubbing brush and standing on a wet floor. She'd paused in her labours to speak to someone on the phone. Jaz went in.

'Here she is now,' said Mrs McDonald. 'I call you all back.'

Jaz shrugged and composed her features into a resigned expression. She didn't want to upset Mrs McDonald. 'It's my own fault,' she muttered.

The large woman carefully replaced the receiver. Her lips were puckered into a dismayed 'O'. She gestured for Jaz to sit down and she lowered herself onto a seat, dropping her brush. 'Very bad things with men happen here,' she said. 'Car thiefs come last night. But honey, I manages to get my three sons. That's them, in Birmingham. They says sit tight and they come down. Just as soon as their market finish. They packs up their stall, comes down, sorts it all out for you. No one bothers my guests. Not here. In my own house . . .'

'Who was here?' Jaz interrupted.

'Bad men. They steals your darling little car.'

'What did they look like?'

She thought for a minute, her face impassive. 'They're white boys. Brothers, I says.'

'Big? Bald? Fancy suits?'

'They dress like . . .' She pulled at the air with her hand as if trying to find words in it.

'Footballers?'

She frowned.

'Matching tracksuits?'

She shook her head.

'Fancy pale-coloured suits?'

'That's right.'

'Thirty-five? Look like bodyguards?'

Mrs McDonald nodded.

'Shit, shit, shit!'

'They says they look for you. I'm not worried at first except it's late. Come back tomorrow I says. She isn't here.'

Jaz stood up and started pacing back and forth. Her mind was racing. 'How did they know I was here?'

Mrs McDonald pointed at the kettle. 'Cup of tea, honey?'

'What did they say exactly? Can you remember exactly what happened? What time?'

Mrs McDonald filled the kettle, plugged it in and sat down again. Her gestures were apologetic. 'Just after you leave. Minutes after. They comes to the front door. They says they's looking for you and waiting. They goes round the back and comes in. You forget to bolt the gates. They sits outside bold as two canaries on the bonnet of your car. I don't know – I thought they just wait. I go out there and they says not to worry, us just waiting. I watch telly. Drink my cocoa. Then! What happen? They drives off! Thieve your car! Very fast. As if it emergency . . .'

'They probably had a phone call about the fire . . .'

'What fire?'

Jaz's pulse was beating like a drum. She suddenly realized she had to leave as soon as possible. Ronnie and Reggie might be back. She felt guilty about exposing her kind landlady to this intrusion. 'Did they threaten you? Scare you?'

She shrugged, palms upwards. 'No. Not at all. They is extra polite. Like proper gentlemen.'

'Mrs McDonald. I'm sorry you've had this trouble. Please don't worry. You don't know anything so they can't hurt you. It'll be all right. I'm going now.' Jaz pulled out Elvis's money and peeled off some notes. She put them on the kitchen table. 'Forget you've seen me.'

'But my boys come. They says they get the car back, if it anyone around here. They grows up here. They knows everyone. I tell them you just a young, defenceless child, in my home, with no one to look after you . . . No mum, no dad . . .'

Jaz backed towards the hall and ran upstairs to collect her things.

'Hey now, don't you want your cup of tea?'

Later, parked again in Lincoln's Inn Fields, Jaz tried to collect her thoughts. She couldn't imagine how Ronnie and Reggie had found her this time, but she'd under-estimated them. She thought that having ditched Pete, she'd be able to punish Vinny from a position of safety, but his boys were cleverer than she'd expected.

She mused for a moment. Perhaps the Mazda had been electronically tagged. Fat Andy had told her about this worrying trend and how his thieves on the street overcame it. It hadn't occurred to her to check. In truth, she didn't know what such a device looked like. Her skills were dated. She sighed. Whatever had gone wrong, she needed to be more careful from now on. She took the mobile out of her pocket and fingered it.

Yes, she thought, vigilance was important. She almost put the phone away but instead dialled the gym on the Mile End Road. It was too early for it to be open and she heard the answerphone pick up. 'It's Jaz,' she said, 'with a message for Piggy and Porky. You've got your car back, you fat wankers, but don't think you've won this round, because I haven't finished.'

Later, she went to Boots, bought a packet of sandwiches and a bottle of Evian, some antiseptic and a bandage. Back in the car, she ate one sandwich then tried to dress her knee. The results were less than satisfactory. She took the photo of Peony and Mimosa out of her jeans pocket and examined it. It was becoming rather creased and worn, but the twins still stared out at her, truculent and beautiful, their cardboard haloes out of place, their faces unusually clean.

She tried to imagine Fat Andy as a small boy with a twin brother, but this was impossible. Fat Andy was the kind of person who'd never had a childhood. He never once mentioned his early life. She thought about their times in bed and how he liked to pretend she was a young girl. Sometimes he'd talked in a baby voice and played childish games. Unlike her sisters, he'd been cruelly separated from his natural playmate. Perhaps that was it, she thought to herself, perhaps with her, he'd been trying to create something he'd always missed.

She started the car and drove west to Shepherd's Bush, listening to the news on the local radio. She was disappointed when there was no mention of the fire.

At Wesley's flat, the homeless man was still crouched in the doorway of the pork butcher, wrapped in a travel rug. He was young and reasonably healthy looking, but his face was pale, mournful and detached. When Jaz stopped to ring the bell he took out a penny whistle and began to play. She gave him her spare sandwich, waited for a while, then rang the bell for a second time. Eventually the door opened a crack. It was Harm.

'I'm sorry,' said Jaz. 'Where's Wesley? Did I get you out of bed?'

'Come in, Jaz,' said Harm. 'Quickly. I'm a lot better. I don't want people to see me like this.'

Jaz studied her face. The bruises on her sallow skin had turned purple and yellow in a spectacular way, but the swelling and the cuts seemed much improved. 'You look both better and worse.'

'I look like hell. Hell on earth. That's the truth.'

They went upstairs. Harm was wearing a baggy T-shirt and fluffy slippers. The living room was untidy. She was still sleeping on the sofa and the covers were strewn around. The floor was littered with cups, magazines and ashtrays and the TV was on high volume, showing a morning chat show. Jaz remembered that Wesley's flat was normally spotless.

'Where's Wesley?'

'Oh, he's out somewhere. Gone to see his therapist or something.' She lit a cigarette.

'You going to stay here?' Like Jaz and Trace, Harm had no permanent address.

Her answer was a listless shrug. She seemed depressed.

Jaz sat on the arm of a chair. Harm lowered the sound of the television and flopped down on the sofa.

'I'm sorry about what happened, Harm. It was my fault. I shouldn't have asked you to do it. It was a bad mistake.'

Harm avoided her eye. She stared at the TV.

'Hey, we are still friends, aren't we?' Jaz bit her lip.

There was a strange, unrelaxed atmosphere in the room, which was unusual. Harm was normally so full of fun.

Harm turned and stared at Jaz. 'You staying away from those two heavies?'

Jaz paused. 'Yes,' she lied.

'You better be. Don't forget that time Trace and I had to rescue you from that psychopath in the East End. What was his name again?'

'Keith.'

Harm lit a cigarette and kneaded the flesh of one of her thighs. 'I'm getting fat, lying around here all day.' She met Jaz's eyes. 'You stay away from those guys. Right?'

'Right.' Jaz thought how ordinary Harm looked without make-up and without her glamorous clothes.

'Whatever they did to your bloke, it's not worth getting involved. You know that?'

Jaz tried to smile.

'It's not worth it.'

Jaz pointed to Wesley's desk. 'Can I use the computer for a minute? It's a car thing.'

Harm nodded. She changed channels irritably.

Jaz switched on the machine and slid in the disk provided by Elvis. She felt a flutter of excitement. As she scrolled down the screen she realized it was what Andy had talked about – it was a record of Vinny's illegal trans-actions and his shady European contacts. She licked her lips. Bloody great, she thought. She extracted the disk and pocketed it, then switched off the machine.

Harm was still watching TV.

Jaz crossed the room and picked up a book from the seat of the chair, turning it over absently. It was a paper-back entitled *Psychosynthesis – Counselling in Action*. 'This Wesley's?'

Harm snorted. 'Well, it's hardly likely to be mine, is it?' She paused. 'You listening to me, Jaz? About those men?'

'Yeah, yeah, I've got the message.' Jaz dropped the book and stood up. 'Coffee?' She went into the kitchen and reappeared with two steaming mugs. 'I'm concentrating on finding his brother. Fat Andy had a twin brother.' She handed a mug to her friend. She had decided not to tell Harm about Vinny and her revenge tactics, but explained her need to find a mourner for Fat Andy.

Harm nodded. 'Trace has told me some of this,' she said.

Jaz described the man on television, behind the Home Secretary. 'It's important,' she insisted. 'It's hard to explain, but this is something I really have to do.'

Harm frowned. 'I don't know, kid. I wish you'd drop it, I really do. Wesley would say you're trying to meet your own subconscious needs. Whatever's driving you.'

'Well, maybe I am. It's to do with twins and family and trying to do something right for a change. I can see that.' She hesitated. 'It's about having some kind of a purpose. You know Trace is helping me. She's going to get a new job and help me to track down the twin brother.'

'She told me. She'll do it too. Trace will do anything for you. You know that.'

Jaz had a sudden brainwave. 'Harm, you ever worked in the House of Commons?'

Harm sipped her drink. She giggled.

Jaz was relieved by the return of her good humour.

Harm inhaled deeply. 'You mean have I done the business with MPs and suchlike?'

'That's exactly what I mean.'

Harm grinned. She lay back cradling her mug and looked at the ceiling.

'Really, this is important. Have you?'

'Of course I have. It's a goldmine. They're away from home, they work late nights, they're terrified of getting into anything semi-legit with a secretary or someone, in case the papers pick up on it. I'm in and out of there all the time.'

'What? The actual building?'

'Sure.'

'Harm, I don't believe you!'

'It's true! Don't ask who, though. Wesley will go off it if I talk. He's already pretty worried as it is. He keeps getting his calculator out and working out how much money we're losing, per day, per hour, per bloody minute.'

Jaz explained how this connection might be useful. 'Harm, I know I messed up last time, but if you can help me get to this twin brother character . . . will you?'

Harm was suddenly serious. 'As long as you stay away from those guys in the East End.'

'OK.'

'Anything else I can do that doesn't interfere with my own interests, I'll do. Within reason.' She sighed. 'But I wish you'd drop it. The fat guy's dead.' She sniffed. 'Get a life.' She picked up the TV remote and flicked channels. 'What happened to the pretty ginger boy? The one I used to know at the garage? Trace said you'd pulled him.'

'I sort of went off him.'

'OK. So what happened about your idea of going up north, for a visit?'

Jaz shrugged. 'I'm thinking of taking a holiday, when all of this is over.'

'Do something. Get your mind off this heavy stuff. It doesn't suit you.'

Later, towards evening, Jaz left the car in the safe space, put on her headphones and sunglasses and jogged at a medium pace to Mile End Road. Her knee was hurting but after the first mile it went numb. She checked around the back of Ronnie and Reggie's gym. As she'd expected, there was a brand new Mazda 626 in the staff car park. It was dark blue and elegant. Jaz suddenly remembered the specifications given by Elvis. He wanted something large enough for himself, Big Boy and Peppy. It had to be flash, and he didn't want white. The sports car she'd stolen last time around wouldn't have been suitable anyway. It had been too small. Jaz walked around the Mazda. It wasn't what Elvis had in mind, but it would do. It was a four-door saloon, with long, low contours. Classic lines, Jaz thought. They're back in fashion. It was a top of the range model with a rear spoiler, body-coloured bumpers and tinted glass. Jaz glanced around. Painted on the wall in front of it were the words 'Managers – Resurved'. Above, the door at the top of the fire escape was wedged open with a chair, as it had been before. She took out the mobile and pressed the numbers to connect her with reception inside. She knew that Kormal would have gone home hours before. A man answered.

'Are the bosses there?' she asked huskily, trying to disguise her voice.

'They're busy. Urgent, is it?'

'It can wait. What they doing?'

'Working out. Weight training.'

'Best not to disturb them?'

'That's right. Who is this anyway?'

'Courtesy call.' Jaz hung up. She ran up the fire escape and entered the back of the gym. Taking off her sunglasses, she stopped for a moment to get her bearings then entered a storeroom. Here there were bales of toilet rolls wrapped in polythene, mounds of freshly laundered towels, a Hoover and other cleaning equipment – and what she was looking for: a pile of maroon sweatshirts each in a plastic bag, with the name of the gym printed on the front. She opened one which said 'small' and put it on. She filled a bucket with hot water from a sink and taking this and two J-cloths, she went to reception. She was very nervous. She took a deep breath. A man was lounging in the swivel chair behind the desk, reading the *Evening Standard*. He was young, stocky and tattooed and wore a cutaway vest and shiny red shorts. His hair was shaved into bristles. He looked bored.

'Hello,' Jaz said innocently. 'I've been told to valet the Mazda.'

The young man sat up and tossed his paper down onto the desk. He looked her up and down and appeared unimpressed.

'I'm new,' she continued. 'There's not much doing. No ladies here. The bosses said to valet the Mazda.'

He looked at her steadily.

She forced a smile. 'Afterwards I've got to clean the showers.'

He grinned. 'Great, isn't it? You get a job as a fitness instructor and end up answering the phone . . .'

Jaz picked up the cue. 'Or swilling out the bogs, or washing towels . . .'

'Or going to the deli for pastrami on rye . . .'

She gave him what she thought was her most

appealing little-girl smile. She dropped the cloths in the bucket, fished around for them and squeezed them out. 'I'm Jaz, by the way.'

He turned towards her on the swivel chair and did something to his arms which made his muscles more erect and defined. 'I'm Baz. Hey, that's good! Baz and Jaz!'

She pursed her lips, lowered her chin and opened her eyes very wide. 'Where are the keys?'

He smiled. He had an even, dark tan and no body hair. 'What?'

'The spare keys to the Mazda, silly. I've got to do the inside and be careful of the leather trim. I've got to valet the boot.'

He opened a drawer and tossed her the labelled chrome ring holding a key and a remote.

As he did so, she dropped the cloths back in the bucket. She caught the ring and held it aloft. 'Thanks, mate.'

'Do mine afterwards if you like. Mine's the Honda Civic.'

'Piss off!' She turned to go down the stairs.

'See you later, Jaz. Mind you give it a good polish.'

'Make sure you fill up the drinks machine.'

She could hear him chuckling as she left the building.

Jaz took the Mazda 626 to Lincoln's Inn Fields. She parked it next to the Lotus Cortina and changed its plates for a pair she'd taken from Vinny's garage. She examined it thoroughly, but couldn't see anything which resembled a tracking device. Stay calm, she repeated to herself, like a mantra. Stay focused. Stay cool. She rubbed the bodywork lightly with a cloth, then drove it over to Peckham. She left it in the underground car park beneath the flats. A group of teenagers watched her. They were leaning on a barrier, gossiping and yawning. She went over to them. 'See that blue car?' she said. 'That's Elvis's new motor. You know what I think? I think you should keep an eye on it for him. Make sure it comes to no harm.'

Upstairs she banged and kicked on the armoured door of the flat. Eventually, she was invited to speak into the entryphone. 'Open up, for Christ sakes. It's Jaz. I've been out here for ten bloody minutes.'

Peppy opened the door. He looked better than he had in recent days. He smiled. 'It's little Jaz!' he exclaimed, pleased. He coughed. 'Er . . . we're busy in here. Business meeting. Can't ask you in.'

'Tell the man I've got the wheels.'

After a couple of minutes, Elvis appeared.

'You coming down to see it?'

'Nah, not now. *Stars in Their Eyes*? On the telly?' He pointed in the direction of the living room. Jaz could hear someone singing Madonna's 'Material Girl'. Elvis glanced backwards into the flat, then turned to her and handed over a wad of notes. 'Five hundred.' He blew her a kiss. 'You's the best, doll. Number one.'

'It's a Mazda six-two-six. Top of the range. Loads of Jap gadgets. A lighty-up ashtray and mirror, air conditioning, tilting seat, telescopic steering column . . .'

'Yeah, yeah.' Elvis looked over his shoulder again. He was worried about missing his favourite programme.

Jaz handed him the keys and the registration document which matched the plates. 'Send this paper to Swansea. You'll have to get new glass because the windows are etched . . .'

'Yeah, yeah.'

'Elvis, listen. I mean it. Get new glass off that dodgy guy in East Lane. He'll rip you off but if you don't the car is traceable . . .'

'Yeah, yeah.' She was sure he wasn't paying attention. He was straining to hear the TV.

'Get – new – glass!' Jaz started to walk away, pocketing the money. 'If you don't you'll get even more police harassment.'

Elvis stepped out onto the balcony and gave her the thumbs-up. He smiled widely, showing his rotten teeth. He'd been listening to her after all. 'Star quality, doll,' he called out. 'You? What you got, doll? Friggin' star quality.'

Chapter Fifteen

Jaz decided, after all the excitement of the last two days, to lie low for a brief spell. She checked into a big, modern hotel near Charing Cross and hung the 'Do Not Disturb' sign on her door. After a good night's sleep, she gathered up a pile of magazines removed from the foyer, a copy of *Radio Times* to check the TV scheduling and the room service menu, and spent the next day reading about celebrities, health and beauty tips, and home renovation on a budget. She familiarized herself with the Paris styles for autumn and the most fashionable new eye shadow colours. In between, she watched five soaps, three game shows and several live discussions where audience members interacted with a panel and argued about released paedophiles, Viagra, the future of Tellytubbies, and the problem of chewing gum stuck to city pavements. At regular intervals she ordered small but appetizing meals from room service. They were grilled and decorated with things like radish spirals, rocket, mango wedges and something called coulis. In the bathroom she showered and experimented with the free, fruit-scented detergents. She washed her knee and changed the bandage. She used all the towels. For a few hours she forgot her responsibilities.

She remembered that Fat Andy had introduced her

to the joys of spending money on hotel rooms. He stayed in hotels when he was away on business and he enjoyed emptying the minibar, making long distance phone calls, having his clothes laundered or dry cleaned, then charging the inflated bill to Vinny at the garage.

Andy, she thought. Oh, Andy. She pressed her chest. The pain was there, less obvious than the throbbing in her knee, but still bothersome. Neither places are healing, she decided. Not my knee, nor my heart. She blinked. In an instant she was back in the bedroom with Andy's corpse. There had been blood on the wall, she remembered. It must have sprayed upwards from his neck in an arc, like water spurting from a hose, and splattered the wall in a wide, dark curve. She closed her eyes and took some even breaths. Yes, Fat Andy had loved hotels, she told herself again, and the blood disappeared, replaced by a vision of him basking in the deep suds of a hotel tub, singing and splashing and soaping his armpits.

She smiled. Unlike herself, Fat Andy had indulged his voluptuous nature all the time. To her amazement, when she moved in, she discovered he ate takeaway or restaurant meals every day. 'But you've got a flat,' she'd exclaimed, 'you've got a cooker!' He also drank bottles of whisky without suffering any ill effects and spent money wildly whenever he got the chance. In the short time they were together, he'd bought a saxophone, a camcorder, a 1100cc Yamaha and a part share in a racehorse. All of these he'd given away. She knew he'd once spent hundreds on flying lessons and he'd had a top of the range whirlpool spa fitted in the dim and tiny bathroom. He wasn't a materialist, he didn't value possessions, but he was hedonistic. He believed in self-indulgence and having fun. Jaz knew she was the opposite. Apart from her occasional binges, her nature was essentially frugal.

I have my moments, she thought. She picked up the phone and ordered a glass of alcohol-free wine and honey-glazed kumquats in a brandysnap basket with chantilly cream. Her thoughts strayed to the pleasures of her night with Pete, but like the memory of Andy's body, she put these away. Pete's a bastard, she told herself. She took a deep breath. He's a bastard like Vinny. She picked up the hotel phone. She felt a sudden need to let Vinny know she was responsible for his troubles. It was a kind of vanity. Anonymous revenge wasn't good enough. She wanted a bit of limelight. Just like in the old days when she worked hard to prove to Vinny that she was the best of Andy's car thieves, now she wanted him to understand that he was up against her own brand of urban terrorism, and she was dangerous. She imagined him standing amidst the smouldering rubble of his repair shop shaking his head, overwhelmed by the force pitched against him.

She dialled Pete's number at the flat. 'Hi, it's Jaz.'

'Jaz! Where've you been? I've been trying . . .'

'Listen, you tosser. You probably haven't even got a job any more . . .'

'Too right I haven't, the whole place has been . . .'

'Burned down.'

'Right.' There was a pause. He sounded excited. 'Have you seen it on the telly? I went down there today and I couldn't believe . . .'

Jaz raised her voice. 'I didn't need to see it on the telly. I saw it myself when it happened.' She paused. She sounded both menacing and triumphant. 'I bloody started it!' There was a silence and then some electronic interference on the line. 'Did you hear me?'

'Hell, Jaz, what're you playing at? Whatever made you . . ?

'I'm not playing, right? This isn't a game. This isn't TV. This is revenge. You tell my companero, that greasy little bastard, your boss, that I haven't finished. I'm just getting started. You tell those joke cockney gangsters to lay off me and my friends. Or I'll burn more than a fucking outbuilding.' She hung up. Her heart was beating hard. She decided that leaving messages for Vinny was the best part of the whole exercise. She only wished she could be there to see his face.

Later, whilst watching *Going Places*, Jaz promised herself again that when the fallout from Fat Andy's death had finally settled, she would take the Lotus Cortina and go with Harm and Trace on holiday. She watched a report on English seaside resorts. Torquay, she thought, why not? Or Bridlington, or maybe Margate. They could eat candyfloss, walk on the prom, play pinball and sit in deck chairs listening to a brass band. In her mind's eye, the three of them were wearing big plastic sunglasses and unlikely sixties-style dresses with handbags and baby stilettoes, like Jacqueline Kennedy. Do wah diddy diddy, she hummed to herself. Dum diddy do.

She remembered spending a day in Redcar with her family, a few months before she'd run away to London. It was a hot, fine morning and Blow announced a picnic on the beach. Jasmine made the sandwiches, Blow tinkered with his car, the twins, incoherent with excitement, searched the outbuildings for an old bucket and spade while Lola complained about the heat.

They travelled to the coast in a Jaguar Mark II 3.8 which Blow had fixed and resprayed. Peony had a pet duck in a cardboard box which she refused to leave behind. Her mother was grey-faced but insisted the sea air would do her good. However, immediately after they parked, as close as possible to the sands, she disappeared into the nearest pub. Peony and Mimosa introduced the duck to the sea and it bobbed around happily, eyeing some distant seagulls with mistrust. Jasmine spread out a blanket and the twins ate their sandwiches and crisps and fought over a bottle of lemonade. After a while they decided to go shoplifting in the town. 'Look after Deirdre duck,' they called in unison as they climbed up the break-water, heading for Woolworths and WH Smith.

Blow retrieved a tennis racquet from the car and he and Jasmine played French cricket. The wide, golden beach, despite the sunshine, was almost deserted. The sky was cloudless apart from the vapour from two tiny aeroplanes. Jasmine could feel the heat pricking her bare shoulders and arms. After a while Blow bought them each a raspberry-topped ice cream and he laughed as it melted and ran down his wrist. He sat on the blanket and read his newspaper. Jasmine took the twins' bucket and spade and built a sandcastle on the shoreline. It had turrets and a moat and each time a big wave broke it was surrounded by water. She sat next to it for a while, hypnotized by the steady, soft rhythm of the sea. The twins came back with throat sweets, pencil sharpeners, mascara and a pair of bathroom scales. They removed their clothes and joined Deirdre, splashing in the shallows. Eventually, as the sun sank in the sky, Blow went to find Lola and told the three of them to pack away. Mimosa carried the duck in her box back to the car. Peony dragged the blanket. Jasmine lingered on her own, on the beach, tidying the carrier bags and hunting for her sisters' shoes. She was tired and her skin was burnt but she knew it was the happiest day of her life.

In the evening, Jaz asked room service to provide her with a laptop computer. She typed a letter on Ronnie and Reggie's headed notepaper, addressed to their members, informing them that the gym was closing immediately for essential repairs and renovation. She said this was a result of fire regulations and the Health and Safety At Work Act. She apologized and recommended that all members attend another gym where good service would be provided. She then checked in Yellow Pages and named a rival establishment, not far away, on Commercial Road. When she'd finished, she phoned the hotel desk again and requested that they make seven hundred and fifty photocopies and provide envelopes. She then began the long and laborious task of addressing the letters to Ronnie and Reggie's customers.

She lay on the bed, intending to watch *Wild at Heart* on Channel Four. She heard a strange noise which she first thought was an alarm, until she realized her mobile phone was ringing.

It was Trace. 'Jaz, I got this number off Harm. Where you at?'

Jaz explained where she was staying and outlined how she'd spent her day. 'Tell Harm,' she said again. 'You know how she worries.'

'Sold a car or something?'

'Yep.'

'That's good news, Jaz.'

'Yep.'

Trace was speaking from a phone box, Jaz could tell from the special tone in the background. 'Listen, I think I've got it all sorted at the Home Office.'

Jaz sat up sharply, scattering letters. 'Bloody great.' She glanced at the TV on the wall. Someone was being brutally murdered. 'What exactly are you doing there?'

'I'm night relief tea lady.'

Jaz laughed. 'Straight up? What's night relief?'

'No, Jaz, it's not night relief. It's night – dot – relief. Some people work late here. That means I'm night shift, four to twelve, and I'm relief, which means I help out. Depending how busy it is. If it's not busy I'm supposed to be in a canteen somewhere, collecting and washing crockery. I haven't done that yet.'

'Bloody great, Trace,' Jaz repeated.

'The money's awful and the work's out to contract. That means everyone in an overall is probably an illegal immigrant. In the Home Office. Funny, right? It's a horrible building. I've got to use a payphone and there's no facilities. It's not the Grand Banana.' She sounded a little low.

'Where you staying?'

'That's the other thing, Jaz. It's a problem. What can I do? I'm back at the hostel, but only because they know me. You know it's supposed to be for under eighteens.'

'You showed anyone that photo yet?'

'Give me a chance. I've only just got my overall.'

'Keep in touch.'

'Will do.'

Jaz remembered Elvis and his TV programme. 'You've got star quality, Trace. You know that? Star quality.'

'I've got a trolley and an urn.'

Jaz had difficulty relaxing after Trace's call. It had returned her to the world and as far as Fat Andy's brother was concerned, she didn't have a clear plan. She thought about ringing him up at work, and telling him about the murder, but this seemed too brutal. She would have to arrange a meeting, as she'd done with Princess and Andy's mother. Trace would be the link.

She turned off the television and made herself a cup of instant coffee. Then she paced about the room and considered checking out, but the alternative was aimless driving, so she decided to stay put. She spent hours addressing the envelopes and rang down for someone to collect and mail them. She returned the laptop and managed to get a couple of hours' sleep.

At six forty-five the mobile rang again. 'Hi, Jaz. It's Trace. You asleep?'

'Yes.'

'Sorry. I'm ringing from the hostel. There's been a big fight here. Everyone's awake. The good news is I may have something. I asked around at the Home Office last night, showed the photo. Most people just laughed. I think it's because he needs a shave in the photo and his hair's a bit, well . . .'

'Messy?'

'Yeah. Well anyway. I explained I wasn't looking for him, I was after his brother. This made a difference. Apparently he's the spitting image of someone called Charles Merchant. He's like a main man there. Important. You know, fitted carpet, real coffee. He's a political adviser or something. Works with the Home Secretary.'

Jaz was excited. 'That's right. That's him, Trace.'

There was a pause. Trace put another coin in the hostel payphone. There was the sound of shouting, a door being slammed and a girl crying. 'Well?'

'Well what?'

'What d'you want me to do now?'

Jaz hesitated. 'Are you going to meet him?'

Trace laughed. 'I don't know. There's millions of us catering staff here, right? And it's like mega-big, this place. Chances of me bumping into him must be like winning the lottery. I'll try and get on his coffee rota. But what if I do? What'll I say?'

Jaz thought for a moment. 'I tell you what. Ask around. Get the gossip. Find out what he does. Maybe where he lives. You know, snoop about. I need to think about this.'

'OK, Jaz.'

'Thanks, Trace.'

After a full English breakfast, Jaz went outside. Beyond the air conditioning of the hotel lobby, London was hot, airless and cloudy. She jogged to Oxford Street to see Davey, the ex-student *Big Issue* vendor. Her knee was worse, but she tried to ignore it. She was aware that she was running with a limp.

Davey was in his usual place although looking less sad and dishevelled – he was wearing a bright red cotton shirt and he'd had a wash and a haircut. Even his dog appeared more cheerful and stood up and wagged his tail when Jaz stroked his head.

'Hi, Davey. How's it going?'

He smiled, showing his toothless gums. 'Can't complain.' He handed a magazine to a passer-by and pocketed the pound. 'Thanks, mate.'

Jaz stood for a moment, watching the swelling tide of Oxford Street. A familiar feeling overtook her. The compelling business of the real world, the routine and bustle, the morning repopulation of shops and offices, the whole complicated mechanism of capitalism – it had nothing to do with her. She lived on a different planet. She was a perennial outsider. She took a deep breath. 'What happened when you spread the word amongst the gang?'

'About Fat Andy?'

'Who else?'

He was suddenly sad. 'Shock and dismay, little Jaz. Shock and dismay. He was well liked. Always did right by us, did Andy. He cared about us. Not like that bastard, Vinny.' Davey turned his head to one side and spat on the pavement, reinforcing his point.

'You told them Vinny was responsible?'

'Sure.'

'What happened?'

Davey drew himself up to his full height. 'I called a meeting. They all remember me, of course, and they all came. They wouldn't have it at first. Argued. Didn't believe it. Said they'd seen Fat Andy and Vinny laughing and joking together only days before. Said business was good. They'd had an order for five Citroën Xsaras and eight Renault Lagunas from Holland. And the luxury class of car is still in demand – pulling high prices too, seeing as how they've made them so bloody difficult to steal. Vinny was on a roll . . .'

'Well? What happened? Did you tell them what I said?'

Davey turned and looked her in the eye, missing a potential magazine sale. 'Of course I did.'

'They remember me?'

'Remember? You kidding? You were one of the best.'

Jaz didn't smile. 'I was the best.'

'OK. You were the best. I told them you saw it happen. Told them little Jaz saw Vinny do it.'

'And?'

'He's finished – on the illegal side, that is. Hasn't got a gang any more. They just melted away. Gone. Disgusted. That's the only way to describe it. Disgusted.'

'So what's happening?'

Davey shrugged. 'Nothing's happening. What's he going to do? Fat Andy took care of the streets, recruited the boys. Vinny doesn't know how to put a gang together. Not a class act like Andy's. He hasn't got the contacts. He hasn't got the interpersonal skills.'

Jaz let out a relieved sigh. 'That's great, Davey. Thanks.'

'That squint-eyed little sod had it coming.' Davey grinned. 'Without Andy there was only trouble, apparently. No bonuses, no incentives, no job security. No one liked working for Vinny.'

'I'll bet.'

'How you feeling now, Jaz? All shook up?'

'Angry,' Jaz confided. 'I want to drive Vinny off the Island. I want to finish him.'

'That's a tall order.'

'I'm going to do it. I'm paying him back for Andy's murder. It's compulsive.'

Dave regarded her seriously. He thought for a moment. 'Let's make us medicine of our great revenge,' he quoted, 'to cure this deadly grief.'

Jaz set off back to the hotel, choosing back streets to avoid the growing crowds. A group of dishevelled teenagers blocked her way, waiting behind a big restaurant.

They were hot and quarrelsome. Jaz knew what they were doing. She'd been there herself a few years ago. Very soon, the refuse would appear from the night before. The manager was sympathetic. The edible food would be bagged or wrapped in foil, and they would scuffle amongst themselves and grab it and run off with it, like hungry dogs.

Jaz thought she might stay at the hotel for another couple of days, waiting to see if Trace contacted Fat Andy's twin. She was just about to push the heavy revolving door, when she saw two men sitting in the reception lounge. She stepped to the side, allowing the uniformed doorman to assist an old lady with her luggage. She peeped in again. There was no mistake – Ronnie and Reggie were waiting for her.

They hadn't seen her. She ran around to the back of the hotel, checked the underground car park to make sure the Lotus Cortina was still there, then jogged towards the service entrance. She was tired. She wished she'd not run all the way from Oxford Circus. Her limbs were heavy and protesting, like they'd been during the aerobics class at the gym, and her knee was agony. She ran up the back stairs to reception. She had to cross a corner of this wide lobby to get to the main flight up to her room. She put on her sunglasses and waited until her pursuers were facing each other, exchanging words, then she flashed through. Within four minutes she'd accessed her room, picked up her few belongings and was back down. As she entered reception again one of Vinny's men looked up. Her eyes met his. He jumped to his feet. She swerved across the marble floor, making for the service stairs. A guest, standing at the desk, let out a small scream.

Jaz felt panic. She practically fell down the concrete

steps. She crashed through the swing doors and bounded the seventy yards to her car. She fiddled in her pocket for the keys, found them and with shaking hands inserted one in the driver's door. Stay calm, she thought. She wasn't calm. It wouldn't turn. It was sticking, reluctant, in the way it had done several times before.

Jaz paused, took a deep breath, wiped the sweat off her hands and tried again. 'Come on, baby,' she whispered desperately. 'Please. Come on.' She wiggled the key gently. Forcing it would only bend it.

There was a slap-slap from the doors and a shout. She looked over. Ronnie and Reggie were pointing at her. 'Hold it!' one of them shouted. 'We just want to talk to you!'

Jaz rubbed her forehead with her sleeve. She fumbled again in her jacket pocket and found the small silver tube given to her by the beauty therapist at the Grand Bahama. Stay focused. Her hands were shaking but she managed to smear a line of lipstick on the edge of the key. She dropped the tube and willing her hands to a degree of steadiness tried for a third time to open the door. Come on, she thought. Don't let me down. She felt the lock release. You angel. Oh, thank you. Thank you. She opened the car and slid in. Dumping her bag in the back, she slammed the driver's door, turned on the ignition and threw the car into reverse. The engine roared and the Lotus Cortina jumped backwards. She dragged the wheel hard through both hands and swerved. She was suddenly facing Vinny's men who were almost upon her. Stay cool.

They stopped, their expressions contorted and surprised, and held up their arms in front of their chests, their palms towards her. 'No,' she saw them mouth. 'No, no.'

She changed gear and stepped on the accelerator, pushing it to the floor. With a furious snarl the car leaped forwards, heading directly for them. Jaz didn't flinch or alter the steering. She drove straight at them. Her breath was coming in painful short bursts. Fear and anger had sent her heart and brain into overdrive. I'll kill you bastards, she thought. Just let me run you down.

They each dived sideways, almost comically, like rugby players. Jaz's tyres squealed in protest as she spun the car towards the exit. In seconds she was out and away. She glanced behind several times but she wasn't being followed. In minutes, taking back alley short cuts, she disappeared into the hubbub of central London.

Chapter Sixteen

Jaz drove fast, then was forced to slow in dense traffic. When she found herself on a four-lane highway, she speeded up again. She had no particular destination in mind. She concentrated on her driving, her eyes flicking between road and mirrors, the interaction of hand and eye, her face set and her body recovering from both fright and exertion. Her knee was throbbing rhythmically. It was hot and the air smelled of exhaust and tarmac. The sun bounced off the hard surfaces of road and bonnet with a glare that her sunglasses couldn't ease. Her sweaty skin stuck to the seat and her mouth still tasted of fear but she felt freedom in this unnatural motion. She enjoyed the car. She felt in control. The Lotus Cortina drove like a dream, its engine purring and growling like a haughty pedigree cat. She felt connected to it. After a while, as well as sensing the disturbances in her own body, she became aware that the left front suspension was wallowing slightly on sharper bends. She remembered Fat Andy mentioning that it leaked fluid. When all of this is over, she decided, I must give the Lotus Cortina a proper going over. The works.

Fifty minutes passed and she was somewhere in north London. She turned down a leafy residential street. The moment she turned off the engine, the memory of

Vinny's heavies, both running towards her in the car park, returned with dazzling clarity. She buried her face in her arms and took several gulps of air. She wanted to cry but fought the impulse. After a while she sat up and noticed the street name and looked it up in Fat Andy's A–Z. She was in Haringey.

She lay back in her seat and closed her eyes. She had evaded her enemies again but next time she might fail. Her mind kept returning to the same question. How did they find me? She decided she'd been careless. The call to Pete had been reckless and stupid. She'd used the hotel phone and hadn't withheld the number. It was easy to match the number with the hotel and he'd clearly passed this on to the brothers. She thought about the letters she'd sent out to the members of the gym. They'd be delivered tomorrow, probably franked with the name of the hotel. In due course, Ronnie and Reggie would put two and two together and realize that as well as everything else, she'd been responsible for this act of sabotage.

Gradually she grew calmer. She reviewed recent events and felt a sense of pride. A lot had been achieved and she was still in one piece. She had never been so purposeful, so directed, so driven. More must be done to punish Vinny, but maybe soon she would be able to stop. She pressed her chest with the palm of her hand, then pressed gently on her injured knee. Stay calm, she thought. Stay focused, stay cool. A few more days. Maybe a week. I'll suggest the seaside trip to Harm and Trace. I'll spend the rest of the summer on holiday, taking a well-earned rest. She opened Fat Andy's road atlas and decided to pick a resort. She closed her eyes and pointed at the map of Britain. She lowered her hand, opened her eyes. She smiled. Her finger had landed in the sea, but the nearest coastal town was Weston-super-Mare. That'll do, she thought. We'll take the car and we'll go there. Weston-super-Mare. What a crazy name. In her imagination she could taste a salty tang and hear the gentle splish-splosh of waves. Children, not unlike the twins, ran back and forth across the shoreline, filling a hole with water. An old couple walked arm in arm, their clothes hitched up above the swirling foam. These people inhabited a safe, predictable world. They were happy. Overhead, sunlit birds wheeled and dived.

Jaz immobilized the Lotus Cortina and walked up the road. She passed a big garage. It was another dealership for Mazda – just like Vinny's place. The same line-up of new models gleamed in the showroom. She noted down the name and address. Afterwards, she had a meal in a café, then used the mobile to phone Harm. 'It's Jaz,' she said. 'D'you fancy a trip to the coast? Stay for a while, eat fish and chips, go to funfairs?'

'What?'

'You heard me.'

'You mean go on holiday?'

'Yeah. We never go on holiday. Why's that? Other people go on holiday. It's what people do in the summer.'

Harm hesitated. 'Are you all right, Jaz?'

'What d'you mean, am I all right? Of course I'm all right. Why should I not be all right? I'm just asking a simple question. Do you want to go on . . .'

Harm interrupted. 'You sound pretty strung out to me.'

Jaz was indignant. 'Well maybe I am! Fat Andy's had his throat cut, two gorillas are trying to kill me, I've got a sore knee that's turning septic . . .'

'Two gorillas? What happened?' There was a silence. 'You've broken your promise!'

Jaz raised her voice. 'No I haven't and I don't want to even bloody discuss it, right?' People on surrounding tables turned to stare. She spoke more quietly. 'Do you want to go on holiday? Yes or no?'

There was an angry silence, then Harm sighed, exasperated. Jaz heard her light a cigarette and inhale. 'I wouldn't mind going to the Costa del Sol.'

'I want to go to Weston-super-Mare.'

'Where the hell's that?'

'I'm not sure. But I've got a road map. I'll drive, Trace can sit in the front and play the record machine and you can map-read in the back. It'll be great. Honest, it will, Harm. It'll be fab. We'll sit in deck chairs and go on the pier.'

'OK.'

'What?'

'I said OK.'

Jaz was delighted. 'Great. That's great, Harm. We'll have to make a list. You know, of things to take . . .'

'You've had contact with those two guys? Be honest. Those brothers?'

'No,' Jaz lied.

'What did you mean when you said . . .'

'I didn't mean anything.'

'You sure?'

Jaz sighed, in mock exasperation. 'I'm sure.'

'OK, then.'

'One more thing. I've got to see a man in Haringey about something. A car thing. How's your poor face? Are you presentable? Will you come with me?'

'Why?'

'I just want you to.'

'If you like. I'll look normal again in two days.'

Jaz felt very cheerful about the prospect of the holiday. Her mood became positive. She consulted the *A–Z* and drove to the Whittington Hospital. She sat in the waiting room for two hours then watched in horror as a young, dark-skinned doctor anaesthetized her knee and with gentle-fingered care and dexterity, dug out a piece of glass. 'Where are your mother and father?' he asked.

'I haven't the faintest idea.'

He gave her a nervous, appraising glance.

'I'm twenty-one.'

'I see,' he said, clearly disconcerted. He cleaned and dressed the wound and gave her a prescription for antibiotics.

'I don't do them,' Jaz told him.

'I'm sorry?'

'I don't do them. I don't do drink, drugs or antibiotics.'

He raised his girlish eyebrows. 'Is it a religious thing?' he asked.

'You could say that.'

He smiled, shrugged and tore up the form.

'It's not infected. I think it was helped by paint thinners. They're antiseptics.' She smiled at him. 'I'm very grateful,' she insisted. 'Don't get me wrong.'

Her knee felt better. She jogged tentatively across the car park. As she was getting back into the Lotus Cortina the mobile phone rang. It was Trace.

'Listen, Trace. I've got this great idea. Harm and I have decided to go on holiday. We thought all three of us should go. Weston-super-Mare. We'll go in the car and stay in a guest house. Like, you know, a bed and breakfast. We could sit on the beach and eat candyfloss . . .' She paused. 'What d'you think?'

Trace coughed. She sounded afraid. 'I don't know, Jaz. I've never been out of London.'

'What? Never?'

'No.'

'Even more reason to go then.'

Trace laughed in an unconvinced way. 'I've met someone who says she can help you,' she said.

'In what way?'

'She's a temp. Maternity leave replacement, from an agency. She works for Charles Merchant. The only trouble is she says she wants paying.'

'How much?'

'She's got some papers she says are valuable. She wants four thousand pounds.'

'Trace, I'm not after leaked documents. Who does she think I am? Kenneth fucking Starr? I just want to find the guy Merchant and talk to him. No big deal.'

'I told her that.'

'Tell her I'll buy her a meal at Planet Pizza, Euston Road. We'll take it from there.'

Jaz heard the muffled sounds of Trace relaying this offer.

'You're on,' she confirmed. 'I can't come, though. I'm on duty. You'll have to see her on your own.' She described the woman.

Jaz gave a time and started the car.

*

Jaz had suggested an early meeting to avoid the rush. She sipped a glass of mineral water and played with the menu. Trace's contact was late but she was instantly recognizable. She was short, with dyed blonde hair, very ordinary, about fifty and wearing a red wool blazer with gold buttons, despite the warmth of the evening. Her shoes matched her bag and she carried a raincoat and some Marks & Spencer shopping. Jaz signalled with her menu and she approached with small, jaunty steps.

'Hello, dear,' she said cheerfully.

Jaz was reminded of social workers from her childhood.

A waitress appeared to take orders for drinks. 'I don't drink,' said Jaz. 'I'll have more water. Do you want wine?'

The woman smiled and nodded. She had careful, lacquered hair and pencilled eyebrows. 'A carafe of house red.' She started chatting amiably about the weather, the length of her journey back to High Wycombe and the fact that the train service was deplorable. She was middle class and effusive. She had the kind of voice people mistakenly describe as 'having no accent'. She was wearing a lot of costume jewellery. When her wine arrived she ordered minestrone and a four seasons pizza.

Jaz asked for a mixed salad.

The woman mentioned her new kitchen and conservatory. She said her husband, Malcolm, was retired but super-fit as a result of playing golf. When she started talking about her niece's exam results Jaz interrupted.

'D'you mind if we get down to business?'

She looked offended. 'Certainly,' she said huffily. 'Of course.'

The food arrived. Jaz picked up an oily leaf in her fingers. 'You know Charles Merchant. I want to arrange a meeting with him. It's personal. I have news for him which would be best delivered in person. Family business.'

The woman was still ruffled. 'Why don't you go through a solicitor?'

This hadn't occurred to Jaz. She thought for a moment. It wasn't a bad idea, except she never trusted professionals. She preferred straightforward transactions where clear needs were instantly met. 'I'm going through you, aren't I? Can you help or not?'

The woman tipped her bowl and chased the last slippery noodles with her spoon. She nodded. Within seconds her pizza arrived and she carefully cut a small piece and chewed it. Her table manners were restrained and prissy.

Jaz waited. 'Well?'

The woman suddenly put down her knife and fork, frowned and became less housewifely. Jaz looked into her eyes and, with a shock, realized she was intelligent. She was also shrewd. She'd underestimated her.

'I can tell you things about him which are reasonably well known. I can tell you things about him which are relatively unknown. I can tell you where he lives and where he eats and drinks. I know what club he belongs to. All this will cost you a hundred pounds. As well as this, I can show you something else which is not in the public domain, but which is very interesting. The last item is only a few days old. It hasn't been offered elsewhere. It will cost you four thousand pounds.'

Jaz imagined this apparently inoffensive, but self-important little woman eavesdropping, poking around in drawers, reading people's e-mails while they nipped out for a cigarette. She pictured her sitting at a word processor, printing off confidential documents whilst pretending to type minutes in a mindless way. She was the opposite of what she seemed.

Jaz was impressed. She could relate to this kind of duplicity. Because she herself looked ineffectual, she also gave people the impression of being harmless, when really she was very strong. They had this in common. 'I think I just want the hundred pound deal,' she said. 'That'll do me for now.' She smiled.

Jaz didn't doubt the woman's information. She'd learned through Trace's access to places of wealth and power that security was no more than expensive tokenism. It only worked if everyone believed in it, and this was never the case. Too many people were needed to service and maintain the rich and the successful. They came and went like an invisible conscripted army. They were low paid, resentful, and usually devoid of loyalty. Because of them, secrets were leaked and the mighty went unprotected more or less all of the time.

'All I want to do is speak to him.' She touched Elvis's roll of money in her hip pocket, then took it out and peeled off five twenties. 'I can't get through to him on the phone.'

'His calls are filtered three times, by three different people. You'll never get him at work.' The woman proceeded to talk for forty minutes, finishing her food and wine. She became more animated as she worked her way through the carafe.

Jaz tore a strip off the paper tablecloth and made a few notes. She learned that Charles Merchant was elusive and publicity shy. His boss, the Home Secretary, was a polished and handsome TV performer, who'd spent a lot on cosmetic dentistry and image consultation. However, it was Merchant, the political adviser, who had the brains and the imagination to make policy. Merchant was envied and feared. He seemed oblivious to sycophancy, flattery or intimidation. He had no known vices or skeletons in his cupboard. The woman compared him to other key figures in the government and used the word 'machiavellian'. 'He's perhaps the most brilliant of them all,' she added. 'He's a politician. An unelected politician. The most gifted of the age.'

Jaz disliked this hyperbole. 'I don't like any of them,' she said. 'None of them know what's really going on. I pay no attention to them at all.'

Her companion was undaunted. 'I think you're underestimating him. Merchant is a man with a mission,' she said. 'He calls it his new deal on Clean Cities. He wants to clean up the streets. Literally and metaphorically.' She gestured out the window. Huddled together in the soft evening, beyond the neon lit plate glass of the café, a young boy and girl in ragged overcoats held out their hands for coins.

'He wants to outlaw vagrancy, expand the prison population, make it illegal to sleep rough. He wants to quadruple hostel accommodation in big cities and raze all no-exit housing estates to the ground. He wants to overturn care in the community and reopen mental hospitals. He wants to tighten up pub licensing laws. He's got an agenda on defeating car crime. He's seriously anti-drugs. He's even devising innovative policies on refuse recycling. He says he wants everything neat and tidy in post-millennium Britain.' She swigged her wine. 'No litter, no riff-raff. Abolition of the underclass.'

Jaz snorted. It wasn't often she heard of a political programme which might affect her own lifestyle. 'Come on.' She laughed. 'That's just a joke.'

'At the very least he wants to hide it from view.'

Jaz smiled and shrugged. 'Hot air,' she muttered. She checked the details of where she might find him. 'Can I get back to you if I have problems?'

'You're dealing with a very powerful man here,' her new friend repeated. 'Some would argue he's more important than the PM. He trusts no one. He never talks to journalists, never gives interviews. He's a workaholic. He won't see you willingly. His private life's a mystery.'

'Look, I'm just not interested in him. He can try and clean up the whole damned planet, for all I care. That'll keep him busy. I just want to tell him something personal, right? It'll take five minutes. Then I'll go away.' Jaz attracted the attention of the waitress and paid the bill. She felt a little irritated by her companion's wine-fuelled fervency. 'Thanks for your help. I've got to go now.' She stood up abruptly and left the woman checking her lipstick in a handbag mirror. 'See you.'

In the car, Jaz dialled the number of Charles Merchant's club, spoke to a receptionist and left a message, giving the number of the mobile. She rang his home and a BT answering service asked her to leave the same information. She said it was a family matter and asked him to contact her. She then dialled his cellphone but it was switched off. She felt disappointed. She drove round to the address she'd been given, which turned out to be a private mews in Chelsea. She bribed the porter with ten pounds and wrote down her details on a memo pad. 'Give him this. I don't want anything except to speak to him, in person, for five minutes. Ask him to ring me. Tell him it's about his brother.' She decided to wait outside

in the quiet street, in the Lotus Cortina, to see if he
returned. She sat for several hours, her eyes on the
entrance to his building. A long, dark limousine pulled
up at about two a.m., driven by a chauffeur. A tall woman
in an evening dress emerged, fishing in a gold net bag
for some keys. Jaz decided it was Naomi Campbell. After
this everything was quiet and deserted. At three o'clock
she knew she was about to fall asleep. She realized she'd
slept in the car a lot lately. She wondered if Charles
Merchant meant to make this illegal too.

As she drifted in and out of consciousness, not
entirely comfortable, her head on the inflatable pillow,
dazzled by the lights of passing cars, Jaz remembered
where she'd been living before Fat Andy took her in.

She'd been in a church crypt in Camberwell, with
Trace, where temporary beds were set up during very
cold weather. This service was run by volunteers, who
were generous and nice, but a group of drug addicts from
Edinburgh had arrived and spoilt everything.

Trace's few possessions were stolen and she decided,
yet again, to go back to the Little Sisters of Hope in the
East End. Jaz moved into a squat in Kensington where
Harm had been living for three months, using the room
of a cellist who was in police custody. It was a beautiful
old house, full of paintings and delicate, threadbare
carpets. Jaz slept on the floor of the living room where a
skinhead chopped up valuable-looking furniture for firewood. There was no gas, electricity or running water.
When the outside temperature dropped to minus fifteen,
he began demolishing the ornate carved staircase. He
suggested burning the cello. Harm became discouraged
and went to stay with Wesley for a few days. Then she
moved into a small hotel in Vauxhall. The Australian

owner let her stay there rent free, in return for what Harm called professional services.

Jaz mentioned to Fat Andy that she had nowhere to live. First he offered her the settee in his living room. He was attentive and kind. He treated her like a child, sitting her on his knee and telling her stories. Within two days, he'd bought the Minnie Mouse nightdress and she was sharing his bed. He persuaded her to give up stealing cars.

Huddled in the back of the Lotus Cortina, Jaz thought to herself, I'm back to square one. I've got nowhere to live. But at least I'm unpredictable. Vinny can't find me if I keep moving.

As she drifted into sleep, Jaz dreamed that she was living in a lighthouse. The sea broke and sighed around her and the black sky was empty and calm. She lay in a strange curved bed, moulded against the round wall. The light flashed regularly and the steady beat of its mechanism was soothing and safe. It was lonely but peaceful. It was like being the only person in the world.

Chapter Seventeen

In the morning, Jaz immobilized the Lotus Cortina and left it outside the Chelsea mews. She dropped all her change into a parking meter and went to get some breakfast. Walking up the King's Road she caught the scent of an upmarket coffee shop. She went inside and ordered a baguette, a croissant and a cafetière of Colombian. She fingered her knee. It was almost better. She pressed her chest. The pain was still there.

She sipped her drink. She was immediately reminded of Sunday mornings with Fat Andy. He always drank a pot of coffee in bed, reading the *News of the World*. It was a ritual. She remembered cuddling up to his vast body as he cradled his mug. 'Little baby,' he said to her tenderly. Then her imagination suddenly veered to the blood-soaked bedclothes, the chill of the room on that final night and one of his limp, dead hands, open above his head, cupped as if asking for mercy. In the corner of her mind's eye, a leg of Vinny's sharp suit, and his gold-ringed monkey hand, holding the dripping knife, moved out of frame.

Hastily, she picked up a complimentary broadsheet. There was a picture of the Home Secretary on the front page. He was smiling, tanned and appeared even younger than usual. He was due to attend a Cabinet meeting that day. She scrutinized the edges, but there was no sign of Charles Merchant. Not even his fat arm or a button on his oversized jacket.

The accompanying column inches said a package of reforms called the new deal for Clean Cities would almost certainly be announced in the coming week. The government's waning popularity would be given a boost by the strong new direction to be taken in home policy. Jaz remembered her companion's comments the previous evening. She turned to a feature article on an inside page where the headline read 'New Deal for Homeless Angers Speculators'. Three paragraphs were full of conjecture but they seemed to be suggesting that as well as expanding prisons and reopening mental hospitals, the government had plans to sequestrate empty offices in big cities and turn them into temporary housing for street people. Even new buildings would not escape if they were unoccupied. They would become shortlife hostels and night shelters. Not surprisingly, many vested interests were unimpressed by this idea. The journalist was suggesting that the Home Secretary would have a fight on his hands, although he was likely to receive support from both the party and the country.

Jaz folded the newspaper and put it to one side. She leaned back, sipping from her oversized cup. The coffee was strong and fragrant. She thought about Charles Merchant. This was Fat Andy's brother. He was an innovator with a vision. He was both shadowy and clear. Instead of being self-seeking and egocentric, like elected politicians, he seemed to be driven by a personal view of how things should be.

Jaz decided there was something admirable about this. He seemed to have genuine ideas that were designed to help people. It is nice, she thought, identifying with him, to be absolutely sure about your aims. She felt that like Merchant, she too had goals. She was just as determined to carry them out. Hers were less grand but no less pressing. It was good to have direction.

Slowly she ate her breakfast. She wondered what Charles Merchant would be like and how he would behave when she finally tracked him down. She was intrigued, even a little excited. She felt less dismissive of his policies than she had the previous evening. She imagined telling him about her life on the streets and offering him insights and suggestions. She wanted to convince him that homelessness was as much about choice or luck or fate as it was about deprivation, that nothing was straightforward and big cities could never be tidy places. She pictured him questioning her, agreeing and disagreeing, quoting her in Ministerial speeches. She felt connected to him in a curious way, as if the two of them were somehow destined to know each other. She wondered if he shared Fat Andy's hedonism and specific sexual tastes. For a brief moment she thought about leaning against him, tucked under his heavy arm in the back of a swift moving government Daimler, her fingers teasing open the buttons of his hand-made Italian shirt.

Jaz tried Charles Merchant's numbers several times. She spoke to the day porter at the mews, bribed him as she had his evening colleague and left another message. He thought that no one had been back to the house, and intimated that it was often unoccupied. All in all, she spent a frustrating couple of hours. She felt at a loose end, unable to make progress.

Jaz hated this feeling. She decided to go for a run. It was a cloudy day, but hot. She took the bandage off her knee and found that it had healed in a satisfactory way. Putting on her sunglasses, she jogged up the King's Road, crossed the river and circled the lake in Battersea Park, where she stopped for ten minutes to eat an ice lolly. She hadn't pushed herself hard but the effort had boosted her circulation and cleared her mind of repetitive thoughts. She set off back at a steady jog, through Nine Elms and Vauxhall. Eventually she found herself in Westminster. She was tired now and her knee was aching. She slowed to walking pace, realizing that since she'd been driving Fat Andy's car she'd allowed herself to get out of condition. For years she'd averaged a ten-mile run every day. Since taking the car, she'd done much less. This had to change. She resolved to stay fit. It was important to be in tip-top physical shape. It was part of her personal code and necessary for self-preservation.

She wondered about going up to the Home Office, near St James's Park and having a look round outside. She might catch a glimpse of Charles Merchant or even get the opportunity to speak to him. She knew this was unlikely, but she was curious and anxious to make contact. As she proceeded up Whitehall she became aware of a gaggle of reporters, photographers and a TV crew. A road was cordoned off and half a dozen policemen were on duty. She realized she was at the end of Downing Street. She drew level as a shout went up from the small crowd. Three men with cameras broke away towards a string of long black cars. Without thinking, Jaz followed them, breaking into a fast sprint. The vehicles were moving sedately and behind there was an explosion of flash guns. Without effort, she outran the press pack and caught up with the cavalcade. One of them slowed in a leisurely sweep, before turning out into the main road. Jaz looked inside. A man in the back seat glanced up, startled, and for a moment stared into her face. Through the bluish tinted window she could see him clearly. It was the Home Secretary. Her damp palm slapped against the glass, in a decisive gesture, before the driver was able to accelerate away.

Later, when Jaz got back to the Lotus Cortina, she could hear the mobile ringing in the glove compartment. It was Trace. She was excited. 'I've seen him!' she squeaked. She explained she was in a phone booth in the Home Office building. 'I've seen him and he's exactly like your fat bloke. I can't believe it. It *must* be his brother!'

'Tell me slowly.'

'Well, actually, he's sort of fatter and I think his hair's a darker colour, but otherwise he's the same. Apart from the suit and the shiny shoes and suchlike. I wasn't expecting to see him. I got such a shock, I nearly wet myself!'

'Did you speak to him?'

'Get real. He was surrounded by a mob of flunkies holding clipboards and briefcases. He sort of swept past, out the door and into a big car.'

'Did he notice you?'

'I doubt it. There's just been a Cabinet meeting and he's off to speak to the Home Secretary. To discuss business. He's what we call NTG, here, straight down from the very top floor.'

'What's NTG?'

'Next to God. Hey, but listen, Jaz. I've got something else for you. A fax number and an e-mail address. There's a directory here. My friend Shirl looked him up.'

Jaz wrote these down. 'Trace. You've got to try and speak to him. Can't you go up there tomorrow with a plate of biscuits or something?'

Trace laughed. 'Sure, Jaz. I'll do my best.' She sounded very cheerful.

'Do you like it a bit better?' Jaz was tentative. 'Have you made some new friends?'

'Oh yes. There's two lovely women here. Iris and Shirl. They're a great laugh. I've joined a lottery syndicate . . .' She continued chatting about this for a minute or two.

Jaz was relieved. When she hung up, she reflected, not for the first time, on Trace's endless capacity to make the best of things. Wherever she lived or worked, her innocent friendliness and ability to see the good in people meant that she was OK. It wasn't a quality that Jaz envied, but she was touched by it, nevertheless. She thought about Trace's damaged past and her fear of sex. When this is over, she told herself, and we go to Weston-super-Mare, we'll all three of us be happy. We'll be Cortina crazy. She remembered Blow's old cars and his descriptions of his youth. She hummed his song to herself. Do wah diddy diddy, dum diddy do. We'll make our own sandwiches, wrap them in newspaper and eat them on the beach. We'll make flasks of tea. We'll hire deck chairs. We'll meet some nice, ordinary men who aren't perverts and go to the pictures. We'll queue up for the matinee. She let her mind linger on this. We'll hold their hands in the Ghost Train. We'll let them kiss us in the Tunnel of Love.

*

Jaz phoned Harm at Wesley's flat. 'Can I come over and use Wesley's computer again?'

Harm was suspicious. 'What for?'

'To send an e-mail. I want to use his fax. It'll only take a minute.'

Harm sighed. 'Jaz, why do I think you're not confiding in me? What's going on?'

'I'll tell you when I get there. Promise.'

'Wesley isn't here. He's gone to a conference. At the South Bank University.'

'A conference? What about?'

'It's called "Experiencing the 'I'. Psychosynthesis in Action." ' There was a pause and then a giggle. 'Don't ask.'

'Don't worry, I'm not going to. That Wesley's amazing. He's something else.'

Jaz arrived at the flat and gave a thumbs-up to the homeless penny whistle player in the doorway of the pork butcher. He didn't respond. He looked depressed. She dropped fifty pence into his hat.

Upstairs in the flat she was just in time to catch the news headlines. She held up her hand to silence Harm. 'Just let me see this, will you?'

There was film of Cabinet members leaving 10 Downing Street and getting into a waiting line of cars.

'Watch this,' said Jaz.

As the cars pulled away it was possible to see policemen and onlookers and then an untidy crowd of photographers and journalists which broke into a run. Suddenly, in an instant, Jaz appeared.

Harm let out a small cry.

Jaz was shown, dashing ahead of the rest, pursuing, then gaining on the lead car as it slowed at the junction. She looked like a pint-sized autograph hunter.

'That was you!'

The picture on the screen reverted to the newsroom and the next item.

Jaz laughed.

'It was you!' Harm turned to Jaz, her eyes wide. 'What the hell are you up to, Jaz? What's going on? I've just had Trace on the phone. She's obeying your orders as usual. She's tracked down this VIP bloke in Whitehall – the one you think's the fat man's twin. Does this let me off the hook at the House of Commons?' Anxiously she drew on her cigarette, stubbed it out, lit another. Her hands were shaking slightly. She fired questions like bullets. 'This whole thing, it's like the movies. You better tell me more about what's going on. I don't like this. I don't like mysteries. I'm worried about Trace. What are you getting her into? When have we ever had secrets from one another?'

Jaz slumped into an armchair, still grinning but suddenly tired. 'Stay calm,' she murmured. She looked around. The room was even more untidy than the last time she'd visited. The sofa was a tussle of twisted blankets and pillows. Clothes, underwear and tissues were strewn around and there was a tottering heap of partially empty boxes which had held pizzas and Chinese takeaway. Dirty cups were everywhere, and an overflowing make-up bag, full ashtrays and Wesley's CDs, all out of their boxes, littered the floor. 'It looks like a bomb's hit this place.' She glanced at Harm. 'Although you're looking better.'

Harm sat on the arm of the settee. She was wearing an outsize black T-shirt and black and gold leggings. She flicked open a mirror compact and studied her face, applying more lipstick. She was heavily made up, but looked almost normal.

'How d'you feel now?'

Harm sighed. She stared at Jaz, as if not expecting any answers. 'I'm OK. More or less. I'm staying off work till Wesley gets back.' She folded away the compact, threw it on the floor and placed her hands on her hips. 'Are you going to tell me what's going on, or not?'

'Can I use the computer first?'

Harm nodded.

Jaz switched on the machine, pressed a few keys and composed a message to Charles Merchant. It said 'Please make sure Mr Merchant gets this. It's personal. It's about his long-lost, deceased twin brother. It's important that I speak to him.' She added her name and the number of her mobile phone, then sent the message via fax and e-mail, using the information provided by Trace. 'Can I have a wash now, Harm?' she asked. 'You can talk to me while I'm having a soak.'

Harm led the way into the bathroom. She drew down the window blind, put the plug in and turned on both taps. She opened a long-necked bottle and poured green liquid into the gush. There was an immediate billow of foam and a smell which was sharp, pungent and uplifting. 'Get in. I'll make you a coffee.'

Jaz breathed deeply and stepped out of her clothes. She turned off the taps and lay down gratefully in the hot water. She was caressed by bubbles. The scent was wonderful, like an unpeopled Scottish hillside.

She was reminded of another bath, years before, when she'd smelled this same out-of-doors, woodland perfume. She remembered lying in the vast, old-fashioned bath in her mother's house, taking deep, exhilarated breaths. Cardboard was stuffed into a broken window and the steam condensed in thick clouds in the freezing air. To her left was the ancient lavatory with its rusting cistern high on the wall. An expanse of scored, worn linoleum lay between her and the door. She felt the water warm through to her bones.

She was going to a party. Earlier in the day she'd been trudging through the fields, cradling an armful of frost-bitten turnips, when she'd heard the sound of an engine. Hurrying to the front of the farm, she'd seen a motorbike with a sidecar bouncing away down the rutted track. She ran inside and dumped the vegetables in the sink. Blow appeared in the doorway. He seemed flushed and happy. 'That was the curate,' he said. 'I don't know why, but he's invited you girls to the Sunday School Christmas party.' He paused. 'It's a disco.'

The twins appeared. They'd been listening on the stairs. They were wearing matching bobble hats and filthy outsize woollens over their nightdresses. Their bare legs and feet were stained with manure. 'We're not going,' they said in unison. 'We don't like Sunday school, or Monday school, or Tuesday school.'

'We don't like Wednesday, Thursday or Friday school, either,' added Mimosa.

'We don't like discos,' agreed Peony. 'We only like classic West Coast rock.'

Blow looked concerned. 'I said you'd go.' His voice was plaintive. 'I said you'd be pleased.'

'I'll go,' said Jasmine. She was excited. 'I've never been to a party.'

Blow built a big fire and pulled down the damper to heat a tankful of water. He led Jasmine upstairs. In the bathroom he put the plug in the old, cracked porcelain tub and turned on the stiff taps. Jasmine struggled out of her layers of clothing. She hadn't had a proper bath for years. Shyly, Blow produced something from his trouser pocket. It was a small foil cube with a picture of a tree. 'I took this from your mother's dressing table,' he offered. He unwrapped it and crumbled the white block into the water. The dense air was immediately filled with perfume. It was a thrilling smell – the scent of pine forests. Jasmine stepped out of her oversized knickers and Blow's hands stroked her chest and bottom before she slid into the sweet depths. 'I'll wash my hair,' she offered.

Later, wearing a torn, net party dress, stolen from the back of Lola's wardrobe, and a pair of elastic-fronted plimsolls, Jasmine drove Blow's car in the direction of the village. She was cold and Blow fiddled with the heater. She steered carefully, moving up through the gears. He currently owned a well-preserved Hunter GT which was perfectly tuned and smelled of leather and oil. 'I'm going to see a man about a car,' he said, as she pulled up outside the church hall. He climbed into the driving seat. 'Pick you up in three hours.' He squeezed her arm. 'Have a great time.'

Inside, Jasmine hesitated in the corridor. There was the sound of pop music and teenage laughter. The walls were painted a dingy cream and she stared at a notice-board which mentioned Girl Guides and the church roof appeal. There was a smell of Lysol and something else which Jasmine couldn't name. Instinctively, she felt it as piety, conformity, restriction. She knew she was in the wrong place. She went back outside. It was sleeting heavily and Blow had gone.

She forced herself to go into the hall. A man was

sitting at a table in the entrance. He wore a clerical collar and a leather jacket and had a pop singer's haircut. He gave her a big smile. 'You're very welcome,' he said. He handed her a leaflet. It was about a new Bible study group for young people.

Wordless, Jasmine edged inside. It was dark. At the far end of the room a semicircle of coloured lights haloed a man at a record deck. He spoke into a microphone but his words were distorted. He put on another song and waved his arms in the air.

A group of girls began dancing in the centre of the floor. All of them, even those as young as Jasmine, were wearing miniskirts, tight sweaters and clumpy shoes. Their hair was long, shiny and loose and they tossed it about as they swayed and twisted in the gloom. Boys wearing trainers and tracksuits stood around in groups, drinking Coca-Cola from cans and watching the girls.

Jasmine didn't know anyone. She had seen all this before, but only on television. She remembered that Blow had talked about a disco. A disco must be a dance. She realized her expectations of party games and paper plates with cake were both childish and misjudged. She retreated into the darkest corner, fingering the hard mesh of her mother's net dress. It was black and long, almost to her feet. It had a baggy sequinned bodice, cut low and trimmed with moulting feathers. It smelled of mothballs and ancient patchouli oil. Lola called it her Deep Purple dress, because years before she'd seduced a member of the band when she'd been wearing it. Jasmine knew now that it was ridiculous. She was furious with Blow, who had supplied it, telling her it looked all right. She felt like a clown.

Two girls walked by. They were wearing white jeans

and white tops which glowed eerily in the peculiar light. They glanced at Jasmine and sniggered. She felt tears spring to her eyes, but she blinked them away. Her rage was growing. She was angry with Blow for bringing her here, she was angry with the curate for inviting her, she was angry with her sisters for being more aware than herself. Most of all, she was angry with Lola because she was drunk and in bed and had never taken her to a party or bought proper clothes or told her about discos. I hate my mother, she thought.

She edged towards the door. Another group of leggy girls arrived. They had bare arms, shimmering tights and tinsel in their hair. They giggled together and pushed one another. As the curate handed them their leaflets, Jasmine slipped unnoticed outside.

It was snowing and there was a strong wind. The sky was dark, with no moon. She closed the door, extinguishing the music. On a building opposite, a pub sign swung and creaked, but the place was in darkness. There was a rush-rush of turbulent trees. The snowflakes swirled, fell, then melted on the wet road. No vehicles approached in either direction. Jasmine shivered, her canvas shoes soaking up water. The cold air struck her naked arms and chest like a blade, raising her stiff skirt like beetles' wings. She swore to herself and looked around. The curate's motorbike was parked off the road, half behind the corner of the church hall. She approached it, glancing about, then examined it. He's got a nice taste in bikes, she thought. It was a twenty-five-year-old Ariel Redhunter. It was well cared for, with unpitted chrome. She opened the sidecar and found a pair of leather gauntlets and a soft pouch containing tools. She slammed the door and turned her attention to the immediate problem.

Selecting a thin screwdriver she pressed it hard into the lock and tried to turn it. It was no good. She tried again and again, but she couldn't penetrate it far enough. She found a pair of pliers, then tossed the rest of the tools aside. She picked up a broken brick and smashed it down on the ignition. She yanked out the wires and joined them, using the pliers. She mounted the saddle and, with all her strength, tried to drive the kickstart down. She slipped and there was a searing pain as cold steel tore the skin off her ankle. She shut her eyes, and held her mouth tight to prevent herself crying. She was determined. Pulling hard against the handlebars, just able to reach, she repeated the movement. The engine rumbled, turned over, then roared. The sensation between her legs reminded her of sex. She put it in gear and turned the throttle. As the combo moved forwards, she changed up. Gathering momentum, she put on the gloves.

Speeding along the road, away from the village, straddling the big machine like a pantomime midget, Jasmine became unaware first of her arms, then her shoulders and then her neck. They froze. Her feet and knees were numb. Her face was a stiff mask and the moisture that leaked from her half-shut eyes turned to ice. A strand of hair cut into her cheek but she was unwilling to leave go of the controls. She took the bike up to top gear. The engine was well maintained, responsive. On a straight stretch she checked the speedometer. She was doing eighty. The combo bounced and roared, following the dipping and soaring arcs of its yellow headlamps as they illuminated hedgerows, stone walls, telegraph poles. With a swerve and a shower of stones she turned onto the track to the farm. The bike climbed the steep slope, willing and still lively.

Lights glimmered in the distance signalling the farm-house. Three quarters of the way up, she stopped. To the right of the track, the land fell steeply away and below this, a rocky precipice scarred the hillside. She knew that at the bottom was a boulder-strewn stream and the lowest reaches of her mother's barren fields. She stopped and dismounted, the engine ticking over.

Jasmine had no real love of motorbikes and the curate had to be punished. She manoeuvred the machine near the edge of the drop, then she gathered four big stones and wedged them under the section where the sidecar and bike were bolted together, lifting the back wheels above the ground. She put the bike in gear and watched its rear wheel spin. She removed the petrol cap. Then she took off Lola's dress, lassooed it around the stones and dragged them away. The combo moved forwards, driving itself towards the drop. After three seconds, its front wheels found only air and slowly, reluctantly, it tipped. Jasmine ran to the brink and watched it bang and clatter, its crazy lights veering, jumping, blinking. Within moments it was lost to the cold north wind, the snow, the blackness of the night. She waited. She didn't hear it hit bottom, but after a few seconds there was a dull bang and a flash of flame.

The next morning, Jasmine lay under her blankets, her mother's muddy party dress on the floor by her side. Her ankle was hurting. The telephone rang. She heard Blow arguing and she tiptoed to the landing. 'OK then, you tell the police,' he said assertively. 'She's twelve years old. She's barely four feet tall. You really think they'll believe you?'

*

Jaz lay in Wesley's bath, savouring the warmth. Harm reappeared with a mug of coffee for her friend and a bottle of Bacardi Breezer.

'OK,' said Jaz, taking her coffee, 'listen to this.'

Harm sat on the toilet, her feet propped on the side of the bath, tipping the pink bottle to her mouth and smacking her lips.

Jaz explained again about her need to find mourners for Fat Andy. She mentioned Princess and the woman in Pimlico and how they'd both been unsatisfactory. 'The thing is, Harm, like I said before, a man's died and it's like . . . well, it's not nothing. See? It's simply not nothing. I'm sick of it being seen as nothing. I'm sick of no one caring. Something has to be done. It's up to me. And this bloke Charles Merchant has got to be his twin. He's physically identical. The trouble is, I can't get hold of him. He's like . . . he's inaccessible.'

'No one's inaccessible,' said Harm. She thought for a moment. 'You've got Trace in the Home Office, cleaning bloody toilets or something . . .'

'Making tea.'

'Whatever. You asked me the other day if I turn tricks at the House of Commons. You've asked both of us to help you.'

'You said you'd help me if you could. Does that still hold?'

Harm hesitated. 'I guess so. What do you want me to do?'

Jaz pursed her lips. 'I'll think of something.' She picked up a bar of soap and washed her feet. 'Thing is, he's not returning my calls or messages. It's like people are screening me out. I'm not getting through to him.'

'Could be his decision. Maybe he doesn't want to talk

to you, doesn't want contact with his past. Maybe he wants to keep his past sealed up, like in a box. A lot of people feel that way.'

Jaz considered this for a moment. 'I don't buy that.'

'Why not?'

Jaz paused. 'It's a twin thing. He was an identical twin. He'll feel something's wrong. He must want to find out what it is. They always do, they're psychic. I know about twins.'

Harm shook her head. 'Let it go, Jaz. This murder has made you nuts. What's the matter with you, anyway?'

Jaz continued. 'I grew up with twins and they made me feel left out all my childhood. Always together. In bed, the bath, everywhere. You asked one of them a question and they'd answer, "We think this . . . We want that . . ." They had one mind in two bodies. They were inseparable.'

'So you think he's got to be interested?'

' I don't know. Something's happened. I feel different. I've just got to do this. I feel as if for the first time in my life I've got something that I believe in.'

Harm snorted.

'Don't laugh.' Jaz sipped her scalding drink. 'I've been thinking about this a lot lately. This whole thing has changed me. I feel as if I've got a job to do, a responsibility over and beyond just looking after myself.'

Harm stared. She took another long swig from her bottle.

Jaz put her mug on the windowsill, submerged herself then rubbed shampoo into her hair. 'I mean, what've we got, the three of us? All we've ever been clear about is what we don't want.' She thought for a moment. 'That, and getting money.'

Harm considered. 'You're right. I want to make enough money to do exactly as I please. So that I don't answer to anyone. Do my own thing. Make my own decisions.'

'Don't you see, Harm? That's my point exactly. All we've ever been concerned about is our own survival.' She suddenly thought about Charles Merchant and his agenda for change. 'What I'm saying is, maybe there's more. Maybe we should be concerned about what we're doing for other people.'

Harm stood up. 'God, Jaz.' She put her empty bottle on the side of the bath and flicked her hand in a dismissive gesture. 'What are you on about? I spend my whole life doing things for other people. I'm an object who's used by other people, for heaven's sake.' She paused. 'I'm concerned about getting more for me. They want me, they pay. They'll pay enough and finally, in the end, I can escape.'

Jaz hesitated. She lay back and washed the soap from her hair, then sat up again. There seemed no reply to this. She knew Harm had missed the point, but she felt unable to argue. 'I owe it to Fat Andy,' was all she could offer. 'I'll get this sorted, I promise. I'll get it all fixed. Then we'll go on holiday. We'll go on holiday and everything will be . . . it'll be . . .'

'It'll be what?'

Jaz stood up. Water cascaded from her small frame. Her fists were clenched. 'I don't know. We'll go to Weston-super-Mare and it'll be . . .'

'*What?*'

Jaz took a deep breath and stepped out of the bath. She thought of Blow again and his nostalgia for a simpler world. 'It'll be like . . .' She nearly said the words Cortina crazy. She thought for a moment. Blow's song came into her mind. Do wah diddy diddy, dum diddy do. 'I don't know. Everyone will have a smile on their face.'

Harm handed her a towel. 'Oh, yeah?'

Chapter Eighteen

Later, Harm fried some eggs and made sandwiches with tomato ketchup. 'I still can't see the point of causing all this trouble for yourself,' she said. She hesitated then handed Jaz her plate. 'You may not like this, but I phoned the ginger boy from the garage. I had a chat with him.' She paused nervously and lit a cigarette, then immediately extinguished it. She sounded guilty. 'I was worried about you.'

'You did *what*?'

Harm was clearly on thin ice. 'Trace said he'd been looking for you. That he was concerned. She gave me his number because he's been trying to find you. I remember you said you'd gone off him, but I told him you were coming here. He cares about you, Jaz, and he seems a very nice person.' She paused. 'I know you like being independent and everything, but we thought . . .' She stopped.

Jaz put down her sandwich. There was a silence. The atmosphere was tense. 'Who? Who are we talking about here? Who thought what exactly?' Her voice was cold. She waited a few seconds. 'Well?'

'Trace and me.' Harm spoke quickly. 'We discussed it. We never realized the fat bloke was such a good influence. He looked after you, didn't he? And you were more relaxed when you were with him. Less wired. Less driven. We thought maybe that's what you need. You know. A boyfriend.'

Jaz jumped to her feet and grabbed her jacket. 'Are you nuts? I don't want to see him. He's one of Vinny's boys. Fuck, Harm, why are you screwing things like this? I told Trace I never wanted to see him again!'

Harm looked anxious. 'I'm sorry. It's just that he seems . . . sweet. You know. Caring . . .'

'He was a shag. Have you got that? He was nothing. How would you like it if I started telling your fucking punters your address? Some of those weird, kinky ones? Just how would you like that?' Jaz was very angry. She was shouting. 'I can't believe you've fucking done this. What's fucking happening? You told him I was coming here? Are you mad, or what?'

'Stop swearing at me, Jaz.' Harm started to cry.

Jaz pulled on her jacket and made for the door. 'I'm out of here. And you tell that Pete to go fuck himself.'

Jaz slammed the door as she left. Below, the homeless man had disappeared but the pork butcher greeted her cheerily as he locked up his shop. She ignored him. It was growing dark outside and the sky was streaked with red. The air was still and warm. She kicked a can into the gutter. As she approached the Lotus Cortina she saw someone alongside it, leaning against a street sign. His long, thin legs and casual ponytail were unmistakable. It was Pete. He was reading a folded newspaper and his posture indicated he'd been waiting for some time. He hadn't noticed her.

Jaz swore at length under her breath. She stepped behind a parked van. This is too much, she thought, I don't believe this. She crossed the road and hid in a doorway. She put on her sunglasses and looked around. Ronnie and Reggie were probably staked out somewhere, waiting for her to make a move towards the car. She imagined Vinny, his mouth a thin line, clicking the joints of his small, hairy fingers, waiting in a Mazda in a lay-by, his Japanese air conditioning turned on, expecting his phone to ring. Stay calm, stay focused, she thought. On impulse, she pulled the mobile from her pocket and dialled his number.

It was answered. 'Vinny Stasinopoulos speaking.' His voice was even higher and more effeminate than usual. He sounded stressed.

'Companero?'

'Jaz?'

'Vinny, you lousy slimeball. Just tell your ugly gorillas they've lost me. I'm out of there by miles. I'm way off base. I'm in Milton Keynes. I'm in Tavistock. I'm in fucking Doncaster.'

'Jaz? It is you? One moment . . .'

'Fucking Doncaster. Right?' She hung up.

The street lamps came on and the rose-pink sunset wash was eclipsed from the evening, replaced by the usual city glare. Two young boys sauntered past. 'Got a light?' one of them asked, trying to sound hard. He was the same size as her.

Jaz stepped backwards. She felt the money in her pocket. 'I'll give you a hundred quid for your jacket and cap.'

The boy sniggered.

'I mean it.' She pulled out her money, thumbed through the notes and proffered a bundle. 'Now. Just do it. Do it now or forget it.'

He tried to appear in control. Whistling, he unzipped

his nylon jacket and handed it over. He removed his cap. In a sudden gesture, he grabbed the cash.

'Now piss off,' muttered Jaz.

The boys melted away.

She pulled on the garment, over her own. She looked at the cap. They were both blue and white and bore the words 'Toronto Blue Jays'.

The street was almost deserted. Pete still leaned patiently, reading, picking his ear. A wino raked through a rubbish bin, talking to himself. A bus went past, almost empty, followed by a taxi cab.

Jaz fastened the jacket higher than her chin. It smelled of cigarettes and sweat. She twisted her hair and covered it with the cap, pulling the front down low. She walked up the street, away from the Lotus Cortina at a fast pace and turned a corner into an alley.

Suddenly, she felt a pressure against her back. Her breath was forced out of her chest. She toppled forwards, aware of two pairs of feet behind her. A heavy, rough cloth smelling of petrol was thrown across her head, obscuring her vision. Strong arms encircled her, hurting her, then she was lifted off her feet. 'Let her have it!' she heard. She tried to scream. She struggled. She heard a car pull up and realized she was being tipped sideways and bundled inside. She struggled and kicked until a heavy weight pressed her down. Someone was sitting on her. Her cheek was pressed against leather. She fought desperately for air.

Chapter Nineteen

Jaz's mind swam into consciousness. I must have passed out, she thought. She took a deep breath. Her mouth and nose were now free but the air smelled bad. She became aware, slowly, that she was in a car and she was tied up. Her ankles and wrists were bound tightly and her hands and feet were numb. The motor throbbed, idle, its gears in neutral. It was dark and she was alone. She had a sense of being inside a building. She blinked and squinted at the illuminated numbers on the dashboard and to the side, the tiny flash of red that meant the security was engaged.

She tried to turn around. The tail lights illuminated the brick walls of a confined space, the back of a metal door. She was in a small garage. You bastard, Vinny, she thought. You evil fuck. I'm in a lock-up. She struggled against the twine which tied her.

The car spluttered an instant, then resumed its rhythmic judder. She concentrated on the dash. There was a tank full of petrol and the windows were all open an inch. Already, the air was thick and heavy. She squirmed and wriggled but she was trussed like a dead bird. She was drowning in exhaust fumes. Her captors had left her here to die.

The realization made her cough. She gagged and

choked. Her lungs wanted to explode. She twisted and thrashed and sweat broke out on her brow. She was light-headed. Lying on her back and raising her legs, she swung her feet over the passenger seat. The toes of her trainers thumped against plastic as she tried to locate the ignition key. From this position she could see nothing but the roof of the vehicle. She attempted to use the steering column as a guide. Failing, her feet awkwardly tied together, she kicked out wildly. There was a sudden burst of noise. She froze in surprise. The reception was poor but it was a man's voice. She'd turned on the radio. Without meaning to, she listened. Hearing his muffled but reassuring tones, she relaxed. Her brain was turning sleepy. Her muscles, starved of oxygen, were suddenly unwilling to move. The man was making a speech. It was the Home Secretary. Jaz recognized his soft, Northumbrian burr. 'Homelessness and destitution are the scourge of our cities,' he said. 'Hopeless, demoralized individuals, frequently young, have completely lost their way.'

We've lost our way, thought Jaz. We're hopeless and fucking demoralized. She forced herself to think. I've got to get out of here. Unless I get out of here, I'm a goner. With a big effort, she kicked again. Her shin hit something hard and her shoulders began slipping off the back seat. Her neck felt like it was breaking. With each breath, her brain was foggier. The air was now poison, like pure vapourized gasoline.

'Directionless,' he continued, 'they lie around our streets, begging, untidy, frequently intoxicated . . .'

The words had a sense beyond their meaning. They were seductive. Jaz eased backwards. Her feet dropped back to the floor. Again, she stopped struggling and slumped sideways. Intoxicated, she thought. The car seat

felt welcoming – her head seemed to sink into it and
then sink still further. She wanted to sleep, to drift, to lie
still. Her body felt leaden, her mind cloudy with gas. She
couldn't resist. The man's voice was calm, measured. Jaz
thought it was the most beautiful voice she'd ever heard.
The words blurred and became mere sounds. Their gentle
resonance seemed in time with the car's heartbeats. I'll
just lie here, she thought, I'll just lie here and go to sleep.
It's peaceful here. She had a sense of spinning, then
floating.

Suddenly, she was aware that the man's tone had
changed. For some reason, he was angry. Jaz pulled
herself back into consciousness. She forced herself to
listen. He was haranguing his audience. What was he
telling her?

'We are not, I repeat not, prepared to tolerate this.
This situation is a criminal waste of resources. It squan-
ders our education system, it drains our health service.
It is a waste of the gift of life itself.' He paused. 'This
government needs to act and I can assure you, it will act.
We will gather, we will unite, we will stand up, we will
confront this evil . . .'

The Home Secretary was excited now. Jaz remembered being overpowered, dragged into the car. Let her
have it, someone had said. That bastard Vinny. Her old
fury welled up. That murdering son of a bitch. She
struggled to sit. We will gather our strength, confront the
evil. Just like the man on the radio had told her to. 'We
will not rest until we've won . . .'

Something was glinting on the floor. The air was too
foul to gulp so she held her breath. She slid onto her
belly, manoeuvred her head downwards and picked up
the heavy object in her teeth. It was a tyre lever. Stay

calm, she thought. The cold, metallic taste, along with her anger, somehow cleared her mind. Stay focused. With new energy she shoved the lever between her knees and rubbed her wrist bindings against its chipped metal edge. I'm out of here, she thought, you fucking bastards. I'm not staying here to die. We will not rest until we've won. One strand of twine broke, then two. She felt life flowing back into her hands. She unravelled the rest then shook her arms. She unfastened her ankles, lunged forwards and struggled into the driver's seat. She slammed the car straight into reverse and stamped on the accelerator. It leaped backwards and smashed against the door. There was a crash, a tinkle of glass, a groan of metal. The engine roared. She jerked forward a couple of feet then reversed hard again. She looked over her shoulder. The door bulged and buckled, coming off its hinges. She backed into it a final time and it gave way, bouncing and cata-pulting out into the road. Vinny, you evil shite, she thought, I'm not ready to die. I'm not wasting the gift of life itself. She almost smiled. Stay cool.

The Home Secretary, in agreement, concluded his speech. 'We will go on, and then we will go on!'

Jaz backed the car into the street, winding down the window. We will go on, she agreed. The outside world flowed around her like sweet wind. She coughed, retched, doubled up, spat, coughed again. She filled her aching lungs. She rammed the gears into first and pulled the car round. She'd driven one of these before. It was a Citroën Xantia. That's strange, she thought. It's not a Mazda. Vinny must be desperate. He's buying in extra help.

Chapter Twenty

Jaz looked up the street. She was disorientated. She also had a sense of déjà vu. She put both down to carbon monoxide poisoning. There was no traffic and it was night. The air was still warm and motionless. She looked at her watch. It was two a.m. She leaned over the steering wheel, fighting nausea. She massaged her wrists, then her ankles. She felt in her pocket. She still had her roll of money. A group of Asian youths walked by on the other side of the road. They looked at her curiously, but passed without comment, circling the damaged door in the road. She saw an all-night grocer's, an Indian video rental shop, a swiftly moving grey cat. There was a smell of foreign food. A black cab went by, its 'For Hire' sign extinguished. It was then she remembered. Shit, she thought, I really have been here before. I'm not imagining things. She clenched her fists. The cobbles had been recently covered in tarmac, the buildings were even more dilapidated than before, but it was the same place. She'd been brought here by a weirdo called Keith, five years ago. She'd been just sixteen. He'd parked his two-tone Zephyr in one of these lock-ups. A Mark II, she remembered. Spotless chrome. Highline. Canary yellow over cream. Then he'd taken her to an old cinema, showed her films and threatened to kill her. He said he was going to put her body on a bonfire.

Jaz opened the car door and was sick in the road. How could Vinny have known, she kept thinking as her stomach heaved and expelled its contents. How could he possibly have known? She wiped her mouth on her sleeve. Stay calm, she told herself, but she felt anything but calm. She was shaking and full of fear.

Stay focused. I am focused, she told herself. She turned on the lamps full beam and revved the engine until it screamed. Her feet were juddering on the pedals. Her knees knocked together. Keith's smiling face seemed to gaze at her through the windscreen. She hadn't thought about him seriously for a long time. She remembered his Millwall anorak, his small pointy teeth. He's been locked away, she reminded herself. The posse of tramps beat him senseless in the cinema after putting out both his eyes. He was taken off in an ambulance and ended up at the Old Bailey where the judge threw away the key. She hadn't given evidence. She'd stayed out of it, not wanting to be involved, but he was convicted anyway. Broadmoor. Indefinite period. She shoved the gear lever forwards and stepped on the accelerator. The car lurched and took the corner on two wheels. There was a bright flash as metal hit stone, a clatter as the broken rear bumper disengaged, a stench of burning rubber and the roar of the abused engine as the car took off like a rocket.

Jaz felt she was taking control. She drove at high speed, bursting through red lights, racing into round-abouts, junctions, right-hand bends. She scattered a band of revellers, her hand hard down on the horn. She forced a taxi onto a pavement, swerved round roadworks, sped illegally up one-way streets. For reasons she couldn't understand, she headed towards Peckham. When she got to the estate where she'd lived with Fat Andy, she squealed to a halt in front of the flats. There was no one about. She looked up at the window of the room she'd shared with him.

In an instant, she was back inside. She was standing by Andy's body touching his cold, lifeless hand. She remembered it had felt like wax on the point of setting. She had drawn away her own hand, repelled. She had stared at his neck. It was open, like a vagina in a pornographic magazine.

She shook her head, trying to dispel these images. She looked at her watch. It was still the middle of the night. She left the key in the ignition, the driver's door wide open, the attention-seeking radio on.

She felt better. She jogged off in the direction of Camberwell. First there'll be joyriders, she decided, sixteen-year-olds, skiving off school in the morning. They'll spend the day hotrodding around the estate practising their handbrake turns. Then, after dark, their younger brothers will use it to ram a sports goods shop on the High Street, smashing the plate glass. The shop will be looted and they'll drive off with their haul of stolen Air Max trainers, Kappa jackets and Adidas popper pants. Later it'll be abandoned and the hyenas will arrive. This will be the fathers and uncles. First to go will be the stereo, then the wheels. The engine will be stripped down quicker than Pete could do it. Quicker than Andy could have done it. Someone, unaccountably, will decide to make use of the seats. By the next morning it'll be an unrecognizable shell and some little kids will set it on fire.

*

Jaz sat in an all-night café near Ruskin Park listening to the conversations of three elderly black men who'd come off night shift in St Thomas's hospital. They were eating breakfast. She still felt sick and drank two mugs of hot, strong tea. It was very early. She took out the mobile phone and tried Charles Merchant again, on his various numbers. There was no reply and she didn't bother leaving more messages. She was still frightened. She turned to the overweight, cockney proprietor who wore a greasy white coat and a collapsed chef's hat. 'You remember that guy, a few years ago, in the East End who was killing homeless girls and putting them on bonfires?'

The man pushed back his hat and scratched his head. 'Can't say I do, darling.' He grinned. 'Jack the Ripper?' He was making sandwiches for the lunch-time rush. Despite his fat, short fingers, his chopping knife moved at the speed of light. He called over to his regulars. Cheerfully, he repeated Jaz's question.

'Have they let him out?' she enquired.

The three men turned around and smiled at Jaz. 'Fred West?' replied one.

'No man, he was down Devon. Or was it Somerset? Or Gloucester? Fred West. He hung himself. She means Dennis Nilsen. He didn't put them on bonfires. He flushed them down the pan.'

'No, not him,' said the third. 'This was another one. Out east. Stepney way. He was killed by vigilantes. Hell's Angels.'

Jaz gave up. They remembered nothing. She nodded politely, stood up and left. She ran swiftly to London Bridge and got on a train. She was worried about the car.

*

As she walked from Shepherd's Bush station to Wesley's flat, it started to rain. The air was hot and humid and the sky grew so dark it was as if dawn hadn't broken. Large drops fell straight down and bounced on the pavement. Within seconds, Jaz was soaked. This isn't English rain, she thought. There was a smell of wet dust and the traffic swished by listlessly. People huddled in shop doorways, their thin summer clothes sticking to their flesh. The Lotus Cortina came into view. Jaz sprinted towards it. It was undamaged and gleaming, but the water was no longer running off its bonnet in wormy droplets. She was relieved. It needs a polish, she thought. Poor thing. Its front grille and quarter bumpers greeted her like a wide grin. She stroked its pale roof. There was a piece of sodden paper on the windscreen. Jaz picked this off, got into the car and closed the door. Her sports bag was still on the back seat. She unfolded the disintegrating sheet and saw the blurred signature 'Pete'. His words, however, scrawled in felt tip, were unreadable. The ink had run together in purple streaks. She opened a window, made a ball of the note and threw it outside.

I've got to be very careful now, she thought. She remembered Keith again. Get real. It wasn't him. He's locked up and safe. It was that bastard Vinny, and he tried to kill me. I nearly died. She pressed her chest. The pain was still there as well as a curious tightness which was the result of the gas.

She took out the mobile and pressed Vinny's number. He didn't answer. She left a message. She forced herself to sound light, even jolly. 'Hey, companero? Jaz here. I'm just checking in. The Citroën's stripped in Peckham. I'm still here, fine and dandy, and I'm not fucking finished with you yet.'

The car started without effort. She drove past Wesley's flat. The penny whistle player was sheltering with two *Big Issue* vendors. She wondered about visiting Harm and trying to make it up with her, but decided it was far too early. Harm never got up before eleven.

The relentless downpour drummed on the roof and the wipers beat time slavishly. It was the first occasion she'd driven this car in rain. She felt secure in its familiar interior. Her wet clothes were steaming up the windows and she turned on the blower. She increased speed. Five and a half J wheels, she thought to herself. Michelins. There was no problem with grip on the bends but the leaf springs sometimes made the back end skippy. She slowed back down to thirty-five, concentrating solely on the car. Servo-assisted brakes. Fat Andy said they were responsive but they needed to be respected in the wet. She remembered seeing him in Vinny's repair shop with a high pressure airline, blowing clouds of asbestos dust out of the rear drums. She'd stepped back, worried about her lungs.

The rain started to come down even heavier. It was a wall of water. The more cowardly cars pulled up on verges and pavement kerbs. The road ran like a river and the noise inside the Lotus Cortina was deafening. Two small boys, almost naked, ran up the rushing, flooded gutter, screaming with joy.

Jaz thought of the twins. With one hand, she smoothed out their creased photo on the passenger seat. She remembered a heavy rainstorm on the farm when a broken gutter on the gable end had sent a cascade of water into the yard. Peony and Mimosa had raced in and out, cradling their pet duck, first removing their shoes, ankle deep in mud, then their coats, then their cardigans and dresses, then their underwear.

She ploughed on slowly, her wheels churning up waves that washed against the underside of the vehicle. Fat Andy had taken off the old underseal when he'd done the restoration. She made a mental note to check below for rust. When all this is over, she thought again, I'll give this car the service it deserves.

After a few minutes the rain eased. The traffic became dense and slow and the sky cleared. It was all at once sunny and hot again. Outside, the world began to steam. Jaz switched off the wipers and the blower and everything was curiously quiet. She sat in a jam. She took off the nylon bomber jacket and threw it in the back. She put on her sunglasses, avoiding the curious and admiring glances of other drivers. The mobile phone rang.

It was Trace. She was in a payphone and she sounded agitated. 'Jaz, you won't believe this. I've got the sack! This spotty bloke with a wig and tweed jacket's just been down from personnel. He said I'm a security risk.'

'What's happened?'

'I've not been paid, that's what's happened.' She broke off. Jaz could hear her voice muffled as she talked to someone else. 'Jaz, I'm going to take the money from the trolley. There's thirty pounds here in change from the teas and snacks. My friend Shirley says take the lot and scarper. She says she'll cover for me. She says she's never known the like.' Trace was excited and upset. There was more muffled conversation. 'She says the wig man has never been that abrupt with anyone before . . .'

'Tell me what happened,' Jaz interrupted.

Trace paused to collect her thoughts. 'Well, I did exactly what you said. Honest. Exactly as you said.'

'Go on.'

'I went into the fat bloke's office with tea and biscuits, although they weren't ordered. A china cup for the NTG. Top floor. Chocolate biscuits in silver paper instead of plain. Sugar in a bowl, milk in a jug. Not those little packets. I did it all right. I did it properly . . .'

'Get on with it.'

'He was in there, standing next to a filing cabinet. I just walked in. "My friend wants to talk to you," I said to him. "About your twin brother." I gave him his tea on a tray. He put it on the desk then took three biscuits and put them in his pocket. "She wants you to ring her. Write her number down," I said to him.'

'Did he do that?'

'No. He just stood there and sort of stared. He looked surprised. Then he turned around and walked out the door. I followed him but he'd disappeared. He didn't say a word. It was dead weird. I went back to my trolley downstairs and an hour later, what happens? I get the sack. It must have been him. He reported me. I don't know what I did that was so terrible. All I said was . . .' Trace was beginning to sound tearful. 'It's just so unfair . . .'

'Never mind,' said Jaz, trying to be reassuring. 'You might get back in at the Grand Banana.'

At that moment, Trace's money ran out and she hung up. As Jaz stared at the phone in her hand, inching along in the car, her foot poised above the clutch, it rang again. 'I'll meet you tonight,' said Trace. 'In the Planet Pizza. Where you were before, with the temp. Eight o'clock.' She hung up for a second time.

Frustrated by her lack of progress, Jaz turned down a side road. Poor Trace, she thought. She's upset and it's my fault. But it'll be OK. Very soon, we'll go to Weston-super-Mare. Me, Harm and Trace. She imagined a row of pastel-coloured guest houses with bright flowers in their front gardens, chintz sofas, china tea cups and plates of bread and butter. We'll go there, as Cortina crazy as can be. We'll have a good time and be happy and together again, just like we were before.

Jaz's mind kept returning to the harsh words she'd flung at Harm. She felt guilty and insecure. Life was too precarious to fall out with her friends. After all, she reasoned with herself, Harm was only trying to help. She was wrong, but her motives were pure. She dialled Harm's number at Wesley's flat.

The phone rang for a long time. Eventually Harm answered. She sounded sleepy.

'Harm? It's Jaz. Look, I'm sorry for blowing you out.' Jaz swallowed. She never found apologies easy. 'I'm sorry, right?'

Harm yawned. She didn't say anything.

'You listening? I've just said I'm sorry.' There was a silence. 'That's three times, now, altogether.'

Harm sniffed. 'It's OK.' She sounded non-committal.

Jaz's mind was buzzing. 'Listen. You remember you talked about that nutter in the East End who took me to that cinema a few years ago and threatened to kill me?'

'How could I forget?'

'They haven't let him out, have they?'

'Why?'

Jaz paused. 'I dreamed about him.'

'There's been nothing on the telly. Not while I've been off work. I would've seen it.'

'Thought not.' Jaz chewed the end of her ponytail. Several ghostly electronic voices echoed down the line.

She coughed. 'I know you think I should drop the Fat Andy thing . . .'

'Too right I do. I've never known you be so strung out, so driven, so bad tempered . . .'

'Harm, I've nearly finished. I'm nearly there. I've had a great idea. Two great ideas. I need your help.'

Harm yawned again. 'What time is it? God, it's early. What d'you mean by waking me up at this time?'

'Two ideas. Ready? I want you to come with me to see the man in the garage in Haringey. Be nice to him. You know, wear a short skirt, that kind of thing.'

Harm was suspicious. 'What for?'

'It's nothing dangerous. We'll just give him some information. A computer disk, that's all. He's a Mazda dealer. He'll use the disk to prove to the Japs that Vinny's crooked and Vinny will lose the Mazda concession. It's simple. Then it's bye-bye Vinny. No garage. No repair shop. No team of car thieves. He'll be finished. That'll be the end of the Vinny thing.'

'What about those gorillas? His bodyguards?' Harm was anxious.

'This won't involve them, I promise. We'll be nowhere near them. Or him. There's no danger.'

Harm thought for a moment. 'Why d'you need me?'

'He won't listen to me. My appearance is against me. I'm too small. He won't take me seriously.'

Harm thought for a while. 'All right, then. What's the other thing?'

'I still haven't contacted Fat Andy's twin. Trace tried but she's had no luck. You remember you said you had clients in the House of Commons? He's got an office there. Maybe you could get a message to him somehow.'

Harm sighed. 'I wish you'd drop it, really I do.'

'A few more days. I promise. Vinny'll be sorted. I'll have a mourner for Fat Andy. I'll have done it all. Then we'll go on holiday to Weston-super-Mare.'

Harm laughed. 'I saw something about it on the telly. It's . . . well, it's not Fuengirola.'

'It'll be brill. I'm really looking forward to it.' Jaz paused. 'Are you going to help me or not?'

Harm sighed and drew on her cigarette. 'Guess so.'

Jaz gave her the address in Haringey. 'I'll meet you at three, OK?'

Chapter Twenty-One

Harm arrived in Haringey in a taxi. It was very hot. She wore a skimpy white cotton top which was low-cut with hidden underwiring. Her cleavage was spectacular. Below, she had on a tight white leather mini-skirt and her legs were bare. On her feet were patent stiletto sandals. Jaz examined her face. The swelling had disappeared. Any faint bruising was now merged with her normal dusky colour. Below each plucked eyebrow, and on each ear lobe, she'd stuck tiny silver sequins. Her lips were thick crimson gloss and her braided hair was secured in a loopy bun.

The two girls went into the Mazda showroom. There was a smell of polish and new car interiors. A young man in a suit appeared. He stared at Harm as if she was an apparition.

'We want to see the boss,' said Jaz. 'Now. Immediately. No bullshit. Take us straight through.'

Still open-mouthed, glancing at Harm out of the corner of a nervous eye, he led the way to an office. He knocked on the door, gestured to two chairs in the lobby and ran off. They didn't sit down.

'Stay cool,' whispered Jaz.

After a couple of minutes the door opened. The owner looked at Harm, blinked, tried to appear composed, then smiled. He gestured for her to enter. 'What can I do for you?' he asked. His voice was practised in politeness. He seemed unaware of Jaz, as if she was a child. He sat behind his desk.

Harm grinned, showing the gap in her teeth. 'D'you mind if I sit?'

Jaz watched the manager force his eyes from her breasts to her face. He blushed. He was trying to be professional. 'No, please, go ahead.'

Harm sat down and crossed her legs. Her skirt almost disappeared.

He was a large man, about thirty-eight, overweight with a garish tie. His shirtsleeves were rolled up and his jacket was draped over the back of his chair. Two semicircles of sweat soaked below his armpits.

'Do you know Vinny Stasinopolous on the Isle of Dogs?' Jaz remained standing. She was abrupt, business-like.

The man turned to her. 'I know of him, yes. Not personally.'

'He's a crook. Bent as they come. I can prove it. You show the evidence to Mazda, they'll close him down. They'll pull the plug on him.' She paused. 'You'll have it all your own way up here, with this dealership.' She gestured towards him, palms upwards. 'You listen to me and you can take out the competition in a single stroke.'

He smiled automatically, tried to shrug, unsure of how to react. Then he looked into her eyes and realized she was serious. He was caught off guard. He had no pat phrase or cliché suitable to act as a reply.

'Are you interested in success?' Jaz went on. She held his gaze. 'Are you interested in making money?' She

ANDREA BADENOCH

removed the computer disk from her pocket. 'I'm holding your future in my hand.'

The man turned helplessly to Harm.

She grinned again. 'Don't underestimate our little friend here. She knows exactly what she's talking about.'

'Er, what . . . what is it exactly that you have there?' He stared at the disk.

Jaz took a step forward and slid it into the disk drive on the computer next to him. She switched on the machine and pressed a few keys. Columns and rows of numbers appeared. The man took a pair of half-rim spectacles from a case and put them on.

Jaz picked up a pencil and used it to point to the screen. 'These are the Dutch accounts.' She tapped knowingly.

The man inched forward, interested.

'Look,' said Jaz. 'These are cars. Here's the original registration numbers and alongside are the new ones. The cars were stolen and given new identities. The new identities came from write-offs. All the details are here. Every single one. Model and engine numbers, colours. The next column is the date they were shipped. This column here shows how much Vinny's Dutch contact paid for them. Further on is evidence of these sums being deposited into one of Vinny's bank accounts.' She scrolled down the screen. 'It's all here. Look, these are the names, addresses, phone numbers and e-mail addresses of each of Vinny's shady associates in Europe. There's evidence relating to four separate illegal operations in four countries.'

The man's eyes began to gleam. His mouth twitched expectantly.

Jaz went to the end of the disk. 'This is the best bit.

It's a record of faxes and e-mails sent via the computer for a period of six months last year. They've been saved. They have the address of the garage, everything. The names of everyone involved at the place on the Isle of Dogs.' She slapped the top of the computer. 'This is watertight, mister. You can't go wrong with this. Get this to Mazda. Download it today.'

'It'll cost you three thousand,' chipped in Harm.

Jaz turned and stared at Harm, alarmed. She hadn't intended to ask for money. She looked back at the garage owner. He hadn't flinched. He continued to stare at the screen. 'Is this genuine?' he muttered, with difficulty. He sounded as if his throat had gone tight and dry.

'Of course it is. I stole it off Vinny myself.'

He stood up and took off his glasses. He adjusted the waistband of his trousers on his belly. He suddenly become more decisive. 'Right!' he said, looking from one to the other.

Harm took a damp cigarette from between her breasts and held it up to her mouth.

The man fiddled in his pocket, produced a lighter, leaned over and lit it for her. 'Three thousand? I'll get it.'

Later, giggling and shrieking and pushing each other, the girls climbed into the Lotus Cortina. Jaz drove and Harm counted the money again. There was three thousand in new fifties. 'I didn't even have to take my clothes off!' she exclaimed. 'Bloody great!'

Jaz wound down her window and put on her sunglasses. 'One man went to mow,' she started singing, unaccountably. 'Went to mow a meadow. One man went to mow, went to mow a meadow.' She laughed again.

'Harm, you must take half the dosh. I couldn't have got in there without you.'

'Nicking things and flogging things. It's your line of work, not mine. You keep it. You deserve it.'

Jaz remembered Trace's phone call. 'Fancy an Italian meal later?'

'Sorry, I'm meeting Wesley. It's back to the grindstone. It's the funeral directors and crematorium operatives conference at Earl's Court. Opening night tonight. He's got me a full schedule. It'll be a busy couple of days.'

At ten past eight, Trace still hadn't shown up. Jaz took out the mobile phone and rang Vinny.

'Yes?' he answered, sounding weary.

'Is that you, slimeball?' asked Jaz. 'My little companero? Guess what? Mazda's got your disk. The one Fat Andy pinched, with all your fucking European contacts. The one you killed him for.' She paused. 'Have a nice evening.' She hung up.

The waitress arrived and she ordered a pizza margherita, tomato salad and a Kaliber. At eight thirty, Jaz saw Trace's head bobbing behind a queue at the door. She beckoned and waved. Trace walked towards her, tall and gawky. She was accompanied, two steps behind, by the temp from Charles Merchant's office, who was still wearing her red blazer, but appeared less purposeful. Neither of them smiled. They sat down. Trace looked anxious and the woman had a guarded, impassive expression, as if she had no desire to be in their company, but would rather be on a train, returning to Malcolm in

High Wycombe. Unlike the last time, she pushed the menu away, declining food and wine.

'We've both got the sack,' said Trace.

Jaz looked at the woman.

She stared at the paper tablecloth. Her lips were tight.

'They know you talked to me?' Jaz was curious.

The woman shook her head.

'It's not that,' interrupted Trace, 'I think they're clamping down on temporary staff . . .'

'It's bigger than both of you,' said the woman suddenly. 'This is bigger than any little cat and mouse game you two have decided to play. There's something going on here. It involves at least two people at the highest level of government. It's to do with Charles Merchant's policy ideas and his new deal for Clean Cities. Something's happened which is holding things up. I know. I made . . . certain discoveries.'

'Why did you get the push?' asked Jaz.

Her reply was hasty and defensive. 'I sent two e-mails, that's all. Two e-mails to a lobby correspondent. Nothing directly incriminating. Next thing I know, I'm out on my ear. No references. I'm finished at the agency. I've got no job and my house is ransacked.'

'Oh, no!' exclaimed Trace, as empathic as ever. 'Really? I didn't know that last bit. I'm sorry . . .'

'I phoned my husband half an hour ago. He was out playing golf. Came home to absolute chaos. Nothing's been taken, no valuables. It's a warning.' She stood up. 'I've got to go.'

'Thanks for telling me,' said Jaz mildly. She wasn't sympathetic. She felt sure the woman had been observed pilfering documents. It never pays to get caught, she thought. Careless. There was nothing mysterious about her dismissal. Jaz looked at her. She wasn't really interested in her problems. Her mind was full of what she'd done today to Vinny.

'You stay out of this,' the woman warned Jaz. 'That's why I've come here with your friend tonight. If anyone asks, you've never met me. You never gave me money. Keep your distance. There's something dangerous in the air.' She pushed a piece of paper across the table towards Jaz. 'That's my contact at the House. He used to drink with Charles Merchant occasionally at their club. Apparently, they were at university together. I don't want it. I'm well out of all this.' In an instant, she'd disappeared.

'I think I'll have a pizza,' said Trace, staring at the menu. She hadn't been listening. She seemed unconcerned. Now that the woman had gone, she'd forgotten her. She was shedding her experience at the Home Office like a discarded skin. 'Have you got any money, Jaz? I didn't take the trolley money in the end. It seemed like stealing. I'm skint and I'm starving. The food in here smells so nice. Have you got enough for a deep pan vegetarian deluxe? And garlic bread? And a tiramisu?'

Chapter Twenty-Two

Jaz spent the night in the car in Lincoln's Inn Fields. She didn't sleep much. The near-death experience in the Citroën had made her nervous. She knew she should be anonymous and untraceable, but her enemies were cunning. Harm had promised never to speak to Pete again, but the thought of him made her jumpy.

Early next morning, Jaz went for a run. The exertion, combined with the soft light, the gentle murmur of London stirring from sleep, the faint breeze rippling the grey silk of the river – all of this made her happy. She jogged along the embankment, her hand pressed to her chest. The pain was still there, she decided, it still ached. She knew that if she concentrated hard and brought to mind the images of Fat Andy and Blow, then she could still feel sad and abandoned. However, her fury was ebbing. With each act of revenge against Vinny, the anger had shrunk. It was like closing windows against a storm.

Later, she drove east. She parked two streets away from Ronnie and Reggie's gym and approached it cautiously. At the back, there were no vehicles in the car park. The door above the fire escape was closed and padlocked. She walked around the front. The glass entrance was locked and barred with metal grilles. A notice in familiar handwriting was taped to the window.

It said 'Shut Temparrarily'. She stared at it, unable to resist a grin.

A passer-by stopped and spoke. 'Been closed a day or two,' he offered.

Jaz turned to him.

He was tall and black and wearing a football strip. He carried a Head bag. 'I got a letter.' He shrugged. 'Everyone got one. We're all going to another place, down on Commercial Road. It's better, as it happens. Try it. More machines. More staff.' He nodded and carried on his way.

Jaz got back in the car and headed south-east, down to the Isle of Dogs. As she approached Vinny's garage, she slowed. A huge transporter was parked on the forecourt and three men in yellow overalls were driving the brand new Mazdas out of the showroom and up its metal ramps. They're here, she thought. They didn't waste time. The space was already almost cleared. Two salesmen in suits stood by helplessly. They looked perplexed. One attempted to remonstrate, but quickly gave up. Jaz was cautious, but there was no sign of Vinny.

He's finished, she decided. She pressed her chest. Yes, the pain was definitely going. She turned into the alley behind the main building. The repair and body shops were a blackened shell without a roof. There was a lingering smell of burning, and sooty flakes drifted in the air. Jaz wound up her window, wrinkling her nose. A small boy rode a bicycle across the cobbles. She moved over to avoid him and he gestured obscenely. You too, Jaz muttered at him. You too, sonny. She smiled at the ruined buildings. And all the rest of you. You fucking bastards.

*

Jaz bought a bacon sandwich from a kerbside vendor and parked up beside the Thames to eat it. On the opposite bank, cranes dipped and swivelled. The Millennium Dome squatted like a bug, its thin insect legs at rest. Small, buzzing launches and tugs busied about. There was a squeal of gulls and a low, occasional boom coming from down river. Jaz had heard this sound many times, but couldn't identify it. It was too deep to be explosives, too irregular to be any kind of a warning. It was something mysterious, to do with shipping, she decided. Commerce. Trading. Work. It was something from the real world.

Her mind wandered. She recalled an afternoon on the farm when she was thirteen years old. It was towards the end of her time there, in April, but spring, always late on that inhospitable hillside, was more delayed than usual. The ground was hard, still frozen in sheltered places, and the weather had been unusually dry. The grass was sparse and any buds on the wind-damaged trees were brown and firmly closed. It was cold and dreary. The seasons held their breath. The country-side was bound in chains.

Jasmine trudged along, checking the sheep. She was wearing worn-out wellingtons and an old car coat of Blow's. Her hair was tousled and pushed inside her collar. She carried a hazel wand. The sky was patchy with broken cloud and a thin, reluctant sun touched the desolate fields. It glittered on the back windows of the hilltop farmhouse. There were no birds, except for a solitary crow, hovering above the chimney pots. Lambing was almost over. She'd managed it on her own. A few remaining ewes were still in the shed and she went in to water them. It was warm inside and dark with the smell

of animals and hay. A shuffling alerted her. One of the
sheep was giving birth. She stood alongside, watching
the bluish-red slimy lamb emerge from its mother. Halfway, it stopped. The ewe moaned a little and stamped.
Jasmine tugged on the lamb gently and it came away,
plopping onto the straw. There was a smell of blood and
dung. She knew immediately that it wasn't right. It had
an odd, twisted shape and its face was tight shut. It didn't
move. She picked it up and there was no breath, no pulse
of life. It was deformed and stillborn. Jasmine put it to
one side and went to a neighbouring pen. Here the sheep
had twin lambs. She picked up one of them and carried
it over, giving it to the unlucky ewe. The baby bleated for
an instant, then began suckling, whilst the blank face of
the bereaved mother showed nothing but resignation.

Leaving the shed, Jasmine tossed the corpse onto a
pile of debris behind the abandoned stable. She heard an
engine and spotted a Royal Mail van swirling in a hasty
U-turn outside the front door of the house. It skidded,
then tore down the track towards the road, hooting at
Peony and Mimosa. Jasmine watched as it disappeared
in the direction of the village.

Later, as the pale sun started to sink in the sky, there
was the sound of an explosion. It was too low and too
long to be gunshot. Then there was another. Jasmine
hurried towards the twins. They were down the track,
out on the ridge at the same spot where Jasmine had
once sent the curate's motorcycle over the drop. She
knew what they were doing. They were throwing bombs.

Peony and Mimosa had a pile of their mother's old
wine bottles, a bucket and a siphon. One by one, they
were filling the bottles with liquid from the bucket, then
hurling them into space, where they took several seconds

to plummet towards the boulders of the scanty stream. As each bottle fell they yelled a strange incantation. 'Un-tah, un-tah, billie rosie ply,' they called in unison. When it hit the earth, it shattered and a ball of flame rose eerily, before dying. Then there was a deep, dull boom. 'Yes-sah, yes-sah, yes-sah,' they called as the ghostly and terrifying disturbance rent the still air.

Jasmine watched them. She knew they'd mixed weed-killer with sugar and that the unstable concoction was very dangerous, but it was pointless telling them to stop. They were exorcizing their own private demons in their own determined way. They drained the dregs into the last bottle. Peony threw it and unlike the others it climbed high into the air. At that moment there was a scream. It came from the house. Jasmine turned and ran up the slope, the twins following. Behind them, the final bomb burst noisily in the dying afternoon. As they entered the yard there was a succession of wild calls from within. It was Lola.

Jasmine crashed into the kitchen, the twins hard on her heels. Lola was standing at the sink, the sharp carving knife aloft. Her stained nightdress was undone. In her other hand was a letter. She screamed again. The cry was hysterical, forced, over-dramatic.

'Put that knife down,' said Jasmine in an authoritative tone.

Lola turned and saw her three children. Her eyes changed. They had been dead and lifeless. Suddenly they went black, hard and full of something that Jasmine could not name. She screamed again and this time her voice was full of pain. It was a wail of hopelessness and despair.

Jasmine took a step forwards. Lola spun in a pirou-ette, wielding the knife. She slapped her letter down on the table. Glancing at its logo, Jasmine could tell it was from the bank. Her eyes fixed on her mother's face. There was a frozen moment when no one made a sound. The wall clock ticked and some embers shifted in the stove.

'Mam,' said one of the twins.

'Stop it, Mam,' added the other. They sounded scared.

Lola screamed again and with a strange twisting gesture thrust the knife in and through her long, tangled hair. A clump of it came away like a matted, dead creature. She threw this on the floor then dashed to her bedroom. The girls followed, to find her breathless, frantic, slashing the grubby sheets, the down-filled coverlet, the pillows. The overheated air was filled with a billow of fake snow.

Jasmine grabbed each of her sisters by the hand. She dragged them forwards. Together, they pounced on Lola, forcing her forwards onto the bed. Jasmine grabbed the knife. 'Sit on her!' she ordered. She ran into the hall, grabbed a bottle from the cupboard under the stairs and threw it onto the bed. 'Right, come on!'

The twins jumped down, linked hands and made for the door. Swearing under her breath, Jasmine bundled them into the hall, grabbed the key and locked the door from the outside. They leaned together in a huddle, panting. After a while, Lola started crying. They heard her pour herself a drink.

'Where's Blow?' whispered Peony.

'We need him,' agreed Mimosa.

'He's coming,' Jasmine assured them. She tried to sound normal. 'He'll be back. He'll sort her out.'

*

In the Lotus Cortina, Jaz's mobile phone rang. It was Harm. 'I've moved into a hotel in Earl's Court. Just for a while. Wesley's little place was making me depressed. It's called the Kyle of Lockalsh.' She sounded breathless. 'I've managed to get discount from the owner. He's a Scotsman, only he's from Birmingham. He's called Mr McTavish and he's very friendly. Plays the bagpipes.'

'Right,' said Jaz, her mouth full of food. She jotted down the address and telephone number.

'It's really handy at the moment,' added Harm, 'you know, business-wise. The Exhibition Centre's booked solid for weeks.'

Jaz swallowed. 'Harm, when you've got time, and if you happen to be in the vicinity of . . .'

'I know,' Harm interrupted, 'the House of Commons. I haven't forgotten. Charles Merchant. Check him out and tell him you want to talk to him.'

'I don't think you'll get to him, Harm. Honest. He's just not . . . accessible.'

'I'll try.'

Jaz sighed. 'I don't think he's into vice.'

Harm thought for a moment. Jaz heard her light a cigarette. 'What is he into? He must be into something.'

'Changing the world.'

Harm was silent.

'I'll tell you what. Try this guy.' Jaz gave her the name of the lobby correspondent supplied by the sacked temp the previous night in Planet Pizza. 'He's an old friend of Merchant's. He might help.'

There was a pause while Harm made a note of this. Jaz imagined her writing the name in biro on her wrist. 'By the way,' Harm added, 'our Trace is here.'

'Where?'

'This hotel, where I'm staying. She's living in, full board. I recommended her. She's assistant breakfast chef and relief waitress. She's got to wear a kilt.' Harm laughed. 'She's just been trying it on, looks a right dickhead. See you, Jaz. Bye bye.'

Later, Jaz drove over to Earl's Court. She found the hotel without too much difficulty and parked in the small space reserved for patrons at the rear. She was still hungry, so without checking in, she went to find a McDonald's where she ate a Happy Meal and drank Coke. Afterwards, she picked up her sports bag from the car and entered reception. The place had a mock-Highland atmosphere with tartan sofas and curtains, travel posters of Loch Lomond and a moth-eaten deer's head, with antlers, mounted on the wall. A tape played a keyboard version of 'Mull of Kintyre'. She rang the bell.

Suddenly, there was a menacing, low growl. Jaz took two steps backwards. A huge dog appeared from around the desk, its hackles raised. Her heart began pounding. She grasped her sports bag in front of her and held out a hand to fend it off. 'Go away,' she whispered. The dog's lips moved back revealing rows of enormous teeth. Saliva hung from its jaws. It was as high as her elbow with a chest like a barrel. It advanced towards her, its growl deepening.

'Rocky!' A man appeared. He was grinning. 'Rocky, come away!'

The dog glanced at him and wagged its tail. It looked Jaz in the eye conspiratorially, and its tongue lolled out in friendly greeting.

Jaz placed her bag on the floor.

Mr McTavish was burly and Scottish-looking with a

full ginger beard. 'Sorry about Rocky,' he grinned. 'He's an actor.'

Jaz smiled weakly.

'He went to animal drama school in Haslemere. Been on lots of telly. *The Bill*, *EastEnders*. He was quite a star, a while back. He's retired now but he still likes to tread the boards, so to speak. Trying to appear hard.'

'Mr McTavish?' Jaz picked up her bag and motioned towards the register. She was relieved to discover that he was wearing ordinary clothes. There was no sign of his bagpipes. She checked in, making sure she had her own bathroom, and he handed her a key.

Upstairs, she found that her room was tiny and plain, but very neat. There were framed prints of Ben Nevis and a small plaster bust of Robbie Burns. She closed the curtains, undressed and using the complimentary bath gel washed her underwear, socks and T-shirt, hanging them on the towel rail to dry. She showered and changed her clothes. She flicked through the TV channels, but there was nothing worth watching. She dried her hair then opened the curtains and looked at the Lotus Cortina, parked below at the back. She decided it too was in need of attention. One of its quarter bumpers was at a slightly low angle. Also, it wasn't absolutely clean. She borrowed a couple of towels from her bathroom. Back downstairs, she found Trace hoovering the lobby.

'Where's your kilt?' she asked.

Trace grinned, switching off the machine. 'I don't wear it for cleaning, it's for waiting on tables, at breakfast. I've got a tartan hat as well. It's quite nice. The man's just been showing me how to make real porridge.' She yawned. 'He says it's an art rather than a science. What're you doing here?'

'I'm a guest. I just passed the initiation test. I've met the dog.'

Trace laughed.

'I need to wash the car. Can you bring me out a bucket of hot soapy water in about fifteen minutes?'

Outside, Jaz rummaged in the boot. Fat Andy had kept it well supplied. She sprayed WD40 behind the chrome bumper bolts and worked the nuts free. Using a small hydraulic jack, placed on a block of wood for height, she pressed the bumper back into position and fastened the nuts. She walked around the car. The rubbers around the front and rear windscreens were dull and grey. She scrubbed them vigorously with T-Cut then ran the cloth over the glass. Andy had told her not to do this, but she'd always found it brought them up to a shine.

Trace arrived with the hot water. 'Can't stop hoovering,' she said. 'I'm trying to make a good impression.'

Using a hotel towel, Jaz splashed the suds onto the rubbers and washed off a layer of slime. She then soaped the windows, rubbing them thoroughly, before washing and rinsing the whole car. The bird shit she'd picked up in the East End had burned into the cellulose paint. This was upsetting, but, she decided, hardly noticeable. Using the second towel, she dried the car quickly, avoiding smears. She then applied Turtle Wax to the rubbers and they came up black and glossy. Using a soft cloth from the boot, she polished the entire vehicle, buffing up the chrome until it dazzled. When she'd finished, the car shone like a jewel. She stood back, satisfied. A young man walking on the pavement behind the parking area called out, 'Brilliant nick.'

Jaz nodded to him, pleased. Replacing the tins, cloth and jack in the boot, she came across a chrome pipe. She realized it was a tail pipe extension which Fat Andy had never fitted to the exhaust. She shoved it on and tightened the nut. It looked shiny and neat. She walked around the Lotus Cortina several times. 'I love you, baby,' she said.

Chapter Twenty-Three

At seven o'clock, Jaz leaned against the mantelpiece in the small TV room off the reception area, watching *Wheel of Fortune*. The atmosphere smelled of pipe tobacco and air freshener. She picked up a small plastic dome and shook it. Inside, fake snow whirled around a garish model of a highland piper, standing alongside a bright blue loch. The words Fort William were inscribed on the base. She replaced it and turned towards the outside door as it swung open then banged closed.

Harm came in with a client. She saw Jaz and pulled a rueful face. She held up all her fingers twice to indicate that she would be twenty minutes. She pressed the buttons on the lift. Jaz noticed her companion was sombre. He wore a dark, old-fashioned suit and carried a hat. He's probably an undertaker, she remembered.

Her mind leaped to an image of Fat Andy in an outsize coffin. He was muffled in a white shroud, his hands arranged as if in prayer, but blood, insistent and bright, soaked through the draperies at his neck. His face was waxen, his eyes closed. He looked very unlike the corpse in the flat in Peckham. Somewhere in the background, in shadowy, religious darkness, hymns were playing. She pressed her chest. 'Andy,' she muttered aloud. He didn't seem real.

Jaz went to find Trace. She was drinking tea and eating ginger snaps in the kitchen with Mr McTavish. At seven forty-five the three girls met in the lobby. They linked arms and, giggling, piled out into the street. 'Let's get the Lotus Cortina,' suggested Jaz. 'I've just cleaned it. It looks fab.'

'Let's go up west,' agreed Trace.

Harm relaxed in the back, the inflatable cushion behind her head, smoking and dabbing her armpits and chest with French perfume. Trace fiddled with the radio, tuning into a disco beat. It was a Celine Dion dance mix. She shook her arms and shoulders. 'Let's go clubbing,' she suggested. She rapped on the dashboard. 'Party! Party! Party!'

Driving up the Brompton Road towards Knightsbridge, Jaz felt excited. She put on her sunglasses. The car purred contentedly. Its steady rhythms were almost sexual. Her feet caressed the pedals in an effortless heel-toe. Her left hand grazed the gear change like a lover. She felt her skin prickle and her heart thud with anticipation. This is just like old times, she thought. This is the old days. In a place in her brain beyond the jangle of the car radio, she heard Blow's song. Do wah diddy diddy, she hummed to herself. Dum diddy do.

Harm reapplied her make-up and sprayed her dreadlocks with glitter.

'Watch the headlining!' said Jaz. 'Bloody hell!'

Trace sang along to the Bee Gees, getting the words wrong. Complaining of the heat, they both took their tops off. Jaz glanced at them appreciatively. Harm now wore a black silk bustier embroidered with pearls. Trace sported a blue cotton crop top which revealed her long, concave stomach above the waistband of her jeans.

All the windows were open and the warm evening carried both the smell and the light of the city. The sun dropped low over Hammersmith. This is why I came here, Jaz thought, this is why I ran away. For a moment she forgot Fat Andy, Blow, Vinny and the rest. She was more than happy.

They parked in Soho and Jaz disabled the Lotus Cortina. Harm rummaged in her bag for some dangly earrings and put them in. Trace took off her shoes and left them in the car because the pavements were hot and smooth. Two young beggars approached them warily. They were wearing Manchester United strips and their faces were tanned. Harm gave them a pack of cigarettes.

They walked up Old Compton Street, holding hands. Harm waved cheerfully at a group of gay friends. They went into a bar. Harm ordered cigarettes, strawberry daiquiris, vodka tonics and a jug of lime and soda for Jaz. She paid with a hundred-pound note from inside her bra. 'This is undertaker's money,' she told the barman. 'This is proceeds from a brass-trimmed oak coffin.' He smiled at her with tolerance and bewilderment. He gave her a free bowl of tortilla chips.

After half an hour they moved to a café, then a pub, then another bar, then another. Harm and Trace's taste for exotic cocktails seemed to grow. They ordered blue fizzy ones, purple fruity ones, and tall ones decorated with plumage and pomegranate slices. Jaz stuck to soda water. At ten o'clock, in Wardour Street, they jostled into a Greek restaurant and squeezed around a window table. Here, they mopped up oily feta cheese, olives and sweet tomatoes with hunks of warm bread. Harm called for Retsina. She was quite drunk and loud but the waiters encouraged her. They brought her a leather bottle with tassles, on which was inscribed, incongruously, 'A Present From Barcelona'. She stood up, trying to drink by throwing back her head and squirting the wine into her mouth. It went everywhere, soaking her hair and bare shoulders. Trace shrieked and Jaz pretended to cover her face with her hands. It seemed like the whole restaurant was looking at them, grinning. A Greek man with an accordion came across to their table and Trace clapped her hands in time to his folk tunes. When he finished she shouted, 'Do you know this one?' She started singing huskily. The song was something about innocence, guilt and road rage. Harm latched onto this and started up the chorus with Trace, her voice a high, trilling soprano. The waiters started singing, the accordion player picked up the tune and the people on the next table started swaying, holding up their glasses, chanting in unison. The atmosphere was electric.

Jaz stood up and made for the toilets. As she passed through the tables she heard tipsy couples in the queue join in the song. Smiling, her mind full of the catchy chorus, she turned a corner and then stopped in her tracks. Her heart missed a beat. Tucked away out of sight, behind a dense artificial palm, his head propped in his monkey hands, sat Vinny. Instantly she moved out of his line of vision. Stay calm, she murmured. She took in the scene. He was oblivious to the hilarity at the other end of the room. He was wearing an oyster linen suit with a diamond tiepin and his hair was slicked back and oily, but he seemed tired and worn, his face grey, thin, lined. The deep channels down the sides of his cheeks looked gouged out by tears. He appeared shrunken and ill.

He was accompanied by a teenage boy of such

exceptional beauty that Jaz at first thought he was a girl. He had black curly hair, jutting cheekbones and a full, pouting mouth. He was wearing a matador's embroidered bolero. He looked bored. Vinny was talking, his voice low, his gestures intense. His companion hid a yawn behind his elegant hand.

At that moment, Vinny's mobile rang. It lay on the table next to his sleeve. He stared at it anxiously.

Jaz stood very still, smiling. He thinks it's me, she thought.

Vinny picked up the phone and seemed relieved. He issued a couple of orders and stood up to leave. Jaz stepped into an alcove. Vinny dropped two banknotes on the table and emerged. 'I'll see you later, back at the flat,' he said to the boy. Jaz noticed his wandering, squinty eye. He smoothed the sides of his head with both hands and nodded to a waiter. 'Put it on my account,' he said. He disappeared out the door.

Jaz watched the boy. Stay focused, she thought. He picked up the tenners then dropped them again. He seemed unhappy and resigned. She approached his table and sat down. He glanced at her and hastily pocketed the money. He looked suspicious.

'Hi,' Jaz grinned. Stay cool, she told herself. 'You don't remember me, do you?'

The boy shook his head. She noticed his eyes were large and brown, his lashes long. His strong cleft chin was unshaven.

'We met at a wedding or something,' she lied. 'Not long ago. Why don't you come and join me and my friends?' She gestured towards the noisy end of the restaurant. 'We're just relaxing after a hard day's work.' She stood up and he followed through the narrow spaces between tables. 'I'm Jaz, by the way.'

If the name meant anything to him, it didn't show in his face. He was impassive. 'I'm Pedro,' he offered, 'but you can call me Trevor.' He had a cockney accent.

Jaz pulled over a chair for him. Harm and Trace had stopped singing and the accordion player resumed his normal repertoire. Harm called for another bottle and another glass. The restaurant was even more noisy and crowded than before. In the opposite corner, a birthday gathering fired party poppers and opened champagne.

'This is Trevor,' Jaz said. She introduced her two friends.

Trace regarded him with interest. 'I like your Spanish waistcoat,' she said.

Later, standing outside in the street, a faint breeze warming their skin like a kiss, the foursome discussed what to do. Harm leaned drunkenly against Jaz, smoking a cigarette, her arm round her neck. Trace held onto a road sign with Trevor politely supporting her elbow. 'Lessgo dancing,' she suggested. 'I wanna dansh with this bullfighter.'

In the end they went to a club below the pavement, somewhere off Piccadilly. Harm knew the doormen and they got in for free. She pointed at Jaz. 'She's twenty-one,' she insisted.

Inside, Harm ordered grappas, Pernods and a jug of watery Sangria. 'Come on,' insisted Trace, dragging Trevor onto the dance floor. They disappeared in a press of bodies and flashing lights.

'Trace seems quite keen on him,' Jaz shouted above the music.

'She never follows through,' Harm replied. 'Just you watch.'

At about four a.m. Harm was asleep, snoring, lying out on the red plush bench seat. Trace was slumped forwards, her head in her arms, in a puddle on the table.

'Know Vinny well?' Jaz asked Trevor.

'Quite well,' he answered tonelessly. He looked at his watch. 'Shit,' he muttered.

'You late for Vinny?' Jaz persisted.

'Yeah.'

'Why don't you forget fucking Vinny and come home with us?'

Trevor tried to laugh. 'No can do.'

'Owns you, does he?'

He scowled and stared into his half empty glass. He looked at Jaz. 'Who are you anyway?'

'I'm Vinny's bad fairy.' She paused. 'I'm trouble.' She gave him a hard stare. 'I'm Jaz.' She stood up and delved in the front pocket of her jeans, then drew out a wad of money rolled in a brown envelope. It was the pay-off from the Mazda garage in Haringey. 'There's three thousand here. You can have it if you come home with us. If you dump Vinny. That is, permanently.'

Trevor's big eyes opened very wide.

Jaz peeled off the envelope, revealing a bundle of notes. 'You want it or not?'

He reached out his hand tentatively.

Jaz pulled the mobile phone out of the pocket of her denim jacket. She pressed a few numbers and waited. A lazy ballad played on the jukebox. 'Vinny? Companero?'

She gave a short laugh. 'Jaz here. Listen, you slimeball. I've got someone with me who wants to speak to you.'

She passed the phone to Trevor. He looked uncertain. He held it in the palm of his hand, as if unsure what to do with it.

'Go on, tell him.' She put the money on the wet, crowded table next to Trace and moved it a little towards him.

'Vin?' Trevor said. 'It's Pedro. I'm in a night club.' There was a silence as Vinny responded. He grimaced as if in pain. 'That's the thing, Vin. You've got it there, mate. I'm not coming back.' He looked at Jaz and shrugged. 'No, I'm not. That's just how it is. Sorry and all that.' He leaned back in his chair, scratching his balls, feigning unconcern. Jaz imagined Vinny remonstrating in his ear. Trevor picked up the money in one hand, weighed it in his fingers, fanned it, then in a deft gesture, folded it. 'And you,' he said firmly into the phone. 'You too, mate.' He switched off the phone and handed it back to her. His expression was unreadable. He pocketed the money. 'Right,' he exclaimed, his face brightening. He stood up. 'Let's get these two sleeping beauties into a cab or something. Where are we headed, exactly?'

Chapter Twenty-Four

The next day, Trace had a bad hangover. She offered to clean the hotel windows as penance for missing the breakfast rota. Mr McTavish said it was just as well he liked her, or she would have been out on her ear. Jaz, without confidence, took Rocky for a walk. Harm and Trevor each stayed in their rooms all day. Harm slept with her phone turned off and Trevor watched Sky Sports.

Jaz tried to ring Charles Merchant a few times, with no success. She drove over to the Chelsea mews and talked to the porter again. He was sympathetic but unable to help. She left another note then sat around waiting outside in the car for a few hours. He didn't show.

She opened her sports bag and took out her photo of the twins. For the umpteenth time she noted how their angel costumes did nothing to disguise the wilfulness in their eyes. Peony looked ready for anything. Mimosa held onto the hem of her sister's dress, clearly trying to suppress a giggle. I miss you, Jaz thought. She wondered who had cast them in the nativity play. They hardly ever went to school. That teacher, she decided, whoever she was, clearly had a sense of humour.

Jaz went back to Earl's Court, dispirited. She wished she'd given Trevor less money. She'd been over-generous, but then she hadn't known if he'd rise to the bait. She still had some of Elvis's cash, but it was leaking away. She didn't want to be facing penury. She'd had too much of that when she'd arrived in London. Bread-line poverty was difficult. It presented far too many challenges.

She knocked on the door of Trevor's room. She didn't intend asking for the money back, but she wanted to be sure he was keeping his side of the bargain. 'Come in!' Trace called.

Jaz was surprised to see Trace sitting in the window, swathed in a towel, having her hair cut. Trevor stood behind her, holding a silver tail comb and scissors, snipping at her shapeless wet locks. He looked confident and professional. He tilted her head forwards. Jaz noticed that he was tall and lean, wearing Levis and an acid yellow shirt which made his perfect complexion glow.

'Trevor's been telling me his life story,' Trace said. 'He was a trainee stylist.'

'I should never have left.' He paused, snipping carefully. 'Soho was a bad scene,' he added. 'Old men with old dicks. Everybody on the make.'

Jaz looked around. The room was full of half unpacked clothes, CDs, and hairdressing magazines. She was relieved. He'd moved in. 'You're not going back to Vinny then? It's bye-bye, Soho?' She hesitated. 'Bye-bye, Pedro?'

'Bye-bye, Pedro,' echoed Trace.

'I've made up my mind.' He bent his knees and manoeuvred his scissors around Trace's ears. 'I'm going back to hairdressing. I've got creative urges. I'll learn tinting and perming.' He said this without irony.

Jaz realized in an instant that he was a simple soul. Despite his sensational beauty, he was straightforward and honest, like Trace. He wasn't devious. He would keep his word. This meant Vinny was now without his lover. Vinny had lost everything. She turned to leave the room.

'There's been some people here looking for you,' said Trevor.

She stopped in her tracks. 'Who?'

'First of all, a tall guy. He looked familiar. I think I saw him working as a mechanic at Vinny's garage.'

'Oh, him!' Trace snorted. 'He's always after her!'

'Was it him, Trace?'

'Dunno. I didn't see him. Did he have ginger hair?'

'Ginger ponytail. I was careful, Jaz. I always am. I told him you'd left. He said he'd seen the car and jumped into a taxi and followed it. He'd tried every guest house in the road.'

Jaz felt a rush of panic. Pete had betrayed her so often. 'So he knows I'm here.'

'No. I was quite clear. You were here, but you'd left.'

'Is he going to go back to Vinny and tell him where you are? Is Vinny going to come and get you?'

'No, calm down. Definitely not. He didn't know me. I'm not sure he's ever seen me before. I just remember him, in his overalls. I was waiting for Vinny in the office once, watching him under the bonnet of a car. I thought he was sexy.'

'He is,' agreed Trace, 'but silly old Jaz thinks he's a wanker and a liar.'

Jaz gulped. 'Who else was here?'

'Two heavy-looking guys.'

'Oh, my God. Brothers? Bald heads? Flash clothes?'

'No . . .' Trevor thought for a moment. 'One was fair, the other dark. They were wearing jeans and bomber jackets.'

'Well, who the hell were they?'

'No idea. I didn't like the look of them. I told them I'd never heard of you.'

The next morning, Trace served Jaz with porridge in the dining room. She was wearing her Scottish outfit.

'Take your hat off a minute,' suggested Jaz. 'Let's see your hair.'

It was very short and stylishly rumpled.

'Fantastic,' said Jaz enthusiastically.

'He's good,' agreed Trace. 'He trained with Antoine at Fabio's.' She frowned, puzzled. 'Whoever that might be.'

'Are you two . . . you know . . .' Jaz waggled her hand suggestively.

Trace blushed. She picked up her tray. 'Sort of . . .' she offered, very embarrassed. 'We haven't done anything yet. You know. Apart from kissing. Trevor says we have too many wounds which need time to heal.'

Jaz nodded seriously.

'He says we should take time to get to know each other. To establish absolute equality and trust.' She repeated these words like an innocent child.

'I'm sure he's right.' Jaz stirred her porridge vigorously. 'You should speak to Wesley.'

Trace went back to the kitchen.

Mr McTavish appeared. 'Excuse me, madam.' His eyes twinkled. 'You're wanted on the phone.'

It was Harm. Jaz heard her yawn. 'Is it really morning?' she asked. 'I'm at the House of Commons with Wesley. I've had quite a heavy night.' She sounded tired. 'Turns out, would you believe, Wesley actually knows this lobby correspondent person. I mentioned it to him, and then, when I was through with my last client, I found them together in the bar. They used to play squash or something. We've all been having a drink.' She yawned again. 'They've just been discussing how their jobs are exactly the same.' She sighed. 'It's all a bit above my head.'

Jaz was excited. 'Have you asked him about Charles Merchant?'

'Not really, but he's prepared to see you.'

'When?'

She heard a muffled exchange. 'He's going to get his head down for a bit. He'll meet you at two. His house.' She gave Jaz the address.

Jaz parked the Lotus Cortina at the end of a row of polite, tiny Victorian houses in Lambeth. She glanced along the terrace. The restored shutters, the immaculate paint-work, the cultivated postage stamp gardens all suggested gentrification. So close to central London, these bijou residences were probably all worth a fortune.

She tugged the old-fashioned bell-pull of number four-teen. She took off her sunglasses. A small, dapper man answered the door. His automatic smile was immediately replaced by a look of astonishment.

'I think you're expecting me,' Jaz said.

He stood aside to let her in. He was only two or three inches taller than herself, and clearly surprised by her appearance.

Jaz had seen this consternation many times. She knew he assumed she was very young. He thinks I'm about fourteen, Jaz thought. She decided to gamble on this misconception. If he thinks I'm a child, she reasoned, he won't find me threatening. Stay calm, she thought. He'll think I'm innocent and this will help me get to

Merchant. 'I'm glad you've agreed to see me,' she chirped in her pretend, little-girl voice. She sounded slightly breathless. 'I won't take up too much of your time.'

They went into the living room. It was sparsely furnished in bachelor style, with leather furniture, a good hi-fi, black wooden shelving units and matching coffee table.

'Would you like a drink?'

'Got a can?'

'Coke? Lemonade?'

'Anything.'

He disappeared and returned with a glass, a can of lemonade and a large gin and tonic for himself. 'Sit down.'

Jaz sat on the sofa and studied him for an instant. Stay focused, she told herself. He was about forty-five, very boyish, with an unexceptional face and a neat, undersized body. His fair hair was thinning and he wore gold wire glasses. He seemed uneasy.

'Wesley's a friend of yours, is he?' she said, making conversation.

He shrugged and smiled, then took a big swig from his glass.

Jaz poured her drink and tossed the can into a metal waste bin. There was a noisy clatter. She decided to get straight to the point. 'I want to speak to Charles Merchant. It's no big deal, but it's a personal matter. I need to see him face to face. Half an hour, fifteen minutes, maybe, that's all, then I'll disappear. I've not been able to get in touch with him. I was hoping you might be able to help.'

He was staring at her.

'As I said, it's a personal matter. It's nothing to do with his job, Home Office policy, any of that kind of stuff . . .'

He removed some newspapers from the sofa and sat down next to her, even though there were two empty armchairs. He smelled of gin and scent. Jaz resisted the urge to slide along the seat, away from him.

'Can you help me or not?'

He gave her a sideways glance. 'That depends,' he muttered. 'Wesley told me you're a friend of . . . what's her name? Harm?'

'That's right.'

'Are you . . .?' He hesitated. 'In the same line of work?'

Jaz felt a lead weight sink to her stomach. Stay cool, she told herself. She wasn't going to prise anything out of him for free. She thought about getting up and walking out, but then she remembered Vinny, his unattractive squint, and how close she was to ending this whole damned thing. I'm nearly there, she thought, I'm just about finished. It's nearly over. Very soon I'll be on holiday. She imagined the repetitive wash-wash of the sea, the clean air, the ribbed, glittering sand.

She took a deep breath. 'Yes,' she lied.

He leaned over and cautiously put his arm around her.

'How old are you?'

'Old enough,' she piped childishly. Let's get it over with, she thought. She stood up, grasped his hand and pulled him to his feet.

Wordlessly, he led her to the bedroom. He closed the curtains and turned to face her in the gloom.

Quickly, she took off her clothes and climbed in between the bed covers. He joined her, fully dressed. 'I never expected . . .' he whispered, 'I never expected anyone like you.' He sounded as if he might burst into

tears. 'You're the answer to all my prayers . . . That is . . .
Yes . . . sorry . . . I mean that. My prayers.'

Jaz lay motionless, trying to get the measure of the
situation. 'What were you expecting?'

'Oh, you know, someone older. Harder. Too much
make-up. I hadn't intended . . . I hadn't intended . . .' He
was unable to speak.

Jaz remembered Mike, with the red Mondeo in Cambridge. He seemed like a long time ago. She had destroyed
his illusions by appearing too experienced. She turned
towards the lobbyist but didn't touch him. 'You hadn't
intended to do this?'

'No.' He sighed and ran his hands over her body.
They felt nervous and cold. 'Just let me hold you,' he
whispered. He cradled her in his arms. There was a
silence.

Jaz felt the hardness of his erection inside his stiff
cotton trousers. His shoulder bone dug into her cheek.
'What d'you want?' she said eventually.

'Nothing,' he murmured. 'Nothing.' Then he volun-
teered, 'I haven't seen Charles for a while. We used to
meet regularly for a drink and a game of chess. No one's
seen him socially, as it happens. In fact, no one's seen
him at all, recently, apart from his Home Office lackeys.
And, of course, his boss. But it's only odd to those who
don't know him well. I'm not surprised. You see, the
policies are so controversial . . .'

There was another silence. Jaz listened to a clock
ticking. She rolled over onto her back and his hand slid
onto her stomach.

'So controversial, Charles won't be taking any
chances. There are some very powerful interests, deeply
upset by what he wants to do with his new deal on Clean

Cities. Property developers. Financiers. Charles could ruin speculative office and city leisure development at a stroke.' He paused. 'At a stroke!' I mean, what an idea!' He took a deep breath. 'Can you imagine all those lofty billion-dollar buildings, with their glass and steel atria, their fig trees and modern art . . ' He sighed, ' . . . those Roman inspired plunge pools, those air-conditioned, high-tech, twentieth-century palaces – all filled up with dirty riff-raff and drunken tramps?'

Jaz digested this question but didn't reply.

'He's lying low. I know him. He doesn't want to be pestered by journalists and lobbied by interest groups. There's even talk of him being in some kind of danger. He doesn't want to be deflected or side-tracked or bothered. He's busy, determined. He'll wait for the storm to break, weather it, and then move on to the next stage of his vision. The Home Secretary will deflect the flak and absorb the shock – that's what he's good at. They both know the party and the country are behind them. Charles knows what he's doing. He's masterminding this thing. And at the moment he's just keeping an even lower profile than usual.'

Jaz hesitated. 'So he's not seeing anyone?'

'Not even me. And I've known him over twenty years.'

'So you can't help me?'

'I'm advising you to wait.'

Jaz felt her body go tense. 'I can't wait.' She brought to mind her vision of the Lotus Cortina bowling down the M4 in the inside lane, heading for Weston-super-Mare with Harm and Trace, a picnic hamper and an antique plastic transistor radio blaring tunes from Manfred Mann. 'I can't wait,' she burst out emotionally. 'That's just it. I've got to finish this thing. Now.'

'Shush, shush, little one.' He leaned over and she could smell his gin and tonic breath, his armpits. 'Shush.' He stroked her thighs.

'I can't wait,' she repeated, more calmly.

His fingers moved between her legs and deftly penetrated her. He was insistent but gentle. 'You know who you're just like?' he murmured. 'My little sister. Little Jennifer.'

So that's it, Jaz thought. Oh, well. She turned back on her side, facing him, without dislodging his hand. 'Help me, please,' she whispered. 'You know how I rely on you.'

He propped himself up on one elbow, gently withdrew his fingers and licked them.

Jaz's eyes were now accustomed to the dim light in the room and she could see his face.

He smiled at her dreamily. 'OK. Listen to me. He has a Turkish bath twice a week. Tuesdays and Thursdays.' He mentioned an address in Southwark. 'It used to be a public wash house. Fabulous tiled interior with great gushing taps. Upmarket now, of course, private. He's there at seven a.m., twice a week. Never varies. Don't you dare tell him I told you.'

'Thanks.'

There was another long silence. Jaz was unsure what to do. 'You'd better go back to your own room now,' he murmured, forgetting himself.

Without speaking, she got up and got dressed. He stayed in bed. She went downstairs and let herself out of the front door.

Chapter Twenty-Five

Worried about her unexpected visitors at the hotel, Jaz decided not to return immediately. She phoned and spoke to Mr McTavish. 'Let my room go,' she told him, 'but tell the others I'll be back soon.'

'Are you all right?' he asked kindly.

'Yes. Why?'

'There were a couple of men here, asking for you. Trev said they'd been before. We didn't like the look of them. I told them I'm the proprietor and that you've never stayed here. I was most insistent. Rocky came out and he earned an Oscar.' He chortled. 'I hope I did the right thing.'

'Thank you. I don't want to cause you any trouble.'

'What's living without a little trouble?'

'I'll be back soon, OK?'

She decided, as a precaution, to spend the night in the car, parking it in another of Fat Andy's safe havens – an enclosed area reserved for medical waste at the back of Guy's Hospital. It was completely out of sight of the road. She felt nervous. I'll just get this over with, she thought, I'm almost finished, then I'll be away.

An occasional porter, topping up the bins with plastic sacks, regarded her without interest. She watched a constant plume of smoke from an incinerator inside the building and tried not to think about body parts, disease and death. She tried not to think about the corpse in the flat.

Before dark, she got out of the car, did some warm up exercises then went for a brisk run around the narrow, Dickensian streets, knowing that this exertion would help her lose consciousness.

She awoke at five o'clock. The windows were cloudy with condensation. A refuse wagon roared into the space alongside her. The noise and the smell were overwhelming. She wound up her window. Men in orange overalls swarmed over the bulging bins.

Her limbs were stiff, and because her inflatable cushion had slipped onto the floor during the night, she had a crick in her neck. She climbed into the driving seat feeling bad-tempered. She backed out and parked in a narrow bay which said 'Consultants Only', but it proved to be impossible to get back to sleep.

At six thirty she set off for the bathhouse. It was on the edge of a high-rise estate. She got out, wearing the Toronto Blue Jays bomber jacket and cap, traded in Shepherd's Bush just before she was kidnapped. She pushed her hair out of sight. She wanted to look male. She was about to disable the Lotus Cortina when a small boy, no more than nine years old, smoking a cigarette, sauntered up to her. 'Can I watch your car, mister?'

Jaz understood that to refuse would probably mean damage to the paintwork, at the very least. 'Watch it or wash it?'

'It don't need no washing. What's it anyhow? Antiques Roadshow?'

Jaz placed her hand on the roof. She took a deep breath. 'This, you ignorant little shit, is one of the most respected saloon sports ever made. This is a Mark I, twin cam, Lotus Cortina. But you wouldn't know it because you're a sad, small person and you understand nothing. I feel very sorry for you. That's why I'll give you this.' She fished in her pocket, pulled out a two-pound coin and flipped it in his direction.

He caught it with the minimum of movement, blowing a triple smoke ring.

Jaz smiled. 'Now piss off.'

He stamped his cigarette butt under his heel and regarded her steadily. 'Mister, what I am, right, is a man of my word.' He paused. 'Yes? You've paid me, so to speak, so I'll guard this useless heap of old junk as if it's really worth something.'

'Suit yourself.'

Apprehensive about her appearance, Jaz approached the baths and went inside. There was a sign for the Turkish suite, pointing downstairs to the basement. She read the information. Tuesdays and Thursdays were 'men only' sessions. She paid at the desk without being challenged and descended the marble staircase. So far so good, she thought. I wonder what the dress code is.

At the bottom were a pair of heavy velvet curtains. She took a deep breath and went through. She found herself alone in a small room. It was thickly carpeted and luxurious, with heavy floral wallpaper, a battered leather sofa, an arrangement of gilded salon chairs and a hookah. On the walls were ornate framed mirrors and pictures of partially clad maidens bathing or reclining in classical settings. Neatly folded newspapers were available in a rack. She passed through and down a corridor which opened into a large, blue tiled space. It was warm and damp, smelling vaguely of sandalwood. The ceiling was a serrated, coloured dome. A horseshoe of curtained cubicles elegantly circled two huge marble slabs. An overhead fan turned slowly. Jaz thought of sultans, harems and jewelled, curved daggers.

A black man with bulging cheeks, wearing a white buttoned jacket and trousers, dozed next to a pile of fresh linen. Jaz coughed quietly. He opened one eye and handed her two towels and a rubber wristband with a key.

'Istanbul,' she said thoughtfully, looking upwards.

'Constantinople,' he corrected her, in a deep, lazy voice. He didn't question her gender. He closed his eye.

She went into a cubicle which contained a bed, chair, basin, mirror and a wooden locker. I could live in here, Jaz thought. On a table were a hairdryer and a white hand towel spread open with a razor in a sterile wrapper, a shaving brush and soap. Behind the door hung a silk dressing gown. She took off her clothes, keeping on the ridiculous cap to hide her hair. She wrapped herself in a towel, then peeped around the curtain. The attendant still slumbered and there were no other customers.

She lay down on the bed and slept for a short while. It was soporific, with the drip-drip of plumbing in the distance and the quiet whirring of the fan.

She awoke to the sound of voices. Her heart started beating very fast. She opened the curtain a chink. Two naked men walked past, their towels draped over their arms. They were followed by a third. Jaz gasped. The vast back with its folds of flesh, the sagging buttocks, the rope of tawny hair caught roughly in an elastic band – they were almost as familiar as her own body. She nearly cried out. He's identical, she thought. It's incredible. He's Fat Andy's double. It's the same freakish cloning as it was with Peony and Mimosa.

Jaz waited a couple of minutes, then followed, clutching her towel above her nipples. She walked down another corridor and felt the temperature rise. The tiles under her bare feet became hotter. She opened a door and gasped. She tried not to cough. The room was dense with steam. She breathed in steam. Steam filled her eyes. The door swung shut and she sat on a wooden bench. It was almost impossible to see in the thick mist. She took deep then shallow breaths, unsure of the effect of the wet heat on her lungs. She started sweating.

The three men faced her. She pulled down the peak of her cap and looked out from under it. Her eyes adjusted to the gloom. Charles Merchant was in the middle, but his companions sat close on either side as if they were bodyguards. She studied him. His jowls were sunk onto his chest and his eyes were closed. His penis dangled below the edge of the bench and above it hung his big belly. He had the same sparse chest hair as Fat Andy, the same ham-like hands spread out on his knees. It's incredible, Jaz thought. The only difference seemed to be his expression. Fat Andy had an alert, cheerful look. He was always smiling. This man was careworn. His mouth was pulled down as if his mood was permanently morose. His colour was poor, probably from spending too much time indoors.

The four of them sat for a while. Jaz felt she'd never been so hot in her life. Sweat ran down her face. She licked her lips and they tasted of salt. I'm melting, she decided. Suddenly, Charles Merchant raised himself to his feet. He wrapped a towel around his waist and lum-

bered towards a second door. Instantly, the two others
followed. Jaz waited a minute then pursued them.
Beyond, the next room was well lit and dry. At first it
was a relief but after a few seconds it was even hotter
than the steam room. The three men had resumed their
positions. Charles Merchant seemed again to be asleep.
Jaz thought of deserts, parched trees and the bones of
long dead animals.

After several moves between wet and dry, dry and
wet, Jaz felt both sleepy and debilitated. Finally, she
discovered Merchant spread out on a marble slab next to
the cubicles. She stared at him, trying not to think about
Andy in a coffin, a mortuary or on a pathologist's table.
This was difficult, because the still body of Merchant
looked like a monstrous corpse. The black attendant had
woken up. He came over and began kneading the fat.
The minders had disappeared into the sitting room, each
wearing a silk dressing gown. Jaz went into her cubicle.
She put on her robe and rubbed her head and neck with
a towel. She looked in the mirror. Her face was bright red
and the oversized garment and baseball cap looked very
eccentric together. It's now or never, she decided. She
emerged and stood next to the masseur.

Charles Merchant was face down, his tangled hair
covering his features. Jaz watched the black hands
pummel and vibrate his off-white flesh. 'Mr Merchant,'
she said with fake confidence, 'there is a private matter
I need to discuss with you. It's nothing to do with your
job.' There was a slap-slap and a small groan. Jaz waited,
breathing in the scent of exotic oil. 'Well?'

With difficulty, the fat man raised himself on his
elbows. His hair hung forwards hiding his expression,
his face. The masseur stepped aside and re-oiled his

hands. 'I'll meet you tonight in Chelsea,' Merchant whispered. His voice was urgent and hoarse. 'You know the address. Eleven o'clock. Now get out of here. Quick.' He collapsed down again and the black man resumed.

Jaz slipped into her cubicle, triumphant.

Outside, the car had gone. Her elation evaporated and was replaced by a feeling of panic. Several women walked by with pushchairs, leading school-age children by the hand. She set off on foot towards the estate, cursing her own carelessness. That little bastard, she kept thinking. His legs were barely long enough to reach the pedals. She wandered around pointlessly, overheated from the baths, with the sun beating down and the windless air giving no relief. She asked a couple of teenagers if they'd seen the Lotus Cortina but they only shrugged and stared. Suddenly, she heard a voice. 'Hey mister! Hey! Over here!'

She turned. The small boy was sitting on a wall, enjoying another cigarette. As she approached him he winked and gave her a thumbs-up.

'Where's my car?'

'I moved it, so to speak. It's all right.' He jumped down. 'Come with me.'

She followed his jaunty, self-important little body down through an avenue of municipal trees, past a burnt-out community centre and through a courtyard reserved for overflowing wheelie bins. The Lotus Cortina was half hidden by shrubbery and refuse. It was undamaged.

Jaz felt in her pocket for the keys.

'There were these geezers much too interested,' the boy said, lighting up again. 'Walking round, staring.'

'What sort of geezers?'

'No one from round here.'

'Did they go into the baths?'

'Yep. Shortly after you.'

'Three of them?'

'Yep. The other one, he stayed outside, staring at your car. Walking round it. Kicking the tyres. Interested. Who knows why. Then he got back into this bloody great limo they'd come in and started talking on his phone. I thought to myself, this twat's up to no good, so to speak. I thought better safe than sorry. So I moved the heap of old junk. Out of there, so to speak. Over here.'

Jaz looked inside. The ignition was undamaged.

'Do me a favour,' he said, understanding her concern. 'What am I? An amateur? You left a window open. This old banger's easier to rob than shit. I was under the bonnet hot-wiring it in twenty-three seconds. No, I tell a lie. Nineteen. Four seconds to drive it away.'

Jaz grinned. 'You did good.' She fished in her pocket.

The boy held up a palm in refusal. 'I've been paid,' he said.

On impulse, Jaz bent down and kissed the top of his head.

He jumped back as if electrocuted. He drew on his cigarette. 'Hey, mister,' he said, 'what are you, so to speak? You one of those pervs?'

Jaz got into the car. She took off her cap and let her damp hair fall around her shoulders. 'I'm just a girl,' she said. She started the engine. 'Thanks very much.'

Chapter Twenty-Six

Jaz parked outside the Chelsea mews at ten forty-five. There was a warm, dust-laden wind and the street was deserted. She was hot. She leaned out of the window and stared at the skyline. A cat ran across the road and she knew she'd seen it several times before. Her long vigils had made the area very familiar. Just before eleven, she went inside. The porter gave her a silent thumbs-up then muttered on the intercom. After the exchange of a few words, he motioned Jaz towards the houses.

Charles Merchant answered the door. His hair was loose and dishevelled and his tie and top button were undone. He wore a silk-backed waistcoat and his shirt-sleeves were pushed up, exposing his massive freckled forearms. He didn't smile. He looked tired and depressed.

Jaz followed him into the living room. It was decorated in a spare and expensive style with a pale wooden floor, discreet lighting and modern bucket chairs covered in cream and gold brocade. A large abstract painting dominated one wall. Merchant picked up a glass of Scotch and sat down heavily. He sighed, but did not speak. A CD played classical music in the background.

'Are you alone?' asked Jaz.

He met her eye for a second, then looked away. He nodded.

'I've been trying to get hold of you for ages. You're better protected than royalty.' She felt uncomfortable. He hadn't asked her to sit down. She perched on the arm of a chair.

He took a gulp from his glass.

She wondered if he was drunk. Just get it over with, she said to herself. This isn't a social call. She got straight to the point. 'There's something you need to know. It's not good news, but I feel I've got to tell you. You know you had a twin brother?'

His eyes met hers again. They were the same colour as Andy's but they had a defeated, blank look.

She raised her voice slightly. 'Do you know this or not?'

He nodded again.

'Is that a yes?'

'Yes,' he muttered.

Jaz hesitated. 'Well, I'm sorry to have to tell you, but he's dead.'

He jumped visibly. He was shocked. Scotch splashed from his glass onto his arm and over his chair. He put the glass down on the floor. Jaz noticed that the little colour he possessed had completely drained away. He suddenly leaned forwards and hid his face in his hands, resting his elbows on his knees. 'What?' His voice was a strangled whisper.

Jaz decided to press on with her story. Sympathy's never been my strong point, she thought to herself. Stay calm. Just tell him and get the hell out of here. Her voice was confident. 'Your brother Andy was my boyfriend. We lived together for six months, over in Peckham. On the nineteenth of June, my birthday, I got back to the flat late at night. Andy was lying on the bed with his throat cut. He'd been killed that evening. The police more or less dismissed it as an estate-based drugs crime and they've done nothing. But Andy didn't do drugs. Not seriously. He was murdered by his boss. A criminal from the Isle of Dogs.' She paused and tried to swallow. Her mouth was dry.

Charles Merchant's hands still covered his face. He opened his fingers and looked out at her. The effect was a little comical, but she didn't feel like laughing. Her heart was beating fast. She'd waited a long time for this moment and all at once, she wanted both to leave the place and to cry. She positioned her hand on her chest, over the spot where she'd consistently felt the pain. There was more to say. 'It's because you're a twin,' she went on. She was less controlled now and her words started coming out in a rush. 'I knew I had to tell you. You see, I know about twins. I used to have . . . I mean . . . I've got . . . twin sisters. I understand what you're like, you twins. I mean, I know you weren't in touch, or any-thing, I know you were separated when you were little, but I know that identical twins are like . . . one person.' She stopped. Tears were running down her cheeks. She sobbed. 'You see, what it is . . . what I'm really trying to say is I know how you feel about Andy because I really miss him too—I feel the same . . . I miss Andy . . . and Blow . . . I really miss Blow . . . and my two sisters. I miss my sisters terribly. I miss everybody.'

Merchant slid his hands to the sides of his face, cupping his head. His cheeks were wet and doughy. His knee jerked involuntarily. He was in shock.

Jaz cried unrestrainedly. Seconds, then minutes passed. He didn't move and she found she couldn't stop. There was a box of tissues next to the television and she got up and pulled out a handful. She mopped her face and blew her nose. 'I'm sorry,' she said. She rubbed her face. 'This is fucking hard,' she whispered.

Merchant suddenly lay back, his eyes staring at the ceiling. He was suddenly more composed, almost resigned. 'Cry,' he said. 'You cry. It's all right. I don't mind.'

Jaz struggled for control of herself and, after a while, succeeded. 'The thing is, I wanted Andy to be mourned. I mean, properly mourned. I didn't think I was enough . . . I sort of felt that I wasn't good enough, or somehow not able . . . I wanted a real, proper mourner. I told his old girlfriend but she was too drunk and I told his old mother but she was too mad, so the only person left . . . was you.' She fought back more tears. 'I'm sorry,' she continued, 'I'm sorry about your brother.'

Merchant picked up his glass and drained it. He stood up and poured himself another whisky, then held it up to the light. 'I know I can't tempt you,' he said, his voice dull, sad. 'Not ever . . . not even for medicinal purposes.' He glanced over, shook his head then sat down again heavily. The chair creaked. 'It's good stuff this,' he added thoughtfully. 'Government issue. Single malt.'

Jaz stared at him. She swallowed hard. 'How do you know I don't drink?' she asked, her voice quiet. 'How could you know that . . .?'

He looked at her. His face was still morose and drawn.

She held his gaze. 'Tell me. Who told you I don't drink? Who've you been talking to? Who do you know who knows me?'

There was a long silence. The ornate mantel clock ticked. The classical music rose and fell in melodious cadences. A video recorder whirred as it switched itself off. Outside, two drunks chanted 'Here we go, here we go, here we go,' in desperate unison. Jaz listened to their voices recede in the hot night. Her fist tightened around her ball of wet tissue. 'Well?'

He sighed. His expression changed and became confiding. 'Why wouldn't I know?' he said eventually. 'You said it. We lived together for six months.'

Jaz let these words sink in. Her heart started beating very hard. She felt something rise from her chest into her throat. 'What?' she asked, 'what?' Her hand strayed back to her breastbone. 'What d'you mean?' His words and all the crying had released something. The pain had gone.

He opened his arms in a welcoming gesture. His wet face and his posture suddenly reminded her of Fat Andy and the time she'd threatened to leave him in Peckham. He'd cried and talked her out of it. 'You're breaking my heart,' he'd said then.

'Andy?' she said, her voice a small quaver. 'Andy? Is it you?' She stood up and uncertainly moved towards him. 'Is it really you?'

'Yes,' he replied simply.

She stood before him and he encircled her in his arms. He felt comfortable like Andy had always done and the smell of his skin, the spirits on his breath and the rough texture of his hair on her cheek, as she bent towards him, were all more than familiar.

'Little baby,' he murmured into her shoulder. 'My little sexy baby's here. She's come all the way here and found me.'

She crouched down on her haunches and stared into his face. They looked at each other for a while, without speaking. Jaz felt enormous relief. Impulsively, she leaned forwards, held him around his vast waist and squeezed him.

He chuckled. His mood had suddenly changed, just like it did in the old days. He struggled to his feet, picking her up. Clasping her to his belly he took a few steps then spun her around. He'd done this many times before. He put her on her feet and pressed a button on the hi-fi. There was a sudden burst of Boyz 2 Men. 'Let's dance,' he growled, taking both her arms and pulling her gently. He moved her around the room a few times. He was a good dancer, light on his feet.

'Hang on a minute,' Jaz said suddenly. She stopped and struggled, freeing herself. She reached over and switched off the music.

He was smiling broadly now and his colour had improved. The old twinkle had returned to his eye. 'Turn that back on,' he said. 'This bloody place is bugged.' He pressed a button and returned to the violin concerto. He adjusted a speaker. 'I couldn't believe it when I saw you at the Turkish baths. It's supposed to be men only. I wanted to laugh but it would have been suicide. I kept changing rooms. I couldn't get rid of you.'

Jaz stood upright, stiff, her arms by her sides. 'Andy, you tell me what's going on. Tell me now.'

He shrugged. 'We better both sit down.' He picked up his glass. He was a little breathless. He paused. 'It all started one day recently . . . as you said . . . it was your birthday.'

Jaz sat opposite him and listened, concentrating hard. Her eyes were fixed on his sleeve.

Fat Andy began talking. He explained how he'd been on his way home from the garage, driving the Lotus Cortina. 'How is it by the way? I saw it outside the baths.

It's got a bird-shit burn on the paintwork. How's it running?'

'It's running fine. It's outside.'

'I called at the flats one night to check on it. It wasn't there. I saw Peppy. He said you'd taken it.'

'Tell me what's going on.'

'Imagine this, right. I'm driving along, as normal. Then there's this Daimler. Big, black. Two guys in neat haircuts and designer shades are following me. It's like a bloody American movie. I pull over, thinking where's the cameras? Where's Andy Garcia? I get in their motor and ask them what their problem is.' He went on to detail an extraordinary conversation. He'd been told that his twin brother, whom he hadn't seen since infancy, was now a big shot political adviser. He was influential, apparently, successful. He was calling the tune in government policy. He was enormously powerful, well off, a key player in the administration. 'The only trouble was,' Andy continued, 'they said he'd had some sort of nervous breakdown. They said he'd gone to a sanatorium near Geneva, to recover his health.' There was a pause.

'So?' asked Jaz

'They said this nervous breakdown was like embarrassing deep-shitsville for the Home Secretary. For everybody. They asked me to sort of . . . stand in for him for a while. Like, pretend to be him. Follow his routines. They offered me a wad. More money than I've ever earned in my life, all together. I'm telling you, compared to working for Vinny, stealing lousy cars, it was an offer I couldn't refuse. They also threw in this place.' He gestured around the room. 'Restaurants, booze, a chauffeur-driven limo . . . the works. They said it would only be for a few weeks. Until my brother recovered. They didn't want any publicity. Things were too delicate at the moment, politically, and important new legislation was about to be announced. They were very, well, persuasive.'

'I can't believe you're telling me this.'

'Didn't you get my letter?'

'Letter?'

'I gave them a letter to give to you, and cheque for two grand. It was made out to you. I told you to hang on in there in Peckham and pay the rent. I told you to chill out, said I'd be back and then we'd both be a lot richer.' He scratched his head and sighed. 'Of course you didn't get it. Bastards, bastards, bastards.' He leaned back in his chair and stared into his glass. After a moment he continued. 'What I've been doing is . . . hiding. When they needed me to wander past a journalist or a TV crew I've done it. I've been driven around in flash cars, here and there, not knowing what the hell's going on. I was given a cupboard full of fancy suits and told to keep my trap shut.'

'What do you think's going on?'

He shook his head. 'Dunno. I'm out of my depth here, by fathoms. These guys have threatened me. I swear I've had a gun in my ribs.' He looked at her. 'No kidding. A gun. And I didn't like it, not one bit.'

'I bet.'

'I've never been famous for bravery.' He paused and gave her an appraising glance. 'Unlike you.' He sighed. 'Now, I act like a robot, obeying orders.'

Jaz described the scene at the flat, the night of her birthday. 'It was a nightmare,' she whispered. 'I thought it was you. It must have been . . .'

Fat Andy let out a deep sigh. He wiped his eyes again. 'The poor bastard. He was never ill. There was no nervous breakdown. That was all lies. He'd never been ill. They wanted him out of the way.'

'Why?'

Fat Andy shrugged. 'I don't know, I really don't. I'm a prisoner here. But one thing I've known from the start is these guys aren't working in my brother's interests.' He looked very unhappy. 'And now you tell me they went and killed him. He's been dead all along.' He sniffed and rubbed his face.

'What're they doing, exactly?'

'Blocking the changes he wanted to make, of course. They've nobbled civil servants. Bribed junior ministers, God knows who else. The Home Secretary's just a free-loading prick, in with them, you know, deep. Up to his lousy sun-tanned neck.' He paused. 'He wasn't before, but now the wind's changed, now these bad guys are making the running, he's backing off from Charles's new policies. You wait. There'll be a classic U-turn any day now.'

'Who are these guys?'

'High-class heavies. Ronnie and Reggie, only with degrees in economics. But it's the guys they represent who matter. Big businessmen, property speculators, financial manipulators. Men who stay well behind the scenes. They're the ones who want to stop Charles's pro-posals, his new deal on Clean Cities. They won't have their property requisitioned, won't have anyone inter-fering with their investments. And I tell you, those bastards will stop at nothing. It's not public yet, but in the back rooms, the policy's already as dead as a dodo.' He swigged his drink, finished it, poured another and sat down again. 'I'm supposed to be Charles Merchant and in a few days it'll seem to the world that he's backed down. He never would have backed down. Never in a million years. He was strong and he was shrewd and he had it all practically airborne. The whole goddamned thing was ready to fly. But not now. They got rid of him. And there's nothing I can do. I'm just their mouthpiece. As I said, I'm completely out of my depth.' He sighed again. 'You know me. Show me dodgy car documents, I'm your man. Show me a pair of stolen plates, I'm laughing. But show me White Papers, shite papers . . .' He sighed. 'I haven't got a bloody clue.'

'So it was them who killed him.' Jaz was thoughtful. She chewed the end of her ponytail. 'The heavies with degrees.'

'Must have been.'

'They frightened off a woman, a temp at your office. She helped me and then . . .'

'Oh, definitely,' Andy interrupted. 'She was over curious. Suspicious of me. She went through my jacket pockets and found an old wallet – Visa slips, my driving licence. Made photocopies. She was onto it. She knew.'

'They shut her up.'

Andy was silent for a moment. 'They will have done.' He paused. 'Oh, God . . .'

'The heavies with degrees.' Jaz's mind was spinning.

'Degrees and black Daimlers. FBI collars and ties. Gun holsters.' Fat Andy's face registered more pain. 'I didn't know they'd killed him. Charles. Not until you told me just now. But it makes sense. Complete sense. And no one knows. No one's interested. In the eyes of the world, a small-time car thief dies in a bedroom on a no-exit council estate. Who cares? Did it even make the South London Press? I think not.'

Jaz shook her head. She felt relieved, unburdened, even elated with the knowledge that the body in the flat, lying grotesque and bloodstained on their bed, had not been Andy, after all. Instead, it had been an unlucky stranger, a person she'd never met. She took several deep breaths. The crying had been cathartic. She felt better than she had for a long time. Her chest, her head, her whole body felt lighter, looser, calmer. She stared at her former lover. You're alive, she thought. You fat, lucky bastard. She almost smiled. Andy's predicament was serious, he was way out of his league, but at least he wasn't dead.

Images from the recent past jostled for attention in her thoughts. She remembered Princess, Andy's former girlfriend and the old woman, his mother, both of them lonely and desperate. She thought of the black masseur in the Turkish bathhouse and the lobby correspondent in Lambeth with his unrealizable desires. She pictured Andy's tormentors, cool and aggressive in their leather bomber jackets and fascist haircuts. She remembered, suddenly, the choking fumes in the Citroën, inside the lock-up in the East End, her nausea, her own brush with extinction. She concentrated on this. Her eyes narrowed. Her mind shifted, then steadied, like the gears of a car. 'They tried to kill me,' she said.

Fat Andy didn't reply. There was a silence. She looked at him. She'd seen this expression on his face many times before. He was trying to muster innocence.

A realization formed in her mind. 'They tried to kill me. The heavies with degrees.' She paused. 'Your heavies.'

Andy attempted a smile. His cheeks formed cherubic mounds, then collapsed.

Jaz's sense of calm ebbed away. In its place, her heart was thumping. 'You told them about the lock-up, about that shit-head Keith who wanted to murder me in the cinema when I was sixteen.' A hot feeling formed in her brain and in her stomach. It was anger.

Andy's lips formed a closed circle and he whistled, quietly and tunelessly.

Jaz raised her voice. 'You did. It must've been you. It was the same place. It was the garage where he kept his Ford Zephyr. I showed it to you more than once. We went there. I told you the whole story.'

He looked at the floor.

'You told them about that lock-up. Where it is. You told them that was the place that would really scare me. Really do my head in.'

'No.'

Jaz bent down and met his evasive eyes. He caught her glance unwillingly, then looked away. He was furtive. She knew he was lying. 'Bastard.' Her heart, light for that one brief moment, gained weight again and sank like a stone in her chest. It's the same old thing, she thought, horrified. He's unreliable, he's selfish. He's unthinking. He only ever worries about himself. And this time he's stepped so far out of line it's almost unbelievable. 'I might have died,' she added.

He pulled himself into a more upright position. He still looked shifty. 'They wouldn't have killed you, Jaz,' he said in unacknowledged admission. 'They were only trying to scare you off. They wanted you out of their hair because you were irritating them.'

Jaz remembered the lock-up, the foul air, the tight bindings on her wrists and ankles, her near collapse into unconsciousness in the carbon monoxide smog. She looked him up and down. He was overweight, perspiring and half-drunk. He was weak, floundering. He'd betrayed her, ignoring the consequences, in order to make life easier for himself. I used to love you, she thought. She turned this over in her mind. I must have been mad.

In an instant, she was in exactly the same place she'd been on the night of her birthday, before she found the body. Her love for him, as she'd known back then, was misplaced, founded on the wrong needs and reasons, and in any case, it was over. It was past tense. Finished. He was unworthy of her. He was undeserving. He had no values. Her anger evaporated at that moment because she knew he wasn't worth it. 'The car's outside,' she said coldly. 'Why don't I drop you somewhere?'

He sighed, almost luxuriantly. His stomach moved down then up. He was glad she'd changed the subject. 'No.' He paused. 'Don't worry, I'm leaving. I'm out of here. But not yet. I've got a plan, but it's got to be water-tight. Two of us are working something out – me and the chauffeur.' He tried to force a laugh.

Jaz held out her hand in a gesture of friendship which she didn't mean.

Andy shook it formally. 'We're planning something James Bond-ish,' he said. 'Car chases, stunts, private aeroplanes . . .'

Jaz looked for the gleam in his eye, but it wasn't there. He was frightened. They both knew he was treading water, slowly sinking, slowly drowning.

Jaz gestured towards the window. 'I'm going to Weston-super-Mare.'

He levered himself to his feet. He was a little unsteady and held onto her arm. 'Do you think we might ever . . . you and I . .'

In your dreams, thought Jaz. You betraying bastard. 'Don't think about it,' she said. 'Not now. Concentrate on the moment, the problem in hand.' She formed her mouth into a smile. 'You know what you always used to tell me when I was out on the streets, nicking BMWs?'

He shook his head. 'What?'

'Stay calm, stay focused, stay cool.' She stared briefly into his eyes then moved towards the door.

Chapter Twenty-Seven

Back at the hotel, the next day, Jaz found her two friends lounging in the small TV room, watching the Jerry Springer show. It was a confrontation entitled 'Keep your hands off – he's mine'.

Harm was painting her toenails purple. A cigarette was wedged in the corner of her mouth. Trace had her head on Trevor's shoulder. He was leafing through *Hair Today*, studying the photos. The air was thick with the smell of varnish. Rocky, the old Rottweiler, was asleep in a triangle of sunlight on the faded carpet. His jaws and feet twitched as he dreamed of mock combat and stardom.

Trace and Trevor moved along the sofa and Jaz sat next to them. There was another person in the room, sitting in an armchair, half concealed by the open door. It was Pete.

She froze, giving him a cold, hostile stare. 'You don't give up,' she said.

'Give the boy a break,' murmured Trevor lazily.

Pete leaned forward, clasping and unclasping his hands. 'Whatever you thought I did, I never,' he said. 'I never did anything to piss you off.'

'You left his door open,' said Trace mildly. 'His flat was stripped bare.'

'He'd have a job today,' agreed Trevor, 'if it wasn't for you.'

Jaz stared at Pete. His pale, poet's face was as handsome as ever. His long, delicate fingers were clean of oil and his nails were manicured. His hair was shining like a halo, wavy and loosely tied back. She remembered desiring him. She remembered what they'd done in his bed. 'You set those two goons onto me,' she spat out, despite herself. 'Vinny's heavies. You told them where I was. You kept telling them. They might have killed me.'

Pete's mouth dropped open. He gasped. 'I never! Jaz, I never did!'

Jaz's hands were clenched into fists, one on each knee. 'Well, some fucker did.' She thought about her recent nightmare days. Ronnie and Reggie had pursued her and found her several times. The kidnapping in the Citroën, she now knew, was the work of Fat Andy's heavies and they'd almost found her here. But Ronnie and Reggie had also come close to tracking her down. They'd been after her and they'd been persistent.

'Everywhere I went, those brothers turned up. I had something they wanted.' She glanced over at Harm but she was concentrating now on her fingernails, apparently not listening.

Trace sat up. 'Two brothers?' she asked innocently. She picked up the TV remote and switched off the set. There was a silence, broken only by the dog's snores. 'Two big guys in sports clothes? Baldy heads? Look like boxers?'

'That's them,' said Pete.

'Oh,' said Trace, suddenly dismayed. Her hand covered her mouth. 'That was me.'

Jaz stood up and faced her. 'What d'you mean?' She was astonished. 'Trace?'

'Whoops,' said Trace. The colour drained from her face.

'Tell me.'

Trevor picked up Trace's other hand in a gesture of support. He squeezed it tenderly, then raised it to his lips.

'Two brothers,' repeated Trace. She thought for a moment. Her voice was hesitant, uncertain. Her eyes were scared and fixed on Jaz. 'They came to the Grand Banana lots of times and the Little Sisters as well. They were looking for you. They said they'd seen the car.'

'What, the Lotus Cortina?'

Trace nodded. She bit her lip. 'They'd seen you leave in it, the first day you came to the Grand Banana. A classic Ford, or something. They were looking everywhere for you, Jaz, and were nice and polite and friendly and everything. They said you had a piece of property and they wanted to buy it off you. Said they'd give you a good price.' She paused. Her voice became a whisper. 'They meant the car.' She was ready to cry. 'Didn't they?'

'No,' said Jaz. Her voice was ice. 'They were after a computer disk.'

Trace swallowed then responded quickly. 'I don't know anything about a computer disk. I thought it was the car they were interested in, that one you're driving.' She was frightened. 'You're always selling people cars, Jaz. That's what you do. You sell cars.' She paused. 'Not computer disks . . . Why would they have wanted . . .' Her voice wavered then trailed away. She looked around desperately. 'I didn't mean to cause trouble for you, Jaz. Or anything like that. Were they bad men? What have I done?' Tears brimmed up in her eyes then rolled down her cheeks. Trevor stroked the back of her hand. 'I kept telling them where you were. With Pete. At Mrs McDonald's. At that flashy hotel in Charing Cross. So you could talk to them about it. About the car.'

Jaz stared down at Trace. 'Why didn't you tell me?'

Trace's lower lip trembled. More tears fell. 'I don't know, I think I forgot. It wasn't important, it was only a car. You told me not to tell him anything.' She pointed at Pete. 'So I didn't . . . I did exactly what you said, Jaz.' She was insistent. 'I always do what you tell me to do. Always.' She rubbed her face with the back of her hand.

'Sshh, sshh,' whispered Trevor consolingly.

There was another silence. Rocky awoke, eased himself up and glanced around. He growled menacingly, fixing Pete with a mean stare. He lifted his top lip, revealing his yellow set of teeth. Pete slid back in his chair nervously, lifting his feet and clasping his long legs in his arms. Satisfied, Rocky turned and left the room.

'The brothers aren't such bad guys,' said Pete after a while, breaking the silence. He sounded young. 'They're harmless. If they've got a problem, they throw Vinny's money at it. You had something of theirs?'

Jaz nodded.

'They would have paid you off. That's their style. They're not violent.'

Harm coughed. Jaz looked over at her. She screwed the top on her bottle of nail varnish and met Jaz's eye. 'OK,' she muttered. 'I lied.'

Jaz clenched her fists. She took a deep breath.

'I'm sorry. It wasn't the brothers who beat me up and I never went to see them. I lied to you.'

Jaz was speechless.

'I was done over by an American country and western singer in the Savoy. I won't say who, but he's very famous.' She pulled a face and admired her nails. 'D'you want to hear about it?'

No one spoke. 'Get this.' Harm took a deep breath. She was trying to make her voice light, anecdotal, hoping to improve the atmosphere. 'He comes out the bathroom wearing a woman's dress. He's a big macho guy, but you know, nothing surprises me. I'm cool. He plays music, very loud. He yells at me.' She shrugged, indicating she'd seen it all before. She lit another cigarette. 'I start to get a bit worried. Wesley's outside chatting to the PR woman and the guy's agent, but he never hears a thing. This guy, he punches me out and all his fingers are covered in rings. They come busting in eventually and rescue me. The guy's out of his head on crack. He thinks I'm his mother.' She laughed, unconvincingly. 'They got us out of there double quick, I can tell you. Paid us plenty to keep our mouths shut. Wesley's still devastated. He blames himself.'

Jaz tried to swallow. 'Why did you tell me it was . . .?'

Harm interrupted, her voice harsher now and more serious. 'To try and stop you, of course. Your boyfriend gets killed and you're in a state, understandably. You're in shock. But you needed to recover, not run around like a nutter, trying to get revenge. It was a mad idea you had, and I kept thinking about the time you nearly got murdered in the East End when you were sixteen, and I could see it happening again. Your judgement isn't good, Jaz. You're too rash. I thought if I told you it was Ronnie and Reggie who'd beaten me up, then you'd stay away from them.' She looked at Trace. 'I guess, between us, we really screwed up because you got completely the wrong idea about them. Screwed up right and proper.'

Pete uncurled himself and got to his feet. He tentatively put his arm around Jaz's shoulders. She stood mute and unresisting. 'I've ruined Vinny,' she said to no one in particular. 'Vinny's finished and I did it.'

'Vinny had it coming,' said Pete, kindly but firmly. 'No one misses Vinny.'

'Why didn't he try to stop me?' Jaz whispered. 'Are you telling me he wasn't even angry?'

Trevor leaned forwards. His voice was knowing. 'No,' he said, 'Vinny gave up when Andy died. He'd lost the illegal business because it was nothing without Andy and his gang. Vinny was finished. He knew that. All the rest was only ever pocket money. Just a front.'

'What's he going to do now?'

'He's going back to Greece,' answered Trevor confidently. 'He decided that ages ago. He wanted me to go with him. His mum owns a souvenir shop in Corfu and he says it could expand. It's got potential.'

Pete led Jaz out of the room. 'Let's go upstairs,' he whispered. He pressed the button of the lift.

Jaz lay in bed with Pete regarding the little motes of dust which floated in the beam of sunlight penetrating the crack in the curtains. Her head rested on his smooth chest and his gentle hands caressed her back and neck. She let him stroke away the tension, the anger and the fear. 'I had a pain in my chest,' she whispered, 'but it went away.'

Fragments of recent events were competing for attention in her thoughts. She saw the small boy outside the

Turkish baths, the dashboard of the Citroën when she'd been tied up and choking, the attractive aerobics instructor at Ronnie and Reggie's gym.

Pete had questioned her a little, but she'd not been forthcoming. They made love several times and this was better than talking.

She rolled against him and he rubbed the insides of her thighs. She stroked his penis until it stiffened again. She pressed her body against his, feeling both tenderness and relief. He kissed her deeply then moved on top of her. Downstairs the dog started barking. He laughed into her hair.

Epilogue

Jaz sat in the driving seat of the Lotus Cortina, studying Fat Andy's road atlas. She'd spent the previous day servicing the twin cam and she was confident it was running at its best. Now, she was illegally parked outside the hotel, as Wesley loaded Harm's heavy suitcases into the boot. 'You're going on holiday,' she heard him laugh, 'not emigrating.'

Harm opened a rear door and slipped inside the car. She was wearing hot pants, a halter top and the kind of zany sixties sunglasses which had featured in Jaz's imagination in recent weeks. She smelled of deodorant. She lit a cigarette.

Trace appeared in the hotel doorway, stuffing a large bottle of Ambre Solaire into a small duffel bag. This was her only luggage. She kissed Trevor goodbye and got in the front next to Jaz. She was giggling with apprehension. Trevor handed her a pile of cassettes. 'For the journey,' he suggested.

Jaz put on her Versace shades and slipped the car in gear. She eased into the traffic. Her window was wound down and she rested her elbow on the warm metal. As she pulled away she glanced in the rear-view mirror. Wesley, Trevor and Pete were framed together, standing on the pavement, grinning and waving. Mr McTavish appeared behind them, holding Rocky by the collar. He raised one arm in salute as the Lotus Cortina accelerated and turned right at the lights.

Somewhere on the M4, stuck in a long and winding jam, Trace switched off the tape and tried to tune into the traffic report. She was wearing Harm's sunglasses. It was hot. Harm was asleep in the back, her head on the inflatable cushion. The sun beat down mercilessly on the roof of the car. Jaz swigged some water from a bottle and handed it across. The news came on the radio. 'Leave that,' she said.

She listened to the main story about a by-election in Birmingham. The government had lost the seat, with a huge percentage swing to the opposition. The political correspondent gave his opinion. 'The expected reforms from the Home Secretary have, on announcement, proved to be negligible and disappointing,' he said. 'The electorate feels like a balloon let down. Huge promises have turned into hot air. Unless he can pull a rabbit out of his hat at this late stage, then the days of this administration seem numbered.' Jaz visualized a rabbit and a balloon and pursed her lips.

The second item was even more interesting. The presenter talked more rapidly. 'News is just in about a plane crash in Sussex. At about ten this morning a light aircraft plunged to the ground in flames in a field on the outskirts of Aldeburgh. Locals believe that two bodies were recovered but as yet there is no official statement. Witnesses describe a mystery car, a Daimler, without number plates, speeding through the quiet country lanes in quote, such a dangerous manner that some residents alerted police.

Two men were seen abandoning the car and boarding a plane which crashed immediately after take-off. Our correspondent Anna Smythe is at the scene.'

The announcer was replaced by a woman speaking to the studio by telephone. She was excited.

'Yes, Gary,' she said, 'the plane crash was preceded, apparently, by an amazing car chase, ending at a small private airfield near the coast. I'm there now.' Her voice was definite and clear. 'I can just see the wreckage in the distance but the site is cordoned off. There is a big black car, two of its doors open, on the runway. Earlier, an ambulance removed two body bags from the wreckage, but we can only speculate about casualties at this stage. One local witness, out walking his dog, describes a Daimler, without number plates, travelling at high speed. At one point it collided with a pillar box. Police gave chase, I'm told, with their lights flashing and their sirens sounding, but the lead car burst through a locked and chained gate onto the field, tore across the tarmac, then stopped beside a small waiting aircraft. Two men hurried on board and the plane took off within a minute. As it left the ground it is said to have exploded and burst into flames.'

'What exactly is happening there now, Anna?'

'Well, Gary, it's not entirely clear. The police seem as confused as the rest of us. As you said yourself, there has been no statement. The owner of the airfield, a local man, is quoted as saying it has been disused for two years and the flight was completely unauthorized. There is a rumour, I have to say unsubstantiated, that one of the men, attempting what seems to have been a spectacular getaway, was allegedly none other than Charles Merchant, the elusive political adviser to the Home Secretary.

But that's just hearsay, Gary. It's caused quite a stir, I have to say, and more journalists are arriving by the minute. The lanes are blocked and no one can move. We'll have to hang on for the official explanation. It's wait and see, I'm afraid. Now it's back to the studio.' There was a beep and the start of a record.

'Any connection with the sensational by-election result, do you think, Anna?' said the presenter hurriedly, speaking over the link.

'It's interesting to speculate, isn't it, Gary? That's one theory being discussed here at the moment. It's certainly possible.' She was faded out, replaced by Simon and Garfunkel.

Jaz glanced at her friends. They were both asleep. She changed up and accelerated gently as the traffic began to inch forwards. She pressed her hand on her chest. There was no pain. She was calm and relaxed. Fat Andy was dead and Blow was dead but it no longer felt like her business.

She pictured the burning aircraft and Blow's burning car on the motorway. They were both consumed by fire, cremated, obliterated. Up in flames, she thought, envisaging twisted metal; glare; heat; peeling, blistered paint; a pall of black smoke, curling towards the sky.

Her mind wandered to a flat, wide, imaginary beach where the tide was so far out, the sea was invisible. In this daydream, the sand was wet and fine, like grey mud, and there was heavy, low cloud. She was standing by the Lotus Cortina which was stationary on the beach, its doors open and its engine running. In the distance, Harm and Trace wandered off, arms linked, in the direction of the town.

Jaz pictured herself with a can of petrol, dousing the

car. She was alone and the light was fading. She stood back and tossed a roll of burning rags into its interior. There was a flash and a roar as it caught alight and she felt the heat as it was engulfed in fire. The dull scene was illuminated by the blaze and a flock of seagulls screamed overhead, their wings beating angrily, their beaks like razors. Goodbye, Blow, Jaz imagined herself saying, as the car burned. Goodbye Andy. So long, cheerio, adios, you fat bastards. I'm rid of you at last.

Later, with the jam behind them, the three girls hurtled along the outside lane of the motorway, overtaking coach-loads of tourists. A sign above them said Bristol, Exeter and the South West. 'What!' shrieked Trace delightedly. 'What does that one say?'

Later, another sign said Somerset and Devon. 'Somerset and Devon,' read Harm, excited. She handed out some sandwiches. 'We're nearly there.'

'Somerset and Devon,' yelled Trace, as high as a child. 'Oh, my gosh! Somerset and Devon! I can't believe it. We're on holiday!'

Jaz concentrated on driving. She felt connected to the Lotus Cortina. Her arms and the steering wheel were one smooth movement. The rhythm of the engine matched her own steady pulse. The muscles in her feet were held at exactly the same tension as the pedals. She felt in control. Her mind was blank except for an autonomic response to curve, speed, incline. I'll keep the car, she thought. It's mine now.

Trace fiddled with the radio. Blow's song, his joyful Cortina anthem, emerged from Jaz's subconscious and began to throb. Do wah diddy diddy, dum diddy do. It repeated several times, then disappeared. A pale glimmer on the horizon, almost blue, suggested open sea. It was then that the pure line of ocean and sky combined together in her line of vision, in her mind and in her heart. Her eyes flicked towards the hard shoulder and she braked, crossing lanes to reach the slip road. Weston-super-Mare, she'd noticed. Three miles. She smiled to herself. She was happy.

Blink

by Andrea Badenoch

It is 1962. The Beatles have released 'Love Me Do' and John Glenn has orbited the Earth. But in this pit village in County Durham, everyone is looking back towards the traditions of the past . . .

Except for Gloria, the local hair stylist. With her narrow skirts, low block heels and her Mini Cooper, Gloria is a modern woman – until she's found dead, floating in the coal-polluted shallows of a nearby pond.

Gloria's young cousin, Kathleen, finds the body but refuses to accept the suicide explanation embraced by the village. Gloria had everything to live for. Twelve-year-old Kathleen is shy and innocent but her mouse-like wordlessness makes her invisible. She is therefore an ideal witness . . .

Andrea Badenoch's new novel, *Blink*, is published in Macmillan hardback in March 2001, priced £10.
The opening scenes follow here.

Chapter One

Kathleen walked gingerly down the rough, coal-strewn track towards the pond, her wellingtons slipping on the loose stones. It was windy and her coat collar was buttoned against the driving cold. Over one shoulder she carried a bulky square camera case on a strap. Under her other arm, she held a flat rectangle. This was a long-playing record which she'd borrowed – without asking her Auntie Joyce. It was called 'Please Please Me'. Her small Jack Russell terrier totted ahead. His name was Nosey and his eyes and ears were alert with excitement.

Kathleen was a slight figure on the monocrome slope and her little plaits blew behind her like micetails. Dying fireweed, its cotton puffs recently shed, stirred stiffly at the sides of the path and dust eddied on the black faces of the pit heaps which rose in high, steep mounds on all sides. Below, the surface of the water was uneasy. The sky was unbroken grey and the sullied landscape was colourless and bleak.

Beyond the pond, a lonely house came into view. This was her destination, the home of her school friend, Petra. Surrounded on all sides by mountains of waste from the pit, it resembled an outpost; a place of grim survival. Smoke puffed from its squat chimney and was immediately carried away. A light shone from between the half-closed kitchen curtains. It looked desolate and unwelcoming.

Kathleen approached the pond. She watched the wind form oily ripples which rolled then broke, sluggishly. The dog sniffed the air then barked. Here, nothing grew, not a blade of grass – not even fireweed. Polluted by the mine, the once legendary sweet waters had for decades been thick and lifeless. Formed in a natural fissure, the pool was deep – some said bottomless – but it was scummy now and stank of coal.

Kathleen's eyes narrowed. She stopped and peered through her spectacles. Still clutching the LP she took off her glasses, breathed on the lenses, rubbed them on her coat, then replaced them. In the distance, on the water's edge next to an ancient, ruined barn, something shone red. It was bright and startling. The dog barked again. A beachball, Kathleen thought. Maybe a lost umbrella. Intrigued, she left the track and walked towards the barn which tottered doorless on the far shore. Her feet sank into the black mud, leaving oozing footprints.

'Nosey!' she called, as he raced ahead, his tail erect and quivering. As she neared the red blotch, she could see it wasn't round at all – now it looked like fabric. It's a bedcover, she decided, blown off Petra's mam's washing line. It was caught between two rotting posts which emerged from the shallows like broken fingers.

She drew alongside the barn. Nosey was running to and fro, by the water's edge, yapping furiously. She gasped. She could see it clearly now – the red cloth was a jacket.

*

Kathleen laid the long-playing record on the ground, unfastened the heavy case and took out Da's old box brownie. She steadied herself, holding the camera firmly upright at waist height, in order to take a portrait shot. The wind was blowing against her and she leant forwards, balancing herself. Peering through her spectacles into the viewfinder she trapped the exact image and with her right thumb carefully pressed the lever on the side that released the shutter. There was a loud click as the mechanism moved, then the lever clicked back to the 'up' position. Carefully, she returned the brownie to its case, then stepped into the foul pond, the cold filling her wellingtons.

She waded forwards. She was afraid. The icy coldness rose up her thighs. The skirt of her coat floated then dragged. She lifted her feet from the slimy bottom to stop them sinking. She grasped one of the posts. The discoloured water was black on the surface but a few inches underneath it was a rusty orange which was both malodorous and dense. She looked again. Above the half-submerged red jacket there were floating tendrils of short blonde hair. She took off her glasses and rubbed her eyes. She saw what was unmistakably a rigid hand, an arm. She polished the spectacles on her shoulder and put them on again. She thought of posed plaster mannequins she'd seen in shop windows on her rare trips to town. Her heart turned over and she grasped the sodden jacket, tugging it hard. The stiff figure was freed from its mooring. Grotesquely, it turned over and reared up.

It was a dead body. A drowned person.

It had a yellowish-cream waxy face and eyes that met hers and stared. Its hair was stuck down, its mouth was open with water streaming out. Its lips were drawn back in a frozen grimace from which teeth protruded. Kathleen cried out and released it. With a gentle splash it sank below the surface.

Kathleen stepped back, unbalanced. She staggered then fell at the pond's edge. The dog barked hysterically. Soaked and filthy from her chest downwards, she struggled to her feet. One of her wellingtons came off and was lost. She gasped for breath in uneven sobs. She picked up the camera then half ran back to the track. The Jack Russell overtook her, excitedly. She turned to look behind. The body was no longer visible but she knew it hadn't been a bad dream. She moved her short-sighted gaze upwards to the pale cloud. There was no break in the flat canopy; not a sliver of blue, not a single bird. Nearby, a hidden train shunted and rattled. Her sobs steadied to a heavy, even rasp. She tried, but failed to remember some religious words. 'Gloria,' she managed to gasp, after a moment. Recovering her voice she shouted loudly: 'GLORIA!'

This wasn't a prayer directed at a godless sky. It was the name of her cousin. Her cousin Gloria was lifeless, waterlogged, dead. She lay drowned in Jinny Hoolet's pond.

Kathleen hammered on the side door of the isolated house of her friend. 'Mrs Koninsky!' she yelled. 'Petra! Open up!' She banged with both fists.

Petra peered through the gap in the kitchen curtains. The electric light made her sallow and suspicious. She opened the door. 'Where's the records?' she demanded. 'Where's Billy J. Kramer and the Dakotas? Where's John, Paul, George and Ringo?'

'Phone the police,' Kathleen muttered, leaning in the entrance, water forming a pool at her feet. 'Phone the doctor.' Dismayed, she realized as she spoke that she'd lost her Auntie Joyce's LP somewhere near the pond. She pushed past Petra into the dim kitchen where the pot-bellied stove smoked and gave off practically no heat.

'You're all wet,' was the reply. 'You're dirty.'

With uncustomary boldness, Kathleen walked through and opened the door into the hallway. The Koninskys were one of the few families in the area with a private telephone. 'Where's your Mam and Dad?'

'In bed. It's Sunday.'

'There's a body in the pond.'

Petra was suddenly wide-eyed and impressed. Her mouth fell open into a silent 'O'.

Kathleen picked up the smooth black handset and listened, tentatively, to the tone. 'What do you do with this? What do you do again?'

Her friend grabbed the receiver. She wanted to take charge. 'Nine, nine, nine,' she said with authority. 'I'll do it. We need to dial nine, nine, nine.'

Wearing only Petra's unwashed dressing gown, Kathleen stood on the edge of the bath and looked out of a small top window. Below, the police had put up a screen which blew like a sail in the wind. Two Alsatians were being led from a van, parked on the hard surface of the track. One uniformed constable was measuring the ground with a tape, another stood hands on hips, his helmet pushed back, gazing across the impassive pond.

'Let me look now, let me LOOK,' insisted Petra from the landing. 'It's my turn!'

They had been told to stay inside. Kathleen ignored her. She wondered what the adult Koninskys were doing. She blinked. She craned her neck as the flashing lights of another police car became visible on the road at the top of the hill.

Petra held Nosey, Kathleen's dog, under her arm. She was on the landing outside the bathroom door. The dog struggled a little because he didn't like her. She clamped him harder. 'Stop it!' she whispered, urgently. 'Keep still, you little bastard.' With her free hand she took a cigarette lighter from her pocket. It was gold with a single diamond in the centre and yesterday she'd stolen it from her mother. She flicked it open, creating a small flame and this she moved towards the dog's front paws. He wriggled frantically and freed himself, falling at her feet. Before she had time to back away he bared his teeth, bit her ankle then raced away down the stairs.

'It's MY TURN!' shouted Petra again, to Kathleen. She was angry. 'Get off there, will you, and let me have a look!'

Kathleen returned downstairs. Her clothes were still damp but she put them on anyway. She pushed a foot into her single wellington and located her camera. She called for Nosey but he didn't appear. She wasn't worried because he knew his way home. She ran a tap, rinsed a glass and drank some water. The sink was stained brown and there was dirty crockery piled up. She noticed cobwebs in the grey net curtains. She glanced around. The room was sombre and the worn linoleum was scuffed and grubby with bits of trampled food.

'Goodbye,' she called loudly and went outside.

Mrs Koninsky, praying fervently, stepped aside to let her pass. Kathleen paused and looked at the ambulance which was perched on the top of the track, its driver clearly unwilling to negotiate the steep, rough slope. Its siren was extinguished but its light was still flashing. Over at the barn, a burly older man wearing a trilby and an overcoat, wrote in a notebook. He had a red face and earlier he'd spoken briefly to Kathleen. He was nice, she decided, and he seemed to be in charge.

Just then a stretcher, carried by two ambulancemen, appeared from behind the flapping screen. Mrs Koninsky, oblivious, her eyes half-closed, intoned in Latin. Kathleen removed her camera from its case and turned the film advance key on the left-hand side counter clockwise to wind on the film. She checked the little red window at the back – she had five pictures left. She held the box brownie sideways in both hands, waist height, to get a landscape shot. She squinted behind her spectacles and tried to stay as still as possible. Gloria's body was covered in a white aertex hospital blanket. Her feet were sticking out the end, toes erect, her legs stiff in death. As the stretcher passed Kathleen centred it in her viewfinder and took another photograph. Gloria was still wearing her black patent court shoes, Kathleen noticed. They were the latest fashion with a thick heel rather than a kitten stiletto. Kathleen was suddenly very, very sad. 'She only just got them shoes,' she murmured to the entranced, chanting woman behind her. 'She loved them. She got them from Dolcis, all the way up in Newcastle. She drove up there specially in her car. They cost her forty-nine and eleven.'

Later, in the dim warmth of Nana's gleaming kitchen, a pot bubbled on the range and the banked up fire cast shifting shadows around the walls. Nana's long body rocked energetically and her knitting needles clacked. She was in her usual place, at the side of the hearth, patchwork cushions heaped behind her to ease the pain in her joints. Nosey was asleep against the fender, his little legs twitching as he dreamed of rabbit hunts across the fields. Joyce, Nana's daughter, leaned over the table, her long hair thick, dishevelled and russet in the red light from the fire. Her uniform was partly undone revealing the dark line of her cleavage, the mound of her breasts. Her little pillbox hat was by her elbow. She heaped sugar into a cup of tea and stirred it vigorously. Nana's rocking chair creaked steadily, the old wall clock ticked and the coals shifted contentedly in the grate.

Kathleen sat half-hidden on her cracket, that is her low wooden stool, in a dark alcove. Her hands were folded over the camera in her lap. She was motionless, watching, listening. She'd put her damp clothes in the laundry basket in the wash-house and she was wearing her school uniform. She had nothing else, except pyjamas. Her glasses occasionally glinted from the gloom of her corner, but Nana and Joyce ignored her.

'It's a bad business,' said Nana, finally. She rocked more furiously for an instant, then suddenly placed both feet on the mat and stopped. She laid her knitting aside. 'It's a disgrace.'

Joyce sighed. She spoke softly. 'I saw it coming.' She slurped tea noisily from her cup.

Nana stood up abruptly, grasped her stick and lurched towards the dresser, her long legs stiff and unbending. She retrieved two glasses and a chipped cut-glass decanter half full of amber liquid. She poured an inch into each glass and handed one to her daughter. 'We'll be the talk of the neighbourhood.' Awkwardly, she sat down again, hooking her stick on to the mantelpiece. 'Never mind secondhand,' she said, mysteriously, 'that damned hussy, she was twenty-secondhand.'

Kathleen didn't move but there were tears welling in her eyes. 'Poor Gloria was a nice person,' she thought to herself. She remembered an expression often used by her teacher at school, although never about herself. 'She's got a very good brain. That's it,' she mused. 'Gloria had a very good brain.' She watched Nosey's little heart beating as he groaned and rolled over without waking. 'She was a brain-box.'

Joyce pushed her tea aside and swallowed her whisky in one gulp. She suppressed a burp. The clock struck the half hour. 'Miss High and Mighty,' she said. 'That was her. OK, I know she was a sort-of cousin, and everything, but I'm not pretending. I didn't like her and that's all there is to it. She gave herself airs. Thought herself Lady Muck.' She began to fasten her overall. She was soon to go to the local cinema where she worked as an usherette. 'Anyway, she was a mess, wasn't she? I'm not surprised she's done herself in. Didn't eat anything . . . much too thin . . !' She placed her pillbox hat on the back of her head. 'Mind you. Da will be upset.'

Kathleen listened attentively. Both women knew she had discovered the body earlier, but their concern had been minimal.

'That business must be worth something,' said Nana reflectively. 'And that flat. That flat will have to be sold.'

Kathleen thought about Gloria's neon-lit salon, with its row of overhead driers, its pink ruched curtains. She'd been a hairdresser – the only one in the village. She'd been planning a refurbishment.

'Da must be the beneficiary,' Nana said. Da was her second husband, not Joyce's father. She sipped from her glass and pulled a face, as if she was drinking medicine. 'That flat and that car will have to be sold.' She licked her lips. 'That's for sure.'

Joyce stood up and pulled on a wide, old-fashioned fur jacket. Her uniform strained against her hips. 'All those shoes,' she said spitefully. 'Those stupid little white boots. Lipstick like chalk. All that bloody Mary Quant. Not much good to her now, are they?'

Kathleen stood up and stepped into the pool of light in front of Nana's chair. 'Poor Gloria's dead,' she said simply. The tears that had been threatening to flow now spilled down her cheeks. She took off her glasses, rubbed her eyes then put them on again.

'Yes, and you'll be dead,' said Joyce sharply, 'if you don't find my Beatles long player. It'll be coming off your pocket money for bloody years.' She opened the dresser, poured herself another finger of Nana's whisky and downed it in one quick movement. She put down the glass and moved towards the door. 'Right? All right, Kathleen?'

Kathleen waited for the back door to slam then slipped upstairs to the airing cupboard. Her coat was still damp but she put it on. She jammed her feet into her school shoes and tied the laces. Silently, she went out. 'I wonder where Da is,' she thought. It was still early but the afternoon had faded to a damp, grey October evening. The winding wheel at the mine was drawing up pitmen at the end of their shift. 'I wonder if he knows.' The street lights at that moment flickered and came on, dimly. Kathleen paused for a second and blinked.

*

Da had been called away by the deputy. The news was broken softly to him, but in very few words. Now he stood in his work clothes and heavy boots, black from head to foot, his soft cap clutched in both hands, his head bowed. He was tall for a miner but the bright, white-tiled cleanliness of the mortuary, with its high ceiling, seemed to diminish him. He was sad and hunched and helpless as the trolley was wheeled towards him. The blanket was drawn slowly from Gloria's face, revealing its pallor, its staring expression, its ghastly, toothy grin. Da shuddered, stepped back and closed his eyes. The attendant muttered something consolatory. He looked again, but this time at a silver chain around his sister's neck. It was entwined with a black strand of debris from the pond. 'Is that . . . Is that . . .?' he stuttered.

The mortuary attendant was calm but helpful. 'Yes, sir?'

'Is that a St Christopher? Around her neck?'

Carefully, the man lifted the jewellery. A little pendant swung between his fingers.

'It's her,' said Da, his voice a dull sigh.

Her camera over her shoulder, Kathleen set off down the street where the neighbours had already drawn their curtains against the coming night. She cut through a cobbled lane to the centre of the village. All was quiet, the shops shut up for Sunday, except Gloria's hair salon. It shone brightly, tragically, its neon lights aglow, with two police cars parked outside. A tall PC filled the entrance. Kathleen glided unnoticed to the plate glass window and peered in through the nylon. A group of policemen, one the big man in the hat and overcoat, sat around, incongruously, under the driers. They were drinking tea from flasks. A young one had placed his helmet in a basket of plastic rollers which stood on a stand. Another leaned against a basin.

Kathleen slipped round to the back, entered the yard, located the key, quietly unlocked and pushed open the rear door. She stepped into the tiny storeroom where Gloria had sipped Tizer and read fashion magazines whenever business was slack. There was rumble of laughter from the men. Kathleen took a deep breath. The smell of the perming chemicals reminded her unbearably of her cousin. She peeped into the salon. At that moment she realized that Nosey was snuffling at her feet. He'd followed her. 'Go home!' she whispered fiercely.

The older, thick-set man had put his cup on the floor and was writing again in his notebook. Kathleen followed his gaze. He was copying some words which were inscribed large, on a wall mirror. The script was wobbly and written in what looked like dark red lipstick. Kathleen glanced down at a jar of combs in disinfectant and two oversized bottles of shampoo. She stared up again. 'DON'T LOOK FOR ME' the message read.